Abigail Mann is a comedy writer living in London and surviving on a diet of three-shot coffee, bourbons, and vegetarian sausage rolls. She was born and brought up in Norfolk, which she says is to blame for the sardonic humour that runs through her novels. Abigail was the runner-up in 2019's Comedy Women in Print award with *The Lonely Fajita*: her first novel.

Abigail takes inspiration from unconventional cross-sections of modern society and the impact this has on identity and the relationships we create. She wrote her first novel after teaching literature for a number of years and whilst working in the fast-paced co-working spaces of East London.

🐦 @abigailemann
📷 @abigailemann
📘 abigailmannauthor
Ⓑ @abigailemannwriter
www.abigailemann.com/

Also by Abigail Mann

The Lonely Fajita

The Sister Surprise

Abigail Mann

Happy reading! love Abigail x

One More Chapter
a division of HarperCollins*Publishers*
The News Building
1 London Bridge Street
London SE1 9GF

www.harpercollins.co.uk

HarperCollins*Publishers*
1st Floor, Watermarque Building, Ringsend Road
Dublin 4, Ireland

This paperback edition 2021

First published in Great Britain in ebook format by
HarperCollins*Publishers* 2021

A catalogue record for this book
is available from the British Library

ISBN: 978-0-00-843070-2

This novel is entirely a work of fiction.
The names, characters and incidents portrayed in it are
the work of the author's imagination. Any resemblance to
actual persons, living or dead, events or localities is
entirely coincidental.

Set in Birka by Palimpsest Book Production Ltd,
Falkirk Stirlingshire

Printed and bound in Great Britain by
CPI Group (UK) Ltd, Croydon CR0 4YY

To Joe
For all the laughing and walking that
brought me back to myself

Chapter 1

A t twenty-seven, I should have outgrown the act of picking glitter from my cuticles, but then again, being Lorrie Atmore's daughter comes with its own set of obligations. Today, I'm covertly multi-tasking. If you were to part the wind chimes at the back door to peek inside our tiny kitchen, you'd see me blasting oak leaves with a hairdryer, using my elbow to pin down the stack that I've already washed and dried. In my head, however, I'm running over lines from the script I've spent every lunchtime working on for the past week.

Mum launches into an anecdote about a supposedly malicious gluten scandal between the PTA mums as I silently mouth the words that I'll present on a live stream tomorrow morning. After five years at *Snooper*, I'm a little *too* well-adjusted to my role as sub-editor, or Captain Comma, as my colleague Max so often calls me. *The Oxford A-Z of Punctuation* is my Bible and I can reference it with the passion of a born-again Christian. It's not the legacy I thought I'd have, so when I was offered a chance to front something of my own, I said yes immediately. Seeing as *Snooper* claims to

1

be 'on-the-pulse media for the anti-news generation', I should have expected that career progression would be unconventional, but going from an editorial desk to a spotlit studio is decidedly out of my comfort zone, not that I've admitted it.

Mum, however, relishes being at the centre of a community that hums around her. She's been the chairperson at Dulwich Green Primary since 1999, a position she refuses to relinquish, despite the fact that I stopped attending fifteen years ago.

I hold two glittery acorns to my chest like I'm plucking the cherry from an iced bun. She frowns, her cheeks dimpled in a barely suppressed smile.

'You look like a burlesque dancer. A really cheap one,' she says.

'Mum!' I shout, as she chugs with laughter like a faulty diesel engine. I flick the acorns across the table, stretch high above my head, and let my mind tick things over. I've been on the cusp of telling her about my work assignment all week, but every time I open my mouth it's like a claw drags the words back down my throat. 'So ...'

'Mmhm?' She threads a silver bead down the stem of an oak leaf.

Now. Tell her now.

'How many more do I have to do? My fingers hurt,' I say, falling back on topics I know to be conversational safe zones.

'Don't be silly. It's too early for that. You've got no idea what a *hardcore* session with half a dozen placards and paint tubes looks like—'

'Back in the day ...' I say wistfully, pre-empting her speech. Thanks to her terrible aim, the acorn she throws in my direction misses by a foot and tinkles as it hits a porcelain teacup on the dresser behind me.

'Cheeky cow,' she says, using her glasses as an Alice band for her mess of over-permed hair. 'But yes, *back in the day* we'd pull all-nighters with the fabric paint. That red blob by the fireplace is a symbol of resistance. And sleep deprivation.'

'The one that makes the living room look like a crime scene?'

'That's it. "You Otter Be Ashamed" painted over four bed sheets. We made the front page of *The Sunday Times* with that one. Best day of my life,' she says, wistfully.

'Thanks ...'

'All right, second-best day of my life,' says Mum. 'Before you came along, obviously.'

I push my chair back to let our pot-bellied cat vault onto my lap. He purrs, kneads my thigh, and looks up at me with sleep-drunk eyes.

'Tea?'

'All right, but then I've got to go to bed. Big day tomorrow.'

I rub my stiff knuckles and knead my temples, tucking a lock of hair behind my ear. I glance at the clock and check my phone through a squint. If I go to bed now, I might be able to get six hours in before I have to travel to Holborn for the hair and make-up appointment that was booked for me. Personally, I don't think my twice-yearly trim needs updating, but apparently when you're asked to present on a live stream it requires a look that'll 'stop the kids from scrolling', whatever that means.

I think back to the steps that led to me presenting tomorrow and struggle to credit it to the Rolodex of self-help books I listen to on my commute. To get ahead at work, *The Career Doctor* suggested 'socialising with your superiors outside the office to build rapport', but Duncan – our Editor-in-Chief – didn't even attend his own birthday lunch, so that was off the cards. *Take the Reins* details a five-point-plan for success that includes 'say yes to everything', but that led to working late on Christmas Eve, checking for typos in a recipe for vegan pigs in blankets.

Snooper frequently gets sent PR products to review, so when Duncan handed out genealogy kits in the conference room for this week's 'Hot in Tech' feature, I didn't think much of it. That was until we each unboxed a plastic vial with instructions to fill it with saliva. The meeting was undignified, to say the least; lots of hacking, spitting, and wiping of chins. Like always, everyone in editorial had to pitch for features linked to the product, and like always, I expected my idea to turn up on someone else's desk. When I let slip that I didn't know who my father was, Duncan sat back and rubbed his jowls, a sign that he was listening.

The notion that I've been given this chance purely *because* there's ambiguity over my parentage has crossed my mind, but I'm not going to jeopardise it by asking any questions. Opportunities like this are rare; like getting through a day without seeing a single Kardashian in your

Twitter feed. Mum still takes pictures on a disposable camera, so there's no chance she'll watch the live stream, but the idea that I'm going behind her back to find answers to questions she never wanted to answer makes me a feel a bit ... squirmy.

Mum plugs in a hot glue gun and taps the worktop, waiting for the kettle to boil. She's always liked the idea of me being a journalist, but new media is a step down from the kind of writing she thought I'd be doing. This is largely due to her fervent mistrust of the internet. Basically, if it's not in print, she doesn't think it legitimately counts; although the same logic doesn't apply to Henry, our elderly neighbour, who writes, prints, and delivers the community paper on his electric scooter.

My stomach squirms like I've swallowed a sandwich bag full of baby eels. For the umpteenth time, I'm within arm's reach of asking about my dad. Mum's in a good mood, so the risk factor is fairly low. Then again, I don't know why it would play out differently today. It's like the very first time I noticed that we weren't like the families around us, the ones with 2.5 kids and a car big enough to fit camping gear in.

I was six years old in the bakery section of Sainsbury's, which would soon become synonymous with traumatic moments I'd rather forget about. Seeing as I'd just been given the part of narrator in the school play, I wanted to show off, and picked up the nearest greeting card to do so. The words confused me, so I patted Mum's leg.

'Does "father" mean the same as "dad"?'

5

'Yes,' she replied, looking elsewhere.

'Why do fathers need a day?'

'They don't,' she replied. 'Put it down.'

'We could send it. To my dad.'

'We can't. You should only send cards to people you love.'

'Why don't you send it then? Mums and dads love each other.'

She squatted down, kissed my head, and gently peeled my fingers off the cellophane wrapper. 'Some do, but lots of mums and dads don't, and that's OK too. Because I'm both, aren't I?'

This was wildly confusing to me, but I didn't say so.

'So, he doesn't have a house?'

'No, sweet pea. He's in the same place Grandma and Granddad are. Shed his mortal coil, so to speak.'

'What does that mean?'

Mum pulled me to one side, away from the wheels of someone else's trolley. 'He's dead, my love.'

'Why?'

'Jesus Christ, Ava. Sorry. Can we not talk about this now? I only came in for milk.'

I thought I was in trouble, so did what most six-year-olds would and started to cry.

'Shit.' She hauled me into her arms and walked us round to the bakery, where rows of birthday cakes sat covered in thick factory icing. 'Pick one.' Thus distracted, I forgot about the conversation and we went home with a ten-person sponge covered in candy bracelets and gummy sweets.

This routine persists; I bring him up, Mum snipes at me, drags me along for the food shop, and we come back with a disproportionately large celebration cake.

I think about it now and feel a bit sick. We've not done the bakery run for a few years.

Mum pours hot water into our mugs and picks up a glue gun, wielding it with the dexterity of a cowboy in a shootout. 'How are you feeling about it, then? Being on camera.'

'Absolutely horrible, to be honest. And excited, in a way. It feels like a really long time coming. I'll finally be delivering the content I write, y'know? It's just the thought of everyone watching my face.'

'You can hardly wear a paper bag.'

I snort and a smile pulls at the corner of my mouth, despite the headache sitting heavy on my brow. Mum runs a hand through her hair, glittery dandruff falling on the table. 'I think we've rehomed half of south London's wood-lice by bringing all this lot inside, don't you?'

'Pickles is too lazy to chase them out, so they're essentially lodgers at this point.'

Mum snorts and squints at the calendar tacked by the door. 'You still all right to take photographs tomorrow? For the Harvest Festival? If you've got something on, I can find someone else.'

'Nah, it's all right, I'll be there. Did Ginger say if Rory was going?'

'I don't think she is, no. Apparently she's busy doing a "Wagamama's crawl", whatever that is.'

'Really? I thought that was just a distraction technique after she broke up with Myles,' I say, sliding a silicon mat under the glue gun before a globule of molten plastic lands on the table. 'I didn't think she'd still be going after – what has been now, a month?'

'She sounds like her mother when it comes to break-ups.'

'Katsu curry is for Rory what Malbec is to Ginger.'

'Your generation. Honestly.'

Mum and Ginger became friends at playgroup when Rory and I were babies, and we've been solid fixtures in each other's lives ever since. Whereas Mum is stubbornly independent, the same isn't true for Ginger, who has welcomed countless boyfriends and five fiancés into their house over the years. Rory and I started to make bets on how long they'd last, with a sherbet Dip Dab awarded to the closest guess within a week.

'I'm surprised Rory hasn't moved back in with Ginger whilst she's in between flats. All that money she could save,' says Mum, wistfully.

'She wants to be independent. I don't blame her, to be honest. Ginger keeps telling her to forgive Myles, but why should she when he has a propensity for Thursday evening cocaine and can't say where he spent the last three nights? Anyway, I don't think that Rory finds living with Ginger particularly ... calming.'

Mum scrapes her hair into a top knot, rubs her neck, and looks at me from beneath a puff of fringe.

'What about that one you went out with? Dan? Demi?'

'Drew.'

'The American. Any more dates on the cards?'

'Pfff, absolutely not. He told me he hates cats because "they have no concept of the alpha male", which is really ... disturbing.'

I slide Pickles off my lap. He lands on the floor with a sizeable thud owing to his near spherical shape, achieved by eating three dinners a night thanks to neighbours who fall victim to his feigned cry of starvation.

I pull out a plastic wallet containing the script I wrote for tomorrow's live stream, my lines neatly highlighted in pastel green. As I re-read it, a band of tension tightens across my forehead. The lines I wrote to sound authentically casual now read like I'm trying too hard, which, of course, I am. Mum puts her hand on the back of my chair and cranes forward. She smells like hemp hand cream and sandalwood smoke.

'Want to practise with me?'

'No,' I answer, folding the page in half. She holds her hands up, as though absolving herself from a crime.

'Sorry for asking! What's it about anyway, this TV thing you're doing tomorrow?'

I pull one leg up, hug my knee, and peek through my overgrown fringe. 'It's not on TV, it's the internet.' I breathe in slowly. It feels like a moth is fluttering in the core of my chest, tickling up my throat until it's between my teeth, ready to be spat out.

'Yes, well, near enough.' Mum rubs her eyes. 'Go on then, tell me.'

'We're going to have our DNA profiles revealed,' I say,

my heartbeat pulsing in my neck. Mum dangles a tea towel in front of her. Pickles lazily bats it with his paw. The kettle flicks off, but she doesn't move to pour it. 'Max and I posted samples to a lab. Well, so did everyone, but we were chosen to lead the feature.'

'What does it tell you, this test?'

'Err, well, something to do with our nationality based on shared genes.'

'Oh!' Mum flicks the tea towel onto a worktop and picks up the kettle. 'Fashion changes all the time. I expect the feature won't age well with the rate that trends move on these days.' She puts a mug down on the table and screeches. 'Ah! That bloody animal! Shoo! Go on, off!' She swats a hand in front of Pickles, who howls and shakes his paw, having stepped on a sticky leaf that he's now wearing like a ski.

'No, not like that. It's DNA stuff. The science-y bits that make up a person. We find out ... we find out—' I stutter, tiptoeing around the edge of a conversational landmine. 'We find out where our DNA is traced to, so there's a chance that my paternal data is—'

A rapping noise turns our attention to the back door, where Ginger is just visible through the window. I can tell she's on tiptoes; the strain is clear in her eyes, wide, wet, and husky blue.

A throaty squeak breaks through chugging sobs that accompany her entrance. Ginger shrugs herself out of a faux fur cape and lets it drop to the floor before collapsing into a kitchen chair with renewed trumpet-like sobs.

'Ginger! Whatever is the matter? Oh, Ginger! Let me get some wine. Ava, a bottle of white. Ava?'

I open the fridge and slide a bottle off the top shelf as Ginger tries to talk through guttural tears. 'I'll get out of your way,' I add, not quite loud enough to be heard above the cooing and sobbing coming from the table. Going by the state of her, I can safely assume that I've won the sherbet Dip Dab this time, but I've missed my last chance to ask Mum about my father before tomorrow.

I leave them to it and plod upstairs, take off what little remains of my make-up, and practise my 'camera face' in the mirror whilst I sweep rosewater serum over my neck. An article I'd read on *Refinery29* said that three litres of water a day and botanical toners would get rid of the dark circles under my eyes, but even after buying every product listed and teaching myself Japanese facial techniques, I haven't seen a change.

'No way, that's unreal! Like, so cool ...' I whisper to my own reflection, trying to make my delivery sound detached and aloof like the fresh-from-the-womb media graduates that Duncan insists on hiring. 'No, I've never wondered about him,' I say, unconvinced by my own smile. 'Not for a minute.'

Chapter 2

'Are ... are you sure this is what Duncan asked for?'
'Yep,' replies the stylist with a curt nod. I blink
beneath false eyelashes so thick I feel like I'm about to take
off. My hair has been scraped back into what I have been
reliably told are called 'space buns', giving my eyebrows an
arched quality thanks to eye-watering tension at my scalp.
The headache that I slept off last night has reappeared with
renewed vigour, aided by white lights framing the mirror
I've been wheeled in front of. Not only do my eyes hurt
from the brightness, but I'm now reacquainted with every
long-lost pore and blemish on my face. Nice.

'He's gone for an edgy, youthful look, y'know? Imagine
you're the kind of person who gets drunk tattoos and
shags a member of One Direction whilst listening to Billie
Eilish on repeat.'

Right, so that explains the facelift I've been given cour-
tesy of Natalie's brutal work with a metal comb and an
entire packet of Kirby grips. 'I know it's meant to make
me look younger—'

'Youthful,' interrupts Natalie with a self-satisfied nod.

She shakes a can of hairspray and blasts it in an arc above my head. With no warning, I inhale most of it.

'Sure,' I splutter, 'but ... I feel like it's accentuating the fact that I'm a decade too old for this look.'

'It's just because you're not used to being on camera,' she says, giving my shoulder a squeeze. 'It's all about lighting. This one actress – she was a Dame or something – wouldn't do television appearances unless her team could screw their own lightbulbs in. They were turned up so high, right, that the studio was *humming*. Benedict Cumberbatch sweated through his three-piece. You won't believe the powder I got through doing touch-ups.'

'Weirdly, that *does* makes me feel better.'

***

'Hey!'

I stand on tiptoes and look over the heads of a small crowd gathered at the collection point of a café counter. A harried barista attempts to steam three kinds of milk in tiny jugs, a backlog of KeepCups lined up beside him. A hand waves, a swimmer in an ocean of hipsters. I wriggle through.

Rory's fiercely red hair is piled on top of her head and held in place with a huge clip, a loose tendril running over her shoulder like a snake. She pulls me into a one-armed hug; a little uncomfortable owing to the bag of coffee beans wedged between us.

'Are you buying these?' I ask.

'No, they've given them to me so I don't lose my place in the queue. I feel like a right pillock.'

'I'll take it.'

'You're a peach.'

She handles the bag like a cautious parent with a newborn, transferring it into the crook of my elbow. Manoeuvre complete, she clasps my shoulders and turns me from one side to the other like I'm a patient she's examining. I frown, my hairline taut. I open my eyes wide to relieve the pressure.

'Wow. That's ... that's a look,' says Rory.

'Oh, don't,' I say, massaging my scalp.

'It's very slick.'

'Hmm, that's the word for it. She combed so much gel through my hair I thought she was about to insert me somewhere.'

'You say that, but since I was relocated to A&E I've seen some things that truly confront my understanding of human anatomy,' says Rory. 'Oh, hang on. Yep, that's me! I'm coming! Ava, bring the coffee beans.'

We scurry to the front, where I cautiously hand over our beany placeholder, swapping it for a lukewarm flat white. Outside, Rory and I sit on an old bench by the window. With the parquet flooring, painted bricks, and school gym equipment, I get an unnerving flashback to PE lessons, most of which involved Rory and me chucking a musty beanbag to each other at the back of the hall.

'So glad we could do this, even if it is for ten minutes,' says Rory, her eyes softening as caffeine slips down her throat. 'Ah, that's the stuff. Got a hangover. Before you say anything, I will tone it down from now on. It's getting silly. Thing is, I can't bear the thought of having dead time in the evenings. Too many opportunities to think about Myles.'

'Don't be too hard on yourself. It's not been that long. Couldn't you stay with Ginger for a bit? Use it as downtime?'

'Absolutely not,' says Rory, flicking down a pair of over-sized sunglasses. 'Mum's taken my break-up worse than I have. She randomly wails like Mrs Bennet. The melodrama! She's one step away from smelling salts, I swear to God. I said to her: "Mother. This stops now. He hasn't cheated on you, has he?" Perhaps if I'd seen *just one* example of a healthy relationship between her and literally any of the men she went out with when I was a kid, I wouldn't be so bloody useless at weeding out the arseholes. I said that to her and all,' she adds, licking coffee foam from her finger.

'Wow, that's brave.'

'Oh, you know what we're like: lay everything on the table, get out of each other's hair for a while, and meet up for a consoling tapas session when we've both chilled out.'

I nod, quietly envious of Rory and Ginger's open – if chaotic – relationship. If I bring up the tiniest grievance to Mum, she reacts like I've made a personal dig at her and then bustles off to do some work for one of the various committees she's on. Later, when she gets home and I'm on the sofa watching *Queer Eye*, she pretends like nothing's happened. That's that. We move on.

'Anyway, I've talked about Myles to death. Distract me. How're you feeling about your first live stream? Exciting, right?' Rory interlocks her fingers in mine and jiggles my hand, making the pot of sugar cubes dance on the table.

'Yeah, I mean ... I'm excited. I am. I'm just feeling a lot of *other* things too,' I say.

'You'll be fine! You and Max have got great chemistry, you've said so before,' says Rory.

'Only when he's not trying to wind me up.'

'It's *because* he tries to wind you up. You can handle it.'

I bite my lip and bounce a chunky heel on the floor.

'What's up? There's a lot of nervous energy radiating off you,' says Rory, flicking her glasses down her nose to inspect me properly.

I close my eyes, the warm autumn sunshine cutting between two austere townhouses. When I open them, Rory is poised like a blackbird, listening.

'It's the DNA results that I'm worried about. Not in a *Jeremy Kyle* way, but I don't think they're going to be ... straightforward.'

'Well, isn't it that the point of a reveal? Like, the surprise element is the hook, right?'

'Yeah, obviously. But ...'

'Oh! Oh!' Rory grabs my knee, her eyes wide. 'Do you think you're the love-child of someone famous? Mick Jagger? You could have, like, twenty siblings by now.'

'Not quite ...'

'Go on, put me out of my misery.'

'Well, you know there are questions about who *he* is. My dad.'

'I know that him and Lorrie weren't properly together,

right? She bonked him during her activist days, didn't she?' I grimace, but nod regardless. 'You must know his name though.'

'Nope.'

'Really?! Bloody hell. Lorrie really went for the "dine and dash" approach. Dark horse.' I put a finger to my lips, willing Rory to talk a little more quietly. She grins and scratches lipstick from her front teeth. 'You must have asked at some point,' she says.

'Yeah, but not recently. Every time I do, she ignores the question and overreacts, as though the idea that I'm curious about him is proof that she's failed at bringing me up properly. As far as my father goes, the only thing I know is that they met during a protest about dolphins. Or whales. Some sort of sea creature. Anyway, he died when I started primary school. Not sure when exactly.'

'I can't imagine that's going to make for an uplifting watch,' says Rory. 'Do *Snooper* know about your family history?'

'Only what I told Duncan in the first meeting. Basically, that it's kind of a mystery.'

Rory props her chin in her hand and taps the table, thinking. 'What kind of vibe are they going for during the live stream?'

'It's *Snooper*, isn't it? So, light-hearted banter and wide-eyed reactions. Something they won't have difficulty editing into little clips for short attention spans.'

'That doesn't sound *so* bad. Still, it's a pretty extreme way to explore your family history.'

'Trust me, this is the better option. It's not just an

opportunity to show Duncan I can do more than check for misplaced commas, but I get to find out about *him*, whoever *he* is. This is one way to do it.'

'I'm surprised it's taken you this long. In all the time we've known each other, you haven't *once* gone into Full Ava Mode. I thought you'd be pinning a bunch of Lorrie's old receipts and photos to the wall to map her movements during 1991 with red string and a stack of Post-its.'

'As much as I love the thrill of a colour-coded research project, this one is too complicated,' I say, massaging my scalp. My leg jiggles so much that our teaspoons rattle on their saucers. Rory holds my wrists, performing a slow inward breath. I copy her.

'Do you remember when you sorted through five years of medical school notes for me? Three thousand pages stacked and categorised with coloured tabs and so much highlighter you could have self-referred to a solvent abuse clinic?'

I nod, feel my brow soften, and allow my shoulders to retreat an inch or two away from my ears. 'I had to dust off my industrial hole-punch for that. It was a good use of annual leave.'

'There we go. Feel better?'

'A bit.'

Rory grins and plucks a loose blonde hair from my jumper.

'You can always pretend you're ill if don't want to do this today. I'll write you a doctor's note.'

I pick at my thumbnail, which has been painted a lurid

shade of green. 'Seriously, it's fine. I just feel a bit weird because Mum goes twitchy and awkward whenever I bring him up. Getting my ancestry results on a live stream feels ... underhand.' I run my tongue across my teeth. The coffee is making my heartbeat throb, the effect more debilitating than restorative. 'I don't feel prepared enough and I'm not sure Max has even read the script. We had one snatched conversation about it last week by the vending machine. Did you know he's the middle child of three brothers? Think we all could have guessed that ...'

'Try and relax into it. It won't be as bad as you think,' says Rory, squeezing my hand. 'Come on. I'll walk you to the station. Take this.' She slides her Lotus biscuit over the table towards me. I pick it up and hold it to my chest. 'I'm honoured.'

'Just in case you need a sugar hit at some point.' Rory stands up, swings a bag across her chest, and flicks a lighter until her cigarette glows amber.

'Oh, hang on. I owe you for this coffee trip,' I say, consulting an app on my phone. So far, your tab stands at £32.70 and mine is £26.60.'

Rory laughs, the cigarette puckered between her lips. She takes a drag and blows the smoke over her shoulder. 'I'll get this, on one condition,' she says, pulling me to my feet.

'What's that?'

'That you give Max my number.'

'Are you sure? I can't verify that he's had all his jabs.'

'If it comes to it, I'll walk him to the clinic myself,' she says, bumping me with her hip. 'Fancy coming out after work? Waterloo? Me and some of the hospital gang are planning to get drunk on pink wine.'

'Maybe another time? I promised Mum I'd help out at this school thing tonight. Kind of hoped you'd be there.'

'Ah, of course. I can't face a children's choir tonight, especially if they're doing split harmonies. Right. I've got to go. Good luck! I'll be watching from here!' she says, tapping her phone.

Chapter 3

I swipe into our building, hang my bag on the back of my chair, and scan down today's schedule in my bullet journal. I'm nine minutes behind. Bloody train strike. My phone buzzes with a calendar reminder telling me to head to the dressing room, where I'm given a white crop top and baggy trousers to wear. My emergency measure of over-the-counter migraine medication followed by a takeaway porridge pot hasn't had a chance to kick in yet, so when I lace up the patent Doc Martens that I've been given (unnecessarily, seeing as we're only going to be on camera from the waist up), I feel my heart beating behind my eyeballs and the effect is nausea-inducing, to say the least.

I didn't know it was possible to feel wildly tired and drastically awake at the same time but, alas, this seems to be the case. Max hasn't responded to the five messages I've sent asking if he's ready for a run-through. As he's not at his desk, I go on the hunt, my feet clumpy and unfamiliar. I push the door open to the work kitchen and stifle a yawn to avoid straining my hairline.

Alongside me, a stretch of windows looks down onto

a throng of street-level activity, as a ribbon of red buses, cycles, and beeping Hackney cabs jostle for space on a road split by pedestrian crossings and tall Georgian buildings. Giselle is perched with an espresso by the door, her head bent in concentration as she shakes beauty samples out of a padded envelope. She squints at the underside of a lipstick, taps a note out on her laptop, and rolls her sleeve up. From a distance, her skin looks like it's covered in a number of puce-coloured burns, but then I notice the arc of lipsticks before her, each with a corresponding swatch on her skin. Phew. No clingfilm bandage necessary.

'Hey, have you seen Max anywhere?' I ask, tapping on the back of a chair.

'He came out of Duncan's office earlier, but that was first thing this morning,' says Giselle, holding her arms parallel to compare identical shades of burgundy.

'Hmm. *Shit.*'

'You all right?' says Giselle, looking up. 'You look a bit sweaty.'

'Yeah. Sorry, I'm just a bit distracted,' I say, reaching up to rub my eyes.

'No!' shouts Giselle, her chair tipping backwards as she slaps my wrist down. The lipsticks scatter across the table. 'Your make-up looks insane! Don't touch your face!' She tips my chin from one side to the other. 'Is this the new Charlotte Tilbury palette?'

'Maybe?'

'How could you not know?' she asks, incredulous.

24

'I was thinking about other things.' I stretch the back of my neck and wince. 'I swear it's getting tighter,' I say, cautiously tapping my hairline.

Giselle sits on a beanbag and pulls her heels onto her lap.

'Have you practised your surprised face yet?' she says, tying her hair back with a sequined scrunchie.

'No ...?'

'You might want to. I've seen Max do his and it's pretty good.'

'Why would we need to practise?'

'Well, you've already seen your DNA results, right? You've got to make it seem authentic.'

'What do you mean? It's meant to be revealed live!'

'It's got to *seem* like it's revealed live. Max was going on about it earlier. Something to do with being related to King Louis the Sixteenth ...'

I exhale sharply and pace up to the windows and back again. 'Oh, God. This is a nightmare. I'm living in an actual fucking nightmare.'

Max blasts through the double swing doors.

'Morning, all!' He wipes his palms on his jeans, rocks back on his heels, and rubs his nose. He nods in my direction, but reels into a conversation with two tech hands by the fridge that contains few words but plenty of over-enunciated laughter.

I take a half-step towards them. 'Max,' I hiss, trying and failing to attract his attention in a subtle manner. 'Max!' He whips around and smacks his lips like he's popping bubble gum.

'Ava? Man, didn't recognise you. You look good. What happened?'

My neck grows hot and I now regret the urgent email I sent to lighting about using the high wattage bulbs. I pull him out of the kitchen and into a darkened corner of the studio.

'I've been looking for you everywhere. Did you have an appointment this morning?'

'What kind of appointment?'

'With the stylist?' I say, tugging at my space buns in an attempt to loosen them.

'Didn't have one,' replies Max. He throws an arm across my shoulders and grins down at me as he steers us towards the studio. I jab a knuckle into his ribs and face him straight on, arms crossed over my scooped T-shirt that shows three inches more cleavage than I'm comfortable with showing.

Max and I met on our NCTJ journalism course five years ago and became an unlikely pair; I'd save him a seat during lectures, he invited me to parties, and our friendship was uncomplicated by sex, which is how he burned his bridges with the rest of our cohort. We ended up at *Snooper* within six months of each other and he delivers peanut and prawn dumplings to my desk if I'm on a tight deadline, so there's genuine friendship there beneath the bravado.

'Duncan literally told me I wasn't allowed to appear on camera if I refused to go.'

'Call it natural beauty,' says Max, posing with his fist propped beneath his chin. He does look annoyingly cool, if dishevelled.

'You excited?' he asks, glancing around at the technicians taping cables to the floor.

'No. I'm ... annoyed at you.'

Max places a hand on his chest and pretends to look affronted. 'Me? No.'

'Please – for the love of all that is holy – can we go over the script.'

'Sorry, looks like we're about to start,' says Max with a wink.

Lowanna, the floor manager, pulls aside her headphones and runs a finger down her clipboard. 'Can we get you in position? Max? Ava? We need to set up the shot.'

I sit down on set and clutch my forehead, squinting. The lights are so bright that everyone's silhouette is stamped on the back of my eyelids. My head throbs. I never thought I'd relate to Harry Potter so strongly, but if I didn't know better, I'd say Voldemort was close by.

Max sits down next to me on a plywood cube and pulls his leg up.

'So, you know the set-up of the feature,' says Lowanna.

'Yes,' says Max, at the same time as I say, 'No.'

'Great,' says Lowanna, ignoring my response. She scrolls through the auto-prompt on her iPad. 'Intro, couple of jokes, quick description of the spit samples, then results. Oh, and if you want to throw in the phrase "Who do you think you are?" that'd really help our Google ranking, but not too obvious. We can't afford to get sued. Make some guesses about what you think you'll discover. Ava, you're up first, Max second, a lil' reflection to close ... and we're done!' Lowanna locks the iPad and hovers, the cups of her headphones held just above her ears. 'All good?'

'Yeah, s'fine,' says Max, nudging me with his arm.

'Don't forget, push all your feelings into your face,' says Lowanna, snapping her headphones back on. 'Subtlety doesn't work on camera.'

'Yeah, about that. Can I have a quick look at the DNA results? I didn't know we were meant to know them in advance.'

'Uhh, no. Slight change of plan. We've decided to keep your results sealed until the big reveal. Max has been prepped for it. He's got your back. Trust me, it'll make for a better delivery.'

Max picks his teeth and flashes me a school photo smile. 'Time to shine, buddy.'

I take a shallow breath as the set swims in front of me. Industrial lighting, the smell of heavy aftershave, and a drum-skin tightness across my forehead swash together and catch in my throat like bile. At the back of the studio, Duncan unfolds a chair in the gloom. He settles into it, his legs crossed at the ankle, observing all before him like the family patriarch. Max raises a hand to wave, but I'm barely keeping my cinnamon porridge down as it is, so don't risk any non-essential movement.

'Something must have caught his attention. Thanks, Tia.' Max drops his gaze, heel jiggling, as Tia turns to me. She removes a wide brush from her holster and dusts my T-zone so thoroughly I'm sure she's trying to lift fingerprints.

She steps away and I sense Max beside me, sitting tall

and poised. He squeezes my knee and nods towards the camera, red light blinking. Lowanna clicks her fingers to get my attention and traces the line of her mouth, urging me to smile like an over-zealous pageant mum.

'Quiet on set!' comes a voice from the darkness. 'Energy! Enthusiasm!! And we're live in three, two, one ...'

Chapter 4

Max nudges me with his elbow. I blink, barely able to focus on the prompter, which has slowed down to a crawl. Lowanna's eyes bulge with impatience. I sit up straight. I've been tiptoeing around Duncan for five years, and now he's right in front of me, leaning forward in his chair as Max goes off-script. I urge my brain to engage as Max buys me some time, but my head is full of noise, all of it loud and distracting. Up until today, I thought of the live stream and the DNA test as two completely separate things, so much so that I hadn't quite processed how publicly I'd receive the results.

I hear my name and it snaps me back into my own body. *Engage brain, Ava.* I catch sight of myself in a monitor off-set: a squinting mole woman, albeit with meticulous winged eyeliner. I can't open my eyes any more, because I'm sure that my skull will split down the middle like an overripe watermelon if I do. Maybe smiling will help? I try, but combined with the squint, it's like I'm in the throes of an acid trip.

Lowanna looks between the monitor and me before smacking her forehead with a clipboard.

'OK, so we better explain how it's going to work. Ava, you ready for the science-y bit?' says Max, pretending to push glasses up his nose with a wink to the camera. He's working the viewers like they're sat round his table in a pub. In that scenario, who am I? The mute who sits in the corner with a soda and lime? Duncan shifts in his seat, poised and attentive as a tennis umpire.

I mimic Max's laissez-faire posture and prop my heel on the stool, looking to him with a smile that I hope comes across as girlish and cool. 'Well, I did get an A in GCSE Biology, but my knowledge is limited to the life cycle of a plant cell nowadays, so you might have to break it down a little.'

Max laughs. I feel my shoulders retreat from their defensive position up by my ears.

'Right! So basically, we sent some saliva samples off to our friends at The Ancestry Project, who analysed our DNA to find out what's going on behind the scenes of our genetic make-up.'

Oh my God. That was *almost* word-perfect from the script I wrote. This is good. I look down the camera lens, chin up. I know what to do from here.

'So how much have you thought about your results since we sent our samples off?' I ask, glancing past the camera to Duncan at the back of the studio. He gives me the tiniest of nods.

'Quite a bit, actually,' says Max, feigning nonchalance. 'But I'm not expecting any curveballs. My dad's a massive history nerd – sorry, Dad – so I know a fair bit about where the Oswolf–Brownes come from.'

'Oswolf–Browne?'

'Yeah. We were quadruple-barrelled at one stage, but my grandfather knocked two names off by Deed Poll way back when. Bit of a mouthful, isn't it? Ironic, seeing as he was an auctioneer, but there you go. Anyway!' says Max, clapping his hands together. 'Ava, what do you know, or think you know, about your heritage?'

'Err, not a whole lot to be honest,' I say, propping my chin on my fist like a crop-top-clad version of The Thinker. 'I haven't grown up with knowledge of my dad.' I weigh my words, unused to hearing a voice so candid coming out of my mouth. 'Only that I must have had one, otherwise I wouldn't be here, right?' Max smiles at me but doesn't interrupt. 'My only family are the ones Mum's pulled into the fold over the years. It sounds weird saying it to other people,' I say, clutching my hands in my lap. 'But before I went to school, Mum and I lived all over the place with The Earth Mamas, so my version of a normal family is … not other people's normal. The Earth Mamas were essentially a nomadic commune, which facilitated some pretty committed activism, back when it was uncool to be an eco-warrior, you know?'

'So, ever since then it's just been you and your mum?' says Max, his fingers tapping his thigh.

'Yeah. I think so.'

'You *think* so?'

'Well, it's like … We've always been a two-person unit, you know? We moved into a house that my grandparents left her, so no more sleeping under canvas. The fight continues, she's just channelled it down other routes. More PTA warrior than eco-warrior nowadays.'

'Well my DNA results are going to be an anticlimax. Sorry, everyone,' he says, looking to the camera.

'You never know, we might turn out to be cousins.'

'That'd make our snog at last year's Christmas party a tad awkward,' says Max.

'Max! You had mistletoe,' I say, rolling my eyes. Duncan and a few others laugh behind the camera. I feel buoyed. The LED viewer count at the front of the studio ticks over into its first thousand.

'Here we go!' says Max, as two envelopes are dangled in front of us. I take the one with Max's name on and he takes mine. The crew are fixed on me, their gaze flicking between me and the envelope in Max's hand. Annoyance prickles up the back of my neck. This is really happening. There's a handful of people here who know that I'm about to get some pretty fucking huge news and their priority was to push me in front of a camera first and ask me how I feel about it second. My hands are clammy. The teleprompter displays a question. I repeat it aloud.

'Nationality. Any guesses before we dive in?' I ask, reading the words in monotone. *Just get through the next few minutes,* I tell myself.

'Ah, easy. A hundred per cent legend.'

'Hundred per cent delusional?' I ask, giving the camera a side-eye as though the viewers are in on the joke. Max grins like he's trying to ruin his school photo.

'You?'

'Couldn't say. I have an ... unsubtle jawline, so ... a bit German?'

'And your dad's side?'

'I have no idea.'

'Shall we?' says Max in a sing-song voice, wiggling the envelope at me.

On set, an off-key sound effect plays to build suspense, but it's more like entrance music for a pantomime baddie. I clutch the side of my stool, my nails scratching the painted MDF as Max slips a finger under the envelope flap. He pulls out a folded piece of card and maintains a neutral poker face, giving the camera a conspiratorial glance.

'Someone lied to you, mate. There's no German, but there is evidence of recent ancestry in Russia on your mum's side.'

'Wow. OK. Maybe it was an awkward time to be part of the Soviet Union?'

'I have always wondered why you get so upset at the unequal distribution of stationery around the office,' says Max. More laughter ripples across the studio.

'Ready for your dad's side?'

In the monitor, my face fills the screen, make-up intact thanks to the sheer quantity of hairspray that serendipitously locked it onto my skin. It was worth the face full of carcinogens.

'How do we feel about haggis?' says Max, peeking at me from behind the gold envelope.

'Never had it,' I say, my stomach tightening.

'Odd, considering that your DNA has a strong Celtic link, which indicates a close ancestor according to our expert over at The Ancestry Project.' I feel my eyebrows retreat up my forehead. 'We're not talking a bit Scottish here. This is a paint-yourself-blue-and-scare-off-the-Romans level of Scottish,' says Max. He launches into a poor imitation of Mel Gibson's *Braveheart*, which sends laughter round the studio.

'How're you feeling?' says Max, his excitement palpable.

I rub my collarbone and take a staggered breath in, nodding slowly as my heart rate levels out. Rory was right. This wasn't as bad as I thought it would be. Now I know that my father is from Scotland, I can find a way to tactfully ask Mum about any trips she's taken up there and work backwards without risking her going into a spiral of denial. Good. This is progress.

'Guys,' says Max at the camera, running a hand through his floppy hair. It falls into annoyingly perfect waves. 'We're glad you're here for this, because Ava's about to get a bit of a treat.'

'I'm good for treats,' I say with a laugh. Max pushes his chair out as a flat-screened TV wheels into view. Oh God, what now?

Max taps the screen. A map of the UK comes into focus, a handful of countries shaded in blue. Up in an area of north-east Scotland, a tiny outcrop of land is ink-dropped by the deepest colour. He taps it again. From London, an animated arrow travels up to a place called Kilroch, where it bounces on the spot, demanding attention like an over-excited toddler.

'Let's give it a look,' says Max, grinning past the camera

to where Duncan sits. He knows already. Everyone must know, except for me. I smile. Behind it my brain is thick like overcooked porridge, but 16,437 viewers are watching the live stream, so I nod in agreement. 'OK, sure.'

Max rubs his hands together and winks at the camera. I don't hear what he says, distracted as I am by an invisible hand that clenches my ribcage and squeezes.

'You have a half-sister,' says Max.

'What?'

'Moira.'

The phrase doesn't register. Max could have asked my opinion on Coco Pops and I wouldn't know what to say. 'I ... don't have a half-sister.'

'Turns out you do. How about that, guys? Our own family reunion here at *Snooper!*' Max nods to catch someone's attention and starts clapping, his eyes crinkled from a broad grin.

I stare at the screen, eyebrow twitching. What the *actual* fuck? This has got to be a wind-up, some gimmicky idea trotted out by an intern to boost our views.

I snatch the envelope from Max and spread the card on my knee as a confetti canon explodes on either side of us. The air is thick with fluttering pastel discs and whooping from the studio, but I hardly notice. I stare at the page, trying to make sense of the figures listed beneath Moira's name and mine. It looks too technical to be fake.

If Mum's relationship with my dad was as fleeting as she's implied, who's to say he didn't father someone else before me? It's not like he would have looked Mum up to tell her, especially when The Earth Mamas' cross-country convoy had no fixed address for the best part of a decade.

I pull a spiral of gold ribbon from my head as Max slaps me on the back in congratulations. The clapping subsides like burst microwave popcorn as a rainbow of detritus settles on the floor.

I stand up, my head throbbing from the sudden movement. Lowanna jabs a finger towards the prompter, which scrolls the message 'KEEP IT LIGHT!' but I don't seem to have control over my body, let alone speech at this particular moment. Max barks out a laugh to fill the terse silence. I close my eyes, willing this all to disappear, but when I open them again the studio shunts sideways and I have to grab Max's shoulder to steady myself.

'Woah, Ava. It's a lot to take in, I know.'

What a fucking joke. He knows, does he? Six years we've been friends and this is what he does for extra views and few brownie points with Duncan?

'Let's sit you down,' he says, gently tugging on my forearm. I yank it away. There's too much light and the silhouettes I can see come in and out of focus like I'm looking through a kaleidoscope. 'Talk us through your feelings,' says Max.

'I'm … I'm feeling a bit weird,' I say, my stomach heaving. An acrid taste pricks the back of my tongue and I hold my mouth slack, horribly uncertain of the warning signs at play.

'Well, that's understandable. This is a surprise! Tell us

what's going through your mind,' says Max, willing me with his eyes to sit down.

'I don't feel good,' I say, draping a forearm across my brow. Max's eyes dart between the camera, Lowanna, and Duncan. At the back of the room, the viewer count rises, 31,589 ... 31,611 ... 32,734.

'Mixed feelings are normal. It's not every day you realise you're not an only child, right?' says Max. He laughs until the sound putters out, the odd piece of confetti drifting down from the lighting rig.

I'm unduly proud of the fact that I haven't been sick since I was nine, the result of a birthday party fuelled by candy floss, off-brand fizz, and a tightly-sprung trampoline. Such an accolade was never destined to last long.

'I'm going to ... I'm gonna—'

Max nods along, realising too late that my puffed cheeks are not, in fact, an ill-timed impression of a particularly sweaty hamster.

There's no time to flee. Heat travels up my throat with alarming speed. Objectively, the pace of delivery is outstanding. I clap my hands over my mouth, but this only succeeds in spraying vomit outwards in a fan, leaving me coughing and spluttering for breath like I've taken in a mouthful of seawater. The camera lens twists, zooming in as I stand slack-jawed on set, the sound of plops hitting the floor as the viewer count ticks over into six figures. I turn to leave, but the floor is so slick that even my Doc Martens can't seem to gain traction. I slip, steady myself, and bolt for the doors, Max's voice ringing in my ears.

Chapter 5

Iblink in the half-light that cuts between the curtains, my skin cold and clammy like a plucked chicken. I push the duvet to one side and yawn, but my jaw is stiff, as though I've been leaning on something and, yep, there's my phone on the pillow, an oily smear of make-up on the screen. Never before have I so deeply regretted making a Twitter account that lists my employer in the bio. I flick through my notifications, but there doesn't seem to be an end to them. Feeling panic rising from the pit of my empty stomach, I jab at my phone, deleting all my social media apps until the notifications slide into one another and disappear. A handful of texts remain, the first from Rory. It must have come through just before we went live.

Break a leg! You look like an X Factor contestant! In a good way!!

Max has got to have some skeletons in his closet with a signet ring like that ... still give him my number though, please and thank you xxx

OH GOD this is it! Buckle up, baby!

Speak, my child, speak!

OCH AYE, Scotland! Excellent! This explains a lot about your ability to cope when the temperature goes above twenty-two degrees.

I hope this 'treat' is a trip to the Edinburgh Fringe. With spending money. And a plus one. Or Iron Bru? Lots of it.

A SISTER. YOU HAVE A SISTER. OH MY GOD. THIS IS HUGE. I'm on shift now, but call me later???

On my break. Just watched the end. Are you OK?? Where are you? Do you need rehydration tablets? I can steal some!

Seriously, let me know you're all right. Not meaning to alarm, but you're all over the internet. As are your stomach contents. Maybe stay offline for a bit. I LOVE YOU.

I groan, pull back the curtain, and blink in the low light. Apart from the post-migraine feeling that the world is covered in cotton wool, I feel OK, despite the faint whiff of vomit that I suspect is coming from my hair. Thank God for the triple-strength Thai painkillers that Mum keeps in her bedside drawer.

I pull my laptop onto the bed, dim the screen, and log into my work account, scrolling until I find an unopened email that contains a link to my results on The Ancestry Project website. I wait for the page to load as a carousel of sepia photographs fills the screen, each smiling face morphing into one from the generation before. The messaging is clear: ancestry is *fun*! Or at the very least, an interesting anecdote to recycle at uneventful barbeques. I click through.

My DNA map loads and I see it played out before me once more. A gold line tracks north from my borough, crosses the Scottish border, and angles towards the east coast. When I click on a place called Kilroch, a faceless avatar glows like a hallway light in winter. My half-sister.

Of the 212,857 linked family members listed under my DNA tree, there's an aunt I already knew about in Peterborough and a bunch of third and fourth cousins scattered across Western Europe and the USA, all decidedly less interesting than Moira.

I click on her avatar. The rough coastline of the Scottish Highlands zooms past jagged peninsulas and land spliced with lochs until a lattice of single roads converge by a harbour. I tap my plastic keyboard and think. If Moira is listed as an immediate relative of mine, does that mean I've come up on her list too? I double-check my preferences and am strangely relieved to see the default settings flicked to 'private'. I'm not quite ready for that.

I've never felt deprived growing up as an only child, but I *have* wondered what it might have been like to know there was someone else around, especially as a kid. Mum and I were so often like bookends, seeing each other at the beginning and end of a day. I spent a lot of time with sticker books under committee tables, crawling out when orange juice and Kit Kats were on offer. Adults liked me, an accolade that ensured other kids didn't. I convinced myself I didn't mind because adults made sense to me; I knew what to ask, when to ask it, and they didn't play made-up games with confusing rules that changed all the time. Mum sometimes arranged sleepovers with the daughters of her friends, but Rory was the only one that stuck. She found me funny for the same reason others found me awkward, like when I laminated the Monopoly rules and founded The Sandwich Club, a lunchtime group that involved tidying school classrooms for fun. For *fun*.

I bring up another internet tab and Google 'Kilroch'. An extract from its Wikipedia page says it's a 'civil parish in the Highland area with a population size of 319'. Bloody hell. You could house the whole village in our local Wetherspoons and still have a few packets of pork scratchings left over. I drop the orange pin onto a lane called Little Vennel, where a series of squat, whitewashed houses materialise on a hill that tips down towards a broad, steel-coloured bay. In the distance, light reflects off the metallic arm of a crane bent over a series of deconstructed rigs.

Rigs ... Mum's mentioned them before. They've got something to do with a pod of dolphins she and the other activists were trying to protect, which makes sense because her dolphin obsession is extreme. Our house is a two-up, two-down but packed into the living room is a dresser full of dolphin memorabilia that Mum has collected over the years: glass-blown dolphins, hand-whittled dolphins, laser-cut crystal dolphins, and, worst of all, a second-hand nail brush shaped like a dolphin. If these are the rigs she spoke about and she was there in the Nineties, my father must have been too.

My stomach flip-flops and my heart races like I've mainlined one too many espressos. I snap my laptop shut. Nothing about Kilroch seems wild enough to justify Mum being so coy about it. It feels like a mosquito bite that I've tried not to touch, but now that I've scratched it, the itch is worse than ever. I don't want to upset her by bringing it up, but I don't want to be lied to either.

Roused by the change of activity, Pickles crawls out from under my bed and leaps onto the window sill, knocking a row of books to the floor. I pull a jumper out from the linen basket and throw my arms into it, nudging him with my foot. 'Go on, go and chase some birds,' I say, pushing my window open and manhandling Pickles onto the garage roof, where he yawns and stretches in the dwindling autumn sun.

In the bathroom, I squint at the mirror. I need some time to figure out what to do with this new information, but the seed of it has planted in my head and I feel full of energy. I arm myself with a hot flannel and a bottle of micellar water. I look like a Picasso portrait. The foundation used to contour my nose is smudged across my cheek, thick and dark. I lean over the sink to scrub and rinse until the water runs clear.

Back in my room with a mug of tea and a fully charged laptop, I'm settling in for another armchair exploration of Kilroch, but as I flick through pictures of seafront houses flanked by fields and a grubby lighthouse, my pillow vibrates. I pull out my phone. Mum's picture appears, flashing on the screen. I slide the bar to answer it, my stomach tight. From her end, there are sharp instructions over a background din of jabbed piano keys and the periodic shrieking of children. At some point I'll have to explain why I need to find a different line of work, something entirely anonymous and preferably remote so I never have a chance to reappear on the homepage of *Snooper* whilst covered in sick. I try and push this thought to the back of my head, quietly raging at whichever web editor decided to punish me with this much coverage. *Take a breath, Ava.*

I haven't got the capacity to lend my anxious brain to work when the sensitive subject of my unknown sister is on the line.

'Ava?'

'Mum? Take me off loudspeaker, I can't hear you properly,' I say.

'Sorry, I've got you balanced on the paper plates. One sec.' I tentatively sit up, my head hollow like a barren pigeon egg. 'You sound awful. Where are you?' she says.

'In bed. Well, I was in bed. Migraine.' No need to go into detail now. Or, perhaps, ever? 'I think I slept it off.'

'Oh, that's a nuisance. Didn't you have that big thing at work today? No – get Geoff to bring round the coffee urn,

otherwise it won't be hot by the time the parents turn up.'
She must be at the school. *Shit.*

'You're feeling better, though? Good. Wonderful.' She
sighs. 'I tried calling earlier, but ... I'm sorry to do this
to you.'

'Do what?' I ask, trying to keep my voice neutral.

Mum shifts to a whisper. 'I can't think of what to do
that'll get us back on track. Not tonight, anyway.'

My stomach lurches. I didn't see 'The Dad Conversation'
happening like this. What was I thinking? After years of
tiptoeing around the subject like a cat on hot tiles, I've made
the whole thing far messier than it was before. Making hints
about the other side of my family never worked in the past,
so why would it now? I feel six years old again, standing
at the top of the stairs in an oversized dressing gown to
eavesdrop on Mum and Ginger talking about something
I couldn't understand. Even today, the stakes are a mystery
because I've got no idea if she knows about Moira's existence either. Realising I've got a sister in Scotland is one
thing, but now there are a hundred other questions I need
the answer to. How many of those would hurt Mum?

'Ava?' she says, 'Are you still there? Shall I come home?'

'No, Mum. I'll be all right,' I reply, my breath shallow.
'What's wrong?'

Mum sighs. 'Nothing's ready. We had the biggest faff
trying to get the bloody leaves up. Father Carmichael has
gone over to Blackheath because he needs to read the last
rites to an ancient parishioner who's had the audacity to
catch pneumonia. Inconvenient, but you can hardly ask

him to postpone. We've got the deacon from St Mary's down instead.'

'Dandruff Dan?' I say, clasping my forehead with relief. She hasn't seen the video. Of course she hasn't. Mum still uses a brick-sized Nokia that plays polyphonic ringtones and only needs charging once a fortnight.

'That's him. Let's hope he's not wearing a black cassock. I was going to ask if you could pick up two or three boxes of wine on your way over. Laura was meant to do it, but her youngest ate the top of a glue stick so she's had to go to A&E.'

'Um, I can—'

'I only ask because I thought you'd be leaving soon. Oh, make sure you're here before the little ones are on stage. The dancing is spectacularly bad,' she says, stifling laughter. 'Possibly because Miss Burford's choreographed it and she's eight months pregnant, so the movements are fairly limited. Anyway, we'll have a giggle if nothing else.'

'All right. I'll be there soon,' I say, biting my hangnail.

I hang up and drop my phone onto the bed. The lock screen lights up; a picture of Mum and me behind a stacked plate of scones laden with clotted cream, our faces covered in crumbs and contentment. I swallow, but it feels as though a pine cone is lodged in my throat.

Chapter 6

The smell of overcooked rice pudding hangs in the air as I step through a side door propped open with a breeze block. My Doc Martens squeak on the parquet as I sidle across the hall towards Ginger, who spots me from a distance and makes a swooping gesture at Mum to let her know I've arrived.

On stage, a group of children dressed in vegetable costumes dance in a wobbly circle, heads whipping round to find their parents in the crowd. A carrot with neat French braids accidentally jabs a broccoli in the eye and he clutches his face as though it's fallen off, his mouth held open in a silent scream. There's a ripple of muttering through the audience as a frazzled woman in a beaded necklace scoops the wailing boy off stage. The remaining vegetables shuffle together to fill the gap, as though this is a practised manoeuvre.

A woman in a neatly pressed linen jacket walks towards me with the short, purposeful stride of a person whose most used phrase is 'Yes, I would like to speak to the manager.' She mouths something at me, but I can't make it out, distracted as I am by the singing.

When she gets closer, I recognise who it is: Mum's arch-nemesis, Vanessa. Mum usurped her chairperson position and Vanessa's run against her at every AGM since. Rumour has it that she bribed the headteacher with a hefty supply of black-market book tokens, but when the head moved on, the new board weren't so easy to influence. The dog poo we had posted through our letterbox in 2003 had to have come from Vanessa; she's the only person we know who has a dog small enough to produce such a turd (an inbred, yappy dachshund with bulging eyes and a nervous disposition).

'Are you Lorrie's girl?' she says, her veneers sparkling.

'Yes.'

'She said you'd be here an hour ago.'

'Well ... I'm here now,' I say, handing her a carrier bag with the wine in it before scooting around in my rucksack to retrieve my camera. I pull the strap over my head and flick the power on.

'We need some pictures of the children, mid-song, cherub-like, that sort of thing. You better be quick – they'll finish in a moment. Avoid Charlotte on the second row; she's got chicken pox and we don't want to advertise it. You've done this before, haven't you?'

'Yep.'

'All right, off you go then.'

Vanessa shoos me towards the children and hovers by my shoulder until I start clicking, her many bracelets tinkling as she dumps my bag on the trestle table Mum is trying to clear of used napkins and plastic cups.

I snap a few photos before the show ends, wildly clicking to ensure there are enough pictures to pacify demands for the school calendar. When the lights are switched on, a horde of oversized vegetables dash towards their parents, most of whom have formed a line in front of the cheap wine I picked up. Vanessa lets Mum serve, using the time to apply a particularly garish shade of mauve lipstick, which smears on the front of her pearlescent teeth. I make a choice not to tell her about it.

'You're a star, Lorrie,' I hear Vanessa saying, as she glances over at Mum. 'I don't suppose you've ever experienced the *total* fucking nightmare that comes with maintaining acrylic nails. The upkeep is such a burden, you know. Forty-five pounds every three weeks. Nigel can't understand it. You're lucky in that respect, darling. Must be nice not to worry about keeping up appearances.' Vanessa picks her teeth with the corner of a blunt-edged nail. Mum straightens, pink-cheeked, and pulls her Per Una cardigan a little tighter around her waist. 'Is there anything left for me to do?' Vanessa adds, her voice dwindling with reticence.

Mum takes a moment to think. 'Well, there's the—'

'Oh! Look who's turned up when everything's finished!' interrupts Vanessa, barking out a laugh as she pretends to spot me for the first time. She squeezes my elbow. 'Do excuse me. I must catch Giles before he heads off. We're at couples' golf on Sunday and I haven't had a chance to ask about a luncheon. You don't mind, do you, Lorrie? Nothing keeping you?' Vanessa unclasps her stiff handbag, runs a wide-toothed comb through her bob, and rubs her lips together, smearing the colour in a clown-like rim around her mouth. 'You *are* good,' she says, swerving around a caretaker who wheels a stack of chairs behind him.

Mum's smile twitches and she blows her fringe out of her face.

'You shouldn't let her speak to you like that,' I say.

'Ah, it's nothing. Vanessa's like an orange; from a distance you'd assume she's sweet inside but you soon realise she's ninety-nine per cent pith.'

'She's definitely got a mean Carol Vorderman vibe about her.'

'She's also the reason we acquired eight M&S sandwich platters for tonight. You have to pick your battles.' Mum pushes her palms into the small of her back and sighs. 'Help me with the tablecloth, will you?' We lift the corners and walk towards each other. She takes it off me and tucks it under her arm. 'You're on edge today,' she says.

'I'm just ...' I look at Mum. She seems older in a way I hadn't noticed before: dark eyes, stooped shoulders, standing with her right hip jutting forward. 'I'm just annoyed with people like her.'

'People like what?'

I nod towards Vanessa, who is busy accepting compliments for the glittering leaf display that she contributed nothing towards. 'All this stuff that you do for the school, and the WI, and the play group – they don't realise how much you take on for them. Vanessa's only here because her husband can't stand her being at home.'

I bite my hangnail and look around the hall. I don't

like this version of myself. I shouldn't be able to say how many times the wall displays have changed, or when they re-laid the parquet flooring. You're meant to remember your first school as a golden haze of sugar paper, poster paints, and pudding-faced dinner ladies, blue crash mats, cloakrooms, and wearing Hula Hoops as wedding rings. With the amount of times I'm pulled back, I've never had a chance to grow nostalgic.

Mum has sewn herself into this community. Her presence isn't remarked on, but assumed, otherwise how would anything function? She loves it. There's nothing that gives her greater joy than arguing over the correct placement of sausage rolls at a finger buffet. But is it my thing, too? Other than work, this is what I do the most. Her social life is *my* social life, because it's only ever been me and her. Until today. Now there's Moira and God knows who else up in Scotland. If I go there to find out, is it like I'm abandoning her?

Mum ties up the handle of a bin bag. 'You know, Vanessa never spends time at home because her husband has been having an affair since 2003 and she can't leave him because he tied up their finances in the pre-nup.' I scuff the floor with the toe of my boot. I can feel Mum's eyes on me, but I don't look up. 'We've all got different reasons for doing things.'

We stand side by side and lean against the wall bars at the same time, Mum sighing with weariness. We look out in comfortable silence as the last few parents sing goodbyes and wheel scooters towards the exit, miniature rucksacks swung over adult arms. Mum bumps her shoulder against mine and my stomach flip-flops, as though physical proximity might increase the likelihood of her accidentally absorbing what I know.

'Are you happy?' I ask.

'Jesus, Ava. What, right now? In life? In spirit?'

'Sorry, I didn't mean that to sound so ... meta. Like, generally?'

'Yeah, more or less. I've got a few good reasons to get up in the morning. Pickles would starve rather than catch anything to eat, for starters. Then there's Ginger, who would probably be the third wife of a serial polygamist if it wasn't for my intervention on those God-awful dating apps. And I've got you,' she adds with haste, feigning an afterthought.

'I'm actually shocked that I come after Pickles,' I say, disguising laughter.

'It's not personal, sweetheart. He keeps my bed warm and doesn't flail about half as much as you did when you were little.'

'Unbelievable.'

'Would you get those for me?' says Mum, gesturing to the bin bags. I pick them up as the caretaker stacks chairs around us, whistling through his teeth. Back in the hall, we collapse tables.

'Oh, before I forget – I said you'd come to the Hastings beach trip with the Brownies Saturday after next. We have to allocate one adult to eight kids now, so we could do with the extra body. Anyway, I thought you might like to get out of the house. Sea air and all that good stuff.'

'I, err ... Can I get back to you on that?'

Mum looks at me, her head tilted to the side like a confused spaniel. A shrill laugh bounces off the walls, flicking our attention to the furthest corner of the hall. Vanessa is trying her best to cordon Giles off from his wife, a woman whose irritation is made obvious through her clipped responses and the persistent tapping of a crocodile skin shoe.

'I thought she was after Simon the Hotelier?' I ask.

'His wife came out of a coma, so she's had to move on,' Mum mutters, flashing a fake smile in their direction.

'Are we sure Vanessa didn't have anything to do with Simon's wife going *into* a coma?' I ask.

'It's the mystery plaguing Dulwich,' says Mum. We put the bin bags down by the door step and say goodbye to a mum who clutches the sleeve of her son's coat as he tries to wriggle out of it.

'Imagine if I didn't have you around? I'd end up like Vanessa, drinking expensive gin at eleven in the morning, wondering why the house was so quiet.'

My pocket buzzes with a text message. It's Max. I scowl and shove it back in my jeans. Mum nods towards the door.

'You get home. I'll finish up.'

'You sure?' I say, not used to being let off early.

'Yep. Just make sure the kettle's filled up if you're going to bed. Ginger'll be round later and I'm keeping her off the wine.' She squeezes my hand, walks to the front of the hall and slots herself next to Vanessa, giving Giles the chance to slip away. A stellar manoeuvre from our Lorrie Atmore.

I open a message from Max as I step outside.

Hey Ava. First of all, are you OK? Secondly, yes it did all come out in the wash, thanks for asking. Today was something else! More details soon. A bunch of us are heading out in Shoreditch. Buzz me if you want the location. Peace!

Is he having a laugh? Seems like I'm not the only one taking a break from reality tonight.

Chapter 7

My eyelids feel gritty as I wake up to the sound of bickering seagulls, an odd alarm call considering how far inland we are. I push myself up in bed, but my fingers get caught on the wire from my earphones. I fell asleep watching a webcam feed of Kilroch harbour, which explains the unusual alarm clock. Autumn has already swathed the east coast of Scotland, with dark mornings and pockmarked fishing boats pulled up onto the slipway, the industrial silhouette of an oil rig outlined by an inky black horizon.

Last night, I skimmed through dozens of web pages that refer to Kilroch: travel blogs; TripAdvisor entries for its one pub and two cafés; and endless Wikipedia pages on its history to the point where I'm now starting to understand references made in the shipping forecast. I'm not sure what else I was hoping to find. Perhaps an old photograph of a man pale enough to blame for my inability to tan, or a record of Mum's activity that explains why nearly half my DNA comes from inside a tiny Scottish village. By the time I'd read a seven-page forum spat between two rival fishermen over who really *did* land the biggest herring haul of 2007, my research was at a dead end.

I pad past Mum's room and brush my teeth with one hand, the other switching my phone off flight mode. There are many things I fall short on, but coping with a barrage of overwhelming feelings is something I'm *really* good at. It's learned behaviour, as Mum exercises this method frequently. It's like taking a holiday from your own emotions. One press of a button and you can filter who can contact you and when, thus – *fuck*.

I double-tap on an email from Duncan. This is it. This is when I get refused a reference and have to spend my days racing the clock to earn a toilet break in a distribution warehouse. My stomach drops like a Slinky down a mineshaft as I take my phone down to the kitchen and pull a half-eaten packet of Bourbons towards me, shoving two in my mouth and reaching for a third as I wait for the email to load through our ancient broadband.

> *I'd like you to come into the office ASAP re: DNA livestream. 8AM. Bring a pastry.*
>
> *Duncan*

Bring a bloody pastry? Am I supposed to organise the catering for my own dismissal? He knows I'm a meticulous filer of expenses; there's no way this is coming out of my last paycheck.

I want to care about it. I *should* really care about it. I've plugged away at the Junior Editor role since I left Kings;

the grey area between writing and reporting that every graduate is forced to compromise on, but I didn't think I'd still be here years later. Although I have an excellent knack for matching amusing GIFs to listicles, it's not where I thought I'd be at this stage of my career. I write well. I know my way around a metaphor and always deliver on time. But the skills I learned whilst training are barely applicable at *Snooper*. I offered to cover the student riots a couple of years ago and Duncan told me to 'take the bomb-proof vest off, we don't do that shit here,' and so it was back to proofreading a piece on '12 YouTube Videos that Will Change the Way You Think About Make-Up'.

Pickles licks his sandpaper tongue across my toes. 'Is that necessary?' I say with feigned annoyance, pulling him onto my lap. I bury my face into his fur, which triggers a protest meow.

'What are we going to do?'

I look down at him. He stares back, a globule of happy dribble dangling from his toothless mouth.

***

I tuck a paper bag of cheese twists and cinnamon swirls into my rucksack. This way, if the pastry comment was a joke, I don't have to reveal my inability to read sarcasm in emails (and can scoff them at my one-person pity party on the way home). If it wasn't, I'll have appeased Duncan and might get some kind of sympathy bonus on my last payslip. I head past reception, but avoid walking past the notorious gossip that is Carl, as he's in the corner of the auditorium shredding paper whilst video calling someone who gasps and tells him to 'shut up' every few seconds.

I'm early, so walk over to my desk and start peeling Post-it notes from my computer screen. Across the court-yard, Duncan paces in his office, gesticulating into the air with a mobile held up to his ear. He turns on his heel and is ... laughing? Hmm. Odd. He catches my eye and gestures for me to join him.

I pick my bag up and wheel my chair in, but the legs bump against something soft and doughy. A snuffling sound, like a pig with a bad cold, comes from under the desk.

'Morning, sunshine,' slurs Max, who squints at me from under his Canada Goose jacket.

'Max! What the fuck! Why are you sleeping under my desk?'

'Went out last night after work and didn't make it home. Turned into a big one, actually. Haven't had that much powder since New Year's Eve.' Max stretches slowly and runs his tongue along his gums. 'I did text you, didn't I?' he says, holding out a hand for me to grab. Pff. *As if I'm going to help him up.* Max rubs his palm against his jeans.

'I've washed it, promise,' he says. 'Although I should be asking you that question ...' he says, grimacing at my hands.

'Oh, here we go,' I say, rolling my eyes. I should have known he'd prepare stand-up material for our next run-in.

Max gives me a lazy grin and staggers to his feet. He looks like he's stepped out of a Tim Burton film, all insect limbs and hollow eyes. 'You missed a good night out.'

'Yeah, I was a bit preoccupied,' I say tersely, looking in the other direction. Max doesn't take the hint. Instead, he swings an arm around me and rubs his knuckles against my head, which is infuriating, although somewhat satisfying considering how bruised my scalp feels after yesterday's hair trauma. I duck under his elbow and sit on the corner of my desk where I can scowl at him more obviously.

'Are you pissed off because I knew about the sister thing and didn't tell you? Moira, isn't it?' he says, rubbing the joints in his fingers. I feel like I'm going to spew again, but this time it'll be a tirade of profanities rather than actual vomit, which is marginally better.

'There are two things about this situation that are grossly unfair,' I say, launching into the speech that I'd mentally rehearsed on the train. 'One: that I've lived my *whole life* not knowing that Moira exists and then *you* find out about her first,' I say, adding an accusatory finger in his direction. I didn't consider hand gestures before now, but it feels right, so I'm working with it. 'Two: that you thought the *perfect* time to reveal that *teensy* piece of information was on air in front of 35,000 people.'

Max swallows his smile and a deep furrow appears between his eyebrows. 'Look, I didn't think you'd react like that. I genuinely thought it would be a nice discovery for you. I knew about your dad not being ...'

'Alive?'

'Yeah. And, well ... you've got that lone wolf thing going on, so I thought it'd be a nice surprise.'

'It was,' I spit, my jaw clenched.

'Are you sure? Because this,' he says, circling his face, 'isn't screaming joy ...'

'I am happy! It's just ... it's not as simple as "Wahoo! Ava has a sister! Let's start planning a Christmas sleepover!" It doesn't just involve me, does it? I literally grew up in a household where the motto was "Don't look back, look forward" and I know that's largely because of my dad, even though Mum can't bring herself to talk about him. Is it cool I have a sister? Yes. Could this have been timed better? Absolutely. Is this going to upset my mum? Probably, and that's why my brain feels like scrambled egg.'

'Why? Was she the sexy other woman?' says Max, his chin tipped back.

'It's astounding that you can be pervy about someone who isn't even here. Especially my mum.'

Max pulls me into a reluctant side-hug, squeezing my arms flat against my side.

'There's one *tiny* detail amiss,' he says.

'What do you mean?'

'It wasn't 35,000. If you count replays, yesterday we tipped into six figures.'

'Oh, God. *Shit*. Are you serious?'

'Yeah ...' says Max, somehow managing to look proud and sheepish at the same time.

'Even the sick bit?'

'Especially the sick bit.'

'Ah, no. No, no, no,' I chant, squatting to the floor. I tuck my head between my knees and breathe deeply.

He pulls me to my feet, his voice without the slick of

bravado that he often uses at work. 'I know yesterday might have *felt* like a very bad day in the office –'

'That's a total fucking understatement.'

'– but trust me, it really kicked things up a notch or two around here,' says Max.

'Can you just tell me where I can find a cardboard box? I want to take my succulents home and I don't want to do it whilst everyone's here gawping.'

'Ava – stop. Just go and see Duncan. Please.'

I try very hard to swallow my pride, but it feels like a gobstopper stuck in my throat.

'Fine,' I say, hitching my backpack higher on my shoulders. Max ruffles his hair, steers me towards the corridor, and holds open the door with mock chivalry.

'Do you know what's really unfair?' I say, turning back to face him. 'That you can rock up after an all-nighter and *still* look like you're shooting a *Rolling Stone* cover. Is there no justice?'

Max winks. 'Laters, treacle,' he says, saluting me as the doors ping closed.

***

My stomach rumbles.

'You hungry?'

'I am a bit, yeah.'

'Why don't you crack those pastries open?' says Duncan, leaning back in his chair. He crosses his feet at the ankles and props them on the corner of his desk, arms folded over an ugly knitted tank top.

I try and read his expression. Is he being nice, to soften the blow? Or is he just hungry and time poor?

I pull out the paper bag and slide it across the table towards Duncan, who peers inside like he's a police detective inspecting particularly gruesome evidence.

'No pain au raisin?' he asks.

'No.'

'Shame.'

He pulls out a cinnamon swirl, rips off a chunk, and dunks it in his tea.

'Here's the thing,' he says, his words muffled as he sprays pastry flakes across the table. 'You know as well as I do what the problem is here. I get it,' he says, raising his hands in admission, 'it's a generational thing isn't it? You lot grew up with tick box exams, participation prizes, toys in cereal boxes, all that "follow your dreams" rhetoric. I have to dangle carrots to get writers your age to take risks. Don't take it personally, you can't help it.'

I open my mouth to say something, but hold back because I'm so confused about the direction this is going in.

'Point being—' He takes another bite and sucks his fingers clean. 'You've got my attention now.'

Duncan sits back in his chair and starts tapping on his phone. He places it down on my side of the table and swivels the screen to face me.

'Site traffic for the past twenty-four hours. Have a guess at the precise moment you blanked. Oh, and vomited on camera. Can't forget that. Go on.' This feels like the time I got pushed off a twenty-five-foot diving board at the leisure centre. The free fall was horrific but knowing that all that water was rapidly coming up to smack me in the arse was worse.

A graph unsubtly tracks a huge peak in web traffic at midday that only briefly dipped in the early hours of this morning. I knew the live stream was a total bloody car crash, but the scale of the pile up has only just hit me.

'Umm, I can explain,' I say, my neck hot.

'Can you explain how every single area of the website saw the biggest jump in click-through traffic since last year?'

'Because I spewed like a Catherine wheel? But in my defence—'

'And that's where I'm gonna stop you. Max said you'd try and deflect, but—'

'With all due respect, Duncan, if I'm getting fired, can it just happen already? The past twenty-four hours have been ... a total nightmare. I know Max is a far better presenter than me, but considering the circumstances, I was hardly going to outperform him. I was bait for the piece, wasn't I? I *like* working here, but it's felt like *Groundhog Day* for the past couple of years. In short, I can't write any more variations of "23 Jack Russells That Look Like Leonardo DiCaprio" or I'm going to be sick,' I say, immediately regretting my choice of words.

'Bit late for that, isn't it?'

'If I can't work here anymore, can you tell me straight? Because then I can start emailing out the dozens of pieces you've rejected over the years so that someone, somewhere, can pay me for them.'

'God, I should have switched to coffee before this,' says

Duncan, wincing as he rubs the back of his neck. He looks exceptionally like a basset hound today, right down to the rheumy eyes.

'We've had more advertising revenue come in overnight than we have done in the whole of the last quarter. Two major lifestyle brands want to run homepage campaigns and, collectively, we've gained ...' He picks up his phone and scrolls for a moment, the white light from the screen illuminating the unshaved salt and pepper bristles on his chin. 'Nineteen thousand subscribers to our live stream, and three times that across all our social media platforms.'

'Oh, Jesus. This is because I made a total tit of myself on camera, isn't it?'

'It's safe to say that you made an impression.'

I concentrate on jiggling my foot up and down because I can't bear the thought of shedding even one single tear in front of Duncan in what is so far the longest conversation we've had in the six years I've worked here.

'Have you looked at the comments?'

'God, no. I'm completely mortified, Duncan.'

'I'll give you a flavour of what we've had,' he says, clicking through pages on his iMac until a thumbnail of Max and me appears on the screen. My stomach swoops like I've been pushed off a swing.

Duncan clears his throat. '"Where have you been hiding her? She's HILARIOUS!" That last bit is typed in capitals, by the way,' Duncan adds, breaking the high-pitched voice he's adopted to characterise them. '"This reveal was a ride! Where the hell is Kilroch and why isn't she on her way there to find her sister?!" There *are* a few that focus on the vomiting, but objectively it was funny, even if the studio smells like a bad coach trip.' Duncan rocks forward in his chair, grinning. He puts the tablet down, leaving the comments hanging in the air between us.

'I know you've got some issues with how we set this up, but the results speak for themselves,' he says, gesturing to the screen. 'I don't know how much of that you planned, but frankly I don't care. You did a good job.' Duncan smiles, despite the concertina of frown lines on his forehead. 'Ava, I'm giving you a compliment, so write it down or something because they're not handed out often.'

I bite my thumbnail, the skin around it already pink and sore. 'Thanks, but, um ... I'm not sure this is the reputation I want.'

'Look, I know this isn't conventional. It's not like you're a bad writer. But what we do here is find a different source, a different perspective, and then present it with a fresh kick. I couldn't pick out something you've written from any of the other kids that come in here knowing how to use a semi-colon, which, by the way, is far less important than having a bit of grit. That live stream, though? Internet gold. Your script was good. You're funny, whether intentionally or not. It's the direction we need to be going in.'

I look out of the window and watch two pigeons jostle for space on a window sill, chests puffed out, toe-tapping along the ledge.

'If you never thought I was a good journalist, why have you kept me in editorial for so long?' I say.

'It's *because* I think you're good that I'm asking you to leave.'

'What?' I say, my voice small. *Jesus*. I didn't know it was going to be quite this brutal. I thought I'd at least be able to collect my mug from the kitchenette before handing my staff pass back.

'Not like that,' he says, waving a hand in the air. 'Sorry. The husband and I have been watching a lot of Swedish crime recently. I can't seem to stop making everything sound like a homicide plot. Where was I? Right. The way I see it, you've got a choice to make.'

Duncan holds his hand up, ready to tick points from his fingers.

'DNA tourism is on the up. You've got a personal angle and an audience waiting for more content. If you want to pursue this story, it's there. If you don't want to do it, I'll understand. It's not my family on the table, so ultimately, it's not my call.'

I jiggle my knee. Ever since I found out about Moira, I've been fixed on the idea that if *only* the timing had been better, if *only* I'd found out more gently, I'd have more clarity about what to do. But that's not true, is it? There's no such thing as *good* timing, not with something like this. If I go up to Kilroch, I can look into my father's side without having to broach the subject with Mum, thus avoiding the likelihood of her shutting down like an angry clam. If I find Moira, it'll have been worth it. If I don't find her, things can go back to normal. At the very least, I'll know something more about the place my parents met.

I tap the front of my teeth and take a deep breath. I've never travelled alone, let alone the far end of Scotland. If Mum knew where I was going, she'd ask too many awkward questions, which isn't unreasonable when you consider that we've only holidayed apart once, and even then it was a Centre Parcs forty-five minutes out of London. I'll have to say I'm going to Edinburgh for a work trip, otherwise her suspicion levels will be off the chart.

'I've not left the country before,' I say.

Duncan grins, his joy undisguised.

'It's Scotland, Ava, they eat the insides of a sheep and call it normal, but that's as weird as it gets.' Duncan rocks forward in his chair, folding his arms. 'Look, our audience want to be on this journey with you. If you're going to explore your family connection anyway, you can take them. Combine it with a diary series – something quirky, eccentric, funny – that's the vibe we're angling for.'

'But I don't think I'm any of those things,' I say.

'You are. The live stream proved that,' says Duncan, tapping the graph on his tablet. He sits back, eyes narrowed, and raps the table with his knuckles. 'Let's say you find your sister, sit her down, announce yourself ... you may as well turn it into a video feature, right? We can use it as a follow-up; the viewers get a happy ending, and you get more space on the homepage.'

I nod, but it's only to buy myself some time. I don't need to look for ways to justify it anymore. It's obvious, both for my job and as a way to stitch together the mismatched pieces of my family history. The only problem is figuring out a way to appease Duncan's need for clickbait content whilst I try to find Moira, thus gently broaching the subject of our father's Lothario approach to procreation.

'How long do you think you'll need?' says Duncan. He shuffles back in his chair and gives me a hard smile.

'Six weeks? Maybe less? I'd want to try and integrate within the community. I don't want to freak anyone out by scribbling things down in shorthand, you know?'

'Hmm. Just one small factor to consider. If you wait that long, our audience will have moved on by the time you deliver the goods.'

I nod, more to reassure myself than Duncan. 'It's not just about the job, though. I don't know Moira. She might not want anything to do with me, especially if I charge up to the Highlands and announce myself without knowing more about the circumstances.'

'Take a week,' he says, swallowing coffee.

'I don't know ... What if it takes me a while to find her? I'll keep busy, content wise. I'll write a bunch of diary entries, travel guides, whatever you want. *Snooper* aside, this is a big deal for me. I need more time.'

Duncan's purses his lips to the side. 'We can figure out the logistics when you're there, but I can't guarantee how long this assignment will last. If you're going to go, go soon.' He holds his hands up, his shoulders hunched aggressively. 'Clock's ticking.'

I nod, swinging my rucksack over my arm, and hover by the door. There was a time I was envious of those who walked out of Duncan's office with new job titles and bylines. Now that it's me, I don't know how to feel. At this point, I can't sit back and wait for someone else to decide for me.

'Duncan?'

'Hm?' he grunts.

'I'll go. This is my story, isn't it? I'll figure out the right way to tell it.'

Chapter 8

'I just don't understand why you need to go up there. What are they expecting you to learn in Edinburgh that they can't teach you down here?'

'Well, it's to see a different side of the magazine, I suppose. They've been encouraging more of us to go up to the Scotland office anyway. The desk cost is way cheaper. I think they're trying to make it the bigger of the two UK headquarters. Something to do with Brexit. I don't know the details,' I garble across the kitchen table. Mum frowns as she snips thyme sprigs from the planter outside.

'Ava, can you take these off me?' I get up and walk to the open window, pulling my dressing grown tight around my chest. Mum reaches through and hands me a bunch of herbs, their smell woody and fresh. 'Pop them in a glass of water, would you?' I nod and turn the tap on. Mum disappears below the window frame. 'It seems a bit last-minute. Are you sure they're not exploiting you?' she continues. 'You're with a union, aren't you?'

Opening the fridge, I glance at the half-eaten mackerel that was there a few days ago. Tempted by the smell, Pickles winds around my legs, a globule of saliva dripping onto the kitchen tiles. 'It's a good thing, Mum. They don't give these opportunities to everyone.'

Mum frowns and dips below the windowsill again. I close my eyes and breathe in slowly, partly from nerves, partly from the fish juice that has leaked on my hands.

'Here you go, slugger,' I say, scraping oily fish skin into Pickles's bowl. He trots over, his deep purr a token of simple contentment. 'How is it I'm envious of you right now?'

***

Duncan wants me on a train by next week so I've spent the last few days trawling the internet for accommodation. I was hoping to stay on the outskirts of Kilroch to keep a low profile, but with the North Sea on one side and a roughly stitched patchwork of fields on the other, there isn't such a thing as a suburb. The two B&Bs I've called so far have already closed up for the winter, so I've turned to my last resort.

I found it on a volunteering forum, hidden on page five of Google under 'Kilroch home stay'. Braehead Farm. And not a scrubby urban farm like you get in London featuring fat goats, a depressed donkey, and bags of pellets for toddlers to chuck at the animals. A proper, working farm with a muddy track, sun-strewn fields, and an assortment of disused machinery rusting in the driveway.

A farmer named Kian needs a volunteer to 'help with the family's rare breed pigs and chickens, as well as extraneous duties in exchange for free bed and board'. Although I'm dubious about how legitimate this is, the reference point I've latched onto is 'no experience necessary'. The nearest I've come to animal husbandry involves pulling fledglings out of Pickles's mouth back when he was fit enough to climb trees, so this suits me. With no phone number listed, I ping Kian an email. If Duncan wants me to get 'stuck in and chase a story', that's exactly what I'll do.

I lie back on my bed and click through photographs of the farm: a whitewashed house smothered in wisteria, set within patchy heathland. It looks idyllic.

'Where is it you're staying again, Ava?' shouts Mum from across the landing. This is a trick question. She's framing it as though I've told her already (which I can't have done, as the only bed I've booked so far is a single berth on the Caledonian Sleeper train up to Inverness) so she must think I'm lying about something. Which I am. Sort of.

'Not sure yet, someone is going to meet me at the station.'

I glance over the half-filled suitcase and sigh as Pickles climbs on top of a neatly rolled jumper. He paws it, his purr throaty and self-satisfied. I haven't got a clue what to pack. I've tried checking the east Highlands forecast, but between October and December it's like a weather tombola: rain, sleet, sun, or fog in any combination, sometimes multiple times a day.

As I attempt to manhandle my stiff, sun-bleached rain mac into its zip-up hood, my laptop pings with an alert. I stuff the mac into a trainer, open my email, and experience the now familiar pang of anxiety that comes with knowing I've pulled off a plan that part of me was hoping would fail.

Hey, Ava!

Thanks for responding to the volunteer call-out. I was starting to think I'd have to prepare the farm for winter on my own! We've got a spare room in the house that you'd be welcome to use. It's an old building, but we're well prepared for whatever Storm Sandra decides to fling our way when she lands next week. Bring thick socks and you won't go too far wrong.

You didn't mention whether you'd done any labouring or farmhand work before, but don't worry because you can shadow me. I'm learning the ropes again myself after spending some time away, but I'll explain all that when you get up here.

Hope the train journey isn't too painful. The Caledonian Sleeper can be a wee bit temperamental, but as long as you hold on to the bed rails round the corners you shouldn't fall out of your bunk. I'll pick you up outside the station near the war memorial.

Apologies if this all sounds rushed—the internet is temperamental so I have to get this sent off before it disappears again.

See you soon, if I haven't put you off!

Kian

I read the email again, my foot jiggling against the bed frame. Pickles opens one grumpy eye and stares at me.

'Mum!' I shout into the hallway. 'Have you got some fleecy socks I can borrow?'

***

'God, what's that smell?' I ask, as Rory opens the door to Ginger's flat. Mum kicks her boots off by the door and smacks a kiss on Rory's cheek before breezing through to the kitchen.

'Dried porcini mushrooms. Mum found them at the back of a cupboard and she's trying to boil them into a soup. Don't worry, I've ordered us pizza. I've told the delivery guy to post it through the window.'

Inside, Ginger greets me with red eyes and a staggered sniff between each word.

'Oh, Ginge. You didn't have to go to all this effort,' says Mum, blinking at the gelatinous grey liquid bubbling on the stove.

'I can only apologise on Mum's behalf,' says Rory.

'See how cruel she is to me?' says Ginger, jerking her thumb at Rory.

'It looks lovely, Ginger. We had a nibble before we came out, but I'm sure a little bowl wouldn't hurt, right, Ava?' says Mum, fixing a smile. Bloody liar. I'm absolutely starving and I know she is too because the only thing I could find in our fridge was a single bendy carrot.

'Well, I hope you've got a robust digestive system,' says Rory.

'I'm sure it'll go down just fine,' says Mum. She turns to Ginger, folding her arms. 'What's going on with this bloke then?'

From the stove, Ginger's shoulders judder. Rory raises an eyebrow and nods towards the corridor. We slip out and head to her old bedroom, where we pull out a futon to lie back on. Rory smacks my leg, her glee uncontained.

'A sister?'

'Half-sister,' I add.

'Pfff, like that makes a difference. Does Lorrie know?'

'No. You know what she's like when you bring up anything remotely uncomfortable,' I say, tucking my feet underneath me.

'She makes a speech about not living in the past and then cleans the house for five hours?'

'Exactly. You haven't told Ginger, have you?'

'God, no. She can't keep secrets for shit. She's distracted, anyway. Some bloke.'

'Who is it this time?'

'Hmm. I think he's called ... Richard,' says Rory. 'Richard the Third. Pretty textbook, if the previous two are anything to go by.'

'Recently divorced, recently retired, and a new member of the golf club with "no partner" for the annual dinner dance ...'

'... which Mum will expect an invite to, only ...'

'... he's taking his wife back.'

We've been through this routine every few months since we were twelve or thirteen and it's only funny now because of its familiarity.

'Have you watched it back yet?' asks Rory, her voice softening.

'Oh God, no. That would be a form of masochism.'

'Have you messaged each other yet? What's she like?'

'I guess I'll find out when I see her,' I say, biting my lip in anticipation of her reaction.

'What?' says Rory. I shush her as she smacks my arm repeatedly.

'Yeah. I've told Mum I'm going on a mini sabbatical to Edinburgh, but I had a job stopping her from looking through my suitcase. I've not exactly packed for the city.'

I tell Rory about the geo-tag that came up on The Ancestry Project, Kian's farm, and the diary I'm planning on writing for *Snooper*.

'Maybe don't tell Kian where you work. It makes it sound ... dodgy.'

'No, I'm going to avoid bringing it up at all. I don't want anyone to think I'm taking advantage, but it's not like I can go around admitting that I'm on the hunt for a sister I only discovered a week ago. There are only 300 people in the village, so someone's bound to know her, right?'

'Good point. If a random English girl turned up in my neighbourhood looking for me, I'd assume I owed them money.'

'That's because you've taken out too many store cards.'

'Now is not the time for lectures, peach. I'm not downplaying this though; it is mad, right?'

'Yeah,' I say, leaning my head against the bamboo bed frame. I feel uncharacteristically relaxed. The only thing missing is a cup of Ovaltine and half a Nytol tablet, a form of deep relaxation that I treat myself to on a strictly once-a-month basis. Generally, I rely on a certain level of neurosis to function.

'Do you know anything else about her?'

'Moira? No, other than her hometown. Luckily, there's

nothing else near Kilroch and it's not like you can pass through it because it's surrounded by sea on three sides, so there's a strong chance she's there.'

'What about her age? Are you big or little sister? Both have their ups and downs, speaking from experience. Remember when Amélie used my Ghds to straighten her pubes? Unforgivable. I can't wait until she brings her uni boyfriend home. The ammo I've got to hand ...'

I laugh. It feels good, like someone's kneading the furrow out of my forehead. 'I guess a lot depends on what kind of person our dad was, right? There could be ten of us. I just don't know.'

'Good point.'

'That's why I've got to tread carefully. Get a sense of what went on before I pop the confetti cannon and shout, "SURPRISE!"'

'You didn't pack a confetti cannon ...' says Rory, her voice two octaves lower.

'No, I'm not a total maniac.'

'Ha! Good. Look, I'll drip-feed Lorrie some info about this *sabbatical* you're on via Mum. If anything kicks off here, I'll get a message to you.'

'I wouldn't bother texting. The reception is terrible, Kian's warned me about that already.'

'I'll figure out something. Leave it to me, I'll be your eyes and ears back in London.'

We both turn to the window when a man wearing a motorbike helmet appears, pointing to a pizza box held against his hip.

'Is this a mad idea?' I ask, my stomach tight.

'Nah, window pizza delivery is the only solution to Mum's shite cooking.'

'No, going to Scotland. Trying to find her.'

'It is,' says Rory, bending the box to squeeze it through the window. 'But that's also the reason why you should do it. Don't worry about Lorrie. Mum will keep her busy.'

I smile. Rory has plucked out the thought hovering at the forefront of my mind. 'Hey, I owe you one.'

Chapter 9

I've done my fair share of sleeping on public transport. When you're jostling between a hundred other passengers, tactical napping becomes an art form, one that requires a specific toolkit. You want a hat (berets work well), headphones (noise cancelling), and The Goldilocks Seat (middle of the carriage, headrest, least crowded). As a Londoner, I'm well trained in making the best of bad travel, which is probably why my cabin on the Caledonian Sleeper was such a pleasant surprise. Sure, you can touch every wall from the bunk bed, but there's a duvet, mini toiletries, and a nice porter in the corridor who asks if you'd like tea or coffee as part of your wake-up call. On a train!

I pull my suitcase out from under the bunk and sift through layers of thermal vest tops to find my laptop buffeted by my tightly rolled M&S knickers. I sit on the lower bunk with my back against the wall, a can of mojito and a packet of pitta chips wedged between my knees. I check my email in case Kian has experienced a last-minute change of heart, although there's not much I can do about it now if he has.

A restless energy is lodged somewhere in my throat that makes me want to walk laps of the train. Seeing as two people can't pass each other in the narrow corridor without grazing cheekbones, I resist. Instead, I wriggle into a pair of fleece pyjamas, accidentally flashing my boobs to an old couple at a level crossing in the process. Before I have time to feel embarrassed, the train picks up speed and heads out of the city.

***

As I step down from the carriage early next morning, the wind hits me like a slap in the face. I only just manage to hold onto the tassels at the end of my scarf before it's pulled from my neck by the wind, its length whipping behind me like a flag. My suitcase rolls backwards at an alarming speed in the few seconds that I've not been holding it. A glance over my shoulder shows that I'm not the only one, going by the five-bag pile-up that a station guard has managed to intercept with an extended foot.

I swing my rucksack on, hook my suitcase on my elbow, and attempt to steer it towards the exit whilst gusts of wind lure the wheels in different directions. By the time I reach the covered doors, I feel thoroughly beaten up, my hair stuck across my forehead by the haze of drizzle threaded through the air.

It's barely eight o'clock, but the tiny station car park is full of mud-slicked hatchbacks and grumbling taxis. I stand on tiptoes to spot the four-by-four that Kian said to look out for, but so far, I seem to be the only person in

Inverness who doesn't know exactly where they're going. Passenger doors open, hooded heads dip inside cars, and swaddled children are chivvied round the corner. As the station falls quiet (well, as quiet as it can get when the wind sounds like an old man whistling with no front teeth) I start to feel real, acute panic. What in the fucking fuck was I thinking?

I walk back inside to where the Caledonian Sleeper train is and strongly consider getting back on it. How did I possibly think this idea would go down well? I'm so far north that the sun has barely risen, but already it looks to be sinking back down below the horizon, I've got a Pac-a-mac and a pair of barely used trainers in my bag to serve me in what feel like near Arctic conditions, and the only thing I know for sure is that somewhere in a thirty-mile radius is a sister who doesn't know I exist.

I turn around and press my forehead against a brick wall. From behind, it must look like I'm initiating a game of hide and seek, except I'm a grown-up woman and the only things I'm hiding from are the consequences of my ill-thought-out decisions. I try and slow my breathing down, but it's not working. My heart beats faster than the time Duncan took us bouldering on a staff 'away day'; I got stuck three feet up the climbing wall and had to accept a piggyback from Max to get me off the bloody thing.

'Ava?'

I spin, trying to push my hair out of my face (a futile act), and shift from one foot to the other. A man stands by the exit wearing an old hoodie and two-tone trousers that unzip at the knee. I can't imagine a single scenario that would necessitate such a rapid transition into shorts, but it takes all sorts, as they say.

'Ava Atmore?'

'Hi. Yes. Kian?'

'Yeah, that's me. Ah, you threw me a bit there, against the wall, like. Are you all right?'

'Yeah, I'm fine. I'm great. I was just ... trying to do up my coat.'

I bite hard on my bottom lip and will a change of subject. Kian, who is much younger than I thought he would be, rubs his palms down the front of his trousers and extends a hand to shake.

'Nice to meet you. Glad we can put you up at the farm. Seemed like you were getting a bit desperate from your email.'

I smile through clenched teeth and shrug my heavy rucksack up onto my shoulders again. Taking sole responsibility for a farm at barely thirty years old would be terrifying. A few weeks ago, I'd rescued a shell-shocked Pickles from the roundabout near our house during a torrent of rush-hour traffic and that was stressful enough, let alone having a whole farm's worth of animals to look after.

'I've been up to my neck in it since I started running the place at Easter. Bad time to be called back, if I'm honest, but can't do much about that. Can I take your bag off you?'

I instinctively clench the straps of my rucksack and jerk to the side when he reaches for my shoulder. 'God, sorry. That's my London muscle memory kicking in.'

'If I was going to rob you, I wouldn't have gone to the effort of driving across the firth in that thing to do it.' Kian thumbs over his shoulder to where a neglected, rust-eaten Jeep straddles two parking spaces. 'She runs, but only just. In warning: the roads aren't great around Kilroch, but if you can see the tarmac through the hole in the foot well, we shouldn't go too far wrong.'

Kian heaves my suitcase into the boot like he's loading a sack of potatoes. It bounces off the back seat, already scuffed with muck.

I climb into the passenger seat and try and look for a space on the floor that isn't covered by food wrappers, dried mud, or scrunched tissues. When it becomes apparent that this isn't a possibility, I swallow and wedge my rucksack between my knees. Kian settles in next to me and tries to smooth his hair down, smiling in apology.

'I didn't have time to clean up. Sorry.' Kian glances over at me as the engine whirrs lethargically to life.

'Don't apologise, it's fine,' I say.

I open Google Maps on my phone and try to make subtle glances out of the window to check that we're heading in the right direction and not to a dodgy lock-up unit round the back of an industrial estate. I glance at Kian, who uses a screwdriver jammed behind the steering wheel as an improvised lever for the windscreen wipers. Despite the mucky clothes and faint, earthy smell of animals, Kian doesn't seem like a farmer. Mind you, my only frame of reference comes from happy days spent watching Matt Baker herd sheep with his border collie on *Blue Peter*.

There's something about chequered shirts, a shrill whistle, and big arms holding tiny lambs that's incredibly alluring.

'I had to come straight from the sows,' says Kian. 'Some of the breeding stock aren't producing enough milk, but I can't figure out why. I've tried massaging their mammary glands, but it isn't easy as it sounds.' Kian sighs, exhausted. 'The vet can sort it out, but I don't want to call her. It costs a fortune.'

One: it doesn't sound easy at all; and two: Kian has crushed my farmer fantasy in an alarmingly short time.

He winds the window down and sticks his arm out, motioning at the oncoming traffic to stop. 'Indicators don't work,' he says as he pulls out, the engine whirring in protest.

'Oh, right.' I tuck my hands between my thighs to try and warm them up.

'Know much about pigs?'

'Err ... I've seen *Babe* a few times. It's the only film that makes me cry.'

'Oh, aye? Bit soppy, are you?'

I openly scoff. 'Ha. I wouldn't say so.'

'Each to their own. But give me *The Notebook* and I'll be howling for days.'

Our laughter fades into titters, then silence, as the wipers hurl themselves from one side of the windscreen to the other. Kian taps on the steering wheel and sucks his teeth.

'So, is Braehead a family farm?' I ask. Kian nods vigorously, delighted that I've found a way to kick-start the small talk.

'Yeah, yeah, I guess it is. My granddad ran the place until now. Some of the wholesalers in the area have been dealing with him for the best part of fifty years. I don't think he ever thought it'd be me coming back to take up the reins, not when I moved to Edinburgh, mind. It should have been Dad, but he passed away when I was wee, so ... yeah. Didn't have much choice really.'

'Oh. I'm sorry. That must have been tough.'

'Ah, I was young. Can't remember it. Granddad's in an old folks' home now. You couldn't take him off the farm for love or naught, but he's eighty-seven with a dodgy back, so it was only a matter of time before something happened. Get the window, will you? Wave your hand a bit so they know we're turning left.'

'Right, got it.' I do as I'm told and stick my hand out into the drizzle. We turn onto a road that takes us out past the town and onto a suspension bridge that runs over the rippled waves of the North Sea.

'What happened?'

'What do you mean?'

'To your granddad.'

'Got kicked in the head by a bull. The concussion was bad and he never fully recovered.'

'Oh my God, that's awful.'

'You'd be surprised how common it is,' he says. Kian catches my eye and breaks into a smile. 'Don't worry about the bulls. I sold them when I took over the farm. It's just pigs, chickens, and sheep now. And trout when we get the lake stocked.'

'I bet you host a killer barbecue in summer.'

'You'd think so, but I'm not a meat eater myself. Can make a crackin' hummus though.'

'You're a *vegetarian* farmer?' I ask, twisting in my seat to face him.

'Yeah, I know. It makes small talk with the fellas over at the cattle market a wee bit awkward.'

'I can imagine. I am too. Well, most of the time. Except for fish and chips. And sometimes cocktail sausages, but only if they're part of a Christmas buffet.'

We climb uphill through a pine forest and emerge between undulating fields speckled with Highland cows who glance at the rattling Jeep from beneath an ombré forelock.

'They're cute,' I say, cringing at how simple I sound. When I glance at Kian, it's clear I don't need to worry.

'Aye. It's why I can't eat them,' he says, his face soft. 'I used to hate it when Granddad loaded them onto the truck for the abattoir. They knew what was happening, no doubt. I switched as soon as I left home.'

Kian chews the side of his cheek.

'The farm isn't my business. I mean, it's my business in that I care about it, but it's not my business career-wise. I was working on a post-doctorate research project back in Edinburgh before the bull incident.'

'What was your research about?' I ask. Kian sits taller in his seat.

'I was testing a drone-based solution to variable weather patterns and its impact on crop development. Basically, we use drones to deposit nutrients in the right part of a field.'

'This might sound dim, but it sounds like a drone strike, except ... with fertiliser?'

Kian scoffs. 'I wouldn't use that wording, but yeah. Sort of.'

The Jeep starts making a loud rattling noise like a penny in the washing machine as we accelerate downhill. Kian smacks the dashboard until it stops and shakes his head. 'Ignore that,' he says.

I grip the seat tighter and try to keep a neutral expression.

'Anyway, the project's on hold now,' he says.

'For how long?'

'No idea. I didn't plan on taking up the farm, but it's not like you can ask sheep to look after themselves whilst you finish a post-doc, especially the breed I've got. It's like *Shawshank Redemption*. Lady Susan got stuck in the brook for two days last week.'

'Aren't brooks shallow?'

'They are. She went down for a drink and her fleece soaked the water up like a kitchen sponge. She was so heavy by the end of it that she couldn't stand up again. See what I mean? It's a wonder they get through a day.'

We turn onto a coastal path, where pockmarked sea defences break waves before they have a chance to claim more of the coastline.

'Sorry for the mental off-load,' says Kian, glancing at me. 'I don't get to speak to many people during the work week. No water cooler to stand and have a moan at, y'know?'

I nod, but I'm not sure what to contribute. We've not been in the car that long and I've barely had a chance to mention the weather, which should have bought me ten minutes according to the English rules of small talk. Elsewhere, meaningful conversation with strangers is strictly reserved for pub toilets at 2 a.m. when your beer-addled brain thinks it's a good idea to gossip and share lipgloss.

As we turn onto the village high street, Kian slows down and pulls up alongside a man whose face is partly covered by a thick scarf.

'Ross. Ross!' calls Kian, yanking on the handbrake. Going by the crunching sound, it's about as effective as sticking a cat to the wall with Blu Tak.

The man bobs down to look inside, a sheen of dew across his brow.

'No umbrella?' says Kian, his voice deeper than it was thirty seconds ago.

'No point, Kian. I haven't been properly dry since I arrived here. Hi, I'm Ross.'

The man leans into the car to shake my hand, but if time has slowed down up to this point, it now speeds up with horrible velocity. I force my clammy fingers into his palm but my hand is too cold to squeeze, so essentially, a stranger is cupping my squid fingers with no explanation from either side. I feel like I'm hovering outside my own body. Surely you need to give warning before throwing an attractive – if damp – man into someone's immediate vicinity. I wasn't bloody well prepared for an encounter like this.

'Ross takes care of Kilroch's spiritual needs,' says Kian.

He shuffles in his seat, emphasising the close proximity between us all.

'Aye, that's right. Although I still haven't convinced Kian that Sunday worship is a good idea.'

'You know what it's like with the farm, always something to sort out. Anyway, Ross, this is Ava. Ava, Ross. She's come to help at Braehead for a while,' says Kian.

'Ah, great! I'll be seeing you around, will I?'

'Yes, definitely.' I nearly bite my tongue off, I say it so quickly.

Kian revs the engine, nodding to Ross, who straightens up and tucks a loaf of bread under his arm, the crust already soggy.

As we gather speed up the hill, I resist the urge to strain against my seatbelt to snatch another look.

'He's got a face I'd struggle to slap.'

Kian laughs. 'He's caused divisions between the married folk, let me tell you. A lot of the older women have recently returned to church with renewed vigour.'

'I bet.'

Chapter 10

As we drive through the village, I struggle to imagine Mum in a place like Kilroch: a clipped Londoner with red hair, hemp clothing, and, if the stories are true, a penchant for protest through the medium of an angry tambourine.

We trundle alongside a dry-stone wall, where a gate is held open by a loop of blue string. Two trees, bent parallel to the ground, flank the entrance, as though stuck in a perpetual gust of wind. Beside us, a field holds two dozen sheep, their wool thick and bellies round. As we bounce up the driveway, they break into a chorus of dissonant bleating.

'They're only mawing because they think I'm here to feed them,' says Kian, glancing over the flock with feigned annoyance. 'Ah, there's the house. I always think it needs a coat of paint when someone else sees it. Now summer has passed, I won't get a weather window for months.'

'Oh, don't apologise. My house back in London hasn't been decorated since 1995. My bedroom is a pretty garish combination of lilac paint and flocked wallpaper. There are Forever Friends stickers on the PVC windows that I can't get off.'

I hesitate, my hand on the door handle. This can't be the same farmhouse I saw online. If the walls were white at some point, they're now streaked with mildew, drainpipes bowed under the weight of moss that creeps like gangrene from the eaves.

'Do you, umm ... want to go in?' says Kian, looking between me and the house.

'Oh! Yes, sure!' I say, a little too enthusiastically to hide my disappointment.

When I step out of the car, it feels like someone has squeezed all the breath out of my lungs. Like London, the air here tastes of something, but it's not the smell of humming pavements and sour bins; it's the clean smell of earth and animals and water. I look down at my feet, the fluorescent blue of my trainers offensively bright against the concrete driveway. Kian pulls out my suitcase and reaches for my rucksack, but pauses when something catches his eye.

'Ah, no. Babs is out. Give me a sec whilst I lock her away, she's not good with new faces.'

Not wanting to loiter, I shoulder my bag and wander around the side of the house to where a handful of frill-necked chickens are clawing at the muck, their downy feathers puffed up round their legs like harem trousers. At the back, beyond a scrubby garden overgrown with snapped, brittle, and browning herbs, endless paddocks blur behind a haze of drizzle. Behind me, the back door opens, my suitcase propped inside out of the rain.

'I've got the kettle on if you want to warm up,' says Kian

from the kitchen. I join him inside. He clicks a stove igniter and a whoosh of a gas sets the stove roaring into flame. 'I thought you might want to find out a wee bit more about the farm, why I need the help, you know? I don't spend a lot of time inside. Ah, I should have tidied up a bit more, sorry about that. Tea?'

'Yeah, please.'

Kian unclips a stiff Kilner jar, pulls out a tea bag, and inspects it under a spotlight by the sink.

'Coffee works too ...' I say.

'Yes, coffee. Sorry, I should have checked the hot drink situation beforehand,' says Kian, embarrassed. 'If you write down a list of groceries you want from the shop, I'll pick them up tomorrow.' He nervously looks around the room, like he's just noticed his surroundings.

'Sure, no rush.'

From the paper-strewn table and single dirty bowl left by the sink, I get the impression that Kian is used to his own company. He's far younger than I expected, and although this is his family's land, he doesn't seem the farming type. Ultimately, it doesn't matter. If he hadn't replied to my email, I might well have sought refuge in an unlocked barn, shoes worn through and reputation in tatters like every single female that features in a Thomas Hardy novel.

I pull off my trainers, the flagstones so cold beneath my socks that the floor feels damp underfoot. Thick clouds mask the sun, so I flick the light switch on, but nothing happens. Kian frantically stacks papers to clear the table, a number of invoices, receipts, and scribbled figures sticking out in a haphazard pile that he shoves on a shelf lined with fluted crockery and waxen candle stubs.

He takes down two mugs branded with the contact details of a silage company, gives them a wipe with a tea towel, and fills them with hot water. 'Could you grab the milk whilst you're up?' he says. I nod, eager to look helpful, and turn to a fridge so clunky and voluminous that I'm sure I could climb inside, close the lid, and survive a nuclear blast.

I take out a glass bottle and give it a shake, but the liquid inside doesn't seem to move.

'Is it supposed to be … not white?'

'Oh, aye. It's as fresh as it comes. John down the road delivers enough for the week and I give him some eggs in return. We get by on swaps and trades a lot of the time. Saves driving all the way to Glenfinnay for the big shop. It's not pasteurised, mind. You got a good immune system?' Kian asks as he slops milk into each of our mugs.

'Bit late to say no?'

He looks at the coffee and then back at me. 'Yeah, I suppose so.'

He slides a mug over the scrubbed kitchen table and I wrap my hands around it to show that I'm complying with the yellow milk. We both fall silent, thaw our freezing hands, and let the house talk around us.

'I don't mean to sound like I'm counting down the days, but you didn't mention how long you wanted to stay.' Kian pushes the sleeves of his hoodie up to the elbow and blows on his coffee, but he underestimates his puff and sprays droplets on the table. Neither of us acknowledge this aloud.

'Well, I was thinking a few weeks,' I say, trying to keep it vague. I need enough time to find answers that will either lead me to Moira or give me enough information to continue my research back in London. Duncan has technically given me a week, but if things go well and my articles are good, I can wangle some more time.

'Are you looking to travel around at all? I don't want to hold you hostage if Kilroch is a stop on a longer journey. I'm glad for whatever help I can get. At this stage, it would be easier to tell you what doesn't need doing rather than what does.'

'I hadn't planned on visiting anywhere else, no.' I can feel my cheeks grow hot. Rather than fabricating a reasonable back story as to why I've travelled nearly 600 miles to collect eggs and push a wheelbarrow about, I need to go easy on the details. 'I'm taking a break from my job in London,' I start. I sip my coffee and am surprised by how silky and deep the flavour is. It's easy to overlook the insipid colour when it tastes so good. 'I wanted to be outdoors, you know?'

This isn't *strictly* true. Ordinarily, the closest I get to proper nature is an evening spent watching *Planet Earth* with a katsu curry on my lap and the sound of foxes humping in the front garden.

'Aye, you'll get the outdoors here,' says Kian, leaning back in his chair. 'The days are drawing in, so we don't get much light, but when I'm not in the fields I'm in the barns, and when I'm not there I'm here trying to get the old man's finances in order. I've got two degrees and can barely make sense of them.'

'There's a good start. At the very least, I can organise these into files for you,' I say, nodding to the precariously placed papers teetering on the edge of the shelf. 'Don't judge me, but the thought of having unbridled access to some hardcore filing makes me quite giddy.'

'Consider the job yours,' says Kian, smiling with tired eyes. 'But until the chickens figure out how to clean their coop, it's down to you and me. Then we've got the sheep to keep an eye on. And the pigs, they get up to all sorts of mischief. Seems like intelligence has been bred out of the ones you get on industrial farms, but our rare breeds are in a different league. What else? The flashing on the barn needs replacing, the orchard trees need paring back. Ah, Christ. A whole load really.'

I start to feel like both he and I have been a bit short-sighted. I thought rural life was all post office robberies, village arson, and gossiping over strong tea. An anxious knot forms in my stomach, and not just about the work. This living situation is intense. Just the two of us? On a wind-battered farm bordered by sheer cliffs on three sides? Although Kian speaks with a soft drawl that would work perfectly for voiceovers in an M&S Christmas food advert, there's also a *slight* chance he's a serial killer. I didn't even ask to see his ID before I jumped in the car.

I thought I was getting a bed and an opportunity to find out about my Scottish family from a safe distance. I won't lie, the idea that I could do without brushing my hair for a fortnight also appealed. But if I've underestimated how much goes into running a farm, Kian has overestimated how useful I'm likely to be. I'm sure he'd prefer a six-foot-two, broad-shouldered bloke who can hoick a pig under each arm and call it a laugh, but instead he's got me; five foot nothing and on the run from a public meltdown that's plastered all over the internet.

When I think about it, this might be the *perfect* place for me to be.

Chapter 11

I sit up, my head leaden, and clunk the bedside lamp on, blinking as the bulb warms up to a dull, amber glow. Hearing my alarm in an unfamiliar room sets everything off-kilter. I hadn't noticed the fusty twin beds and darkly lacquered furniture before I'd climbed beneath the sheets, exhausted. Despite being scratchy and a particularly heinous coral colour, the extra blanket I pulled out of the wardrobe kept me warm, even as gusts of wind pushed a draught through the cracks in the window sill. The radiator knob was so stiff I had to wrap my hand in a scarf to twist it on. The sound of clunking and ticking kept me up most of the night, so I had to shuffle down into a duvet cave, the covers pulled over my head to block out the sound.

I lift the curtain and look beyond the window sill, where a floodlight is triggered by loose straw blown across the courtyard, collecting in the gutter of a hand-pump well. Beyond, darkness swathes the farm. Something doesn't feel right.

I heave my suitcase onto the spare single bed and attempt to co-ordinate my hands in order to pull on a pair of socks, shuffling round the room like Bruce Forsyth performing a Charleston. The farmhouse grumbles in the wind, but I can't make out the distinct noise of Kian moving around, despite it being six o'clock. It feels like a late start for a farmer.

Yesterday, Kian described how quickly gossip drifts up the coastline, so I want to make a good impression, in case word gets out of a Londoner freeloading at Braehead Farm. 'If you fart in Kilroch, you've shit yourself by the time it's reached Cumnaird,' were Kian's exact words. With my public shame quota at capacity, I've got to at least try and reclaim my sense of dignity. If help is what he needs, help is what he'll get, perhaps not in expertise, but enthusiasm.

I plop back down on the bed and scrape my hair into a rough ponytail. My nose is so cold that I'm not convinced it's attached to me anymore. Is the potential loss of my extremities worth all this?

No one knows specifically where I am. I barely hide anything from Mum, but I've long since learned to keep all thoughts about my father to myself, which makes this feel especially devious.

I hold my shivers in, clutch the handrail, and head downstairs. In the kitchen, the radio crackles with raised voices, the hum of a political joust burring in the background as the febrile cockerel I spotted on a fence post yesterday crows from the yard. If Kian wasn't awake before, he must be now. I'll stick the kettle on. Strong tea wins over the heaviest of sleepers.

I find a tablespoon of stale Darjeeling in the back of a

cupboard and run it through a strainer, leaving it to swirl in a chipped teapot. At the table, I push papers aside to clear a space, stacking an envelope marked 'FINAL NOTICE' on top of a lopsided pile. It's a good job Kian isn't paying me to be here, going by the intimidating number of letter-headed bank statements scattered around.

The clock ticks, its anchor-shaped pendulum swinging the seconds back and forth. I scrape my chair under the table, hoping the noise will wake Kian up, but when his face appears at the back door, I wobble on the spot, my foot half in my trainer.

Air sucks through the kitchen as Kian steps inside, his cheeks ruddy, eyes crystalline blue.

'Ah, you're up! Good to see you.'

'Am I late?' I say. 'I thought *you* were late.'

'Nah, I didn't want to wake you up early.'

'Oh, *shit*. I'm so sorry. I set my alarm for six. I really thought you hadn't started yet, or I would have come and found you.'

'Pfff, can't remember what it feels like to sleep past half four.'

'That sounds ... quite inhumane,' I say, no longer wondering at the dark circles underneath his eyes.

'Don't I know it. Come find me in the barn when you're ready,' says Kian, holding his hands over the Aga before pulling gloves back on.

'I'm ready now.'

Kian bites his lip and tucks his tracksuit bottoms into a pair of thick socks. 'Are you sure you don't mind getting that mucky?' he says, gesturing to the fluorescent orange and pink Pac-a-mac I borrowed off Mum.

'Yeah, it's fine. This is old anyway.'

'Don't say I didn't warn you.'

***

I bow my head into the wind as I head towards the open barn door, where light leaks into the darkness of the yard. It looks every bit like the setting for a murder.

The sound of a ripcord engine stutters into life and trips through the air. Inside the barn, Kian is kicking dried clods of mud from the underside of a quad bike chassis, an oily rag flung over his shoulder.

When he sees me, he brushes straw from the bottom of a Thermos and hands it over, drinking from his own with a dopey smile on his face. I sniff the air.

'Hey, how come you get coffee and I get peppermint tea?' I say.

'Call me a caffeine martyr. At least one of us needs to be alert when we get on these things, but we needn't both endure a triple espresso to get outside in the mornings. It's a slippery slope, Ava, and it ends with migraines and unpredictable bowel movements.'

'Wow. Say no more.'

'Sorry. Blame the guys down the cattle market. A bad influence, the lot of them,' he says, grinning.

'Is that a pub?'

'Ha! No. It's literally a market where we sell cattle. And a bunch of other things, but largely they fall within the

106

big three: trotters, testicles, and tractor parts. The testicles are attached to the animal. The rams, bulls, cockerels, you know? They're breeders. We rent them out.'

'Like farmyard gigolos?'

'Essentially, yes.'

I draw a semi-circle in the muck with the toe of my trainer. 'I'll have to go out later to meet some of the others who live round here,' I say, my heart quickening at the thought.

'Yeah, if you like. There's an egg delivery later in the week. Ross is on the list,' says Kian, giving me a nudge with his elbow.

A smile tickles my mouth, but I bite my cheek to keep it down. 'Notable customer, is he?' I ask, folding my arms. I must remain professional, because for all intents and purposes, I'm still working, even if the majority of my new colleagues have trotters and defecate in the same trough they eat from.

'Oh, aye. Extremely notable, especially amongst female members of the community.'

I squat and pretend to examine the overlapping tubes and wires that feed into the bike. 'What's the crowd like in Kilroch?' I ask.

'Mostly older. Some young families. Then there's a big gap. There's not a huge amount in the way of opportunities for people our age. I've got a couple of mates who come back for the odd weekend and a family friend who lives close by. She's sweet.'

'It'll be nice to get a sense of the place.'

'I'll get you in the thick of it, don't you worry. They all know about you, mind.'

I fiddle with a length of straw and try to appear aloof. 'How come?'

'You heard of Belisha beacons? A big fire on a pole, lit to pass warnings through the Highlands quicker than a man on a horse with a scroll or whatever they wrote on back then. It's the same concept now, except she's called Donna and is a fifty-five-year-old woman who spends most of her time commenting on who's left their curtains closed past seven o'clock on a weekday. It's partly why we don't have a constable here, there's nothing that gets past our Donna.'

I pull myself up and knock back my tea, which pools in my belly, warm and sweet. This farming business isn't so bad. So far, the quantity of tea breaks is spot on.

'You ready?' says Kian, his voice strained, mid-stretch.

'For what?'

Kian twists the key to the quad bike. The ignition putters out twice before ticking over into a steady grumble. The smell of fuel fills the barn. Just when he allows himself to look smug, the engine cuts out again.

'Ah, shit,' says Kian.

'Has it maybe ... got enough fuel?'

'Aye, a full tank.'

Well. There goes my short-lived contribution. Kian reties the waistband of his tracksuit bottoms and kicks the chassis a few times, throwing me a frog-like smile when the engine jumps into life.

'You played Mario Kart before?' says Kian, rubbing his hands down the front of his chest.

'Yeah, sure. This is basically the same, right?' I reply, swinging my leg over the seat.

'No, it's the opposite. When you want to speed up, be really careful. The throttle is loose. I smacked my chin on the handlebars testing it out last week.'

'Maybe if I ran alongside you instead?' I suggest, as Kian wheels his own quad bike out from behind the hay stack.

'You'll be fine. Just follow me and don't do anything drastic,' he says. 'This is the quickest way to get round the farm. Or you can get on the back of mine? Be warned though, you'll get the splashback when we go through a puddle.'

I lower myself back down onto the seat and twist the key until the engine jumps to life beneath me, sending jolts up my arms that ricochet to the back of my skull until my eyes feel loose in their sockets. Kian pulls up alongside and nods.

'Let's do this.'

Chapter 12

By the time I reach a speed I'm comfortable with, my sore knuckles are white from hovering over the stiff brakes and the salty wind which slaps down in stinging bursts along the back of my hand. Streaks of orange paint the underside of thick clouds as I trail behind Kian. We bounce down uneven tracks, rain cutting deep rivulets into silt-strewn ruts that I'm constantly trying to steer my wheels out of. I briefly close my eyes in the first rays of sunshine that break over the hills, the fields so green that I see emerald on the backs of my eyelids. Sheep follow us along the fence, their heads hung low, coats heavy from the rain. I slide off my quad bike and take small, shuffling steps towards Kian, careful not to step on their hooves. The ewes are far less concerned about personal space than I am.

'Do they get cold?' I ask Kian. He pulls a hay bale to the floor, the herd bleating around him like a disorganised choir as he cuts the string with a pen knife.

'What?'

'Do they get cold?' I look up as Kian shakes a section of hay from the bale and chucks it towards me. I clap it between my hands and sneeze as sweet-smelling dust puffs into a cloud around my face.

'These lot?' Kian laughs and gives one a dull pat on the rump. 'No. They're better off than you and me, and that's without electric blankets and hot dinners.'

What's this? Kian's got an electric blanket? It's no wonder I felt exhausted this morning, I must have burnt 800 calories shivering all night.

'Ouch. Hey!' I wave my hand behind me, where a mean-looking ewe stares at me with bulbous eyes. 'Greedy.'

'Can you do a count?' says Kian, winding the frayed string in a loop around his elbow and palm. 'I'll do the same.'

Four rounds later, I'm still trying to figure out if the one with a brown eye-patch is number twenty-three or twenty-four. From behind, they appear like a crowd of Dulwich pensioners: cotton-haired ladies with tight mouths and watery eyes who complain about the same problems over the top of one another.

'How many?'

'Thirty-nine.'

'You sure?'

'Yes. No. Why, how many should there be?'

'Forty-two.'

'Really? Hang on, I'll count again. You should give them different coloured collars or something.' I scoot around the herd as they tiptoe between each other, nibbling at the hay that is simultaneously being eaten and trodden into the ground. 'Do sheep wear collars?'

112

'I believe you're thinking of *One Hundred and One Dalmatians*.'

'Oh yeah. Maybe.'

I zigzag up and down and surprise myself by recognising a few of them by the way they shake their tails, or how belligerent they are about food. One such ewe clambers over her field buddy (don't judge me, I've no idea how sheep use terms of endearment) and continues eating in a headstand position, her unexpectedly skinny legs pointing towards the sky amid a mass of woollen bodies. It's like a burlesque routine, if you squint hard enough and start humming, 'Ba da da daaaaa, ber da da daaaaa ...'

I look over at Kian, who bites his lip and taps a thigh with one hand. 'You're right. There's thirty-nine. Shite.' He walks around the herd, glaring at each sheep in accusation like a tyrannical dinner lady. 'There's a troublemaker amongst this lot.'

'What shall we do? Make an example of them? First in line for lamb shanks?'

'Ava, no,' says Kian, his eyes narrow. *Not the time to make jokes, got it.* 'I know who it is.' I wait for the big reveal. 'Miranda.' *Ah, there we go. I'm no better informed.* 'She's got a reputation. Led a couple of the others astray. She can't be trusted.'

I step from one foot to another. My trainers are soaked through with a delightful shade of brown which I know for a fact is at least fifty per cent excrement. Who knew that some mud is preferable to others?

113

'We'll hop on the quads and look round the fence, see where they could have got out.'

A few minutes later, I've made it over ten miles per hour. I'm scanning the fence, but the whole process is like the world's most boring Sherlock Holmes case. I've seen a few bits of wool caught on barbed wire and two empty bottles of Iron Bru by the water trough, but beyond that the field looks as generically field-like as ever.

When I reach Kian, the cause of the breakout becomes clear. The trunk of a pine tree has splintered five feet up and fallen into the field, squashing the fence and breaking the electric charge that runs through it.

'Must have happened overnight. I'm surprised we didn't hear it.'

'They must have hopped over,' I say. *Have no fear, Kian, Captain Obvious is on the scene.*

'Ah, this isn't good. I think Miranda is carrying triplets. She's clever enough to climb out, but she's hardly light on her feet when it comes to getting down the cliff edge. Ah, silly sods. We need to find them soon, or we'll be scraping them off the rocks later.'

'Oh God, really?'

'It's happened before. They get spooked and dive off the side like lemmings. You head along the tree line and I'll take the track out towards John's pasture. If you find them, try and herd them back this way, all right?'

'Err, OK, sure.' I nod, hesitating as I walk towards my quad bike in case Kian gives me an instruction more specific than 'stop three sheep from dive-bombing off a cliff', but he's already driven away by the time I twist the key. A reverse alarm bleeps unnecessarily as I drive backwards in an arc. I'm so cautious a slug would have time to slither out of the way before popping beneath the wheels.

I copy Kian's stance on the quad bike and stand up, hunched over the handlebars. I dip, rock, and lurch across the field, feeling braver as my knees intuitively flex in time with the bumps. I don't know what the rules are concerning the quad bike highway code, so when I get to the gate, I stick my arm out to show I'm turning left despite the relative isolation. When I get to the woodland, I take the speed up a little higher, on the verge of enjoying myself (I push the sheep peril to one side for a moment), zigzagging between the trees, my eyes wider and more alert than they have been for months. I scan the landscape. Over the engine thrumming, I hear waves overlapping each other, crashing on the rocks below like an over-zealous drum solo.

I scan the horizon, eyeballs wobbling in my head from the assault course of tree roots protruding from the ground, when—

'Miranda!' I shout, a flash of grey wool bounding over a stump in front of me. The sea forms a backdrop between the trees, blending with the sky in a shade I'd refer to as 'dead salmon', going by what I've seen in the Farrow & Ball catalogues that are posted through our front door in Dulwich. Fuck, where has she gone? I slow down, not wanting to spook her, and turn towards the sound of twigs breaking in the copse, where an almost spherical sheep is indelicately tiptoeing in the opposite direction.

I can't see her two pals. Maybe they lost their nerve and headed back towards Braehead. It's what I would do. Why on earth would you want to get soaked by sea spray and eat moss for dinner when a heat lamp is on offer in the barn? I need to start thinking like a sheep. If I edge her out on this side and block her in, Miranda will have to turn back towards the farm, right?

My engine growls as I manoeuvre round a protruding rock, the back wheel spinning in thick mud. The path I was following is no longer visible beneath dead pine needles, and going by the sudden disappearance of trees to my right, it looks like Kian's land comes to an abrupt stop at the point where it cuts into the North Sea.

From the corner of my eye, I see Miranda's shaggy rump hop over a felled trunk, but when I twist the throttle to make ground on the outside, she speeds up, her matted tail bobbing like a rabbit as her hollow footsteps sink into the ground.

'Oh shit, oh shit, oh shit,' I say, losing sight of Miranda as she bounds round the corner behind a stack of fence posts, their stakes rusting from sea mist that hisses up the cliff sides. Panic sets in. I speed up, ducking just before a low-hanging branch hits me at chest height. A branch snags my hat and yanks it off my head like a playground bully. I lunge behind me to grab it, but my reach is clumsy and I flail, my gaze broken as the handlebars twist towards the cliff edge. Just like that, the quad bike jerks, the seat shunting to one side. I'm holding on by an arse cheek, the engine groaning as it bombs over rough terrain, and like the total idiot I am, I manage to twist the throttle as I attempt to pull myself upright again.

Everything slows down, like the moment in a Bond film where 007 dives out of harm's way, a super-bike exploding below him, a gun in one hand, and an anorexic supermodel in the other. OK, it's not quite like that, but if you swap in an incompetent sort-of journalist from south London and replace the love interest with a rotund ewe, you wouldn't be far off. In quick succession, three things happen. One: the quad bike skids to the side, pinning itself partway through a gap between two trees as the back wheels churn skid marks into the bark. Two: My coat catches on a branch, the elastics of my hood pulled so tight that I now peep through a tiny gap. Three: Miranda jumps out in front of me, crimped wool forming a moppy fringe over eyes set so wide apart it's a wonder she's able to see at all. The little sod.

I don't move. Not through choice, but because the tangled hood situation is reminiscent of the time Big Philippa strung me up from a peg in the cloakrooms and stole my Tudor Day money in year five; I can't move, it only makes it worse. From behind me, I hear footsteps.

'Shhhh! Shh! She's here! Don't freak her out, she's completely rogue,' I hiss under my breath.

'I think you've done enough damage yourself, lass. Get on, back you go, eh! Eh!'

Oh God, it's not Kian. Miranda darts off again, clearly having the time of her life. 'Go on, Jess. Way, way!' A flash of black and white nips past me. A border collie, grizzled and grey, rounds in, stalking. 'Adda' girl, walk by. Hold. Hold, Jess!'

From my half-squat, tangled in my own clothing, I can't see the woman who completely ignores my plight, her bare legs on show beneath an unseasonal chemise skirt and cut-down wellie boots. She leans over to the quad bike, still whirring between the trees, and twists the key. The engine putters out. Her hood is pulled low, but as she bends towards me, I see her eyes; so blue they're marble-like, as though she pops them out and keeps them in a jar every night. The woman pushes my head to one side and I wince as she tugs the elastic free from the mess of branches. They snap back and twang against my face, stinging my already cold cheeks. I stumble to my feet and tug my hood down.

'Thanks, I don't know what happened, I—'

The woman picks up a staff propped against a lichen-covered stump and holds it aloft, looking at me through narrowed eyes. I feel exposed. Her eyes dart across my face as though she's matching me up to a *Crimestoppers* e-fit. Her mouth is pencil-thin, curtailing my reconciliatory smile.

'You the English girl?'

'Yes.'

'Hmm.'

At that, she turns her back to me and strides into the trees, her petrol-coloured coat slick with rain. I look to the quad, pinned in place by a wishbone branch. I don't know whether to follow the woman or to try and yank it out. I hear her whistle to the dog, who works around her, pushing Miranda away from the edge and back towards the farm. An animal like that makes Pickles look completely incompetent as a pet. He's so lazy that sometimes he can't be bothered to wee outside, so climbs into a planter and relieves himself there. We've had three monsteras and he's killed off the lot.

I leave the quad where it is (it's not like there's anyone around to nick it) and head inland, away from the cliffside that I was terrifyingly close to hurtling over in a low-budget homage to *Thelma and Louise*. My trainers are completely saturated with rain and I'm convinced I have the beginnings of trench foot by the time I emerge from the woods. When I reach a gap in the dry-stone wall, the border collie is waiting, head tilted with curiosity, her mismatched eyes locked on me from afar. When I approach, she nudges up and down my leg with her nose. Am I being frisked by a dog? Is that what's happening?

'She wouldn't leave until she saw you catch up. It's strange, because Jess only herds animals that can't think for themselves. Don't take it personally.'

'Thanks?'

'Not my fault, it's the way she was trained,' says the woman, frowning.

Now that my turbo adrenaline surge has subsided, I realise just how cold I am. I tuck my hands inside my sleeves and try to hold my body still, but I'm shaking so violently I can barely stand. The woman sighs.

'Come on, lass. Can't stand there quivering all day. Kian's got enough to be getting on with without running about after you and all.'

Chapter 13

Date: Tuesday 8th October
Location: Farmhouse kitchen
Cups of tea: Two
Sleep: 7 hours and 13 minutes

How much peril can you experience within a forty-eight-hour window? No, this isn't a new quiz for Snooper, I'm talking about actual, real-life peril. Sure, careering down an escalator whilst trying to text is a fairly common occurrence in London, but I've faced my mortality far more frequently since arriving in Kilroch.

My vision of wandering in and out of a wisteria-woven barn with happy pigs and a jolly farmer for company faded within seconds of arriving. For starters, the farmhouse is held together by a combination of mildew and sheer willpower, the yard is patrolled by geese who hiss and bite like feral cats, and I haven't seen a single health and safety notice on display, which is unsettling when you consider that the farmer keeps petrol in a barn full of highly combustible hay bales.

I'll be amazed if I make it back to London without needing first aid.

The next stage of my plan involves finding a reason to leave the farm. Unless my sister is squatting behind the chicken coop, I'm not going to find her by wandering the same field in Kilroch day in, day out – that's for sure.

***

'Honestly, it's no bother,' says Kian. He digs out chicken feed using a milk carton trimmed down to form a scoop.

'It is, though.' I duck and step out of his way, my eyes watering. I sweep the next load of soiled straw into a pile, which is pointless as the wind immediately whips it into a tiny, mucky tornado. I take shallow breaths. The smell of ammonia is so strong it burns my nose, as though I've inhaled swimming pool water.

'We got Miranda back, that's what's important,' says Kian. He screws a plastic lid on the container and wipes his hands on his trousers as a brood of hens burr around his feet. The sound is comforting and homely, like elderly women gossiping over tea and pink wafer biscuits.

'Will it be hard to replace? The quad?' I ask, turning my hand over in a sunbeam that appears through a break in the cloud.

'I might need to source a few parts, but it'll be fine. The folk round here trade scrap with each other most of the time. Unless you're a McCulloch. They'll buy anything that makes farming more efficient, even if it compromises animal welfare. It works for us. Our farm is barely keeping its head above water so we need to save as much money as we can, even if it means more tinkering in my spare time. It's something to do when the evenings are long,' he says.

Kian flicks through the clipboard's wrinkled pages, a furrow deep set in his brow as he taps a pencil on the page. 'Ah, it's the hotel in Cumnaird that needs another tray of eggs this week,' he says, scribbling down a figure.

'That sounds *far* too productive for anything I'd consider evening down-time, but somehow I get the sense that Netflix and Domino's Pizza isn't your thing?'

'It might be if we had the bandwidth,' says Kian. 'The wi-fi is too patchy for streaming videos unless you go down to the car park behind The Wailing Banshee. The landlady had a new router installed thinking it would encourage a younger crowd, but there aren't enough of us here to pack it out at the best of times.'

I nod, mentally fist-pumping at this news. Prehistoric internet means less chance of Kian seeing my live stream meltdown, or the numerous GIFs and edits that have cropped up since.

'I see you met Jacqui,' says Kian, breaking my reverie. We walk around the coop to where a rectangular nesting box sticks out at the back, dusty paint flaking off its wooden slats. Kian unlatches the lid and opens it to reveal three plump hens, who blink up at him in annoyance. He carefully tips the hen nearest to him to one side. Underneath her honeyed feathers are two porcelain white eggs. I can see why she looks a bit miffed; I'd be fuming if I had to push one of these out every day.

'Is that who my surly saviour was? Jacqui?'

I copy Kian's delicate actions with the hens. He is my chicken sensei.

'Yep. I've known her for years. She's always been a bit—'

'Terrifying?'

'Nah, I wouldn't say that.'

'I'm grateful for the whole "rescuing me from a cliff edge" thing, but she's quite, err ...'

'Quite ...?'

'Intense? Like, I might be wrong but I sort of feel like she hates me with the fire of a thousand suns and wishes I'd get sucked away by a tornado somewhere past the Scottish border?'

Kian scoffs and leans over to the basket, somehow managing to transport one egg between each of his fingers. 'She's just practical, is all.'

'Does she live round here?'

'About a mile over, closer into the village. She manages the tearoom.'

'Does she?' I say with ill-feigned credulity.

'Oh, aye.'

'I just can't imagine her reading the specials menu to anyone without sighing.'

'I'll tell her that when I see her,' says Kian, closing one lid and opening another with a sideways smile, where a frilled hen blinks at him, perturbed. 'You might rethink your words when you've had a slice of her shortbread.'

I slide my hand inside the nesting box. 'Well, I guess not everyone makes the best first impression,' I say, thinking back to my live stream.

'Jacqui has looked out for me a lot since I took over the farm. There were a few weeks in summer when Granddad was in hospital and I was seeing out my notice period in Edinburgh. Jacqui was working double days making sure the animals were all right and the sheds locked up. She's one of the good ones, just ... takes a while to warm up.'

Kian sounds sincere, but I'm not convinced. Stick Jacqui next to a fire and I'm sure the last polar ice caps would melt before she did.

I jostle three eggs in one hand and try to move a chicken with the other, but I get the impression that I've met the flock's resident matriarch because she's an absolute unit and resists my lame attempts to shift her.

'Come on, move your arse—'

'Be careful, she –'

'Ouch! Little fucker!'

'– nips.'

I yank my hand away, scraping my wrist against the lid and dropping an egg in the process. It cracks on the floor, the yoke popped like burst sunshine.

'Oh, fucking hell. Sorry.'

'Don't tell me, tell Babs,' says Kian, pointing at the hen. Can chickens glare? Because that's exactly what it looks like; her eyes are beady and so full of malice that I half expect her to draw a taloned claw along her throat to signal that my human days are numbered.

'I promise I'll stop destroying your farm soon,' I say, a sulky undertone slipping into my voice.

'It's only a broken egg. If this is your path of de-escalation and we started with the destruction of a quad bike, we're heading in the right direction. You might make a bad cup of tea before you level out again. I'll try and prepare myself for it,' says Kian with a wink.

I kick some dirt over the egg goop and place the other two carefully in the basket, following Kian as he heads back towards the shed.

'Oh! Hang on, I think it might be a ... yes, it is!' I say.

Kian reaches the shed, props the door open with a brick, and flicks on a naked bulb.

'Quick, take these off me. My phone's buzzing,' I say. Kian stretches his sweatshirt to form a pouch and I carefully drop my eggs inside, unzipping one, two, three layers until I reach the pocket that contains my phone.

'Wind must be in the right direction. Make the most of it, it'll disappear any second,' says Kian, as he pulls open a cupboard stacked with egg trays.

I answer the call and march across the yard, wellie boots flopping against my shins. Inside the barn, I lean against a hay bale. I've got two bars of reception. We're in.

'Mum! Are you OK? How's everything?'

'Ah, there you are. You sound a bit crackly, is that normal?'

'Oh, probably. Might be something to do with the distance,' I lie.

'What do you think of Edinburgh, then?'

126

'It's, err ... yeah, it's nice,' I say, looking to the puddle on the floor, an iridescent sheen of leaked petrol glazing its surface. On the roof, a loosely tacked strip of corrugated iron rattles in the wind.

'Lots of hills, aren't there? You'll get a good bum marching up and down the stairs, they're endless. Did you know you've been there before?'

'Have I?'

'Yeah, when I was pregnant with you. We took it in turns to pitch up outside the Pleasance Theatre during the festival. Pointless really, to try and attract attention when every other person was trying to flog flyers like their lives depended on it. The only positive was that we rarely got moved on because I was pregnant with you. Boy, did I let people know about it. Pregnancy made me incredibly bossy. It took a while to shake off.'

Pfff, that's giving herself a *little* too much credit. I stalk across the yard, paranoid that one of the chickens will start shrieking, and thus out me.

'That's cool, Mum.'

'You all right? You sound a bit off.' Mum lowers her voice to a stage whisper, which is louder than her actual talking voice. 'What are they like? The Scottish contingent?'

'Oh, fine. Really nice. My manager is great, but the coffee is terrible.'

'You know what I say: don't skimp money on the things that perk you up and bring you down.'

'Caffeine and periods.'

'That's my girl. What about your colleagues?'

I cup my hand over the mouthpiece, turning on the spot to escape the wind in an uncoordinated pirouette.

'They're quite loud. Much more so than in London. Massive sticklers for timekeeping, especially when it concerns mealtimes.'

As if on cue, the sheep spot me and slip behind one another as they jostle downhill. They pick out a route with dainty toe-taps like a boisterous ballet troupe, all wide-eyes and crossed knees.

'There is one – Miranda – she's a nightmare. Never where you expect her to be, and when you do find her, she'll use any excuse to do the exact opposite of what you need. She's the ringleader, from what I've seen.'

'Really? That sort of behaviour isn't overlooked for long,' says Mum.

'Oh, the boss is aware. Problem is, he lets her get away with all sorts.'

'Best to keep out of her way,' says Mum. 'You don't want more drama, especially when you're not there for long.'

'I'm trying,' I say. 'But it's only a matter of time before something kicks off. I've got a feeling.'

***

The next day, I set my alarm two hours earlier and think I've beaten Kian to it, but by the time I pull my second fleece on and shuffle downstairs, he's already tapping his foot by the back door, a Thermos in each hand. Out in the shed, I rearrange eggs by size whilst Kian lines every possible surface with empty boxes. I turn over an almost

128

spherical egg in my hand and wonder if there's a category for 'monstrously large'. This one is so big I'm surprised Kian didn't have to intervene with forceps.

I stretch and yawn, my arms heavy. God, I'd do anything for a nap. I only got up an hour ago, but still.

'You're like my mum, Kian. She never bloody sits down. Between coffee mornings and bake sales, she has a busier social life than I do. In fact, she arranges most of *my* social life too,' I say.

'Bit of a handful, is she?'

'Not half.'

'I can see why you wanted to escape for a wee while.'

'What do you mean?' I say. It comes out like an accusation that I try to counteract by casually leaning against the door frame, one ankle crossed over the other. In my head, I have the air of a sweater-clad catalogue model, but inside my stomach flutters like a jam-jar full of anxious butterflies until I'm sure one's going to plop out of my mouth like an ill-timed burp.

'Your ma?' asks Kian, glancing to the side as though he's misread the situation. 'Sorry, I didn't realise it was a dodgy subject, like.'

'It's not.'

'I'll stop going on about it. It's fine.'

'What's this then?' I say, drumming my fingers on the bench. I point to the mess of papers that I now believe to be an attempt to keep track of orders. Kian ignores me.

'If it's any consolation, I know what it's like to have a, errr ... complicated family dynamic.'

I'm brain-weary from tiptoeing around subjects I'm not used to verbalising. It feels like swimming upstream in a baggy T-shirt and trainers, similar to the swimming lessons we had at school. They culminated in a 'safe' simulation of what it feels like to drown, which involved Mrs Hillier plunging you below the surface with her shot-put arm whilst you tried not to inhale chlorinated water.

'Egg delivery, isn't it?' I say, flicking through the notepad. Ten pages back, the handwriting changes. Kian's scrawl is pressed into the paper with a thick blue biro, the letters spiky and clear, but the writing underneath is a mess of a crossings out, smeared ink, and words so illegible it looks like a series of tiny spiders crawling over the page. 'Five minutes with a highlighter and I could sort this out, no problem. Speaking of which, if you fancy letting me have a go at the stack of papers in the kitchen, just say the word. No offence, but it's like a scene from *Britain's Biggest Hoarders*.'

'Aye, knock yourself out, though I could find some more interesting things for you to do.'

'Trust me, I've got itchy fingers already.'

'Suit yourself, I'll not stop you.'

Kian flicks through the clipboard, a slight smile in the corner of his mouth. 'This was Granddad's system. He left school at eleven and didn't see the point in all the literacy stuff. As long as he could read the name of the guest ale down at The Wailing Banshee, he was happy. He nearly keeled over when I said I was going to do Anthropological Geography at Uni. "Nothing interesting about humans after you've untwisted a sheep's testicles using just your pinkie fingers," that's what he said.'

'I guess that's a skill in itself, although not something I'd put on a CV,' I say.

'No, quite. He accepted IOUs instead of payment far too often, so I wouldn't take his business advice to heart.'

I glance at my watch, keen to start deliveries so I can snatch half an hour with my laptop before dinner. According to a one-sentence email from Duncan that reached my phone in the early hours of this morning, my first diary entry went down well, so now I'm pressed to write another in covert snatches between the seemingly endless jobs on the farm. I tried to pitch a new article about the generational divide between the urban young and rural old, but Duncan's criticism was constructive, in as much as 'sounds drier than a camel minge in the Sahara Desert' can be. He wants click-worthy content. The more personal, the better.

Kian slaps the clipboard down beside me. 'Write a name down on the label, stick an elastic band round the box, and stack them in the crate. Crack on, I'll be back in a minute.'

Kian stomps across the yard, the sound of his footsteps softened by the well-worn rubber of his boots. I look down the list. The rumours are true. There's a worryingly poor circulation of last names, like the whole county got half a dozen to share between them, all ending in 'son': Wilson, Thomson, Robertson, Anderson, and one Macaulay. I look at the name again, squinting at the scrawl. Jacqui Macaulay. She doesn't seem the type to give a second chance at a first impression, but I'll give it a good bloody go.

Chapter 14

I walk around the house, holding my phone aloft like a water diviner. I need height. With the farmhouse in a dip, a cliff edge on one side and half a mile of cow fields on the other, demand for a phone mast isn't particularly high on the telecom agenda. Still, I've got to find enough signal to send an email to Duncan, otherwise my next diary entry will be handwritten and sent via the ankle of a crow chucked into a southerly gust of wind.

Borrowed wellie boots on, I pull my sleeves down over my hands and march across the yard, clambering over a fence into the sheep field. The sight of another signal bar makes my stomach bubble with glee. A short way off, Miranda chews a hunk of grass in a grinding semi-circle. Another bar! I squeal. Miranda looks up and acknowledges me with a guttural *bah*. She blinks slowly and drops onto her front elbows, reducing the distance between her mouth and the ground. Do sheep have elbows? Or two sets of knees? If I get up high enough, I might be able to Google it. Kian said the signal can improve if the wind's blowing in the right direction, but I'm not so sure. So far,

I've found it impossible to detect sarcasm, humour, or straight neutrality in Kian because he delivers all three with the same intonation.

As I crest the hill, my clock flicks onto 10.32, but already the sun is dwindling as though it got up for work, looked outside, and decided it couldn't be bothered with the rest of the day. I turn around, trying to find a sweet spot, and ... yes! My phone pings. I send my diary entry out before looking at anything else from yesterday. A quick look on Instagram tells me that Rory is still racking up a huge gyoza dumpling debt, Max is yet to wear a shirt that doesn't feature tropical palm trees, and Pickles has once again been featured on the page @FatCatsOfInstagram. His legacy continues, if not his low-cal dry food.

When an email comes through featuring the interlocked DNA icon of The Ancestry Project, I press it:

Would you like to change your privacy settings to start talking with your DNA matches?

I hover over the button. I could do it. Messaging Moira would mean that this whole charade of a 'farming holiday' is rendered unnecessary (that and the obvious fact that holidays shouldn't involve labour, unless it's the strain that comes from holding a chunky paperback aloft on a sun lounger), but something is holding me back.

How do you start a conversation like that? The only thing we have in common is a man who performed a handful of naked push-ups at some point in the Nineties and a bunch of other things left to chance. However you look at it, it's still a risky way to announce yourself, especially when I've got no idea how Moira feels about having a sister. What if the circumstances were dodgy? Was our father married, with a family, or more children?

I lock my phone and slide it in my back pocket. Today's egg delivery has come at the right time. I need to get off the farm. I need to start asking questions. I need to find a way around these sheep, who have blocked me in a semi-circle, eyes wild and yellow.

I half expect them to start clicking their feet, heads hung low in an ovine version of the opening scene in *West Side Story*, but as I head back down the hill, the herd follow me in Pied Piper fashion. I speed up, worried that they'll headbutt me to the floor. Death by slow chewing is not the way I want to go.

By the time I get back to the kitchen, Kian is draining the last of his coffee, his eyes bloodshot and manic.

'All right, let's go.' He unhooks a set of keys from a nail tacked into the wall, the wallpaper below stained tobacco yellow.

Outside, I squint as the sun cuts behind the house, glistening on the slick concrete forecourt. We load the Jeep with trays of eggs and a piece of machinery that looks like it's been dredged from a river, yet Kian claims it just 'needs a new bolt' before it's put back in the tractor. I strap them in, keen to avoid a scenario that involves a sharp corner and 150 crushed eggs. I walk around the passenger seat, but Kian's already there. He tosses me the keys and they hit my left boob, which would have hurt if it weren't for the three jumpers I'm wearing. I fumble and catch hold of a thistle-shaped key ring before they bounce to the floor.

'You can drive, right?'

'Well, I *can* drive, technically. I know recent events might suggest otherwise, but I have a license. Actually –' I put on the facade of smugness '– I can drive a minibus up to a capacity of fifteen people. Not to brag.'

'Great! You'll be fine in this.' Kian opens the door and settles into the passenger seat, one leg pulled up on his knee.

'I don't think you should trust me with this.'

'Why?'

'Because ... I've not driven in Scotland before. With hills and sheep in the road and potentially mowing down Jacqui because I can't find the brakes.'

'If you mow down Jacqui, I'll know it's not an accident. You'll be fine. Anyway, I've got to see John about this engine. If you deliver the eggs whilst I'm there, you can pick me up on the way back. Might be a good way to introduce yourself to people.'

I can feel my heart pulsing up into my throat. The beans on toast I had for lunch are threatening to make a reappearance. The alternative is that Jacqui has poisoned me with a lemon drizzle she left on the kitchen table. A possibility.

I shift the keys from one hand to another and bite the inside of my cheek.

'All right. But if I take this one off the side of a cliff as well, don't blame me.'

***

136

I look like an owl blinking over the steering wheel, elbows tucked in, eyes scanning the road for hazards that have so far included a portly rook that I swerved around as it pulled squashed rabbit innards from the middle of the road.

Kian waggles his hand out of the window as we reach the high street, so I turn in towards the green and pull up. In fear of the eggs sliding into the footwell, I let the car's momentum run out naturally before squeezing the handbrake on. I wonder if I should shove a wooden block beneath the back wheel before leaving it on any sort of incline?

'God, that was exhausting. I feel like I need a lie-down.'

Kian unclips his belt, gets out, and slides the rusted machinery off the back seat, his hands streaked with oil. He taps on the window, mouth tight with strain. I wind it down.

'You got the addresses?'

'Yep,' I say, tapping the clipboard that I've rearranged and highlighted in order of delivery.

'Great. I'll be a couple of hours, but if you finish before me go into the post office and tell Jules to send Dot round the back. She'll give us a yell over the fence. And don't crash the car.'

Kian slips down an alleyway as I scan the list on my lap, low-key anxiety fluttering in my stomach at the thought of meeting so many people without Kian acting as my social crutch. Back in Dulwich, Mum scans the neighbourhood for new additions and pulls them into her inner circle, where they debate the politics of intimate waxing, swap tagine recipes, and organise fundraisers so that the kids can have reindeer in the playground at Christmas. The husbands? Entirely surplus to requirements.

Mum has novelty eyelashes on the front of her Vauxhall Corsa, sunbathes in the front garden, and knows the best spots in Trafalgar Square to be seen with a placard. It's a bit much for London, let alone somewhere as small as Kilroch. Her time here with The Earth Mamas signalled the end of teenage rebellion and the start of adult responsibilities that I can't imagine dealing with myself. Did I take her away from that?

I lock the car and look down the cobbled high street, my clipboard in hand. Something here drew a line in the sand that she couldn't step back over. The question is, what did Moira's family have to do with it?

Chapter 15

It's pushing four o'clock and I've only gotten round to a measly three houses. Honestly, all this to shift a few dozen eggs, and I've only collected six quid off the punters. Most of them claim to have a tab going with Kian and gave me the odds and sods from their larders instead of actual money. On the seat next to me is my hoard: a roll of butter that looks like pre-packed cookie dough; three tins of pilchards; and half a leg of lamb roughly wrapped in butcher's paper and quite possibly leaking blood onto the upholstery.

I look up from my clipboard and peer out of the window. If people put house numbers on anything round here, it would make delivering the bloody eggs they've requested a lot easier. After 'Arbuthnott Farm', 'Merry Meet House', and the choicely named 'Bushy Gap Cottage', I'm now outside a house that Kevin McCloud would describe as 'handsome' with an 'ergonomic outlook that wrestles with a chaotic vista'.

I leave the car in first gear, as instructed by Kian, and walk up to the house, which is joined to the church on one side and a village hall on the other. Ivy links all three together, snaking in a lattice between bricks and wound across window panes. The doorway is only just visible behind a curtain of vines that haven't managed to squeeze their roots into cracked mortar. Although my experience of religion is limited to church hall jumble sales and amateur pantomimes, I gather that this cottage must be where the priest lives. Or is it a vicar? Parson? God, who knows. Actually, that's exactly who *would* know.

Going by the state of upkeep, I don't bother with the bell and rap my cold knuckles on the door instead. Whilst I wait for an answer, I kick the heels of my wellie boots together like a bumpkin version of Dorothy from *The Wizard of Oz*. Unless a village of this size is fanatical enough for two priests, it's got to be Ross who lives here.

'Coming!' says a voice from behind the door, throaty and low. He doesn't sound like a priest.

'Sorry, I can't find the keys. Hang on.' There's jingling, scraping, and I hear a word that *sounds* very rude but can't be, because priests don't swear. They're bashful and a bit awkward. When they were young, they were probably the kid who ate paper at the back of the classroom and cried when thunder and lightning struck over the school.

The door opens, the wood sticky in the door frame. Ross stands in front of me looking flustered in a thick jumper pushed up to his elbows and a black shirt unevenly buttoned to the collar. Holy Jesus. The only ecclesiastical box he's ticking is that his face is so well chiselled, he looks like a Baroque painting of Jesus, one that nuns would direct their gaze towards during periods of concentrated prayer.

'Hi, you're ... eggs,' says Ross, his gaze dropping to the tray in my hands.

'Eggs. Yes. These are eggs. I'm not an egg. Obviously. Although I suppose I was one at some point. Depends on whether you believe life starts at conception, or ... some other time. Jury's out. Ha, ha, ha!' I say, swallowing.

I stare at a cobweb in the gap between two bricks and feel a simmering heat build from my chest up to my hairline. I'm broken. I need a system restart on this whole encounter.

'Aye, yes. An interesting debate, but not one to have on the doorstep, I'd say,' says Ross. 'Do you want to come in?'

'Yes,' I reply, far too quickly. It's only when I step on the doormat that my instincts kick in. 'I have a clipboard.' What instinct is that? The instinct to be a complete and utter weirdo?

'Right ...'

'Yes. I, err ... need to check something.'

'Let me take those off you.' He pushes his wavy hair behind one ear and reaches over to take the tray from me. I forget to let go and for a moment we both stand, clutching two dozen eggs between us, the memory of why I came here momentarily absent. 'Or you can keep them?' he says, removing his hands.

'Shit, no. Sorry. Thanks.' I push the tray towards his chest and take out the clipboard that I've tucked under my arm. The page crinkles as I run my finger down the list and stop over a name I don't truly believe can belong to him. 'Reverend Dingwall?'

'Dingwall? No. Reverend? Almost.'

'Sorry, I must have written something down wrong.'

'I doubt it. If it's a church you're expecting, this is the only one around for a fair few miles.'

'Oh, right. I'm not familiar with the place yet.'

'Your accent is a bit of a giveaway. Mine is too, according to the locals.'

He sounds the same as everyone else I've met so far, but I'd made the mistake of referring to my Caledonian cabin buddy as having a 'generically Scottish accent' and that went down like a sack of spuds, so I've learned my lesson.

'How's it going up at Braehead?'

'I've been demoted to egg delivery after I crashed a quad bike earlier in the week.'

'I see,' he says, smiling. 'I shan't pass judgement.'

'No. That's, like, your thing, isn't it?'

'We're all judged in the end, so I don't see how doing it prematurely helps.'

'I don't know about that. It would make talent shows pretty boring.'

'That's true.' He holds my gaze for a moment and I realise that I'm staring at him like a weak-willed Labrador.

'The eggs,' I say, surfacing for air.

'The eggs!' He looks down at them and scratches his chin. 'I think we can blame Doug Dingwall for these.'

'I'll tell him when I see him.'

'You can't,' he says, brow furrowed. 'How shall I say it ... He's moved on to a better place.'

'Oh God. How awful. I'm so sorry, I didn't realise, I—'

142

'No, no – not like that. Doug has gone in for a knee replacement.'

'Oh! Ha! Good one!' I say, overcompensating for my excusable gullibility by laughing like a maniac.

'Yeah, I'm on loan. Like a footballer, except –' he narrows his eyes, concentrating '– not like one at all, actually. I mean, we both draw a crowd at the weekend, but their songs use "fucking wanker" a lot more than ours do.'

I feel like I've bitten a lemon, my smile so tight my dimples feel pincered with callipers.

'That'll be a few more years in purgatory for me. Ava – that's right, isn't it?'

'Mmm,' I reply, already replaying the way he says my name on a loop inside my head.

'Ah, nice. My grandma was called Ava.'

I smile, not sure what to do with this particular piece of information. From the wall, a clock ticks, the minute hand ticking round to a quarter to three. Ross notices my side-eye and springs towards the kitchen.

'Sorry, I've kept you. I've clearly been here too long. Couldn't convince anyone to stick around for a chat back in my regular parish, but I've got the opposite problem here. Even the sheep won't stop baa-ing at you when you run to the shop for a pint of milk.'

'Well, I've only met a handful of people so far and wouldn't say that's true of everyone.'

'Ah, Donovan?'

'No.'

'Glenda?'

143

'No.'

'Seamus?'

'No.'

Jesus Christ, what kind of reputation does this place have? I don't know whether I should mention Jacqui, because it seems a bit bold to gossip with a priest, but he did start it, so it seems fair to me.

'Jacqui, have you met her?'

'Jacqui? Unfriendly? I wouldn't have thought so.'

'Oh, not you too.'

Ross folds his arms, a half smile playing on his mouth. His forearms are taut, like he'd be really good at bell-ringing, or tossing a caber. Hmm. Must stop thinking of innuendo-fuelled hobbies.

'Have you made an enemy of our Jacqui?'

'I thought you said you hadn't been here that long.'

'I haven't. Three months. But the cakes, have you tried them? I'd leave my parish in Edinburgh for them on a permanent basis. Can't say the same for the coffee. I wouldn't be surprised if the delivery guy got something mixed up, John Gilmore, I think? He sells bags of manure on the side, so it's not an impossibility.'

'Taste like shit, does it?'

'Your words, not mine,' he says, dropping his chin.

How? How are there quite literally thousands of men in London and yet the only attractive one is here? And a priest, at that? I take a deep breath, refocusing on my clipboard.

'Speaking of Jacqui, she's next on my list.'

'Ah! Fantastic. Can you give her these from me?' Ross jogs through to the kitchen. I hear dishes shifting and cutlery clattering into the sink, before he reappears with two loaf tins, their non-stick sides slick with droplets of water. 'Only if you don't mind. She brought round a coffee cake yesterday. Stupidly delicious.'

'And the eggs?'

'I'll keep them, but maybe we'll go for six next time? I wouldn't want to criticise a colleague, but I think you'd agree that twenty-four in a week is excessive.'

'I'd say so, yeah.'

'Right you are. Look, if you want to drop in again or come to the service next Sunday, don't hesitate.'

'Not really the religious type, but –' I could be? Too keen? '– I'll think about it,' I say, my hand on the doorknob. As I duck to head beneath the ivy, I turn back towards Ross.

'Hey, if you've been here for three months, surely you've been getting a tray of eggs every week before now?'

'Yeah,' he says, rubbing his jaw. 'Your appearance has made complete sense compared to my last theory. I've only ever been a city boy – didn't really know how things worked in the country. The rural villages are known for being a bit old-school in their ways. Anyway, I thought the eggs were like some kind of goodwill gesture to keep the cows healthy, you know? I always found them on the back step. If it was Kian, he never rang the doorbell, so hopefully that explains my confusion. Somewhat.' Ross pulls his face into an awkward grimace.

I laugh and pull my sleeves over my hands, clasping

them inside my fists. It's an annoying habit from when I was a teenager, but I can't seem to shake it.

'If you want to help me get through this lot one evening, I wouldn't complain,' he says, glancing down at the eggs. 'But I'll warn you now, it's omelettes and soufflé.' Ross smiles into the corner of his mouth and pushes a curly lock of hair from his face.

'Yeah, sure,' I say, taken aback, firstly by his direct invitation and secondly by my willingness to accept it. In London, it takes two months and a string of WhatsApp messages to organise a coffee date, and even then, people usually flake out the night before. But this isn't a date, is it? It's dinner with the local priest, Kilroch's officially chaste consultant for all issues moral and religious.

'Good luck with Jacqui!' he says, holding up a hand as he shunts the door closed.

***

Back in the car, I flick down the sun visor to assess my appearance and squint at my scuffed reflection. Oh, it's bad. Really bad. I look like I've just fled a war zone. My fringe is stuck to my forehead, my hair is matted and mushroom-like from tucking it inside my scarf for extra warmth, and my cheeks are so pink I look like I've head-butted a blusher palette.

Jacqui happens to have put the biggest egg order in, so it's in my interest to make sure I get her on side, as I can't be the only person in the village etched onto her black list. I walk from the Jeep to the post office-cum-tearoom, my steps slow and considered. My shuffle down the high street coincides with the departure of a man with deep-set wrinkles, who holds the door open for me. As I step inside, he calls over my shoulder.

'She's here, Jacqui!' With that, he nods in my direction, his bottom lip pushed up like he's using it to scaffold the rest of his face.

A hush descends over the tearoom as Jacqui comes out of the kitchen at the back, a Cath Kidston apron tied around her waist. We face each other. A woman with candy floss hair says something to her companion from behind her hand, eyes fixed on me. My stomach is an oil-slick of anxiety. In the corner, a small toddler drops half a cream-smeared scone on the floor and starts crying, his head dropped backwards, mouth agape in horror. Jacqui dries her hands on a tea towel, whips it over her shoulder, and jerks her head backwards, gesturing that she wants me to follow her.

This is ridiculous. I'm Lorrie Atmore's daughter. I haven't been trained in the rules of navigating PTA mums and bossy divorcées for nothing. For years I've lurked by collapsible tables lined with tray bakes, watching Mum navigate groups of women with the deftness and determination of a small-town Michelle Obama. I need to step out. No one knows me here. No one knows that I've ever been any different. It's time to channel my inner Lorrie.

'Jacqui! I can see why your tearoom is heaving, I can't walk past someone in Kilroch without them raving about your buttercream.'

Jacqui frowns and points to the clock behind my head, one hand on her hip.

'I close in half an hour. What good are these to me now?'

Ah, this might be harder than I thought.

'Sorry, Jacqui. I was doing a loop and, well, to tell you the truth, it's turned into a big meet and greet. Everyone here is so welcoming.' I do my best to smile as I talk, which feels unnatural but necessary in these delicate times. 'Ross, up at the rectory? He asked me to bring these back down to you, with his thanks, of course. I think he'll be losing teeth at the rate he's eating your cakes.' I'm small-talking. This is small talk, right? It feels strained enough to be small talk.

'Losing teeth? I don't tell him how quickly to eat them, lovie.'

'No, of course not, I meant it like—'

I pause. She's thrown me. There's a limit on how many times you can compliment a cake you haven't eaten. I'm not bloody Mary Berry.

Jacqui takes the tins off me and leans against the kitchen counter.

'When Kian delivers the eggs, he comes to me first.'

'He must have forgotten to mention that.'

'I had four lemon drizzles, two coffee and walnuts, and a fruit loaf to make today. The loaf was for the boys down at the harbour before they went out to do the crab pots tomorrow morning.'

I don't want to say sorry, but I should for the sake of peace talks. What does she expect me to do, tune into the shipping forecast?

'Sorry about that, Jacqui.'

'Nothing much to be done about it now.' Jacqui turns away from me and unstacks three trays of eggs across the counter. She counts them with her index finger, her mouth silently forming numbers, up one row and down another.

'There are sixty-four,' I say.

Jacqui raises one hand to silence me. This woman! She makes Nasty Vanessa from the PTA look like Kate bloody Middleton. I involuntarily sigh and shift my body weight from one foot to the other, rolling my head to stretch the muscles down my neck.

'Have you got somewhere to be?' she says, her voice dripping with sarcasm.

'No. This is *the* most important part of my day.' An angry claw scratches at my temples.

Jacqui blinks, her mouth a rosebud. She turns her back to me and starts counting again, moving from one egg to the other with a precise, measured tap on the shell. I have a strong desire to perform an aggressive dance behind her; one that involves an excess of middle fingers and a silent scream. Imagining it will have to suffice.

'There are sixty-three,' she says, throwing me a look that suggests I fell predictably short of her expectations.

'Oh.'

'So I'll have the missing egg by eight o'clock tomorrow.'

'Sorry?'

'You'll bring me the missing egg by eight o'clock in the morning.'

'Eight o'clock?'

'Aye.'

'I could run to the shop next door and get one for you.'

'No, I only use Bantam eggs for my cakes. I like Gillian, but her hens are no' up to scratch. Like I said, I'll have the missing egg by tomorrow morning.'

'Not a problem,' I say as sweetly as possible. I glance towards the door. There are no prams blocking the aisle. Jacqui's hasn't got a weapon within reach (unless you count a spatula). Escape route clear. I sidle along the bench towards the doorway.

'Where did you say you were from, Ava?'

She's using my name! A small success. I cough to clear my throat.

'London.'

Jacqui rolls her eyes. 'I may have lived in a village my whole life, but I know that London is made up of boroughs.'

'Oh, right. south London. Dulwich.'

I've panicked. I could have made up something. It's her strangely pervasive, low-key aggression making me feel on edge. Admitting where Mum and I live was *definitely* on my list of no-go talking points.

'And you're up here to help on Braehead Farm because ...?'

'I wanted to get outdoors. A break from work. Well, the kind of work I did, anyway. Computer stuff. *This* work makes my body hurt.'

Jacqui clearly doesn't care about my answer because she doesn't comment on it.

'I ask because people don't often come here without a reason. We're not the Isle of Skye, and we don't have the tourist appeal of Orkney. Folk come here for specific reasons.'

I don't reply. I can't tell if this is just Jacqui being Jacqui (well, how she is with me anyway), or if she's trying to suss me out. I need to leave now, before I'm clobbered to death with a marble rolling pin.

'OK, I'll be off now,' I say in a sing-song voice, scooping my hat from the side.

'Hmm. Oh, and don't bother yourself bringing any more tins down from Ross,' says Jacqui, smoothing down her apron. 'I'll fetch them myself.'

Chapter 16

Date: Friday 11th October
Location: Beneath a duvet in Kilroch, Scotland
Cups of tea: Six
Sleep: 5 hours and 37 minutes

If you're still not sure where Kilroch is by now, switch on the weather forecast and look north to where the land mass is covered in a deep blue, swirling cloud of rain. We're beneath that.

So, how is life on a farm with a herd of sheep and villainous chickens going? Has it sufficiently pushed all thoughts of That Live Stream out of my head? Thereabouts, is the short answer. At this point, it feels like a fever dream.

Farm life is better than expected in some respects, worse in others. After a week, I can balance a tray of eggs on one hand. Mildly impressive. The cold I could do without. There's still no sign of Moira, although in theory I could have walked past her a dozen times already. Is she the woman who takes her pet weasel for a walk every morning? Is she the heavy-handed chippie cashier who pours so much vinegar on your dinner it's like she's trying to turn it into soup? The search continues. Next stage: take a wellie boot round and ask all women in their twenties to try it on, Cinderella style.

It's taken three days for my usual desk hunch to make way for a deep-set muscle ache. I've never twisted, lifted, dragged, or shivered so much in such a short space of time. At this point, I'd struggle to pick up a bag of rice without wincing. I rub my shoulders, crane over the steering wheel, and try to spot Kian on the high street. Where the hell is he? A woman I now know as 'Jenny the Wink' walks in front of the car and waves at me for a third time, but I've slipped so far down the seat I'm practically in the foot-well. I smile back like a frog being squeezed in someone's fist. I know I need to ramp up my search for Moira, but seeing as my time away from the farm has thus far been segmented into tasks, I'm not sure how to start digging whilst staying semi-covert.

I yawn so widely my jaw aches. Today, I was late getting out to feed the pigs and lost favour with the sows. Bertha took it incredibly personally. When I eventually appeared with a bucket of feed and vegetable peelings, she charged me down, teeth bared, screaming like a possessed toddler. In her haste to eat, she bit through my wellie boot and now it leaks. My toes look like dried apricots.

The Jeep's side door clicks open and Kian swings into the front seat, wedging a clunky clip-lock case between his feet.

'Where have you been? I've got repetitive strain injury

from waving at the entire population of this village. Look. Here she is again.' I raise my hand as Jenny the Wink passes back the other way. 'What is she doing, buying her weekly shop one item at a time?'

'I think she might just be lonely.'

'Oh,' I say, annoyed. 'I feel bad now.'

'Nah, only joking. She's a right busybody, Jenny. I don't think that twitch of hers is genuine either. Claims she got struck by lightning, but between you and me I think it's a ploy to keep her disability benefits.'

'Bet she's lethal in a game of wink murder.'

'Can't move for the bodies.' Kian laughs and shakes his head.

The car lurches as I put it into first gear and we both rock forwards like we're mounted on an unruly horse. Despite the potholes and temperamental clutch, driving here is a dream. Unlike London, no one tries to blindly cross the road whilst watching Netflix on their phones, largely because there *is* no one beyond the quarter-mile radius of the shop, post office, and pub.

'Hey, I got you something.'

'Have you?' I side-eye Kian as we turn on the undulating road that leads to the farm.

He rips open a paper bag and the smell of warm pastry fills the car.

'Oh, that's too good,' I say, reaching over to take it off him. 'If I drive us into a ditch it's your fault. You can't distract me like this.' I rip off a chunk between my teeth and swallow a too-large mouthful in one boiling clod. 'Did

Jacqui give you this?' I say out of the corner of my mouth.

'Yeah,' he says, flicking through a crumpled manual pulled from his chest pocket.

I scrunch down the top of the bag and put it in the drinks holder, wiping my fingers on the side of the seat.

'Where's yours?'

'Ah, I'm not hungry.'

'Am I right in thinking that Jacqui intended this for you and not me?'

'Seriously, don't worry about it. I ate a boiled egg before we came out.'

'I hope it wasn't the missing egg from Jacqui's tray.'

He smirks. 'Fresh from Babs this morning, so no.'

I told him about Jacqui's single-egg request from Wednesday and he could barely stand straight from laughing. He thinks she was mucking about. Mucking about! He didn't see the look in her eye. She reminds me of a honey badger: seemingly cute but would claw your genitals off at the slightest misdemeanour.

'So, are there many people still living here who you knew growing up?' I say, tapping the gear stick in a performance of nonchalance.

'A few. Jacqui's family have been here so long I'm sure there's Viking blood in there. John's from Orkney, but his Mrs was in my year group at school. The McCullochs are a huge family—they make up about a quarter of the village.'

'So, there aren't many other youngsters around?'

'Nah, although I'm not sure I can pin myself in the "young" demographic. I feel like an old man. You know I fall asleep in front of the TV with dinner on my lap? It's embarrassing.'

I flick the windscreen wipers on and slow down by the gates to Braehead Farm. I hadn't considered the idea that Moira might not live here anymore, which feels like an appalling oversight. The Ancestry Project named Kilroch as her hometown, but what if she's living somewhere else? Doing a season in Ibiza? Studying in a completely different city? My stomach flip-flops. At the very least, I can't get the train back to London without knowing where to look next.

The sheep trot alongside the fence as we bump down the track towards the farmhouse.

'Daft things. They give me such a headache. I was going to make some money off the lambs, but that plan is shot to shit.'

'Why?' I pull on the handbrake and strain to open the door. A gust of wind blows so strong it's like someone's trying to push me back into the car.

'A few weeks ago, a ram broke into the paddock and tupped thirteen ewes in one night. He wasn't right for them,' says Kian, shaking his head. 'Just some chancer from a feral herd. I had a really handsome stud lined up for next month but there's no use for him now.'

'Was he expensive?' I ask.

'I saved up my pint money for three months, so, yeah.'

'I'm sorry your sheep orgy didn't work out.'

Kian pulls out the case he collected and frowns.

'That's not what we call it round here, but –'

'– It's pretty accurate?'

'Yeah, I'd say so. John tells me to be more mercenary, and he's right in a way. These lot don't pay for themselves,' he says, waving a hand at the sheep, who spook and scatter when Kian's arm makes a funny shaped shadow on the wall. 'It's the welfare that's important, right?'

I don't deny that they're sweet to look at (nothing on Pickles, obviously), but when it comes to sheep-related business advice, I'm completely out of my depth.

I slip through the kitchen door and slam it closed behind me in a rash attempt to trap the heat inside.

'I can't sit down or that'll be me done for the day,' says Kian, rubbing his chin as he splits into a yawn. He shoves a Snickers multipack in his pocket, pulls his hood up, and opens the back door. 'Take the afternoon off, all right? We've got a lot on tomorrow.'

***

I drag my attention back to my laptop screen, where the cursor blinks at me from a near-empty page. I can't write anything decent when my fingers are inching towards the stacks of letters spread across the table like a patchwork tablecloth. Maybe if I spent five minutes organising them ... Just a light touch. And if I'm doing that, I may as well put them in date order. Kian did say I could 'knock myself out,' but does he know he's dealing with the kind of person who travels with an emergency pack of coloured tabs?

Laptop forgotten, I next look up when the radio pips for the three o'clock news bulletin. If anything exists beyond the kitchen table, I wouldn't know, so engrossed am I in this menial but oh-so-satisfying task. I lift my third cup of tea to my lips, pausing to read a letter heavily stamped and underlined in bold red lettering. My spending habits are questionable at times, but novelty cat socks at fifteen pounds don't seem quite so bad with the farm's outgoings spread in front of me. Guilt lines my stomach like cold soup. I'm not sure Kian would want me to see this. Between the endless errands, debt, and uncooperative animals, it's no wonder he's stressed.

I had a feeling things were a bit ropey from the snatched reference Kian made to Braehead being a 'poisoned chalice'. Although my knowledge of agriculture comes from evenings spent half-watching *Countryfile* whilst sugar-waxing my legs, I know of one key business principle that could be applied here: money needs to come in more frequently than it's going out. From the looks of things, Kian's granddad kept things ticking along through a refusal to open incoming mail.

Despite us being the same age, I'm barely reaching adolescent levels of responsibility in comparison to Kian. Discovering I'm not an only child was a shock, but at least I haven't had to quit my job to revive a family business. Personally, I'd sell up and be done with it. At least then he can go back to building fertiliser farm bombs, or whatever he was researching back in Edinburgh.

The back door swings open and Kian stomps his feet on the mat, his cheeks ruddy and red.

'Hey, what have you done here?' he says, tucking his hands into the pocket of his hoodie.

'I ... umm. I got a bit carried away, but don't thank me. I find this kind of thing far too enjoyable to count it as work,' I say, zipping up my pencil case. I used up my chisel-tip highlighter on Braehead's last financial year, so I'm hoping he's a *tiny* bit grateful. 'Don't worry, I didn't read anything. Nothing much.'

'Oh, aye. No bother,' says Kian, rubbing the back of his neck. 'I'm not so good with the numbers stuff myself. I'm more of a "do first, think later" kind of guy.'

'Excellent, because I'm a "think too much and never do it" kind of girl.'

'Except for now, right? No one travels 500 miles to dish out chicken feed on a whim,' he says, a dimple appearing in his cheek.

I jump. Both our phones go off in overlapping bleeps, mine inside my pocket, his skitting across the table.

'Told you, you can't predict when the wind will blow this way,' he says, his voice unusually upbeat. He fills the kettle with one hand and opens his messages with the other. I wiggle my phone free. This is a nod from Out There, back where there are chicken shops and nail salons on every high street.

When I open my message app, my stomach drops like someone's cut the counterbalance in a lift. Of the many notifications that have pinged through, one name stands out: Duncan. A caps-lock-filled text draws my eyes to a message sent at 9.21 a.m.

I slip outside and shoo a hen off a mucky, upturned bucket so I can sit down.

Duncan's text loads, each shouty, double-spaced word of it.

AVA. SISTER UPDATE PRONTO. IF YOU HAVEN'T FOUND HER, START DOOR KNOCKING. CUT THE EGG CHAT. EGGS ARE A HARD FUCKING SELL. THNX.

A scratching sound comes from the hen house, as Babs, aka The Bantam Menace, strides down the ramp, her eyes sharp and mean. Chicken memories must last longer than I thought.

Chapter 17

Date: Friday 18th October
Location: Back against the Aga for warmth, laptop on knees
Sleep: Six hours and twenty-three minutes. Not bad.
Cups of tea: Three
Sister sightings: 0

Three hundred people doesn't sound excessive for a village, but I think I'd quickly get a reputation if I went up to every woman under forty asking if she's my long-lost sister. Thus, my main investigative tactic involves observing people from afar to see if I can recognise my own features on someone else's body. Unless I want to further ostracise myself, I'll keep my pocket binoculars out of sight. The milk-churning, prairie-dress-wearing fantasy I entertained before has curdled like cottage cheese, but village life hasn't passed me by entirely unnoticed.

Five Misconceptions of the #FarmcoreLifestyle:
No one meanders through a forest picking mushrooms with a wicker basket hooked round their elbow. I value

163

my kidneys too much to risk eating anything growing from a tree stump, whatever the guidebook says.

If you leave a freshly baked loaf of bread on the window sill, the crows will have decimated it by the time it's cooled down.

Drying clothes outside sounds wholesome but be prepared for them to freeze on the line.

Little old locals are cute until they bark indecipherable insults at you in the street for walking on the wrong patch of pavement.

Don't bother asking for the following items in the corner shop unless you want to be laughed at: avocado, hummus, oat milk, halloumi, guacamole, or anything gluten-free.

***

Kian asked for a hand with something this afternoon, but I can't for the life of me remember what it was. At the time, I was only one coffee down and at the very least I need two before my senses work in unison. At *Snooper*, 'lending someone a hand' usually meant they wanted me to check their content piece for grammar, but at Braehead Farm it's far more literal. Kian suggested that I dab surgical spirit into my blisters because 'the calluses harden up quicker'. Depending on how well my search goes, I might not be around long enough to put that theory into practice.

In a series Duncan is indelicately calling 'Just My Loch', my diary entries have jumped up the 'most viewed' bar on *Snooper*, settling into second place below a listicle featuring

Gigi Hadid's best bikini pics of the year. I understand the need to feed the fire whilst it's hot, but it's a struggle to keep up. It might be because I barely last twenty minutes tapping away on my laptop before I'm asleep with my mouth slack and a trickle of drool on the pillow. It's the emotional tightrope that's most exhausting, not to mention how physically demanding farm work is.

Guilt from lying to Mum flares up like eczema I'm not allowed to scratch. Combined with the anxiety of bumping into Jacqui again, it's safe to say I'm not exactly feeling mellow.

Every time I pass someone in the village, I scan their features for similarities in case I accidentally walked past a cousin, aunt, or grandma. I never thought I looked much like Mum, but perhaps that's because I look so much like *him*, whoever *he* is. Does he have the same chin dimple as me? Is he to blame for my strawberry blonde hair?

First impressions tripped off my fingers easily, but now I've been here for a while, things are different. The only developments I've made in the quest known as 'My Long Lost and Likely Deceased Family' have involved failed trips to the village, either side of feeding animals, counting animals, and keeping those same animals alive in a place where the weather is clearly telling everyone to fuck off. So far, I've completely failed to segue talk towards dolphin activism in the Nineties, which is my only jumping-off point into a bigger, far more complicated conversation.

I walk out to the middle of the courtyard and stand still, listening. It's like tuning an old radio; every so often the wind picks up and noises from the farm are blown in and out of frequency. There's the distant sound of waves fizzing against the cliff edge, the shed door whining on rusty hinges, and the throaty grunt of pigs. Pigs!

I pull my gloves on and head down a track to the left of the farmhouse until I reach an open-sided barn that defies physics by standing up at all. The roof sags like the waistband on a pair of old jeans. Nearby, the back door of a shipping container swings open. Kian emerges, a paper mask hanging from one ear. He raises a hand, a grin set on his face as though he's just told a joke that went down well.

'All right?' he calls. 'I did come up to the house earlier, but I didn't want to disturb you. You had this ... dreamy look on your face.'

'Ha. I guess so. I was just re-sorting those papers on the kitchen table. I'm not sure whether a chronological or category-based system would work best for filing. There's compelling arguments for both.'

'I'll bet,' he says, a smirk twitching in the corner of his mouth.

'I'll walk you through it later. Trust me, I know it sounds lame but just wait until you see the page dividers.' I decide not to mention the plastic sleeve I filled with four or five letters stamped 'final notice'. Not the time, I expect.

'What's this for?' I say, pointing to the shipping container. 'They're used for getting sports cars across the Channel, right? Or – if you're in London – they stack them on top of each other and shove a Michelin restaurant inside.'

'The pigs get more use out of them up here. One of the

local freight companies went bust last year but the owner still owed us money for three lambs that were on the dinner table by the time Granddad got round to sending an invoice. We got this as payment instead,' says Kian, tapping the unit with a metallic clang. 'Just remember to stake the door open if you're going in and out. If it slams in the wind, you'll know about it.'

'Noted.'

'Shall we go for it?' A woman with a severe fringe and square jaw steps down from the container wearing a waxed jacket twice the size of her, the sleeves rolled up to the elbow.

'Ah! It's you! Hi!' Before I get a chance to reply, she bounds towards me and envelops me in a hug. A clunky something-or-other is wedged between our chests, but my arms are pinned by my sides, so I wince through the encounter. The woman's hair falls in a curtain and smells of apple shampoo and another scent that I vaguely recognise from the posh girls at school; sweet, hay-like, and musty. Horses. It's got to be horses.

'Ouff,' I utter, rubbing my chest with a forearm. 'That thing's got a lot of sharp edges,' I say, nodding towards the device in her hands. 'Nice to meet you.'

'Sorry! I always do this. My friend – one from college – I go to college in Moray, right? – well, she told me it can be a bit much. The hugging. I can't see myself changing but I should find out if you're a hugger first, shouldn't I?'

'Bit late for that now,' says Kian, tucking his chin into the collar of his gilet.

'You're right,' she says, smiling. The girl looks from me to

167

Kian and back again. 'Let's reverse it. Brl-rl-rl-rl-rl-rl-rl.' She mimics a tape on rewind. 'It's *so* nice to meet you. Kian's told me about the quad bike incident. You poor thing! That was lucky, wasn't it? We lost our family whippet over those cliffs when I was a lass. He chased a seagull right off the side. Silly beggar. I know it sounds like I'm exaggerating, but she basically burst on impact. Horrible. We couldn't get down in time to scrape her off the rocks so I expect she's out at sea somewhere. For the record, what's your position on hugs?'

'Err, I guess it depends, if it's a—'

'Ah, I'm with you,' she says, giving me a wink that alludes to some sort of innuendo I'm not sure I'm on board with. 'It's so nice to have another person around. I've seen the same faces turn into walnuts with walking sticks since I was a bairn. Kian's back though and that's been great, hasn't it, Ki?'

'Yeah, I've coped,' says Kian playfully, swinging an arm over her shoulders. She beams up at him, eyes wide and doe-like.

Jesus, I'm exhausted. She's going to keel over from lack of oxygen in a second.

'We better get on with it. I'm not gonna lie, this is up there with the worst jobs we have to do all year,' says Kian. 'Apart from spraying slurry.'

'Ah, it's not so bad. It's the catching part that can be ... challenging.'

'Catching?' I say. Going by the tone of conversation, it's like we're about to play an unconventional game of rounders: something that takes place over three days with loose rules about violent participation.

'Yeah. Got a pressurised gun for the jabs this year. My buddy in the agricultural department is doing some post-doc research on non-invasive immunisations, so yours truly got his mitts on this bad boy,' says Kian. The woman passes him the device. He turns it over in his hands, lovelorn. Ah, *that's* what was jabbing me in the boobs.

Kian's excitement radiates off him. Even his arm hair stands on end. Initiating full nerd mode in three, two, one ...

'You take the vaccine and screw it into the base, here,' he says, tapping the vial and glancing at me to check that I'm following. 'Then this canister is charged with a pres-surised burst of air that pushes through the nozzle and penetrates the skin without puncturing it. Voila! Happy pigs. Cool, isn't it?'

'Kian's the only farmer in the county using one of these this year,' chirps the woman, looking to him with pride so sincere it makes me bashful.

'Friends in high places,' he says, tapping his nose. 'It's technically a prototype, so make sure you wear goggles if you're going to have a go with it. The last design had a forty per cent malfunction rate. Just a little kick back when you make contact.'

I take a deep breath. A chunky bacon sandwich is the closest I've ever come grabbing a pig with two hands.

The woman bumps Kian with her hip and grins. 'Let's get piggy with it!' She lifts the gun to her mouth and pretends to blow smoke from the barrel.

'All right, best point that in the right direction,' says Kian, 'Don't think you need protecting against trotter rot.'

'I might. My hands are looking more trotter-like by the day,' I say, turning them over.

'Ha! You're funny,' says the woman, laughing. 'Come on, I'll show you what to do.' She goes to hook an arm through mine and as she does, Kian lifts the gun from her like he's cradling a fragile newborn.

***

'Go on, Ava! Grab it. GRAB IT!' I stand in the corner, my front leg bent in a lunge, my back foot squared at forty-five degrees for stability. I've only every known this position as 'warrior one', but today it's far more like 'saluting the swine', such is the frequency with which my hands slap the floor as I lunge for another sow.

I slump against the gate and toss my second to last jumper over a fence post. The wind cools me down, mainly because I'm sweating so much that it feels like a damp towel is draped across my back.

'Kian! Have you got a second?' I say, wiping my forehead with the cleanest part of my sleeve.

'Can it wait?' he says, swinging a leg back over a pig. He shakes a canister and sprays a cross on the pig's backside just before she bolts from between his knees with a high-pitched squeal. What a drama queen. You'd think we were branding them with a hot poker.

'It's a quick one,' I say, straining to be heard above the

cacophony of squeals. He unzips his hoodie and makes his way towards me, shoulders slumped with fatigue.

'I didn't catch her name earlier. It feels awkward to ask now,' I say, nodding towards the woman as she darts to one side and lands on the concrete with a thump. She jabs a pig on the backside, an arm outstretched like she's on centre court at Wimbledon.

'Sorry, didn't realise. It's Moira. Family friend. Known her for ever,' he says, turning back towards the pigs. I grab his sleeve. He looks down at my hand, then up at me. I can't seem to get a breath in.

'Moira? Moira – Moira?' I say, my words squeezed from my stomach.

'Yeah,' says Kian slowly, taken aback. 'Moira McCauley.'

I look beyond his shoulder to where Moira sits balancing on her heels, teetering in wait for another unmarked pig to trot past. She catches my eye and waves frantically. That's my bloody sister. *Moira.* I've found her. I've bloody found her.

'Are you all right?' asks Kian.

'Yeah, I'm fine. It's fine. Super fine.'

'You sure? You look a bit ... weird.'

'No, I'm just hot. Don't you think it's hot?' I say, fanning myself.

'It's six degrees.'

'Is it?' I say, my voice an octave higher than normal. I can feel my heartbeat in my neck. I can feel my heartbeat everywhere, like a jellyfish pulsating blindly underwater.

'Do you ... want to let go of my sleeve?' says Kian.

'Yep. Sorry.'

'It looks like you need a tea? With a sugar, or two?'

'No, it's OK. Can you cope without me for a couple of minutes? I'll be back. Just need a ... yeah.'

I clamber over the fence, my legs wobbling as I hop down on the other side. I tuck myself out of the wind's slipstream and press my forehead against the barn's corrugated panelling until the pressure verges on pain. My breath flutters in my throat. There's a tickle of something, like a slick of cooking oil coating my stomach. Do I say something now, or wait? Should I go into the whole back story, or just come out with it? I drum my fingers against my leg and try to think clearly, but my brain feels like it's been replaced with scrambled egg. I don't know what to do, but I feel like it would be inappropriate to yell 'I'M YOUR SISTER!' whilst pig wrestling.

I turn around. There's a gap between the warped timber beams, through which I can partially see Moira. She has her arms wrapped around a hefty sow, towards which Kian wades through a sea of jostling rumps. He jabs a vaccine into the pig's side. Moira grins, her fringe stuck to her forehead. Her chin isn't as pronounced as mine, but it's obvious now. I can't believe I didn't notice it straightaway. The same groove in mine is there in hers, set within a square jaw which might look masculine if it weren't counterbalanced by high-set, apple-round cheeks.

I examine the parameters of my common sense. Moira McCauley. It can't be a popular name, and definitely not in a village of three hundred, so, yep, that's almost definitely my half-sister. She looks a few years younger than me, so her father – our father – had a relationship of some kind with Moira's mum *after* mine. That, or there are a number of Moiras dotted about the isle. Did she know him when she was little? Does she have any siblings? Which, of course, means: do *I* have any more siblings? Ones that haven't logged their details on The Ancestry Project?

I turn around and slide down the wall, the concrete floor cold through my jeans. This was the whole point, wasn't it? Answers are surfacing, so why do I feel like folding myself into a piece of human origami? This sisterhood project feels so *untidy*, especially when you factor in the diary entries I'm still being asked to write for *Snooper*.

In my bullet journal, I have a clear line down each weekly spread; one for work, one for life. I've got no idea where to place things now; everything is scrawled across the middle. This was never just about my job, like my conveyor-belt life in London was never really about preferring the comfortable option. If you never try to change anything, you can't expect anything to change.

If I'd known about Moira as a kid, I could have presented her with a matching friendship bracelet and offered to badly French braid her hair; aka Friendship 101 when you're eight years old. We could have sent each other letters written with scented gel pens. We could have met in the summer holidays and gone camping. We'd have bought ice-creams with two balls of chemically flavoured chewing gum in the bottom and swapped transfer tattoos. It would have been like *The Parent Trap*, except neither of us are rich and 'summer camp' would likely be a caravan site on a blustery clifftop near Skegness.

We're not kids. I don't know how to *do* the family thing with anyone other than Mum. I've had years of being an only child. In public, anyway. Let's face it, vomiting on the internet is going to be pretty hard to beat, but I still don't want Moira to be blindsided like I was.

I pick at the orange nail polish that has clung on since my last full day at *Snooper*. Chipped flakes fall to the floor, garish against the mud like radioactive lice. I've speculated about the moment I found Moira, but every time it was detached and clichéd, like shaking up a snow globe and watching the scene settle from a distance.

If instinct feels like anxiety, mine is so intense it's like a shard of broken glass lodged between my ribs. Finding Moira is my opening paragraph, metaphorically speaking. I can't dash out the rest of the story without thinking about the consequences. I'm not a cupcake. I can't just spring myself on her and expect a good reaction.

'Ava?' says Kian. He can't see me tucked round the corner. I pinch the skin between my thumb and index finger. My body feels tightly wound, like I could cry or laugh or scream, maybe at the same time.

'I'm here,' I say, stepping out.

'Great. We've still got fifteen to go. It's anarchy out there,' he says, like he's taken reprieve from hand-to-hand combat in a war zone.

I push my sleeves up, swing my leg over the fence, and hop back inside the pen. Moira is standing in the middle like a ringmaster, the pigs jostling in a circle around her. I clap my hands, surveying the scene. This fizzy energy has got to go somewhere.

'We can do this,' I say. 'Kian, pass me that board. Moira –' the name catches on my lips like I'm talking with my mouth full '– pull that fence in tighter. I'll funnel them in the right direction. When you've jabbed, I'll mark them. Kian, chuck that here.'

He takes the spray can out of his pocket. 'Are you demoting me?'

'Sorry. But not sorry,' I say, catching the canister. I want to keep analysing Moira's face for similarities, but don't want to come across as a massive weirdo. We stand, elbow to elbow, the top of her head an inch or two below mine.

We work through the remaining pigs until I'm so hot I've had to de-layer to my T-shirt and jeans. My bra feels clammy and my arms are a delightful shade of corn-beef purple, a look I last exhibited during unenthusiastic netball matches at school. Kian is covered in straw, his jogging bottoms loose at the waist, whereas Moira looks no different, as though catching pigs is her favourite past time.

'Last one!' I call. We face into the pen, a tank-like sow between us.

'A word of warning – Edith is hormonal,' says Kian.

'What do you mean?' I ask.

The only kind of hormonal I recognise involves eating a family-size bag of Doritos and curling up in the foetal position, all whilst my uterus attempts to punch its way out of my stomach. What do pigs do? Cry into their potato peelings after promising yet again to only eat one trough's worth of dinner?

175

'Edith's having a phantom pregnancy. She thinks she's carrying piglets, but there's nothing in there. Makes her over-protective,' says Moira.

Oh God. That's really sad. I shiver as the wind draws warmth from my damp skin. Edith looks from one of us to the other, her trotters tapping on the concrete. She grunts on an outward breath.

'Shall we just let her through?' I say. 'Herd immunity?'

'I can't risk it. It'll be worse if she gets sick. Can't do much about it if that happens,' replies Kian.

'Come in slowly,' says Moira, 'that's it.'

Kian and I pad across the barn. I smile at Edith, hoping she'll take reassurance from it. It takes less than three seconds for our tentative approach to fail. I squat, but she must interpret this descent to eye-level as a hostile move, because what happens next has all the co-ordination of a dyspraxic moth in a cyclone.

Edith launches forward like a porky battering ram and headbutts me with the full force of a skull two inches thicker than mine. My eyeballs feel like they've been knocked to the floor. I clutch my face to check that it's still there and roll onto my side, away from the frantic scuffling of Edith's hard trotters as she tries to heave herself from the floor. Our collective agreement to stay calm is abandoned as Kian grapples with her ankles. 'Do it now!'

My vision is blurred around the edges, but even then, it's hard to say where Kian ends and the pig begins. I push myself up onto my elbows as Moira jabs the vaccine gun in Edith's general direction, but the uncanny human screech

176

that accompanies it suggests that this was a misread target. Kian jumps up with such alacrity that the gun is knocked from Moira's hand, skittering across the floor towards me. What had looked like the fleshy underside of Edith's rump was in fact Kian's left arse cheek, which now smarts with a bullseye-shaped ridge, pink and tender against his pale skin. He rubs it whilst tugging his trousers up, but going by Moira's wide eyes and unwavering gaze on Kian's crotch, I expect she copped an eyeful and didn't hate what she saw.

Edith, entirely unperturbed, has made it onto her feet. In her eyes, I am clearly as intimidating as a wingless mosquito, because she uses my stomach as a stepping stone in order to walk away.

I don't want to body shame, even if it is a 300-kilo pig, but the weight of Edith through a pointy little trotter is enough to inspire violence. Best make it productive violence. I reach for the vaccine gun, tickling the handle with my fingers until it's pulled closer, and jab it into Edith's side.

'Fucking yes!' I scream, as Edith trots away on swollen ankles. I flump backwards, my head on the straw, and expel the last of my adrenaline on an outward breath. I'm radiant. I've got more excrement streaked across my face than foundation, and yet I feel fucking fabulous.

'I don't know about you guys, but I think we need a drink.' Kian rubs his face with his forearm. 'Moira, reckon it's time to open The Locker?'

Chapter 18

The last of the sunshine cuts in at an angle, stretching shadows across the floor. I pull on a pair of fluffy socks and tuck my feet closer, trapping warmth from the hot shower I took half an hour ago. I try and type quietly, using the pads of my fingers. From downstairs, I hear Moira humming in the kitchen. The start of a headache pinches between my eyes, which isn't surprising considering my quite literal head-to-head combat with a hormonal sow.

I twist at the waist, stretching my sore muscles, and scan over the diary entry I've just typed up as a 'vomit draft'. I'm stuck in a frown, which doesn't make my headache any better. As much as I've tried to add high-octane Spielberg drama to the piece, there's only so much peril you can try to shoehorn into a blog post about pigs. It's hardly like fighting a grizzly bear to save a group of Brownies from a fatal mauling.

'Ava, you coming? We'll get started without you ...' says Kian from the corridor, the steam from his shower billowing along the ceiling and into my room.

'Yep, I'll be there in a minute.' I stop over-analysing

and attach the document in an email to Duncan to get a sense of whether I'm heading in the right direction. I know what he's going to say, but I'm reluctant to do it. He wants me to lean into the whole 'My Long-Lost Sister' narrative, but it feels a bit ... *icky*. So far, I've included a super nerdy version of Kian and whacked a pseudonym over the top, but now Moira's on the scene, everything is more complicated. I haven't had a chance to process the reality that I've got a sister, let alone coherently enough to put it in an article. For now, I'm keeping her off the page.

The sound of Moira chatting away grows louder as I reach the kitchen, which makes a nice change. Although it's been a couple of weeks, I've found it hard to adjust to the noise here. In fact, it's more the *lack* of noise. There's so much in London and it's far more aggressive. If Kilroch is Lorraine Kelly, London is Piers Morgan. One soothes you to sleep and the other shouts at you until you're aching from exhaustion. Here, it's like the synthesiser is pushed down, replaced by a constant, heaving wind that pushes up the cliff and smacks the farmhouse walls, writhing and whistling through cracks in the window frame. On the handful of clear days we've had, I go outside and it's so quiet I assume everyone on earth has died and I want to scream just to check I still can.

I go into the kitchen to find Moira warming her bottom on the tea towel rail by the Aga. She grins and shuffles over to make space for me, so I slide in next to her. Heat permeates my thermal leggings and settles on my skin.

'Oh God, this feels so good I'd be willing to freeze my toes off all over again.'

We both glance up as Kian walks through from the living room, a towel pulled tight around his waist.

'I can't find my house trousers.' He wrenches the back door open, peering down the side of the house to check the washing line. Moira catches my eye and glances away, her gaze darting towards Kian's thinly clad backside. It's quite sweet, really. I didn't think that fleece-lined shirts and threadbare towels were icons of the female gaze, yet here is the evidence presented before me.

'A-ha!' says Kian, pulling back a kitchen chair, on which his affectionately termed 'house trousers' are crumpled up in a ball. He disappears into the living room and comes back pinging the waistband tight, a content smile on his face.

'Are you sure we should crack open The Locker?' says Moira, pushing her thumbs through two frayed holes is her sleeves. 'I'm just remembering last time ...'

'Is this some kind of Highland initiation test?' I ask.

'Exactly that,' says Kian. He drags out a bleached wooden chest from the back of a cupboard and puts it on the table, tapping the lid with his knuckles. 'If you can still stand at the end, you've passed. Jesus, I don't think I can sit down,' he adds, rubbing the spot where he was unwittingly inoculated, eyes smarting.

'I thought it was meant to be a "cruelty free" method of immunisation,' I say.

He pulls open the waistband of his pants to inspect the injury.

'It is if you're a pig. They've got thicker skin than us,' he says, rubbing the spot with the heel of his hand. 'You really hit the bullseye, Moira.'

'Ah, I'm sorry. In my defence, it looked similar.'

'Geez, thanks,' says Kian, looking hard done by.

'Not like that, I mean, you moved and I was already there. It's a compliment! Edith's rump meat would fetch a decent price if you sold her.' Moira's eyes are wide and earnest.

'Not going to do that, though, am I?'

'How come?'

'I can make more money using them to work the woodland. I'm going to get truffles growing up there.'

'It was pig racing last week,' says Moira, rolling her eyes affectionately.

'To be fair, I know a few people in London who would see truffle hunting with a bunch of delinquent pigs as a real expedition. It's that quirky countryside thing, isn't it?'

Kian nods as though this has confirmed a long-held theory, then riffles through a drawer. He jots something down, scratches his chin, and looks at the folders I've organised, quietly intimidated.

'You're going to be upset if I don't put this in the right place, aren't you?'

'Ha, I'm not that neurotic,' I lie. 'Leave it on the top. I'll show you where to slot it another time.'

'Right you are,' he says, reaching for a set of dusty tumblers.

'Wouldn't it be good to have the money now?' says Moira, caution softening her words.

'Sure, but I'm not sending any of them to the abattoir.'

'Not even if it would make that pile less scary?' she says, nodding to the invoices that I neatly stacked in a wire paper tray this morning. I'm glad someone has noticed without me having to point it out. I scraped a C in my maths GCSE, but even I know that negative signs usually mean that numbers are going in the wrong direction. 'The bank will hold off, but only if they can see that you're trying to balance things up—'

'Moira. No more business talk, all right? Ava's here, the pigs are fine, I'm more than fine – going by the recent boost to my immune system – and it's Friday. If we were in Edinburgh, we'd be at a bar lining up Jägerbombs by now.'

Moira looks at Kian from under her thick fringe, made fluffy from a slapdash attempt to dry it with a hand towel.

'You know I can't open The Locker without you,' says Kian.

Moira's cheeks twitch with a barely contained smile. 'Oh, go on then.'

***

'I'm still not convinced this is safe to drink, you know,' I say, tilting my glass in the light. 'It looks like it's been dredged from a riverbed.'

'Look, this is the finest whisky that'll pass your lips, lass,' says Kian.

'Is it normal for him to get more Scottish when he drinks?' I ask Moira, whose head is slumped in her hand.

'Oh, aye. He lost a lot of his accent when he moved away for university, didn't you?'

Kian leans back in his chair, a lazy smile on his face.

'Yeah, well, I didn't want to get banded together with the other lads who jumped when a tram went by and only drank the stuff their daddy'd brewed in the cow shed.' I laugh, expecting Moira to join in, but she has her eyes down, tracing a line of wood grain on the table. 'Either that or they went completely the other way, you know? Cocaine five times a day until they got raging heart palpitations in a lecture and had to go home for the rest of the course.'

I take a tentative sip from my glass. The taste is musty, like licking the inside of a tobacco tin. 'I didn't do the whole "university experience" thing. Stayed at home.'

'Ah, I'm a homebird too,' says Moira, brightening.

'Don't you go to college?'

'Oh, aye. But it's only a wee bus ride away.'

'Moira studies veterinary nursing. That's why I can get her down here to sort the animals out and don't have to pay her anything,' says Kian, with a wink.

I've not got the mentalist skills of Derren Brown, but I'm pretty sure that if Moira were 500 miles away and asked to castrate a pedigree Rottweiler in Kilroch, she'd be out the door and on the way before the scalpel clattered to the ground.

'Ah, I don't mind. It's cheaper staying at home. I wanted to save a wee bit of money from my grant, but it got cut right before I started. I give horse riding lessons every now and again, but we sold the ponies to pay for house repairs after the river burst its banks and took half our garden with it. We've only got a wee Shetland now. She's good for the odd gymkhana, but there aren't enough kids who want to learn.'

Kian pulls the cork out of a teardrop-shaped whisky bottle to top up his glass.

'Veterinary nursing is good, aye, but it's mostly snipping tubes and tying off testicles, you know?' says Moira, blowing her fringe out of her eyes, her cheeks increasingly pink.

Kian winces and crosses his legs.

'I like bigger animals. Ones you can't wrap your arms round. Larger than a Golden Retriever, smaller than a camel,' she says, nodding purposefully.

'Could you do a conversion course or something?'

Kian raises his head, his eyes a little bloodshot. 'Hey, what about that thing with the teeth? Ah, Christ. What's it called?'

'Dentistry?' I offer.

He clicks his fingers and points at me in confirmation.

'Animal dentistry,' says Moira, delicately sipping from her glass. 'Equine, specifically. I've got an interview, but ... ah, I don't know.' Moira cups her chin in her hands, a dreamy look passing over her face. 'I can't tell you how much I've read about it. When I close my eyes, I dream of teeth rasping.'

'What's that?'

'Basically, you get a massive metal file and rub down all the sharp bits inside a horse's mouth.' Moira simulates a back and forth motion, her face screwed up in concentration. 'It's the dream job, you know?'

'She's pulled out three of my uncle's teeth,' says Kian, slurring his words.

'That's because he refuses to travel thirteen miles to a proper dentist,' says Moira.

'So you've got an interview? For this course?' I ask, knocking back another mouthful of whisky that singes my throat.

'Aye, but she's not going to it,' says Kian.

'Why?'

'Because she's a walloper who can't see how good an opportunity it is.'

'No, that's not it,' she says.

'What's holding you back?' I ask.

Moira taps her heels against the chair leg as she plucks at the frayed hole in her sleeve. 'The course is all based down south. Even with a bursary, it's too expensive. I want to help out at home with the bills and stuff, but I can't do that if I've blown it all on rent. I don't know, it feels selfish. I like it here, anyway. I can't see myself leaving,' she says, glancing up at Kian. He gives her a small smile.

I feel a little swell in my stomach. If this were a Doctor Seuss book, there'd be a window through to where my wrinkled heart sits curled up in my ribcage, growing plumper with each heartbeat.

Moira swallows a burp. 'What would our dads say if they could see us now?'

I glance at them both, blinking.

'Seeing as my dad pickled his liver until it shrivelled up and died, I'd say he has very few opinions on excess drinking,' says Kian.

He pushes the bottle towards Moira. She takes it, tipping it in the general direction of her glass, which is marginally successful. I wait for her to continue talking, but instead she squints at the whisky, her eyes bloodshot and unfocused. Moira lowers her finger into the glass, pauses, then lunges like a cat over a pond. She fishes something out, holding it aloft on her fingers.

'A pissed fly!' she proclaims, laughing. The moment's gone. I can't swerve back to dad chat now, not without it being awkward.

Kian takes her wrist and pulls it closer to inspect. The light from a brass candelabra casts an amber glow across the table. 'An incredibly *old* pissed fly. This is an artifact, preserved in Scotch. Save it,' says Kian, giggling, 'and they'll put it in the Black Isle courthouse museum with a little plaque underneath. "Found by Moira McCauley, contained in The Locker, exact date unknown, but likely whilst Burns still walked the land."'

My stomach loosens. Too much, perhaps. I don't know what's in this whisky, but it's making me feel slack, like a loose trampoline. 'OK, enough. You need to tell me what the whole deal is with The Locker,' I say, dragging the wooden chest over with both hands.

'It's is a *very* important family tradition,' says Kian.

'Co-family tradition,' says Moira.

'Exactly.'

'What's the tradition, drinking?' I say.

'Ha. Well, no, not officially. But this is.' He takes a pen knife from the side and slides it beneath the lid, the wood straining as he wiggles the hilt. A metal clasp, covered with rust and pockmarked with barnacles, opens to reveal twelve deep slots inside. Six contain the same teardrop-shaped bottles, their bulbous heads dipped in wax. The others are empty, the velvet lining salt-bleached beneath.

'Do the story, Kian!' says Moria, tucking her hair behind her ears and nestling back in her chair.

'Really?'

'Ah, g'won.'

Kian leans over the chest and lowers his voice. 'Once, on a dark and stormy night—'

'It was stormy, to be fair,' interjects Moira. Kian side-eyes her.

'Yes, thank you for clarifying, young Moira,' slurs Kian. 'On a dark and stormy night, two men whiled away the late-night hours on an oil rig out in the firth.'

'Saucy,' I say, raising my eyebrows.

'Not like that. It was my pa and his pa,' she says.

'Oh.' My stomach twangs. That means *my* pa as well. Kian thumps his fist on the table with faux impatience.

'Moira! You're dumping all over my attempt at suspense here!' says Kian, his eyes unfocused as he pours himself another whisky.

'Sorry, sorry.' She physically pinches her lips to keep them closed as Kian clears his throat and belches into his fist.

'Did your dads know each other?' I ask.

'Yeah, worked together,' says Moira.

'Propped up the same bar, more like,' says Kian, swilling another slug of whisky to the back of his throat without a hint of irony. 'Where was I?' he says, yawning widely. 'Moira, you finish it off.'

'Basically, a diver was working on a pipeline under the rig and found *this*,' says Moira, nodding towards the box. 'Then made the mistake of playing poker with my dad and his,' she continues, nodding towards Kian. 'I never saw it myself, but some of the fellas down at the harbour talk about this tag-team approach of theirs – calling bluffs, tactical trips to the toilet to cop a look at someone else's hand, y'know? It was all planned. They'd no money to bet, but that wasn't unusual.'

'Yeah, it's the reason Mum had to take up night shifts stacking shelves at the big Tesco at Christmas. Sea pay is good, but what's the point if you've lost it all before you're back on land?' says Kian.

'Anyway, one night, this chest was on the table and became the joint property of the McCauley and Brody families. Think they were hoping for a bit more than whisky, but it's nice, y'know? A joint heirloom,' finishes Moira with a smile.

'At the rate they drank, I'm surprised –' Kian pauses, a closed fist held to his mouth '– surprised it lasted,' he adds, his voice trailing off as his head slumps forward to rest on his forearm. A few seconds later, his breathing breaks into a guttural snore. Moira laughs and pulls his hood up, tucking his ears beneath.

In my drunken haze, The Locker takes on an almost reverential quality. Touching something my father has touched, listening to anecdotes about him ... I don't know. It feels fleeting and complicated, not least because of Moira's admiration of him despite his overfamiliarity with booze.

My stomach swills like I've swallowed a goldfish. Now's the time. I've got to tell her before the alcohol wears off and my rational brain kicks in.

'I've got something I need to tell you,' I say, wiping my palms on my trousers.

'So have I,' says Moira. She leans towards Kian, listens for a snore, then turns to face me. 'Can I go first, because I've been dying to talk to someone about it and I know we've only just met each other, but I think I might actually, literally pop if I don't get it out of my stupid head.'

'Yeah, sure,' I say, my heart rate picking up.

Moira drops her voice to a strained whisper. 'I like Kian. And I've been putting off saying anything for ages, because I knew you were here at the farm, and, well ... I get a sense that he's quite *impressed* by you and I'm honestly terrible at reading people, so I don't know if you like him, or if you're gonna be mad at me or anything, because ...'

'Woah, woah, woah, woah. No. Nope. Absolutely not.' I nearly smack her hands down in an attempt to physically emphasise how very uninterested in Kian I am. 'What I mean is, I don't fancy Kian in any way, shape, or form. Not at all. It's a very firm no in that respect,' I say. I glance at Kian, whose forearm is splayed across the table, his fingers an inch or two from his empty glass. 'I've got no idea why you'd think he's "impressed" by me.'

Moira breaks eye contact. 'Well, you're from London ...'

'So are, like, nine million other people,' I say, laughing.

'Yeah, but you're ... *cosmopolitan*. He moved to Edinburgh. I stayed here. He always ribs me for it.'

'I doubt he means it that way.'

'I know, it's just ... He was so keen to be shot of Kilroch. I've never left. He wouldn't be here if he had a choice.'

'If he hated Kilroch that much, he would have sold the farm and not come back, bull kick or no bull kick. He's trying to make it work. I don't know him half as well as you, but it doesn't sound like he's going anywhere.'

'Do you think so?'

'Mmhmm. Do you want some water?' I say, my head starting to throb.

'Please.'

I sit back down, my chair scraping on the tiles. Kian snuffles, his lips smacking together like he's chewing something in his sleep.

'Is he the reason you want to stay?' I ask. Moira glugs down an entire pint of water and wipes her mouth with her sleeve. She nods. 'I really like him. I mean, I really, *really* like him. Have done for ages.'

'I think I'm getting a sense of that.'

'You don't think it's weird?' says Moira.

'No,' I say. We both look at him. 'Apart from the fact that he appears to be sleeping with one eye open, he's nice.'

'He is, isn't he?' she says with a sigh. 'But we grew up

together. I don't know how he sees me. There was this one summer – after my Highers – we snogged at his cousin Jim's twenty-first, but he never said a word about it afterwards. He might not remember. I was a late bloomer, but I've got proper boobs now. Too much boob if anything. I don't feel like they fit my body. If I grew three or four inches, I'd—'

'Moira. You're over-thinking it. Have you given him any sign that you're keen?'

'Yeah! I do all the time. I'm always offering to help out. I try to be ... available, you know? I don't need to force myself to laugh at his jokes, because I think he's genuinely hilarious. And brave. One time, he wrestled a badger that was stuck in the sheep dip and it was exactly like that scene from *The Revenant*. The one with Leonardo DiCaprio and the bear.'

I laugh, but Moira is slack-jawed with awe. 'A badger?' I say. 'Like, a Hufflepuff badger? The house known for being a bit soft?'

'They're the largest predators in the UK. Teeth that can crack a conker in half!' Moira retorts. 'I wouldn't call that unimpressive.'

'Look, I'm far from being an expert on romance. The last Valentine's Day card I got was the result of an office prank and the one before that was from my mum.'

'That's quite sad.'

'Yes, I know.'

I have a strong desire to make cheese on toast, but as far as I can tell the farmhouse isn't equipped with a grill. How have these people survived for so long?

'What should I do?' says Moira, biting a hangnail.

'Sow the seeds. Be a bit coy. Big eyes and all that. Maybe it's not a case of *being* there all the time but making him notice when you are. In a subtle way.'

'Eurgh, this is hopeless,' says Moira. She blows her fringe out of her eyes and rubs her forehead as though a hangover has already kicked in.

Outside, the wind howls, pushing through a draught that slams a door upstairs. Kian starts, blinking with bloodshot eyes and a grunt. 'I'm so glad market is on a Sunday this week,' he groans.

'What are you on about?' says Moira, scraping back her chair. She shuffles to the sink, fills a glass with water, and pushes it in front of him.

'The farmers' market. It's on Sunday,' he says.

'No, it's tomorrow, like always.'

'I thought ... because of the cattle convention over in Dingwall. Mad Steve said—'

'You took Mad Steve's word as law? The man who claims he time travelled through a stone circle to see Hendrix performing in 1967?' says Moira.

Kian looks from Moira to me, and back again.

'Ah, no. Ava, this is no good.'

'Why?'

'I'm meant to be selling all the fucking squash.'

'You're selling squash? Ha! You're in luck,' I say, standing up to stretch. 'I can run a squash stand in my sleep. Depending on how many you're expecting, you'll need between five and eight bottles of double concentrate. Don't bother with Robinson's, it's not worth the money. Whack a few packets of Rich Tea biscuits on a plate and you're laughing.'

Kian is looking at me like I'm an idiot, but I've no idea why.

'Well, I've not seen it done, but there's a first time for everything, right?' says Moira.

'You've never seen a squash stand before?' I say. 'Really? The mark up is off the scale,' I say. *Finally*. It's clear where I can contribute.

'Hold on. You know this is a farm, right? We're selling squash. Butternut, winter, coquina, acorn? And they've got to be fresh. Cut the morning of, which means we need to be out on the field in ... four hours,' he says, his words sloshing into each other.

'Right ...' I look at Moira, who chews her lip, glancing at the clock. Kian looks like he's on the cusp of passing out, or vomiting, or both.

'Oh, before I go, what was it you were going to tell me?' she asks, zipping her yellow raincoat up to her chin.

I shrug, pasting a smile onto my face. 'D'you know what, I've forgotten. I'll let you know if it comes back to me.'

I perform an exaggerated yawn, my arms stretched above my head. 'Are you sure you just don't want to do a squash and biscuit stall?'

Chapter 19

Head torches should only be worn by kids working towards a cub scout badge, yet here I am, ankle deep in muck, scanning a thin beam of light across the ground like I'm monitoring a vegetable prison break. Every time I bend down, all the blood swills up into my skull and presses against my forehead until I think I might split like an overripe blueberry.

I locate Kian by triangulating the sound of his groans, which have become more frequent and guttural since the sun rose behind us.

A thump sounds, like a sack of rice falling off a shelf. When I turn around, Kian is curling into the foetal position between two ridges of muck.

'Ava, you're gonna have to go on without me.'

I look behind us to the wheelbarrow, which is only half full of squashes, most of which are so small I doubt if they'd be carved into anything other than a tealight holder.

'Stop shouting,' I say, pinching the bridge of my nose.

'I'm not,' he replies, his voice whiny.

A crow swoops down and lands next to us, raking

195

through the disturbed earth with a taloned claw. It caws, the sound like a rusty spoon scraping round the insides of my head. Kian raises a finger and holds it to his lips but can't bring himself to make the 'shh' sound.

I tap my leg, on the edge of a strop. I'm well aware that tantrums shouldn't be part of an adult's remit, but Kian's lack of organisation and the pain brought on by drinking a hundred-year-old whisky is turning me positively feral.

'If you had just – if we – we could have done this yesterday,' I say, my voice biting with irritation.

'No. Has to be same-day fresh. That's the whole point of the farmers' market.'

'How would anyone know?'

Kian props himself up, elbows quaking, cheeks streaked with mud. He's a picture of suffering. Trench-dwelling soldiers with gangrenous feet might look at Kian and say he was doing worse.

'Nigel would know. He's got a star. A Michelin one. He gets his ingredients from us. Pokes them and prods them and sniffs them.'

'A plant pervert.'

'Exactly.' Kian swallows, steadying himself for a moment before he continues. 'If we can get cosy with him, we can sell direct and won't have to keep chucking odds and ends to the handful of people who come to Kilroch at the weekend.'

I stand up, rub the small of my back, and twist from one side to the other. 'Would it make a big difference, money-wise?' I ask.

'Not much, but I can't be too picky, especially seeing as I'm not selling the animals off for meat.'

'I'm just thinking ...'

'Hmm?'

'I don't know how to make a farm profitable, but isn't this approach – the eggs, the market, truffle hunting with pigs – don't you think it's a bit ... scattergun?'

'Probably. But I need to pay the bills, otherwise this'll all be gone. Sold off. I don't want to be the Brody who lost the family land. If I had more than ten minutes to sit down and figure it out, I would, but it's just been me for nine months now, and, well ...' Kian waves a hand at the field. Now the sun has been winched further into the sky, an expanse of waxy, orange-skinned squashes peeks out from beneath salt-bruised leaves. 'Haven't had a chance to sell this lot, let alone plant more for next season.'

I pick up the clippers and try to ignore the pulsing in my temple. I push the vine to one side, exposing a squash so wide and warped it looks extra-terrestrial. I hack, yank, and twist, but it remains stubbornly attached. Damp earth saturates my knees.

'What do you do if you can't cut through the umbilical cord?' I ask, sweating. Kian appears beside me on all fours.

'Firstly, it's not an umbilical cord. Secondly ... you need to twist and pull at the same time.'

'My first boyfriend gave me that advice.'

Kian snorts. 'Don't, I'll be sick.'

'Maybe if I chop, you can twist. OK, ready?' I step over the vine and adopt a wide stance.

Kian runs a hand over his face.

'Let's get this big boy out. Here.' Kian hands me a curved blade. 'Go for it.'

I saw back and forth with maniacal vigour until the knife cuts through, the sudden lack of resistance sending me onto my back where I lie like an upturned ladybird. The squash breaks off into Kian's hands and he quickly stands to deposit it in the wheelbarrow. My head throbs so much I'm sure it would be better if I took it off and left it in the field like a weird little pumpkin.

The wind catches the church bell from down the hill. It chimes softly, the noise pulled in and out of earshot by converging gusts.

'This'll do,' says Kian. 'We'll harvest the rest another time and store them. If you're left with wee ones at the market, don't linger,' he says, holding up a tennis-ball-sized squash. He flips it back onto the pile and takes a deep breath, both hands gently resting on his stomach. I trot to keep up beside him, low-level anxiety prickling my stomach.

'Aren't you coming too?'

'No, I'm going to see a couple of university pals in town.'

'Oh, right.'

'Moira's helping you out on the stall.'

I nod, a whoosh of excitement tickling my ribcage. I wonder if she's feeling as delicate as I am. If so, we can battle through the day together as I'm sure this is only the baby teeth of a much angrier hangover. It's not been twenty-four hours, but what I learned yesterday is that

Moira likes to talk. A lot. The upside is that she can talk for the both of us.

I scoot past Kian and the wheelbarrow, hopscotch over the cattle grid, and hold the courtyard gate open for him. I'm trying to be as helpful as possible, but candid chats about finances could be overstepping the mark.

He clears a space on a workbench and I devise a system of weighing, calculating, and scribbling prices on the squash with a black Sharpie. I line the squash up in height order like I'm about to direct a class photo. They're a diverse bunch; some wonky, some stout, some decidedly phallic. I'm not sure why anyone would pay upwards of four quid for what's essentially an awkward vegetable, but I'm not going to interfere with finances anymore, if that's what Kian thinks I'm doing.

The church bells chime like a Biblical reminder.

'So, how long have you and Moira been a thing?' I ask. I lean up against the brick outhouse and bite my cheek. That sounded far more inconspicuous in my head than it did out loud.

'What do you mean, a thing?' Kian lines an empty crate with newspaper and frowns.

'Oh, I thought I'd picked up on a vibe between you two.'

Kian scratches his jaw and shakes his head in a bad imitation of denial. 'We've known each other for ever. Since we were kids, you know? She's familiar.'

Hmm. As far as ringing praise goes, I've heard better.

'So, you've never got silly at a party together? You're not related, are you?' I realise that the answer to this question has direct relevance to me. I suppose there's a chance.

'I know Kilroch is far from a cosmopolitan community, but we do draw the line at getting off with family members.'

'I wasn't implying that. Honestly.'

Kian breaks into a smile. 'It's nothing complicated. I just don't see the point in risking a friendship for a snog, you know?'

I can fully sympathise. Max was the first male friend of mine I actively tried *not* to kiss. I've turned at least four good mates into awkward acquaintances due to innocuous actions that I misinterpreted as flirting. I've vowed never to make the same mistake again, especially since an incident last year involving Rory's French housemate. He went for a double cheek kiss that I wasn't prepared for, which resulted in me licking his earlobe by accident. It's hard to come back from that.

I was happily plodding through my new-found platonic existence until Kian introduced me to Ross. In a way, this is the perfect test. He's the most attractive man I've seen but with the added caveat of being a priest, so I can practise talking to men again with wondering what they'll want from me. It levels out the power dynamics quite nicely.

As we load the Jeep, a cockerel crows from an upturned whisky barrel by the front door. Now for the important questions. Can I ask Moira about our dad without raising too many questions in return, and does Kilroch house enough Pepsi Max to stave off a hangover?

Chapter 20

Three hours later and my hangover has gone from a solid eight out of ten (retching behind a fishing boat) to a three (I've managed to stomach a Cup a Soup and have only minor heart palpitations). The oddball squashes have been weirdly popular. A small child laughed for a full minute, running his fingers over the blistered skin of a mini pumpkin, which saw another fiver into the cash tin Kian had all but chucked at me as we left the house.

As the footfall fades, a broad-shouldered man with salt-and-pepper hair stops to speak to Moira about a lame sheep, leaving me in charge of our misshapen squash nursery. Every few seconds, she pushes her hair behind her ears, exactly like I do. It's a habit Mum has always told me off for, saying it made me seem nervous. Seeing it on Moira, a strange sense of joy settles in my rib cage. It feels like drinking tea from a Thermos in the cold: warm and soothing.

Moira waves the man off and stands next to me, our elbows touching.

'Are you Kilroch's go-to expert on all things veterinary?'

'Well, what these guys don't know about raising sheep isn't worth knowing, but they think I've got "proper knowledge" now that I'm doing a course at the college. They don't know I haven't moved on from guinea pigs yet.'

'It's just a bigger skeleton, right?'

'Thereabouts.' Moira smiles at me and hooks her arm through mine, swaying from side to side. 'God, it's nice chatting to someone new.'

An older woman cranking round the pedals of a rusty bicycle waves at Moira from the saddle.

'All right, Lindsey? Gizmo doing OK?'

'Wonderful! Fur's grown back a treat!'

'Great!' Moira turns back to me, her fringe puffed up in a breeze that feels like a tickle compared to yesterday's cheek-slapping wind. 'I lanced a cyst on her dog last month,' she says by way of explanation. 'I don't ask for payment, so I think it's OK. They're all family friends.'

'Do you find it weird that everyone here is reluctant to charge money for anything? It's nice and all, but how does anyone make a decent living?' I say, thinking back to my egg delivery and the miscellaneous collection of items I brought back as payment.

'I've never thought about it like that. It's just helping each other out, like you would do with a neighbour, right? It's all swings and roundabouts.'

Moira scrapes muck out from underneath her thumbnail, frowning at the floor. Silence muscles in like a hand at my back, pushing me to broach The Chat with Moira. I thought I'd be able to watch and assess from the sidelines, circling in when the time was right. But what does that look like? The longer I wait, the harder it is.

Moira wraps her arms around her middle, shifting from one foot to the other. 'You know all that stuff I said last night?' she says.

'What stuff? Everything's a bit hazy around the edges.'

'About Kian.'

'Ah, yep. There was quite a lot about that.'

Moira scratches her forehead. 'I'm not going to say I didn't mean it, because I did. I just hope I didn't come across as *properly* desperate. It's hard when you've grown up with someone. I don't know how to act around him in a way that makes him realise I'm hot rather than cute, you know? Even saying that makes me want to stuff both fists into my mouth.'

I think back to this morning, to Kian and his unconvincing excuses as to why he and Moira wouldn't work.

'You need to see each other off the farm. What about the pub?'

'No, my dad's old harbour mates will be in there. I'd rather not have an audience.'

'A bar?'

'Do you see *anything* that looks like a bar in Kilroch?' says Moira, gesturing to the bunting-lined high street.

'Fair point. Ohmygod,' I splutter, sidestepping behind her. Ross stands by the post office window with two elderly women who talk over each other in their eagerness to speak.

'Why are you hiding?'

'I look like I slept in the chicken coop.'

'Me too. Don't worry, everyone here is used to it. Oh

...' she says, following my gaze across the road. 'Hold on. Rev!' she shouts, beckoning him over.

'No! Moira, I can't.'

'You *like* him,' she says in a sing-song voice.

'I don't! I just ... get quite flustered when he's near me.'

'Rev!' she shouts again, waving her arm like she's trying to signal for a rescue vessel.

'What are you doing?!'

'Calling him over.'

'Why?!'

'Because you clearly fancy him. Just ... let me help you out. OK?'

I clutch her elbows and do a mental risk assessment of the situation. Chance of embarrassment? High. Risk of failure? Exceptionally so, especially as Jesus ranks higher on his agenda that I'm ever likely to. Do I go along with it anyway? I nod.

'OK, fine.'

Ross leaves the women to rearrange their plastic hair caps and crosses the road towards us.

'Pretend that we're talking about something,' says Moira. 'This always works in movies.'

'Right, err, Babs chased me across the yard this morning and pecked a hole through my wellie boot.'

Moira bursts into laughter, her hand on my arm. 'Honestly, what are you like! Ava, he's looking. He's *looking*,' she hisses. 'You're *such* a hoot,' she booms, every bit the amateur thespian. 'Oh, hello! Interested in a misshapen squash, Rev?' she says, a hand on her hip.

Ross stands in front of the stall, the collar of his coat flicked up and a thick-knit red scarf bundled under his chin.

'I had a grand plan to buy decent veg for dinner tonight but seems like I'm too late.' He lifts his elbow, where a small loaf of rye bread is tucked under his arm in a paper bag, the crust blackened and hard from what I can see of it. 'It's a bittersweet gig, this ministerial business. No one wants to charge me for anything, but then I'm palmed off with the bits that are one step from being chucked on the compost. Look at these.'

He slips a strap of his tote bag down and motions for us to look inside. A bunch of spindly parsnips sit alongside a bag of sprouts so small they could pass as malformed peas.

'I feel bad asking if I can swap, but what am I going to do with this?' he says, taking out a micro-parsnip. 'Pick my teeth with it?'

I burst into laughter, disproportionately so going by the hasty departure of a nearby seagull. The two women by the tearoom pause their conversation to glower in our direction.

'Can't you organise a smiting, Ross? Get the Big Man involved to teach them a lesson?' I ask.

He pretends to consider it, rubbing his chin (his well-formed, just-the-right-amount-of-stubble chin, I must add). 'I'm all booked up on smitings this week,' he says. He changes his stance and goes to point a finger at me, but the effect is undermined by the Fair Isle mittens he's wearing. He looks at his hand and frowns. 'Didn't think that through. Just know that I was trying to be intimidating, because you're *definitely* on my smiting list.'

My pulse taps hard in my chest. 'What for?'

'You've caused a problem in the village, Ava,' he says.

Moira looks between us, unable to tell if this is a serious conversation or not. As much as I love being around her, I now want her to vanish, leaving Ross and me alone. Moira slides her hands into the pockets of her fleece.

'Have I?'

'You're playing innocent, but I know the truth. It comes with this,' he says, pulling down his scarf to reveal a dog collar. 'It's like an amulet. Gives me all sorts of insight.'

'Fine.' I hold my hands up like a cornered bandit. 'I'll admit it. Sometimes I don't wash jam jars up before I put them in the recycling.' *Oh, God.* That's got to be in the top five lamest things ever said in the history of spoken English.

'No, that I could forgive. I'm thinking of the health crisis you've instigated. You won't believe the number of terrible scones I've had to palm off on the Bible Studies group to get rid of those eggs you brought me. Glen nearly went into hyperglycaemic shock on Thursday. He was injecting insulin like a junkie. As humans, we are graced with free will, but some people can't be trusted with theirs.'

'Of course. Ted Bundy, Jefferey Dahmer, John Wayne Gasey ... they took some real liberties.'

'I was thinking more Glen and his lack of control when it comes to scones, but we'll get to the serial killers at some point, I'm sure.'

A woman taps Ross on the shoulder, giving my pulsing heartbeat a chance to go down. For a moment, I thought he was going to 'out' me. If Ross has stumbled on the live stream, there's a chance he'll recognise me, even without the heavy make-up and startled expression.

'Minister, will you be doing a service for All Saints' Day? Only I've got a few thoughts based on last year. I know it wasn't you, but that business with the effigy was very politically charged for a celebration. There wasn't the need for so much lighter fuel,' says the woman, clutching a canvas trolley so big I'm sure she could climb inside for a nap.

'Quite right. I'm planning something far more ... venerated.' Ross looks solemn, which seems to appease the woman, who smiles broadly, her wrinkles pinched either side of her eyes and mouth. When she's hoiked her trolley further up the road, he rolls his eyes. 'Killjoy.'

I laugh and touch his forearm. Holy bejesus, I'm touching his forearm (through a thick woollen coat, but still).

'Oh, Rev. How was the committee *Come Dine With Me?*' says Moira.

'Dr Singh sneaked into first place on the final night. It was a bit of a relief because the winner had to donate a thousand pounds to charity, and if I'd known that, I wouldn't have tried so hard,' he says, tucking his hands in his pockets.

'Well, if you need anyone to sample new dishes, you've got a willing participant right here,' says Moira, nudging me with her elbow.

'Funny, that. One of the cricket club guys was supposed to be coming for dinner tonight, but he's cried off. Severed his left thumb trying to unclog the lawnmower. Can't hold a fork, apparently, so that's a problem. Care to swap in?' he says, looking from Moira to me.

'Oh, I can't. I'm helping Mum in the tearoom tonight. The Young Farmers are holding an AGM and want three different kinds of sausage rolls,' says Moira.

'Ah, I won't try to take you off Jacqui,' says Ross.

'Hang on, Jacqui? Jacqui's your mum?' I say, momentarily distracted by this news.

'Oh, aye.'

'Shall we say seven?' he asks.

'Me? For dinner?' I ask.

'I was going to suggest we pray the rosary together, but we'll start with food.'

'Sure. Sounds good,' I say, winding my smile in so I don't look too overenthusiastic.

I look over Ross's shoulder, to where Jacqui stands outside the tearoom. Her apron strings are pulled so tight, the over-all look is that of a sagging sofa cushion. Around her, the same two women I saw lingering behind Ross moments ago are talking behind their hands, unsubtle looks thrown in our direction.

'Ah, I knew there was something else. Moira, your mum said that you know a good ceilidh caller. Can you see if they're free for the church roof fundraiser? The lass I had lined up has pulled out and we've not got long to go.'

'Oh, aye, no problem.'

'See you tonight, Ava,' says Ross, lifting a mittened hand to say goodbye. I wave back.

'Do your cheeks hurt?' says Moira when he's out of earshot.

'No. Why?'

'Because you were gurning like an idiot the whole time he was talking.'

'Was I?' I say, poking my cheeks.

'To be fair, he's got a *very* good jawline for a Scotsman. As have you. Think of the babies! A walking chin with teeny little feet trying to keep the rest upright.'

'Oi!' I say, bumping her with my hip.

'He's never asked *me* to call him *Ross*,' she says, imitating my accent. 'He's just been "Minister". The last one was called that too. It's like Doctor Who; one disappears and a younger version turns up with a slightly different coat.'

I look into the middle distance, thinking.

'I've got an idea. If Ross is organising a ceilidh, why don't you use it to make a move on Kian? You'll have plenty of time to put in some groundwork before then. And if it's a community event, there'll be boxed wine, which has always helped me through awkward situations in the past.'

Moira looks up, thinking. 'That could work. But what am I going to *do* there? I usually get roped into dancing with the widowers, so I might still get some action. They get a bit handsy during The Eightsome Reel.'

'Put a good dress on. Swing about a bit. Strip the willow.' I wink. Moira smacks me on the arm and buries her face in her hands, her fringe sticking up from the fine sea mist that's only just retreated back into the harbour. She squats down to collapse the table legs, pausing to look up at me.

'Here's the deal,' says Moira, tapping the pen against her teeth. 'If I'm going to try something on with Kian, you've got to attempt a bit of casual flirting with The Rev. Even if it is to give them lot something to talk about.' She nods towards the gaggle of pea-coat-clad women hovering by the tearoom who disperse when Moira waves at them, fingers fluttering. 'But you have to report back to me after you go round for dinner.'

I pout to the side and slowly nod.

'Excellent. Wait there,' she says, taking a few coins from the cash tin. 'This deserves a toast, over hot chocolate, of course. Marshmallows?'

'Always.'

Chapter 21

I'm in a conundrum. If I ring the doorbell and wait on the step, the curtain of ivy will force me to stand so close to the actual door that when Ross opens it, I may fall forward onto his face. Not the worst consequence, admittedly, but not smooth. On the other hand, if I stand partway up the garden path, I'll look like a creepy lurker, which is more accurate. Is there a chance I'm over-thinking this?

As I hover by the bell, the door shunts in its frame and a muffled voice filters through.

'Can you push it from your side? The rain has made the wood swell.'

'Yeah, sure.'

I use my shoulder as leverage. When I step away, the spiderwebs strung on the latticed windows stick to my jacket.

'Let's try it together,' he says, 'one, two, and three for a big one!'

I shove, he yanks, and I stumble into the hallway, my boots slapping against the floorboards.

'Ah, y'fucker!'

As the door wobbles on its hinges, Ross appears from

behind it, cradling his left hand. 'Ava, hi! That comment was aimed at the door, of course, not you. I really need to get it fixed, but I'm not so good with my hands.'

Is he sure we can't test that theory?

Ross looks like he's stepped out of a billboard in east London. The only thing he's missing is an ironic form of transport, like an adult-sized scooter (or worse, a penny-farthing, which I did see once whilst walking up Dalston Junction). Ross wears a lumberjack shirt with the sleeves rolled up to the elbow and corduroy trousers that are clearly new going by the packet folds either side of his knees. I hand over a bottle of wine that he takes it from me, brushing my little finger with his thumb as he does so. I'm overwhelmed by the scent of fabric conditioner. It's like he's spritzed it on as aftershave. Is he nervous?

'Thanks! That's so kind.' He looks at the label and grins. 'I'll keep this apart from the cheap stuff we bulk order for Sunday service.'

'You get wine at church?'

'No, you *receive* the blood of Christ. Very different.'

'Sounds ... vampiric.'

'That's what Protestants used to say back when they were burning all the nuns.' He claps his hands. 'Right! I was a bit keen, so it's basically ready to eat.'

I follow him through to the kitchen, where three separate cookbooks are open on the counter, scattered with potato peelings and spice jars. A clunky Eighties oven whirrs in the corner and the smell of warm cinnamon, apricots, and wood smoke hangs in the air.

'Here, take a seat. This one's best. There's a draught that comes down the chimney. Christ, I sound so fucking old. Wine?'

'Yeah, thanks.'

I sit down on an embroidered cushion, the edges stitched with bloated cherubs so pink it's like they've succumbed to scarlet fever. I've barely recovered from The Locker, but there's something subversively appealing about being offered alcohol by a priest.

'Cheers,' says Ross.

'Cheers!' I tap my glass against his and take a far bigger gulp than I intend to, spluttering as it hits the back of my throat. I catch some of it in my hand before it hits the tablecloth like an ill-timed nosebleed.

'Take this,' he says, handing me a linen handkerchief.

I put the glass down and soak up the wine, my neck warm with embarrassment. 'God, I'm so sorry.'

'Don't worry about it. We've already got you apologising to God,' he says, grinning.

'What are we eating?' I ask, my throat hoarse and acrid.

'Well, my brother "gifted" me some of his old books when he moved to Canada. In all honesty, I think he couldn't be bothered to dump them in a charity shop, but I can make a roux from scratch now, so who's laughing? I baked some sun-blushed tomato soufflé things that you cook in a muffin tin, right? Threw in some black pudding and served them to the parish committee. I'll be straight with you, I was sucking up.'

I take a cautious sip of my wine, watching Ross as he

scrapes vegetable scraps into the compost bin. Is it weird to find men more attractive when they're doing menial domestic tasks? If he paired socks on the washing line, I think I'd scream with joy.

'Did it go down well?'

'All our meetings are brunch-based now, so I'd say so. It does mean I have to cook for ten every third Friday, but they've said yes to near enough all of my ideas since, so it's worth it.'

Ross takes my goblet-shaped glass from me, refills it and hands it back. I twist the stem between my fingers and glance down at my jumper, which is now splattered with red wine droplets. Excellent.

I fold an arms across my chest to hide the stains. I hadn't thought ahead to what happens now. The last time I had dinner with a man was over a year ago and I ended up paying for both of us (and his Uber home) because he'd just forked out for his daughter to go on a school trip to Montpellier. Incidentally, that's also when I found out he had a daughter. Ross is different. For one, there's no way anything can happen between us, which is far less pressure than being on a date. Priests love denying impulsive urges, which might be why we get on so well.

'Do you have people round for dinner a lot?'

'Yeah, a couple of times a week. It's a nice part of the job. Not to speak badly of Reverend Dingwall, but he did get one of the local divorcées to cook his tea every night, so there was questionable give and take at play. That thing still had the manual taped to the grill when I first switched it on.' he says, motioning to the clunky oven. As if on cue, it whirrs loudly, the vibrations wobbling a crucifix on the wall above. Jesus looks all the more anxious.

Ross lays the table with chunky Sixties crockery decorated in bold, garish flowers in various hues of mustard and brown.

'This is nice,' I say, turning a side plate over in my hands.

'Not mine. Don't know if you can tell,' he says, a smile twitching at the corner of his mouth.

He opens the oven two or three times and pulls out lidded Pyrex dishes, the sides bubbling with thick stock.

'This looks great. Kian and I are trying to take turns cooking, but to be honest I'm not sure how much more veggie sausage fusilli I can eat before I've reached my life's pasta quota.'

Ross laughs. 'Sounds like my student days. Top-up?' he says, brandishing the wine.

I look down at my glass. I've somehow drained it, possibly because I keep nervously sipping every time I get distracted by Ross's arms. Who does he think he is, having muscles like that? They must be relics of a former life. The Body of Christ can't weigh that much, the man was a stringbean.

'Do you mind if I say grace?' says Ross. He shrugs apologetically. 'Bit of a habit.'

The chair creaks as I wiggle myself into a more comfortable position. Are we doing this in our heads or out loud? I open one eye. Ross is glancing down at the steaming couscous, reverential in his stance. It's quite alluring. No, Ava. Inappropriate.

'Thank you, Lord, for the food we eat, for the hands that made the food – however questionable it may taste – and for those in our community who grew it. Even the rubbish parsnips. Amen.'

'Same to you too,' I say.

He smiles and leans over to slot a serving spoon into each dish. 'Sorry about the potatoes. If you scrape the black bits off, you'll find they're *perfectly* caramelised.' I put one in my mouth and make an effort to chew slowly.

'It's really good.' I'm not lying, either. As we eat, conversation flits over a number of fairly innocuous subjects: the farm, the pigs, the work that needs doing, and the frequent mornings I come downstairs to find Kian at the table looking stressed, an array of invoices spread out before him. Every time conversation drifts outside of Kilroch, I pull it back, but after half an hour, I've run out of frivolous things to say and, quite frankly, want to rest my head on his arm; my tired, foggy head.

I scoop the last few chickpeas from my plate as Ross slouches in his chair, a look of curiosity on his face, like he's waiting for me to announce something. The balance has tipped. He's been talking far more than I have, and I haven't noticed how short my responses have been until now.

'Is it weird? Your house being a church?' I inwardly kick myself for phrasing the question like I'm the token village idiot.

'Well, it's God's house, really. He lets me stay so long as
I pull my weight. I keep the holy water topped up, absolve
sins, that sort of thing. It's a bit like you up at Braehead?
Bit different from London, eh?'

'You could say that.' I stab a round of aubergine that
I'm far too full to eat.

'How do you like it?'

'Like what?'

'London.'

'Yeah, well, it's ... it's London, isn't it?'

'I don't know. Never been,' says Ross, shrugging.

'*Really?*' I say.

'I know. Who'd have thought there was life beyond the
M25?' He grins, accentuating the cleft in his chin. 'You
were telling me about London.'

'I wasn't.'

'You were *going* to.'

I breathe slowly and try to think of something clever
to say. 'It's busy. The parks are nice. Lots of musicals, you
know?'

Smashed it.

'And how about you? Do you like it there?' says Ross,
his look unwavering.

'Yep.'

'You sure?'

I don't reply. Instead, I fork the aubergine in my mouth
and chew like a camel, swallowing too soon. 'Everyone
seems ... *concerned* about why I'm staying in Kilroch.'

'They might just be interested.'

'Or nosy?'

'Or just curious. I am.'

'It's your job to be interested, isn't it?'

'I wouldn't say that. Take Lindsay, for instance. The woman on the bike from the market? If I get another update about her granddaughter's colic next time I'm in the village, I'm going to walk and keep walking until I'm halfway across the bay.'

I smile despite myself. 'London's fine. My job is fine. My mum is great. We still live together. I know it's weird, but it's an expensive place to live, y'know?'

'No judgement here. I own nothing in this house except for a handful of books and a rucksack of clothes.'

'Sounds nice, actually. To be doing something straightforward.'

'Not all circumstances feel like opportunities to begin with.'

'Mmm. Some are more confronting than I thought. More challenging,' I say, rubbing my neck.

'So, coming up here was a break?'

'In some ways. In other ways, it really wasn't. To be honest, I don't think I'm helping much on the farm.'

'I'm sure that's not true. I think Kian feels ... uprooted as well, would you say? A lot of young people don't picture themselves taking on the family farm, but something or other brings them back.'

'Guilt?'

'Possibly. I was brought up in Glasgow, so the lure of the countryside is never something I've really understood.'

'I can see why Kian feels torn. There are about fifty different initiatives he wants to put into practice on the farm, but either side of the daily tasks – keeping 200 animals alive and the like – I don't think there's time for it. I feel like I'm adding to his problems. He has to teach me how to do everything, which takes twice as long.'

'Maybe it's more a case of – and I'm not saying this is true, but – say you're not so great at ... fixing fence posts. Kian's got that covered himself. He'd probably benefit most from getting these ideas up and off the ground. Research, costing, marketing, things like that? How much longer are you here for?'

I mentally tick off the diary entries I've sent back to *Snooper*, remembering Duncan's last email that insisted I provide 'spicier content' or risk being pulled back to the office. Where does he think I am, Coachella?

'A couple of weeks.'

'Great. You can celebrate whatever mark you make on the farm by coming to the ceilidh I'm organising. It's fundraising, really. Arthur fell straight through a rotten pew last month. The timing was excellent; the whole thing collapsed right as we were belting out the last hymn.'

'I wish I'd seen that,' I say, laughing. 'One problem. Ceilidhs ... organised dancing?'

'Yes. But "loosely organised" is probably more accurate. If you're dancing with me, we can be terrible together,' he says, biting the end off a parsnip. A blob of sauce lands on his finger. I answer my own question. Yes, it would be weird if you licked it off, Ava.

Ross dollops another spoonful of tagine on his plate. In the past, I would have held back, not wanting him to think that I had too much of an appetite. Sod that for a laugh. If Ross had an opinion on how much I eat, I'd be long gone. I pick up the dish of burnt potatoes and ladle a mound onto my plates, drizzling them in sauce from the tagine. Ross goes to speak, but I jump in first.

'I've got to ask, how come you ended up doing this?'

'What, Moroccan food?'

'No, this,' I say, motioning to the dog collar. Priesting. That can't be the right word, but I stick by it.

Ross crosses one leg over the other knee. I understand that he's taking a moment to really think about it, but I'm distracted by how unbelievably handsome he is: mouth slightly open, his bottom lip pink from where he's bitten it. It's like the opening shot of a perfume advert: all furrowed brows and the sense that at any moment he'll run through a ballroom of billowing chiffon in search of an unattainable something (it's always Keira Knightley).

'I haven't always done this.'

'Hmm, let me guess. I don't think you're very old, are you?' I ask.

'Thirty-one.'

'OK, that's enough time to have had a proper career. Not that the church isn't proper in the sense of, err ...'

'Normal? Conventional?'

'Yeah, exactly. Teacher?'

He grimaces. 'No,' he says, elongating the vowel. 'Can't

stand paperwork. Also, you're being far too nice with that suggestion.'

'Estate agent?'

'Calm down.' Ross puts on a parody of offence. I laugh and run my finger up the stem of my wine glass.

'Think of a job that sounds really generic but you wouldn't be able to explain it to someone else,' he says.

I take a second to sift through the shouted conversations I've had in bars with interchangeable men wearing expensive suits and unironed shirts. 'Business consultant.'

Ross points a finger gun at me. 'Bingo.'

'Wow.' I glance around at the room, at the bric-a-brac utensils and oppressive French dresser, its wood stained coffin-dark. 'You went from that to this?'

Ross bites his lip and nods.

'Well ... you must have been making a fortune.'

'I was. I thought I was rich. A nice apartment on Princes Street, private booths in clubs, that sort of thing. I had one of those silk pocket squares. I had dozens of them, different colours to match my socks. Can you imagine? I'd buy huge bottles of Grey Goose that came with its own firework taped to the neck, and the cost of it ...' He puffs his cheeks out and shakes his head. 'It would cover a month's pay for the waitress who brought it over.'

'Sounds horrible,' I say, my voice monotone. This is going to come back to Jesus somehow. I've listened to my fair share of heavy-handed evangelists outside Peckham Rye station.

'It *was* glorious, especially if you looked at my highlights on social media. But that's where it ended. I couldn't tell you a single thing about the people I worked with. I *was* rich, but I wasn't wealthy.'

'And you are now?' I ask. I run my finger under the table, over the carpenter's staples and grooves in the wood.

'Not in that sense. Don't get me wrong, I'm never been worse off financially. But I'm really fucking content.'

'Does the bishop know you swear like that?'

'Oh, he's worse,' says Ross, leaning across the table.

We sit in silence for a moment, but it's not awkward like it was before. He drops his arm on the table, his little finger alongside mine.

'Did you choose to come here?' I ask.

'No. Did you?'

I open my mouth, but my reply is stuck in my gullet like a fish bone. Ross leans in towards me. My heart palpitates, but I can't tell if it's the red wine or him. Just as I feel warm breath on my cheek, he leans back in his chair.

'How did you come across Braehead Farm?' says Ross, his eyes questioning.

'Google.' I drink a gulp of wine.

'So, is it farms you're interested in or the area?'

'A bit of both, I guess. I write for an online magazine, so Kilroch's a nice change of scenery. Small. Not much going on.'

'Ah, there's always something going on,' says Ross. 'What made you choose Kilroch?'

'I like pigs.'

'I heard they have pigs down south too ...'

'I like Scottish pigs especially,' I say, cringing at how unsophisticated I sound.

'Hmm. And how do you find the people here?'

'Nice, although there aren't many of them,' I say, pushing a forkful of couscous around my plate. Ross leans in, his eyes soft. I'm in the grip of a red wine haze, which has conveniently stopped me from overthinking how close we are. If it wasn't for the table ...

'There's a real joy in serving a community so small. I've covered every rite of passage since I've been here, and a lot of them in the same family. I've got a simile I've been working on to explain it. Can I try it out?' His cheeks dimple with a smile.

'Go on then,' I say. The moment's gone now that Jesus has found a way to enter the room. It feels a bit seedy, like getting off in a graveyard. Ross gets up and starts to clear the table.

'Edinburgh is like looking at a huge, complicated tapestry. You get an overall sense of the picture, the bits you prefer more than others, but it's hard to see where a version of you could be stitched into it. A place like Kilroch takes up a few square inches, but look at it closely and you can see each thread, where it crosses over, how it's pulled together. You can appreciate how it works. The mechanics of it. How to fix the holes. When you step back, it's not so impenetrable. It makes sense, because you've looked at the back, where all the loose bits are knotted together.'

Whilst he talks, my mind jumps to Mum. She's always known how to stitch herself into a picture. If Dulwich is a tapestry, she's the bloody thimble, always pushing things back into the right place. I'm the loose thread, trailing behind her. But what about when she was here, with The Earth Mamas? I know what she's like, especially when there's a good cause going. She can't help it; she has to get involved. I'm evidence of that.

'I think I get it,' I say as Ross slots a dish into the rack on the draining board.

'What do you think? Too douchey? The ramblings of a mad man?'

'No, I think it's good.'

'You do? Fantastic. Hold on.' He wipes his hands on a polka-dot tea towel and ducks through an archway, returning with a notepad and a pencil tucked behind his ear. 'That solves the problem of Sunday's sermon.'

Ross scribbles on a scrap of paper, pauses, and bounces the pencil against his chin as he scans down the page. My palms feel sweaty, which may have something to do with the overwhelming urge I have to be a rubber on the end of that pencil.

'I've got to find a way to work in something about the oil rigs, seeing as it's October. But I'll come back to that,' says Ross, pushing the notebook into the middle of the table.

'I think Kian's and Moira's dads worked on the rigs. Is it an anniversary or something?'

'Yeah, but not the kind of one you celebrate with balloons. It's probably best if I show you.'

Chapter 22

R oss unlocks the door with an old-fashioned brass key
and pushes it open. A cold draught sweeps through the
gap, the smell of incense lingering in the air. He flicks the
light switches and a row of fluorescent bulbs putter into life,
illuminating two dozen pews. A number of display boards
line the walls, the most colourful of which is decorated
with small, cut-out hands outlined in felt tip and made to
look like tropical turkeys.

'It looks a bit fusty, but it's the records that are interesting.' Ross walks down the aisle. I let him linger at the
front before following myself, if only to indulge in a silent
fantasy about our fictional wedding day. 'Hang on, let me
take these back whilst I'm here.'

Ross picks up a small stack of books and tucks them
under his arm, his shoes squeaking on the marble that
paves a runway past the altar. I walk to the far side of
the pews and scan the inscriptions along the wall. Lots
of Alberts and Margarets, a couple of Lairds and a few
old ministers are listed as 'returned to their maker'. What
you'd expect. Beneath a dusty St Andrew's flag, a different

memorial draws my eye; engraved words precisely set in stone too clean for it to have been there long. An array of flowers in cellophane wrappers are slumped in various stages of decomposition on the flagstones beneath. I step back and read:

Dedicated to the sixty-seven men who lost their lives in the offshore oil rig fire of 2001. Weary hours are past, for now you are at peace.

I scan the dates again. If our father was on the rig at the time, there's a strong chance he was amongst those lost. There's a crinkle of plastic as I nudge one of the bouquets with my foot. A small card slips out, a watercolour illustration of lilies printed on the front. As I bend down to read it, there are footsteps behind me.

'Ah, you've found it,' says Ross. 'The Brodmore rig was just offshore. I heard about the explosion growing up, but it was abstract, far off. A fire in the middle of the sea.'

'Why aren't there any names on it?' I ask. As macabre as it is, I want to see *his* name there in the stone. At least it would be something solid, something to hinge my understanding on.

'They didn't find everybody.'

'How come?'

'Have you seen the rig? What's left of it?'

'Yeah, a couple of times when it's been clear across the harbour.' I think back to the farmers' market. Moira and I had our stall a few strides up from the concrete slipway that tipped down to the firth, beyond which the twisted oil rig skeleton sat claw-like on the horizon.

'That's it. It was all over the news. I didn't make the connection until I got here. Kilroch is the closest village to the rigs, so most of the men who died either lived here or somewhere just beyond. That's a lot of families who woke up without a dad, husband, uncle, you know? It's like a chunk of masonry was lobbed in the sea; there are effects today that ripple back to what happened then.'

He points at the memorial. 'Unemployment, empty houses, women who worked two or three jobs to plug the gap. This village is run by matriarchs, but it's not happened without friction. It's messy. Complicated.'

My hands feel clammy, but it's not because I'm warm. I can see my breath; the church is so bloody cold. 'What was complicated?' I ask.

'Well, maybe it's a sign of the times; people's attitude to the environment is different nowadays. The explosion came because of a resource that a lot of people deem unethical, so sympathy isn't always close at hand. Oil disasters are sad, but not as sad as bush fires, or drought.'

'Yeah, but that doesn't change anything for the families. If you've lost someone, you've lost someone.'

'Oh, aye, I'm with you. The problem is, there was an inquiry after it happened that uncovered a lot of cut corners by the oil company. Then there was an animal rights group who occupied the rig sometime in the early Nineties, which slowed the whole project down. Something to do with dolphins, I think? Thing is, it meant they rushed to get

the oil pumping again and didn't detect a leak. Thus ...'
Ross motions to the memorial. 'No one was able to prove
the correlation, but I don't think it mattered. Grief isn't
known for being rational.'

I nod, my shoulders tight.

'I've been piecing together a bit of local history since
I've been here. Backdated newspapers and the like. Here,
come and have a look.'

I follow Ross to a small side room filled with sagging
cardboard boxes, a heavy-set table in the middle. He's
chatting away, but I can't concentrate on the words. He
said dolphins. *Dolphins*. Like Mum's flotilla of figurines
that line the French dresser back home. That's how she
met my dad; it's got to be.

'Are you all right?' says Ross.

'Yeah, fine.' I try to smile, but I can't stop my nostrils from
flaring and can only imagine how psychotic this looks.

'Here it is,' says Ross, taking a stack of paper from a
shoebox.

I lower my gaze to the table, where a neat pile of newspaper clippings and reproduced photographs are spread
across a felt crafting board. One image dominates the
others. In it, a torrent of black smoke billows from flames
so hot that a crane has melted, bending it towards the sea
like the arched neck of a diplodocus.

'Ah, here it is.'

Ross hands me a newspaper clipping, the corner dog-
eared and torn. I push it back, revealing a headline that
reads:

WE'LL GO DOWN FIGHTING': THE EARTH MAMAS' DEFIANT CALL AS RIG HITS THIRD WEEK OF OCCUPATION

Beneath, a half-page photograph shows three women standing with fists raised behind a handstitched banner strung between the rig's railings. Their faces are cast in rebellion, hair whipped wild in the wind, mouths stretched in mid-chant as dark clouds pool behind them. In the middle, wearing a crocheted cardigan that I recognise from its garish floral pattern, is Mum.

'Pretty ballsy, eh?' says Ross, flicking the picture. 'The police removed them a week after this was in the paper, but I'm surprised they lasted that long. I can't think it was too amicable, sharing 600 square feet with the skeleton crew.'

He doesn't know the half of it. I can think of one *particular* activity that may have whiled away the time.

'Whatever The Earth Mamas did, it worked. Although I don't expect they got a hero's return from the locals when the police dinghy pulled ashore,' says Ross.

'No, I doubt that.'

I look at the picture until Mum's outline appears in bloom on the back of my eyelids. I can't nest this image of her with the one I left in Dulwich. She's always been a bit of an eco-warrior, but I thought it was more the separate-your-recycling and don't-buy-apples-from-New-Zealand kind, not chain-myself-to-a-lump-of-metal-in-the-North-Sea-and-get-pulled-off-in-a-police-boat kind.

Even though the oil company is to blame, I can see

229

why The Earth Mamas were the perfect scapegoat for the hardship that crept in after they left. At the same time, I can't help but feel a tickle of pride in my chest. *Mum*. You total, fucking badass!

'What's up?' asks Ross, noticing the grin I'm struggling to push back down.

'Nothing, it's ... I just remembered something funny.'

I pretend to flick through the clippings, but I can't focus on much else. This begs the question ... How could Mum have ever been satisfied discussing crudités and Easter bonnet parades with the PTA after stepping down from *this*?

'Hey, Ross. I should be getting back. Kian's usually out in the yard for morning rounds about ... five hours from now.'

'Do you want me to walk you?' asks Ross, sliding his hands in his pockets.

'It's three miles from here to Braehead Farm.'

'I know,' he says, taking half a step closer.

'I've got John's number. Moira said he does a taxi service, but I swear Kian claimed he was a mechanic, so it's a bit confusing.'

'He's a train guard too, but only from Thursday to Sunday.'

I laugh and follow Ross back into the church. He pauses at the door and I bounce off his shoulder, his arm reaching out to steady me as I stumble against a pew.

With his hand at my waist, I sway on the spot like I'm finding my sea legs. In a way, I am.

My neck aches from looking up at him as the space

shrinks between us. I worry that Ross can hear my heartbeat, thumping like music through a thick wall. I can't kiss a priest. Can I? But what if the priest is the one initiating the kiss?

Ross grazes my collarbone. I shiver. He searches my face, as though nervous that I'm about to duck under his arm and bolt out the door. I trace an outline down his shirt buttons, poised like a match over striking paper.

The sound of a latch and the accompanying door clunk ping-pongs from one side of the church to the other. Ross and I whip around, looking over our shoulders to a hooded figure who pauses by a candle stand. The lit votives flicker in a draught.

'Jacqui! How are you?' Ross flicks into a smile that's more appropriately public facing and takes a few short strides towards her. Jacqui pulls her hood down, her cheeks ruddy and pink like they've been scrubbed with a potato brush. In the crook of her arm she holds a bunch of lilies and purple freesias.

'Evening, Minister,' she says, smiling, an expression I've not seen before. 'I'm glad I caught you before you locked up.'

'Ah, I'm not as prompt as Reverend Dingwall.'

'Quite. I've come to ...' She looks down at the flowers and across to the memorial, at which point our eyes meet and my stomach freezes into a little cube.

'Ava.' She gives me the slightest of nods.

'We were just talking about the rig tragedy,' says Ross, motioning towards me. He's articulating sympathy with every part of his body, right down to the head tilt and slightly furrowed brow.

'You were? Good,' she says, turning towards me. 'Folk should know what something like that does to a place like this.' The look she gives me is like a taut wire between us. I break away first, sidestepping towards the connecting door, my arms covered in goosebumps.

'Ross, I better call John. Thanks for the dinner, it really was nice.'

'Right, right. Let me show you out—'

'No need, I'll just grab my bits and ... yeah.'

I pull open the heavy door that leads into the rectory and stand on the other side, my lungs heavy like I've been wading waist-deep in the firth.

Chapter 23

I turn over a postcard that Rory has sent me, the purple gel pen blotchy on the back. Underneath a rough sketch of a human body, Rory has drawn three objects with the question:

For ten points, which of these did I remove from a patient's rectum today? A = a toy car, B = a small string of Christmas lights, C = three rocks of crack cocaine. I'll give you a clue. THERE IS MORE THAN ONE RIGHT ANSWER. PS nothing to report from Mumland apart from the standard consumption of Malbec. Peace out, lassie! Rory xoxo

As the kettle builds to a shrill whistle, the back door opens and Moira steps inside, rubbing her bare arms. Her fringe sticks up in a number of directions that she attempts to smooth by licking her palms and running them over her crown.

'All right?' she says, her cheeks ruddy. 'Sun!' Moira points outside with a broad grin pinned to her face.

'Yeah! Good, isn't it,' I say, taking down another mug for her.

'Practically bikini weather. You have to soak up the vitamin D whilst you can up here.' She unties her jumper from around her waist, pulls it over her head, and gestures to the table. 'What happened?'

'What do you mean?' I ask, tucking Rory's postcard under my laptop.

'The table. I can't remember the last time I saw the surface.'

She looks over my shoulder at the open folders, skim-reading the sticky notes tacked to statements and invoices that I've yet to pull figures from.

'How bad is it?' she asks.

'Well, it's hard to say. I don't know enough about the financial side of things, you know? I'm trying to get the farm administration digitised, but I'm struggling to input the numbers in a way that looks ... viable.'

'It's bad, isn't it?'

'Yeah, really bad,' I admit.

Moira grimaces, eyes wide. 'I did suspect so, but Kian gets defensive about it whenever I bring it up. It's not like I don't know what I'm talking about. My family have never owned farmland, but I must visit eight or nine every month with the vet stuff, so I know what goes into it.'

'His ideas aren't all bad,' I say, zipping my fleece to the chin.

'Oh, I know, but he jumps from one to the other without seeing the first one through. I wouldn't say this to him, but it's like trying to shoot a rabbit with a shotgun. If something hits, it'll be luck, not aim.'

I sit back in my chair and tap my fingers on the table.

'I've been trying to think of a way to make it work for him,' I say. 'There are university grants he can apply for, agricultural courses that need farms to partner with, but the applications are properly tedious.'

I gesture to the plastic sleeves in front of me, each stuffed with records so dense and complicated that it takes a strong coffee to read a page without yawning.

'If we make sense of all this, he could apply for one. They want working land and modern farmers who are open to new concepts. That's Kian, right?'

'Oh, aye. I don't think it's a bad idea at all. Ingenuity runs in the Brody family. Before his granddad got kicked in the head by that bull, he used to ride a horse to the pub. He'd tie it up outside and get a leg up from Mad Steve after last orders, then sleep all the way home because the horse knew the route without him having to do anything. Pretty ingenious, right?'

'Yeah. Cheaper than a taxi, for sure.'

'Speaking of which, I've sorted us a ride back from the ceilidh next week. John's got the night off, but my Uncle Mike can drop us back because he's on dialysis so can't drink anyway. If it goes tits up with Kian, I'm going to get hammered and there's no way I'm walking home across the fields.'

'Positive mental attitude, Moira. There's every chance it could be the origin story you tell your kids in the future.'

'Oh me, no pressure. Speaking of which ... dinner with The Rev! How was it? Do you have any reason to say extra Hail Marys?' says Moira, quirking an eyebrow.

'Ha! Nothing quite like that, although there were some prolonged bouts of eye contact that felt *pretty* raunchy, by Jane Austen standards, anyway.'

'Good vibes, on the whole?'

'Maybe? God, it's hard to say. It got really deep really quickly. Intimate, but not physically. Do you know what I mean?'

'Like your brains were making out with each other?' says Moira.

I blink, a little disturbed by the image.

'I know it's lame, but I wouldn't expect to get off with someone on a first date, let alone a date with a priest. That would be weird, right? If he was snogging parishioners on the regular.'

'The last woman he had round for dinner was Teresa and she still wears a girdle, so I'm going to say that's unlikely.'

'I guess I don't know how to read him. It could be that he's *just* being nice to me and I'm interpreting it wrong.'

'Now you understand my predicament with Kian.' She claps her hands to her mouth. 'He's not here, is he?'

'No, he's down at the pigs.'

'Good. Things are *not* going in the right direction there. He popped round yesterday, right? I came through to fill up my hot water bottle and he was stood in the porch talking to Mum, then when he saw me, he said he had to leave because Big Bertha was having phantom contractions.'

I laugh, but Moira looks so disheartened that I want to scoop her up and tuck her in my pocket.

'I'm worried he's going to throw his hands up and leave Kilroch again,' she says in a quiet voice.

'No way – no negativity here! He's probably just preoccupied. Keep at it. I know we haven't known each other long, but if he doesn't sit up and notice how bloody cool you are, he isn't worth the effort, quite frankly.'

Moira's grin pushes dimples into her cheeks.

'Stop now, or you'll give me a big head.'

I tuck my laptop on a shelf, laughing.

'I'll get Mum to pester him about this,' she says, pointing to the files. 'She can be pretty intimidating when she's got a bee in her bonnet, so it might make Kian more likely to sit down and do the application.'

'I can believe that,' I say, feeling sorry for Kian already.

***

After a morning spent picking up sacks of animal feed from a carefully curated list of eco-friendly, Kian-approved suppliers, I take Moira up on an offer of breakfast. Although scoffing Jacqui's leftovers is of clear appeal, I can't shift the low-key anxiety that has crept in since I skimmed through my emails an hour ago. Duncan's most recent request to 'curb the cutesy village larks and get back on the sister search' was followed by an ultimatum: I have two days to give him a solid update or he's pulling me back to the office. For now, I've fobbed him off with a line or two to buy myself a bit of time. I *had* intended to film our reunion, but it's not like I could whip my phone out mid-pig debacle without it feeling weird and inappropriate, like I was using her for an internet sideshow. The problem is, the closer I get to Moira, the more I want to protect her. As a result, I'm so on edge that it feels like I've permanently got an ice cube slipped down the back of my shirt.

'It's here, isn't it?' I say, recognising Moira's whitewashed cottage from a drop off last week.

'Aye.'

'Are we all right leaving the chicken feed on the back seat?'

'Yeah, of course. Why?'

'I don't want someone to steal it.'

Moira scoffs, unclipping her seatbelt. 'Who? The poultry bandits?'

She scrapes the mud off her boots by the doorstep and gestures for me to go inside. In the kitchen, she flicks the heating on, and pulls out a loaf of bread.

'I'm so hungry I swear I'm ingesting myself,' she says, waving a bread knife at me 'I hope you're ready to challenge your arteries.'

Twenty minutes later, Moira clunks a plate down on the scrubbed kitchen table. The oiled monstrosity she's piled on top oozes blobs of cheese between two thick slices of bread, a circular round of sausage, and a slab of potato scone. It's a coronary in a mouthful, with a side order of extra cholesterol. It's also completely and utterly delicious.

'I know I've got food all over my face, but honestly I couldn't give a sheep's arsehole,' I say.

'It's good, isn't it,' says Moira, grinning, her chin smeared with ketchup and a sheen of grease.

'No wonder the life expectancy is lower up here,' I say without thinking. I blink stupidly, but Moira doesn't notice my clumsy phrasing.

'But it's a good life. Worth knocking a few years off, don't you think?' she says.

We eat in comfortable silence as I scan the walls for clues that might tell me something about the way Moira grew up.

'Have you been to all these places?' I ask, pointing at the fridge door. Each inch boasts a different tourist destination in magnet form, from novelty Dutch clogs to the garish skyline of Las Vegas.

'No. They're from family friends. My cousin, mainly. He plays electro-folk violin in a band and tours a lot, so he posts a souvenir back when he visits somewhere new. I've not been abroad myself.'

'Do you want to do something like that? Travel about?' I say, picking Moira's plate up and taking it to the sink.

'I mean, sure. Who doesn't? I've nae seen England, let alone crossed the Channel,' she says, crossing a leg over the other knee. She unzips her hoodie, her cheeks so pink it's like they've been drawn on with a wax crayon. 'If I study equine dentistry, it'll be my first time over the border. The thing is, I don't know if there's any point going to the interview.'

'Why?' I ask, pulling on a pair of pink Marigolds from the cupboard under the sink.

'Ava, you don't need to wash up.'

'Don't be silly, I'm up now. Go on.'

'Well, even if I get a bursary, it won't cover everything. If I get a place on the course, Mum will insist I take it up. That's why I don't want to tell her.'

'OK, I'm not quite following ...' I say, picking up a wire sponge to scrape cremated cheese from a skillet pan.

'She'd convince me to do it, but then I wouldn't be able to help her out with the bills and the tearoom. Gah, she'd hate me spouting off about our finances round the village,' says Moira, wandering over to the kitchen window, 'but Dad wasn't always the most sensible with money. He used to leave his thumbnail long for scratch cards, so that sums it up, really. Mum has taken on a lot of the debts he racked up. Basically, money comes in and goes out on the same day.'

Wow. There's an insight. The more I hear about our dad, the more I'd like to give him a swift kick in the testicles. When did he earn the right to empty the joint account whilst dicking about on an oil rig? Why should Moira and Jacqui carry the burden of his poor life choices? I didn't expect to discover a secret life of philanthropy, but our father's list of redeeming features is so small that I'm struggling to see what Mum found appealing, even if their relationship was three seconds long.

'That's a stupidly big responsibility to have,' I say.

'I know, and I don't mind. Really, I don't. It's partly why I applied to be a veterinary nurse; the training isn't so long, so I figured I could start making money sooner.

Start paying some bills. But you know what's boring about guinea pigs? Everything. If I let on to Mum that I want to specialise, she'll start doing night shifts cleaning the ferries again, and I don't want her doing that just for me.'

Moira looks so jittery I'm half-expecting her to vibrate off the chair like a wind-up frog from the inside of a Christmas cracker. I throw tea down my throat and pull my chair in closer to the table.

'I don't think you should hold back. You've got to let people make their own choices. If Jacqui wants to help you out, that's her decision. You're constantly doing things for other people. I think Kian would have jacked in Braehead Farm if it wasn't for you.'

Moira bites her lip, her eyes pooled and glassy.

'Is that part of it? You're worried that Kian won't be still be here by the time you've finished your course?'

Moira nods, her eyes closed. A tear traces her lash line and runs down the side of her nose. She bats it away. 'What am I? Ten years old?'

'Don't make yourself small unless you've really tried going big. It sounds like you're basing decisions on what other people might need from you.'

'Mmm. Maybe. I need to grow up,' she says, dashing her cheek. 'Nothing like PMT to turn on the sprinkler system.'

I laugh, but the sound catches in my throat like I've swallowed a fat bluebottle. I turn back to the sink and rinse a blob of egg down the drain.

'Could you try and save up as much as you can before your course starts? A pint of amber ale in The Wailing

Banshee costs, what, £1.79? I can see why people drink, it's a cheap hobby,' I say with a laugh, turning back to the table. Moira looks up, her usual pep hidden beneath heavy brows and an even heavier fringe.

'You're wrong,' she says, her voice delicate.

I pause, a mug slick with soap studs in my hand. 'Sorry, did I say something stupid?'

'No, it's fine. But you're wrong. That "hobby" is why Mum's still paying off the interest on Dad's loans.' Moira lowers her voice and shakes her head. 'It's what happens when your dad prefers his drinking buddies over his family. They were his priority for a long time, not us.'

I roughly place my mug down, adding to the rings on the table. 'That's ... really shitty. I know it's reductive to put it like that, but it really is,' I say, my disappointment sinking deeper.

'Yeah. I know. Mum thought it was a good idea when he first talked about working away on the rigs, because "there's no off-licence in the middle of the North Sea", that's what she said. She hid the money problems, but then I found their old bank statements in a cake tin, so it all became obvious. There was other stuff, too. Years before. Even so, she won't badmouth him in front of me.'

'Like what?' I say, turning off the tap.

'I don't know the details, only snatches of stuff growing up. Kilroch wasn't always as sleepy as it is now. Basically, everyone worked on the rigs. Have you seen them?' I nod, remembering the metal structures like spider crabs in the bay.

'Well, there were more of them. Most have been decommissioned, mostly since the accident. But there must have been a dozen at one point and it was stopping the dolphins coming into the shallows to feed. People from all over the country came up here to protest and eventually the oil company shifted the whole operation up the coast. The village was shot to bits after so many lost their livelihood. It's left a stain. After the protests, the oil rigs reopened in a rush. People round here needed someone to blame.'

'Does Jacqui blame them? The activists?' I say, already knowing what Moira's going to say before she opens her mouth.

'She thinks they were middle-class hippies with no sense of the real world. Might be something to do with the fact that they chose to live like poor people because it's more interesting than being ordinary and rich. That's a direct quote from Mum, actually,' says Moira, with a wry laugh.

My stomach swoops with discomfort, like there's a handful of slick worms wriggling inside. My compulsion to fill the silence has dropped away and now my lungs feel empty, like I'm in the deep end as chlorinated water slips down my stinging throat. I desperately wish that I could talk about myself as freely as Moira can. Words seem to bubble up my throat, but as soon as I open my mouth to speak, they pop and disappear.

'Your ... your dad. He worked on the rig that exploded, right?'

Moira takes a big glug of tea and winces at the temperature. 'Yeah, he did.'

It shouldn't matter. I didn't know him. So why do I feel resentful about something I never had?

Moira stands up and stretches her arms over her head. 'Oops,' she says, zipping up her fly. She tucks an old-fashioned rugby shirt into the waistband of her jeans and drains her mug like she's racing someone. The pace at which she's able to shake off a mood is truly admirable. 'Want to see him?'

'Who?'

'My dad,' she says, beckoning me down a narrow hallway.

Chapter 24

'Hang on,' I say, dashing after her as she reaches a staircase lined with floral wallpaper and a chipped dado rail.

'Just up here,' says Moira, not looking back.

I consider leaping from a window and sprinting as fast as my floppy wellie boots will carry me, but I seem to be on autopilot. What does she mean? Is there a chance Mum has lied to me about my father being dead? I grow hot underneath my scratchy jumper, panic setting in.

Moira leads me onto the landing, past a magnolia room filled with boxes of paper bags and cake-tin liners, and up to a narrow bedroom at the end of the corridor. Shimmering butterflies are stuck on the door beneath a metal sign spelling out her name in the style of a Californian licence plate.

She's not leading me to him. She can't be. I bite my lip, annoyed at myself for the flash of hope that tickled at my ribcage before calcifying into a hard, disappointing lump. He's not here, and yet for a minute, I truly thought he was.

Moira opens the door to a bright room with a three-quarter-size bed tucked beneath the window and textured plaster on the walls, painted over with lilac. She slides a mirrored wardrobe door open, revealing a vanity table covered in make-up I've not seen her wear. She passes me a photo frame and shoves her hand in her pocket. The other points to a man in the picture.

'That's Dad: Andrew. And Mum, obviously.'

I stare at the out-of-focus man in the picture. He's tall, that much is clear. Jacqui's Nineties perm barely reaches his shoulders and she's got the height and girth of a rugby prop, with a scowl to match. Andrew squints in the sunshine through dark, curly hair that falls to one side in a style that could seem foppish if it weren't for his thick arms and patchwork tattoos. His jawline is square, like Moira's. Like mine. He's got a hand on Jacqui's shoulder, but going by her awkward stance, you can tell she's holding him up. A half-drunk pint dangles in his right hand, cut off by the frame.

'Mum said that Dad wearing tailored trousers was the best thing to come from a funeral,' says Moira with a smile.

'He's ... he's big,' I say. Now that I know where I got each part, I'm conscious of my face in a different way.

'Oh, aye. Good on the tug-o-war.'

I try to imagine Mum standing in Jacqui's place, but I'd sooner believe that Kian has a second job as a Butler in the Buff. I've seen photos of Mum from before I was born. The abundance of hemp cloth and henna-dyed hair was a *look*, especially when complemented by a ribboned tambourine. Blending in has never been her forte.

I look at Moira and back to the picture, mentally splicing our features apart and dropping them into petri dishes between Mum, Jacqui, and Andrew. Four people, irreversibly connected, but wildly different.

'Do you miss him?' I ask.

'Yeah,' says Moira, with an upward intonation. 'He used to take me mackerel fishing when I was little. He had a little boat in the garage and we'd tow it down to the harbour.'

I feel a pang of something akin to grief. Is that possible if you've never met the person? Moira looks around the room, as though noticing it for the first time. A rainbow of rosettes are thumbtacked to the shelf above her bed. I give the photo back to Moira, my thumbprint stark on the glass. 'Was it nice? Growing up together, as a family?'

'Sure, it was. Mum and Dad never had big bust-ups, but there was always an atmosphere of some kind. I could feel it as soon as I walked in. That's why Kian let me hang around Braehead so much, 'cos we were in the same boat,' says Moira.

'That seems so unfair,' I say, desperately wanting to add myself into the equation, 'that both you and Kian missed out on the chance to grow up with them around.'

'Kian had it worse off than me,' says Moira. I wince, the unjustness of it all brought into light. Deciding whose 'dead dad' situation is worse is a bit like choosing between getting punched in the face or kicked in the stomach.

I don't have a right to feel hard done by. Historically speaking, Mum's hazy references to my father might have been a defence mechanism this whole time. The decision to tell him about my existence wouldn't have been a simple one. Going by what Moira's said about the way she was fathered, I doubt knowledge of a second daughter 500 miles away would have inspired him to don a Batman costume and start campaigning for Fathers 4 Justice.

I pull Moira into a hug, my arms above hers. She giggles and pats my back with T-Rex arms.

'I knew it!' she says. 'You *are* a hugger.'

'Only in special circumstances,' I reply, squeezing my arms together. Over her shoulder, the collage of pictures stuck to the wall comes into focus. 'Um, Moira?'

'Mmhm?'

'Why is your room covered in pictures of Leonardo DiCaprio?'

Moira breaks away, turning to face what can only be called a shrine. The space beside her bed is covered in torn magazine pages and film posters, the faces of his co-stars ripped away.

'He's ... an interest of mine,' says Moira. 'This one is quite rare,' she says, pointing to a box frame. 'You see that? It's an original wood chip from the floating door in *Titanic*.'

'Really?'

'Oh, yeah. I had a *Titanic* birthday party when I was eight. We all wore stripy life rings and made replica "Heart of the Ocean" necklaces out of Blu Tak and tinfoil. What a day,' she gushes.

'Didn't you jump on that bandwagon a bit late? You must have been – what – a toddler when it first came out?'

'No, definitely not. We rented it on VHS from Ted's Tapes

the second we could. He always got stuff in early because an American cousin of his filmed it on a camcorder in the back of the cinema and posted it over by airmail.'

'When's your birthday?' I ask.

'The third of December.'

'What year?'

''92.'

'What?!'

'Why? Did you have a *Titanic* birthday party when you were a kid too?' asks Moira, her lip curled with glee. 'What was your cake like?'

'No, no. I just, umm. I thought you were *way* younger than me.'

'Oh, everyone's surprised, don't worry about it. I think it might be these,' she says, lifting her cheeks with her fingertips. 'Never grown out my baby face.'

'But that means you're like ... six months younger than me.'

Moira contemplates this and shrugs. 'Yeah. Guess so. Oh, that sounds like Mum,' says Moira, as the sound of crunching gravel filters in from outside.

∗∗∗

Jacqui steps out of a faded Skoda, a raincoat slung over her arm. *Six months*. That means that Mum and Jacqui were pregnant at the same time. Did Jacqui know? Did Mum? The latter, of course, is worse, but it's Andrew who wins Biggest Shit of the Decade. Getting a second woman pregnant within a year of marrying the first is a pretty terrible way to display your long-term devotion.

I wipe my cheeks dry and try to skitter down the driveway before Jacqui notices, but as she opens the boot, Jess jumps down and trots over to me with her tongue lolling, head low in playful submission. Jacqui walks over with heavy steps as though she's a sheriff about to shoot a shot glass from my hand. Knowing I'm not going to make it to the car without an inquisition, I stop, hoping my eyes aren't as stinging red as they feel.

'I ... you've had a haircut,' I say, meeting her eyes.

Jacqui runs her hand through a curled lock of honey blonde hair. Catching herself, she drops her arm and shoves a fist in her pocket.

'Yes,' she says, bridling. 'I said they weren't to bother drying it, but they took no notice.'

'It looks really nice,' I say. I mean it, too. 'Is it a ... special occasion?'

'Why, do you think I would no' care to do this ordinarily?'

I don't want to have a sparring match today, so I smile like a simpleton.

'Ah, I've got to head back. Lots to be getting on with,' I say.

As I reach the Jeep parked alongside a gorse bush, Jacqui calls me back.

'Will you tell Kian he needs to turn the sheep out onto the high field? They've all but run out of grass in the paddock and I had to pull two up from the ditch. Not sure why he's left it for so long. Distracted, maybe,' she says, her crystal eyes unwavering.

Chapter 25

I leave the Jeep at Braehead and open the back door of the farm house just to snatch my rain poncho from the back of a kitchen chair. It's not supposed to rain, but that doesn't mean anything here. I've stopped looking at the clouds, because more often than not, I'm in them. The sky blurs with the ground in a cold mist, enveloping my knees and muffling the landscape.

I walk along a track behind the farmhouse that leads to a copse, then a scraggly moor, and finally a public bridleway that runs alongside a field sporting a crewcut of wheat husks. On every fourth or fifth step I have to shake my boots as mud clods build up around each foot like I'm taking part in a solo rendition of the Hokey Cokey.

The walk has given me time to think. At first, I found it difficult to sit with my own thoughts, instead choosing to drown my internal monologue with podcasts and music. But slowly I've replaced my distraction techniques with a different focus: confronting my situation with Moira, however uncomfortable, whilst plodding in wellie boots.

Deep down, I knew the chance of unearthing anything

akin to a love story between my parents was slim, but my half-formed speculations about my father had clearly set the bar too high. How can I tell Moira that we're sisters now, knowing it will send a bulldozer through her already fragile family?

I climb the stile to the church grounds and wriggle between the gravestones, superstitious enough to avoid walking over the mounds, and quick march past the windows of the church hall. Inside, a small group of elderly locals play cards, each with a Thermos of tea on the table in front of them. I reach the back door to the rectory, knock, and peer through the porthole window, my breath steaming up the glass while the building creaks and moans as Ross moves around inside.

I stumble forwards as the door is roughly pulled open. In my haste, I'm halfway over the threshold by the time I realise that it's not Ross at all. I stand, blinking, trying to match the woman in front of me with the Kilroch *Guess Who?* that I mentally flick through in my head. Older. Clip-on earrings. Mean eyes. Could be a few people I've come across.

She steps back as my foot slaps onto the flagstone.

'Hi. Sorry, I was expecting it to be Ross,' I say. 'I wouldn't have just barged in like ...' I catch myself, not wanting to appear over-familiar.

'I'm afraid he's rather busy at the moment,' she says. 'Do you want me to give him a message?'

'No, I needed his advice on a, err ... an issue.'

The woman blinks, signifying that this does not meet the threshold of information required.

'It's of an ecclesiastical nature,' I say, holding my hands in front of me.

'Oh, lovely. It's nice to see the youth engaging with the church. I'm Eileen, one of the wardens.' She taps her front teeth and squints at me. 'Although I haven't seen you on a Sunday. I sit at the back, so I know who comes and goes.'

What's her role, specifically? Crowd control at Sunday worship?

'Do you know when he's free? Because I can wait,' I say, glancing over her shoulder to a wood burner set in the corner of the room, its grate glowing with amber coals.

'Well, he's in the middle of a clear-out, you see. I've got to prepare the house for—'

'Ava!' says Ross, appearing at Eileen's shoulder.

'Hi,' I say, on an outward breath.

Ross is wearing a thick cable-knit jumper with the sleeves rolled up, a week's worth of facial hair sharpening the edges of his jawline. I'm not sure how, but it seems like the more layers he puts on, the more attractive he gets. I can't imagine what would happen to my resting heart rate if he put on a hat.

'This young lady has a question of faith to talk through with you, Minister.'

'Does she? Well, we can't let that stew. Eileen, you're an angel, truly. I can't thank you enough.'

Eileen pats her hair and clutches Ross's wrist. 'Oh, but the study is a mess with the treasury files. I best finish that off, don't you think?'

'Please, you're making me feel terrible. She won't even

let me make the tea,' says Ross, looking to me with a glint in his eye. 'I insist you take a break. Glen's playing bridge next door.'

'Oh, I can't play with Glen,' says Eileen, her hands aloft in protest. 'He's an awful cheat. In God's house, no less. I'll be over tomorrow, Minister. Does seven o'clock suit?'

'Seven it is,' he says. Eileen pulls on a sheepskin coat and heads round the corner, Ross and I waving until she's fully out of sight.

'Seven? In the morning?' I ask.

'Don't. I'm exhausted. I sent her off so I could have a nap. Might have to unplug the main line, too, because she's bound to call. Anyway. You didn't come here about Jesus, did you?'

'No ...'

Ross leans against the door frame and lifts an elbow to let me in. I duck and step into the kitchen, shivering with the sudden change of temperature, despite the flames licking at the stove door.

'Do you want to take your coat off?' asks Ross.

'No.'

'OK.' He pauses, his hands in his pockets. 'Are you all right?'

'Not really.'

'I didn't think so.'

He steps forwards, tucks me into his chest, and rests his chin on the top of my head. The contact feels immeasurably good, like sinking into a bath so perfectly warm you can't feel where your body ends and the water begins. 'Can

I check that this is definitely *not* a church thing, because I don't include hugs as part of my parish duties, as a rule.'

'It's not a church thing. It's a what-the-fuck-am-I-doing kind of thing?'

'Ah, one of those. Will tea help?'

'I doubt it.'

'Shall we start with tea and if you still feel bad after one, we'll move onto a bottle of McCallister's.'

A few minutes later, I'm sitting in the corner of a brown velvet sofa, ugly enough to be ditched at a roadside, comfy enough to sink into due to its sagging frame and excess of cushions. Ross moves a stack of boxes half-filled with books and pulls out a blanket from a Jenner's bag tucked under the coffee table. He throws it over my legs and sits down, seemingly unconcerned that I've railroaded his day. I slide my toes underneath his leg to try and thaw out, the cold tacked tight to my bones. It's quite possibly the most intimate I've ever felt, in the proper sense of the word. He rests an elbow along the back of the sofa and waits for me to get halfway down my mug before asking me what's wrong.

When I start, I can't stop. I tell him everything, from the live stream, to finding out about having a half-sister, and why I've come to Kilroch. I speak in guilty half-sentences that tumble together.

'So, it's Moira? She's your half-sister.'

'I hadn't reached that part yet,' I say.

'It's kind of obvious.' Ross props his head on his hand.

'Is it? How?'

'I've got two younger sisters. The way they go about with each other – I don't think you can replicate that kind of dynamic anywhere else, even if you grow up apart. They had their moments, though. They scratched each other's eyes out as teenagers. It's something about the way their brains work; they're hardwired to band together. Also, you have to have noticed this ...' says Ross, drawing a circle in front of his own face.

'We've both got massive chins,' I admit.

'Not my words,' says Ross, quickly. 'You have a great chin.'

'Thanks.'

'How did you tell Moira?'

'Hmm. That's the thing.'

'Ah. You haven't told her,' he says, putting his mug down on a tiled end table.

'No.' I scrunch my face up and tuck my knees in, scratching at an embroidered dove on the cushion that I've pulled onto my lap. 'I've left it too late. It's like forgetting someone's name at the beginning of a party, except fifty times worse. If you ask again as you're heading out the door, you look like a right twazzock.'

'So, what are you going to do instead?' he asks.

'I don't know. I'm delaying the inevitable, aren't I?' I bite my thumbnail and look at Ross.

'What is the inevitable?'

He lets his question hang in the air and rubs his bristled chin with a curious look in his eye. It's not the neutral expression I've seen him use with parishioners, like an ITV weatherman unfazed by gale force winds. I draw in a deep breath and exhale until my lungs feel small and empty.

'I think that ... I *worry* that Moira will see it as *really* underhand that I've come up here to "see what she's like" before telling her that I'm her half-sister. I didn't have a clue what I was walking into when I got the sleeper train at the start of the month. Oh, and as well as that, I've got no idea how I'm going to convince my boss to let me stay up here longer, especially if I keep leaving Moira out of my diaries. *Snooper* wants the whole trip tied up with a happy family reunion, which isn't likely, is it? How's that conversation going to go? "Oh, nice meeting you. I've been called back to London. By the way, we're sisters. I think your mum hates me because I'm ninety-nine per cent sure your dad had an affair, of which I am the result. Also, I've been writing diaries since the day I got here and soz, but your village sounds about as appealing as the toilet block at Reading Festival." Whichever way you look at it, it's shit. A pile of shit with a fly on top that probably did another shit whilst it was there, just to put the shitty cherry on top of the cake.'

'Is there a chance that the *thought* of telling Moira is worse than the reality?'

'If anything, I think I've downplayed it.'

'Does that mean you shouldn't tell her? This feeling you have – the guilt – it's not going to go away. You said yourself that you wish you'd known you had a half-sister before the DNA test. I don't want to oversimplify about what you're facing, but this isn't just about you anymore. Try imagining this exact scenario, but with positive outcomes instead of the shit storm you're imagining. How might Moira feel when you tell her?'

'I've imagined it on a loop and that's what's making me feel sick. She's already had the burden of dealing with our dad not being around, I don't want to make it worse by suggesting that he shagged about as well. That would be my fault.'

'If that was your positive version, I'm dreading the negative one,' says Ross.

'OK ... positive scenario? That she's ... happy. That's she's understandably angry with me for keeping it to myself, but that she can forgive me in some way. That we're able to see each other, both of us knowing everything. It's not like I can lie about my age.'

'Exactly. If your first reaction is to assume the worst set of consequences, you also have to believe that there's an equal chance for good ones.'

'How should I tell her? Perhaps if I burst a party popper and did a little dance, she might not be so angry at me?'

Ross laughs, shaking his head.

'I can't give you specific advice on that. But as long as you're honest and understanding of how she might react, you'll make the right choice. I'm sure of it.'

I nod slowly and allow my fingers to drift up towards his hand, which dangles from the sofa cushion. He slides his fingers between mine and smiles. My stomach swoops.

'You sound far too logical for a Christian.'

'I'm not talking as a Christian. I'm talking as someone who cares about you and Moira.'

'Be honest. Did you want to throw in a cheeky Bible quote?'

'Eh, I could have chucked in Luke 6:31,' he says, pondering. 'But you're not ready for the Psalms. The language is a bit more ... fire and fury.'

'Isn't that a *Game of Thrones* book?'

Ross grins. 'An unfortunate coincidence. Shall we crack that whisky open now?'

Chapter 26

I use my sleeve to wipe away a spiderweb from the locked letterbox built into farmhouse wall. Inside are two envelopes and a postcard shaped like Prince William's head. No prizes for guessing who it's from. I kick my shoes off in the porch and head through to the living room, where Kian sits with his legs hanging over the arm of the sofa.

'Oh, glad you're here. I want to show you something,' I say, dropping the two envelopes on Kian's stomach.

'What's that?'

'I need my file, hang on.'

I take the stairs two at a time and hover on the landing to read Rory's postcard before slipping it under the mattress with the others. They're getting more and more abstract. Do I need to be worried? Perhaps the Wagamama crawl is pickling her brain with katsu sauce and sake. This time, she's drawn a dumpling on the back, featuring bulbous eyes and a biro speech bubble that states: 'the dipping sauce is suspiciously fishy'. Weird.

I hover on the landing and yawn so widely my body shudders. I didn't switch the lamp off until three-thirty this morning because I had enough reception to use my phone as a hotspot, meaning an uninterrupted deep dive down the rabbit hole of Google. Somehow, I went from watching videos of drag queens recreating iconic Met Gala looks to scouring the internet for ways to bring more money into the farm; a task so dull I should have drifted straight off to sleep. I printed a dozen relevant web pages and stuck them in an old ring binder I found covered in dust and *Jurassic Park* stickers, which I now tuck under my arm as I head downstairs.

In the living room, Kian sits back in an armchair, shoulders round, hands limply resting by his sides. He looks at me with utter defeat.

'Jesus, what happened? I was only gone five minutes.'

He kisses his teeth and nods to a ripped envelope on the seat next to him. 'It's the bank. They want me to start paying back a pretty fucking substantial loan or they'll look into repossession proceedings.'

'Bloody hell. That seems drastic.'

'Yeah, well, it would have helped if Granddad had told me he'd taken out the fucking loan in the first place.'

'Ah ... yeah, that seems like quite an important thing to mention.'

'No shit. I've got to go in for a meeting the day after tomorrow to "discuss our options". *Our* options. Who are they kidding? They don't give a shit about the farm.'

'Even if that's true, can I still show you something?' I say.

'Yeah, but only if it's the folder named "Last Resorts". I need to slot this letter inside and burn the fucking thing.'

'We *can* do that, but would you at least give this a quick look?' I ask, holding up the file like a tiny shield.

Kian nods wearily. I guide him through to the kitchen with the promise of a coffee and Tunnock's Tea Cakes, and open the file on the table. By the time I've talked him through my plan, his cheeks are pink again despite the pessimism ringing through his words.

'I don't see the point.'

'What do you mean?'

'I don't have enough time.'

'All you need is a letter of intent. For now, anyway. Did you read the sections I highlighted?'

Kian lifts a corner and allows each page to pass through his thumb and forefinger like a flipbook, flashing a kaleidoscope of passages that I painstakingly read through well into the early hours of this morning.

'Which of the *many* highlighted sections do you mean? I do get the gist of it, but your Hermione Granger approach to research is a bit ... complex,' he says.

'There's a key, I put it on the front. If you flick to the pink sections.'

'Which pink?'

'Pale pink.'

'Right.' Kian glances furtively at me, a smile playing in the corner of his mouth. I override the desire to skip to the right page for him, although my fingers are itching to do so. 'Research partnerships?'

'Yep. There are grants up for grabs if you can show

potential for a project that combines modern technology with traditional farming practices. This is you!'

'Ava ...' Kian pushes his chair back and rubs his temples. He looks at me with bright eyes, but his mouth is pencil thin. 'I appreciate that you've done all this,' he says, gesturing to the stack of papers, 'but I'll be lucky to avoid total bankruptcy after my meeting with the bank on Thursday. This is a lot of trouble to go to if we're going under anyway.'

'OK, but consider this: if you *are* successful with a grant, it'll mean that you don't need to sell the farm. Surely that's the *last* last resort. There's no going back after that. Won't it be worth it?'

I'm about to drive my point further but pull back when Kian hangs his head like a melancholic donkey. He closes his eyes and jiggles his heels up and down.

'I didn't want to make you feel bad,' I say.

'No, it's not your fault. I'm grateful, honestly. I was just thinking about how worse off I'd be if you hadn't come up a few weeks ago. I've let all this bottleneck in my head, you know?'

'Oh, I'm sure you'd have been fine. Moira's been here, hasn't she? She's far more help than I could ever be. I don't know how to castrate goats, for starters.'

Kian slumps back into his chair with a tired smile. 'Ah, it's the outsiders' perspective, isn't it? Must be that London business brain kicking in,' he says.

'Or years spent watching my mum apply for grants to keep her community clubs going. It *is* a lot of work, but it's better than admitting defeat.' I push my chair back, sit on the edge of my seat, and peer over the pages like a short-sighted academic.

'Didn't you say you worked in publishing?' says Kian, his tone changing.

'No, online media. Why?'

'Because you should be doing this kind of thing more.'

'Nah, it's just my ... productive neurosis. It has its uses. Anyway, it looks like there are three grants you can apply for with different universities that offer agriculture courses. These are all right,' I say, pointing at arm's length towards two blue tabs protruding from the margin, 'but it's the Edinburgh link that's the strongest, because it sounds like your fertiliser drone strike thing is right up their street.'

'Let's avoid saying "drone strike" in the application. It sets the wrong tone.'

I nod, seeing this as a green light.

'I've looked through budget policy documents from Scottish government briefings made in the past twelve months that relate to innovation and investment in the Highlands. They're actually *looking* for ways that universities can partner with farms.'

Kian nods slowly. I wanted to give him an hour to read through the documents I'd printed off, but it's clear I'm going to have to whistle through the key points aloud. Honestly, what's the point in highlighters if they're given no authority?

'What do the green tabs mean?' says Kian.

'Oh, I just wanted to emphasise the fact that I took

one for the team because those were the bits that were especially boring to read.'

'So humble,' says Kian with a laugh.

'I think it's worth submitting. If you don't get through this round, you can try again next year and you'll already have done most of the work.'

'Hmm.' Kian taps his knee and looks at me. I can all but see the cogs turning behind his eyes. 'When's the deadline?'

'Quite soon ... We need a three-year business plan and the conservation status of all the livestock, then they'll send a team round to do a biodiversity survey,' I reply, reading from the cover page with stilted intonation. I've got less than half a clue as to what those phrases actually mean, but I say them with confidence.

'How soon is quite soon?

'Umm, like ... tomorrow.'

'Tomorrow?! There's no way—' Kian breaks off and blinks profusely.

'Sure there is! I'll help with the writing part. It's basically what I do in my day job, so you give me the content, and I'll chuck some proverbial glitter on it. Everything else is in here.' I flop the file up and down and don a manic smile in an attempt to distract him from the intimidatingly large task at hand. Kian looks back to the document, his eyes narrow.

As I'm about to launch into another motivational speech, the back door clatters open and Moira steps in.

'Oi, oi, what's all this?' she says, squatting down to untie her boots.

'Ava's got a crackpot idea to get money for the farm.'

'Crackpot idea? That's your favourite kind, isn't it?'

'All right, cheeky,' says Kian, flicking her waist when she comes to stand behind us. I roll my eyes with feigned irritation and try to rub warmth into my hands. Waiting another week to have The Chat with Moira isn't going to undo any affair that our father had, but I also want to give our news the space it deserves to become a happy memory. Getting ready together before Friday's ceilidh is as good an opportunity as any. Until then, I'm going to channel my efforts into making sure that Kian fills out this bloody application so that he and Moira can one day stop passing through Kilroch like trains running on separate tracks.

'The bank's already expecting repayment on the gargantuan loan that Granddad never bloody told me about. There's still a chance I can keep things going if I start up the eco-tourism side of the farm; getting folk truffle hunting. That way, I won't need to jump through all these hoops for funding.'

'Surely that's riskier? You'll have to deal with groups of southerners turning up in off-the-rack Barbour, swilling two-hundred-quid whisky like they've just discovered the stuff whilst trying to mount Big Bertha.'

Kian scoffs. 'They could try. Can you imagine an Oxbridge posho trying to put their dobber in Bertha's mouth? She'd bite it down to a stump.'

'Gross ... but see! Here's where the grants come in! It's regular income and you don't have to worry about one-star

TripAdvisor reviews for accidental loss of genitalia due to maniacal swine. Consider it my leaving gift to you.'

'Why, are you going?' asks Moira.

'Well, at some point they'll want me back at work,' I say, leaving the details vague. I gesture to the file, refocusing attention towards the grant. 'It's worth a shot, right?'

'I can't see any downsides to this. Think of the bragging rights you'll have if Braehead is *university accredited*,' says Moira, putting on a plummy English accent.

'You needn't have troubled yourself with this,' says Kian.

'Ah, it was nothing. It was all on the internet, I just pulled it off.'

'And doused it in highlighter. I'm surprised you didn't fumigate yourself,' he says, sniffing the page.

'Well, I did feel a bit heady.'

'Seriously, though. Thanks. There's been a lot on and this bloody loan feels like a puncture in the last lifeboat. I underestimated what I was taking on here. I would have sorted it all before now, but there always seems to be so much to do. Fixing things—'

'Chasing sheep,' I interject.

'Crashing quad bikes,' says Kian playfully.

'God, I still feel bad about that.'

Moira must be reading my hungry mind, because she emerges from the pantry holding half a loaf of soda bread and a stick of butter wrapped in greaseproof paper. I tear off a chunk as Kian blinks at the application on my screen. I've got no idea if my suggestions will come to anything, but I've done more research in the past couple of days than I'd done in the past five years at *Snooper*. If we pull this off, it will have been worth it.

Things feel different now. I've stopped thinking about my days here in Kilroch within a London timeframe. Up until last week, I'd catch sight of the station clock in the kitchen, the minute hand ticking round to 8.15 a.m., and imagine myself stuffed beneath someone's armpit on the Tube. Now mornings start with the sunrise, often before. After I've refilled the water troughs, fed the chickens pigs, and checked the fences, I head inside to fill up my Thermos with coffee and can't believe it's only nine o'clock. The day is bookended by feeding times, with a brief midday reprieve, which I usually spend in my bedroom, trying to get warm beneath two snoods and oversized fleeces.

I don't feel like I'm wearing someone else's shoes anymore. I mean, I *am* literally wearing someone else's shoes. My trainers lasted six hours before I stepped into a bog and came out stinking like rancid eggs. It lingered so badly that Kian politely asked if he could put them on the compost heap.

Mentally, I'm not in London. I can recognise dissenting sheep by the markings round their nose. I worry when Babs hasn't laid an egg. I know how to use a pitchfork (you have to wiggle and stab at the same time. Making a 'harumph' noise helps). Last week I saw pink clouds reflected on the bay in a pastel mirror image of the sky and it was so fucking beautiful that I wanted to ask Mum if she remembers a similar landscape, the same view. I want to swap stories with her, but I can't. Not yet. I haven't got control over much, but I can decide when to press the detonator. At least that way, I can minimise who gets hit in the blast.

Chapter 27

When my alarm goes off the next morning, I reach for my woolly hat, sit up, and scrabble for my laptop under the bed. The deadline for my next diary submission has crept up far too quickly and this one needs careful thought. I've had to use some creative licence to retrospectively explain how I found Moira. If I pretend that I've only just met her, there's a good chance I'll buy myself some time and be able to stay for longer. If not, Duncan will insist I cut my losses and head back down south.

> *Date: Wednesday 30th October*
> *Location: In a Jeep, waiting for a herd of cows to cross the road. They are slow. Very slow.*
> *Cups of tea: Five hot, three cold*
> *Sleep: 4 hours and 16 minutes*
>
> *By the time you've read this, my undercover mission will almost be over. After cross-analysing every female I've encountered against my mental Rolodex of potential sisters, I've finally found her. She's the ruddy-cheeked,*

fast-talking, pig-wrangling version of me, and I couldn't be happier about it.

So, how did growing up at opposite ends of the country make a difference to the adults we are now? Well, we both seem to catch sunburn through thick cloud, so it's a comfort to know that we can split the cost of factor fifty if we ever go on holiday together. Aside from that? It's something I was sceptical about before, but it's there in each shared laugh, look, and lunge for the last Tunnock's Tea Cake. A Bond. I feel like it's been tucked deep down, waiting to come out of hibernation at the right time.

Speaking of which, I'm sure you're dying to know how she reacted to the news. Spoiler alert: she hasn't ... yet. After this long apart, I can't risk getting interrupted by reports of Miranda the Sheep attempting to parkour by the cliffside again. A reunion requires a celebration, so you'll have to wait for that. There's no party in Kilroch without a ceilidh to accompany it, so if I can drag Moira away from the thigh-slapping, skirt-spinning chaos for long enough, all will be revealed.

***

'I think my fingers are sweating,' I say, bent double over my knees.

'My ears *definitely* are. Is that possible?' says Moira, blinking. 'I feel like I've opened my eyes underwater, it's so salty.'

'Well done, ladies! Same time next week! Alana, you're

on biscuit duty. No ginger nuts or I'll come out in hives,' says Teresa, unplugging her CD player from the wall. The pulsing tones of Enya's 'Orinoco Flow' are abruptly clipped short, as static gives way to the chatter that drifts across the room like dandelion fluff. I look out of the windows for maybe the fiftieth time since the aerobics session started, but I can barely see the tombstones, masked as they are by thick condensation and rusty ferns.

'If he comes from that direction, I'd be a bit concerned,' says Moira, nodding at the gravestones.

'Shh!' I hiss, fumbling with the window latch to disguise my very obvious surveillance of the church grounds. I push it open and cold air slips inside, cooling my damp skin so quickly I start to shiver.

'He's a priest, so I don't know what the rules are about how public we're allowed to be.'

'You sound *five hundred years old*,' says Moira, jostling me with her hip. 'He's not a priest, anyway. Not in the way you're thinking.'

'Priests aren't allowed to get married. Didn't Reverend Dingwall live alone?'

'Yeah, but not through lack of trying. Everyone said that church attendance had gone down because our generation have "sold our souls to smart phones", but I blame his gingivitis. You wouldn't want to stand within three feet, let alone take Communion off of him.'

'Let me get this straight. Ross – The Rev – he's allowed to ...'

'Have sex?' says Moira, mouthing the word in a

whisper. 'Yep. Pretty sure he is. You'd probably have to get married first. You could do it here! We could train one of the sheep to walk the rings up the aisle, how cute would that be?'

I breathe out slowly and shake my head. Moira grins at me, dimples deep set in her cheeks.

'Fly me to the moon, Jack!' she says, yanking my wrist to spin me round in a circle. We burst into laughter and I feel like a kid again, giggling in the back of a school assembly. Moira stops and I spin to one side, stumbling on the edge of my borrowed plimsoles.

'Ava. Ava!' says Moira.

'Gah! I should have bashed these against the wall outside, I've left a little Hansel and Gretel trail of muck across the floor,' I say, inspecting the underside of my shoe.

'Ava ... I'll see you outside, yeah?' she says, her eyes insistent.

'OK, but do you know where I can find a dustpan or something—'

'Hi,' says Ross, a few feet away. His hair is fluffy, like he's towel dried it too hard, and for some reason, seeing him like this – with a black shirt and a little white dog collar – makes me feel on edge in a way that I didn't before. This time, I have no wine or whisky in my system. Useful for balance, but not nerves.

'Hi yourself,' I say, lowering my foot. Moira zips her coat up and leaves so fast I'm surprised she's not strained her Achilles.

'I wouldn't bother with that. There's going to be about

ten wee ones in here for messy play and I can vouch that it'll be carnage.'

'Right. We should get out of the way, then,' I say, as parents start to drift in, their toddlers stumbling from one side of the room to the other like drunk uncles at a BBQ.

'Egg boxes. I need to give you some back,' says Ross, pointing at me.

'Yep, sure.'

'There are quite a few.'

'I should come with you. To help.'

'Yes! Good idea.'

Ross leads me round the side of the building, where flagstones lead to an overgrown cottage garden, the skeletons of herb plants brown and withered beneath the kitchen window. I follow him as he heads towards the back door, my pulse thumping like I'm about to raid a jewellery shop. I tug my T-shirt down, hoping that it covers the waistband of my leggings. They've somehow cinched tighter in the past hour, giving me the look of an overstuffed sausage.

Inside the kitchen, evidence of Ross's morning is cast around the room. On the counter, an Italian coffee pot and half eaten multi-pack of Kit Kats sit beside an open Bible stickered with coloured tabs. The dining table is bare except for a pair of scissors and a half-mangled milk carton.

'Craft project?' I ask.

Ross blinks and opens one eye as though he's been caught out.

'Shit. Ah, this is embarrassing. I couldn't find my dog collar so I had to improvise.'

I stand on my tiptoes. It's only up close that I can see the textured plastic slipped into his shirt, only part opaque.

'You've not done a bad job here.'

'Cheers,' he says. I rock back onto my heels but he tilts towards me, wavering.

'I'm very sweaty,' I say.

'You're not.'

'I am.'

'OK, you are. Can I kiss you anyway?'

I answer by accidentally standing on his foot, but it gives me some extra height to grapple my way upwards and he's too polite to complain. His hand presses on the small of my back and that's when my lips land on his, heavier than planned. He softens, I pause, our bodies so close that I can feel the buttons on his shirt along my stomach. We stumble sideways, my hip bumping against the pantry shelf. A bag of flour plops to the floor and splits, a white molehill on the flagstones.

'Oops.'

'What?' says Ross, his lips full, eyes searching my face.

'Your dog collar has popped out.'

He looks down and laughs, but when he meets my eyes again the intensity is gone, like we've shifted into the wrong gear.

Ross steps away and taps my arm like I'm a horse he's pleased with, frowning at the flour dust settling on the tiles as he buttons his dog collar back into his shirt. I pull my T-shirt straight and swallow.

***

'What took you so long?' says Moira, following me down the driveway.

'I was fetching egg boxes from Ross.'

'What egg boxes? Did you leave them inside, or—' Moira grabs my elbow and squints, interrogating my face in a way that reminds me of Jacqui.

'OH MY GOD,' she exclaims.

'Shhhhh!'

'I will not! You kissed, didn't you? What was it like? Oh! Oh! Was it *heavenly*?'

'Ha, no. Yes. I don't know!'

'Oh, come on.'

I kick through dry leaves that have gathered in a drift along the wall, the sound crunchy underfoot like Bonfire Night sparklers.

'He does *not* kiss like a priest,' I say.

'That's because he's a minister. A young, fit, highly desirable minister.'

'Hmm. I don't know. He was acting weird afterwards.'

'Oh yeah?' says Moira, misinterpreting me.

'Not sexy weird. Like he regretted it.'

'I'm going to throw one of your lines back at you now. Don't overthink it. He's got his own issues to deal with, just like everyone else.'

'Yeah,' I say, pulling my scarf tight. 'That's about right.'

'What do you think about this?' she asks, pulling her phone out. 'I've been writing and rewriting this text message to Kian, but I don't know if it sounds right.'

'Give it here,' I say, taking the phone off her. It takes three thumb scrolls to reach the end, which is concerning to say the least. 'You know this is a text and not a letter, right?'

'Is it a bit long?'

'Yeah, I'd say so. One more thing. Do you know what these emojis mean?' I say, flicking to the bottom of the text.

'I'm not sure I get you,' she says, her brow furrowed in confusion. 'Mum made a peach pie and I said I'd drop some round, so I added them in.'

'He might get the wrong idea if he reads. "Just wait until you eat this" followed by a string of peach emojis and water droplets.'

'But ... they're juicy.'

'Oh, your innocent mind,' I say, deleting them for her and handing the phone back. 'Keep it simple. "Hey, would be cool to hang out soon", you know?'

'Fine. But you'll have to press the send button because I don't have the nerve.'

I'm about to open my mouth when my phone vibrates in my pocket, making me jump. I wiggle it free and squint at the number as Moira crosses the road to greet a woman walking a wiry dachshund. I answer it, my stomach twisting at the name.

'Hi, Max,' I say, trying to sound more upbeat that I feel.

'Ava! How's the family?' he says, badly disguising laughter by clearing his throat.

'Did you call just to wind me up?'

'What happened, banter buddy? Have your turned feral up there? Olz! Put me down for a kombucha. No, cherry plum, please, mate,' he says, turned away from the mouthpiece. 'Sorry, rushed off my feet, seems like we're both riding off that ancestry video, eh? I did some more digging and it turns out I *am* related to the Plantagenets, so I'm basically royalty. Not a surprise, eh?'

'Is there something you needed to tell me? Because I've got to get on.'

'Yeah, sorry. Hang on, let me go somewhere quiet.'

Blood throbs in my temples. I hear the sound of chatter, clacking keyboards, and the rustling of Max's shirt as he moves through the office. I hold the phone tight against my ear, paranoid that Max's voice will leak out into the street.

'You still there?' I ask. I hear the clunk of a door.

'Yeah. I'm in the plant room. Brings back nice memories. Ones involving Saskia, actually. Do you remember her, she had massive—'

'Max! Please.'

'Yep, sorry. I just wondered if I could read you back one of your diary entries?'

I close my eyes and rub my brow. 'I know what it says, I wrote it. Look, it's not my best, but I had to send something whilst—'

Max ignores me and launches into a breezy reading voice. '"The Hilltop Sasquatch of Kilroch greets me with a glowering eye and thick hands, all the better to push birch saplings out of the way"', he says, over-enunciating in a slow and painful rendition of words that I don't recognise. 'And this bit. "Between a constant series of favours and a collective IQ that would puzzle evolutionary historians, it's a wonder the village functions at all. It wouldn't surprise

279

me to find out that the ale is cheap because they put the decimal in the wrong place.'

'Hang on, Max. Wait. I didn't write that.'

'You did, according to the byline.'

'Duncan said my first few diaries were too dry. I changed them a bit, to be funny, but I *definitely* didn't go that far. I know people up here. I wouldn't write that, it's fucking rude.'

'What about Jenny the Wink?' interjects Max. 'Does she *really* wink every three seconds?'

'No! Well, yes. But that's not why I included her. It was meant to be observational. She's got a twitch,' I gabble. I fumble in my tote bag and plug some earphones in, allowing me to jab my web browser open. I click through to my diary series on *Snooper*, but I only manage to skim-read the first entry before my signal drops and the web page times out. The mocking, mean-spirited passages that have been published under my name aren't anything like the work I sent in.

'Fucking hell. Someone's edited them,' I say, my voice small.

'Y'think? It's not a light touch. Pummelled to shit like an overworked bread dough is how I'd put it. I knew it couldn't have been you, unless you've had a personality transplant since I last saw you.'

A cold, slick feeling of guilt spreads in my chest and pools in my stomach like crushed ice.

'Do you know who did it?'

'Yeah, therein lies the rub. It was Duncan.'

'What?!'

'The Big D. Dunc-zilla.'

'Yes, I know who you're referring to. You don't need to say his name 500 different ways for me to understand how fucking disastrous this is,' I say, slowly thumping my head with my fist.

'Is it terrible if I say congratulations?' asks Max. 'Your diaries are the most read section on the website.'

'Yes – it absolutely fucking would be.'

Hearing Max's voice amidst the background titter of office gossip and snatched laughter throws my situation into stark contrast. What am I doing? I didn't think to read back my diaries after they were published. Other things took precedence, like helping Kian out with the farm, the grant application, and Moira. My sister. As soon as I found her, I knew I couldn't chuck her in as 'content' without telling her why I was here, but I never found the right time and now the window of opportunity is so small, I'd have to get on my hands and knees with a magnifying glass to find it. Thinking back to my first entry, I cringe at how supercilious I sound, let alone after Duncan mashed them up with his ham fists.

John the mechanic-cum-taxi-driver-cum-train-guard pulls round the corner in his pick-up, a wing mirror narrowly skimming the Jeep as he passes. Although he looks older, he's about Max's age, with a little boy strapped into a booster seat behind him. He beeps in acknowledgment and I nod back, blinking angry tears away.

'This is awful. What am I going to do?' I say, my voice wobbling.

'Maybe look on the bright side? Duncan isn't giving anyone else this level of attention, so it could be a good sign for you, career-wise. I'll be honest – if I were your sister, I wouldn't be buzzing about my internet debut – how did you introduce her? "Riding a pig like she was on a bucking bronco?" What's her name again?'

'Moira,' I say, quietly.

'You could have given her a pseudonym ...'

'Please don't tell Duncan that I haven't told Moira who I am.'

'I won't, but look – if it were me – I'd keep my head down, film a fake reunion, and get the fuck out. This could be great for your career. We had a tabloid call up yesterday asking if they could buy your content for an op-ed feature. We said no, obviously.'

'Thanks?'

'Hey, no problem. Your reunion video is due this weekend, right? Do the sister reveal then. Rip the plaster off, and all that.'

'No way. I know that's what Duncan asked for, but I emailed him back and told him I couldn't rush this.'

'Well, I know what I'd do.'

'That's because you have no conscience.'

'It's useful at times. Hey, I've got to go. Keep in touch, yeah?'

'Wait! Can you talk to Duncan? Get him to take the diaries down?'

'Sorry, that's a no-can-do. I've moved to a different department. I cover sports, technically speaking. I've got no sway. Talk to Duncan when you're back. I know I can't force you to do anything, but you know it'll make the narrative stronger if you're able to get Moira's side of the story.'

'Yeah, well, it's going to be a lot harder now that I've apparently authored an entire series depicting her hometown as a backwards dump, isn't it?'

'It's not a problem I'm envious of, mate. Right, Olz is back. I've got a date with a cup of fermented green tea that's supposed to purify my bowel or some other bollocks. Look after yourself, all right?'

Chapter 28

I wake up to the sound of someone trying to be very quiet, which I gather from the clattering sound of a spoon hitting tiles and the swift 'Fuck!' that accompanies it. I pick up my phone, which I keep switched on, even though its use has diminished to that of a clock. Six-forty-five. Practically a lie-in.

I yank the curtains back and sit up to lean against the window sill as the radiator clunks into life, a dull warmth against my side.

The sleep I had last night was riddled with dreams so weird it's like I'd chowed down on half a block of cheese before I went to bed. In one, I'd gone to find Ross, except he looked incredibly like Jesus and couldn't stop to talk because of how busy he was herding sheep out of the church. Every time it looked empty, more popped up, multiplying like amoebas, until I could barely breathe from how closely their woollen faces pressed up against me, their eyes glassy and wet.

I know dream interpretation is inherently bollocks, but this has to have something to do with how rattled I've

285

been since Max's phone call. My cautious plan to find a good moment for The Big Chat with Moira has morphed into a monkey on my back that I can't shake off. Whilst there are secrets between us, my mind hums with anxious thoughts that bounce around my skull like ping-pong balls, keeping me awake at night. I've replaced herbal sleeping tablets with a few pages of the Kilroch village newsletter, but even that isn't enough to hush my brain before bed.

I shed the duvet and pull on my indoor fleece, followed by my outdoor fleece (my new normal), and head downstairs. A chair scrapes in the kitchen. I swear Kian has the same sleep pattern as world leaders who claim they only need four hours of sleep a night and then wonder why they look haggard by forty. As I walk in, he's stuffing papers into the front pocket of a laptop case, a scattering of plastic sleeves on the table. I refill the kettle, still warm to the touch, and place it back on the stove.

'You're in a suit!' I say as he straightens up.

'What? Yeah. Sorry, morning,' he says, his brow an angry furrow. He scratches his neck and shifts papers on the table, glancing behind me to look at the clock.

'Do you need any help?'

'No. Yes. I can't find something. I wrote stuff on an envelope. Sums. I need to type them up for the bank before I go.'

I turn away to hide my face and take a mug down from the shelf. I can't trust my track record for maintaining lies, because I can say with ninety-eight per cent accuracy that I chucked it in the recycling bin when I first started out on Mission Mega File.

'Do you need it today?' I ask in my best attempt at a neutral voice.

'Yes.'

'*Definitely*, definitely?'

'Pretty much, yeah. My meeting is in Inverness and I was planning on finishing up an Excel on the train. That envelope had the profit and loss margins from the last quarter, so ... I'd say it's crucial, yeah.' Oh dear. He looks very stressed, like he's either going to cry or punch something, possibly at the same time. 'I'm going to miss the train now, so as well as looking incompetent, I'm also going come across like I don't give a shit about the farm getting repossessed.'

We both have lessons to learn here. I shouldn't throw things away without saying something first, and Kian should learn that envelopes and cereal boxes are inappropriate items on which to record your business finances.

'Let me drive you.' Kian takes a ragged breath, closes his eyes, and paces the length of the hallway. 'Hey, try and relax,' I say, although I'm hardly one to be making such unreasonable demands. 'You can't be stressed before 7 a.m. It's a universal rule. Let me take you down to the station. That way you'll look forgivably incompetent, but sharp, like this is one of many meetings you have planned so they better listen up because you and that suit have got places to be.'

I follow Kian as he dips and darts around the room, waiting for a reaction that doesn't come.

'So ... shall I get the keys? Or I can piss off if you'd rather be alone? I won't take offence,' I say.

'Yeah, sorry. A lift would be great.'

'Right, just let me put some proper trousers on and we'll be out the door.'

I take the stairs two at a time, and shove jeans on over the top of my fleecy pyjama bottoms that have grown a little baggy. Who'd have thought black pudding sandwiches were synonymous with weight loss? Just before I head back down, I grab my laptop and shove it into my rucksack, tugging at the zips. After ignoring my calls last night, I need to increase my firepower against Duncan without annoying him so much that he fires me. With Kian in Inverness and Moira at college, I can spend an uninterrupted morning hitting redial. I don't want to reach my last resort: holding out until I'm back in London to fix things from there.

Kian grabs the keys from the nail in the porch and opens the door to an unusually still day. I dart past him, he locks up and chucks the keys at me (amazingly, I catch them), and I get in, swinging my rucksack behind the front seat. I try my best to avoid the potholes at speed, which results in Kian nearly clashing his teeth on my forehead as the Jeep bounces down the lane. The car radio comes in and out of tune with club songs that it's far too early for. I switch it off, but if anything the silence is worse.

We drive alongside the harbour, the colour of the sea merging with the sky through layers of fog. I snatch glances at Kian. He wipes condensation off the window with two fingers and looks out across the firth, his hands balled in his lap, shoulders round. He looks younger, like a teenager on the way to parents' evening who knows his reports are going to be poor at best, damning at worst.

'Hey, you should tell the bank about the grant application. It's got to earn you some brownie points, right?'

'I doubt it. I may as well tell them I'm expecting to win the lottery.'

Ah, I see. We're rolling in pessimism this morning.

'Shall I buy a lottery ticket on the way back? Just to cover our bases.'

Kian catches my eye but doesn't laugh. Shit. Things must be pretty serious.

I swallow, clacking my nails on the steering wheel. 'I saw a sign for a dolphin reserve just back there. What's all that about then?' My heart races. It's a blessing I never went into criminal journalism. I can't even ask about the animals that eight-year-old girls have as bedroom posters without feeling light-headed.

Kian breathes in with barely suppressed impatience.

'That's a divisive one,' he says, scratching the razor burn on his neck. 'Kilroch has a bunch of tourists now who bloody love the dolphins, but they're the reason a bunch of mad bints went bananas in the Nineties over the oil rigs. Granddad used to go on about it all the time. The rigs got decommissioned and my dad lost his income. He wasn't so quick to blame the booze, which was arguably worse.'

I nod, the news clipping of Mum flashing across my mind. I can see why she might have achieved a poor reputation and that's without including the illegitimate baby issue.

We finish the journey in silence, the engine clunking like there's something loose inside it.

'I'll see you later then,' says Kian, opening the door before I've slowed the car down properly. I pull the handbrake. We jolt to a stop. He squats, popping his head back inside as an afterthought. 'Whatever happens, thanks for all your help.'

'No worries. Hey, is everything OK?'

'I'll talk to you about it later,' he says, the line in his brow set deeper still. He slams the door. I flex my fingers around the steering wheel, gripping it until my knuckles turn white. Something has rattled him. Has he seen through my increasingly flimsy persona? Does he notice how Moira and I both laugh with a woodpecker lilt? How we tuck our chins in when we're worried?

Back in the village, I trundle up the high street between the faint glow of amber light leaking through curtains, and pull up beside a retired fishing boat, its hull brimming with coarse, salt-burned heather. I need to fish for wi-fi. Let's hope The Wailing Banshee is within range ... I wriggle my laptop free and scan for a signal. Result! I clunk the engine off. It's excruciatingly quiet, aside from the odd seagull screeching overhead.

Forty-seven emails ping through alongside three calendar invites. Going by the incremental use of capital letters and exclamation marks in the messages from Duncan, I see that his tone is increasingly irate. I open his most recent email alongside some older missives, reading them with newfound insight now that I can map Duncan's thoughts over time.

The Sister Surprise

Friday 18th October
Hi Ava,

Thanks for your last submission. Just a few minor tweaks here and there, but I didn't think it was worth sending back for you to check.

Liking the tone, but still no sign of the Mysterious Moira. Any reason why? That line – 'No one seems to live here and the ones that do are weird' – Love it!

Look, I'm happy, we're happy, the readers are happy, but we need a sense that you're moving forward, OK?
Thanks, D.

Sunday 27th October
Ava,

No idea if these are reaching you. We need an update on the sister search and you're not replying to my messages. I thought you were exaggerating about being in the arse end of nowhere, but evidently, I stand corrected. Seeing as you're there on behalf of the website, I feel somewhat responsible for your welfare. FYI: no reunion video by Sunday = train back to London on Monday.

Let us know that you're OK and haven't been strung up by the locals.
Thanks, D

Wednesday 30th October
Ava – got your last diary entry but I've known episodes of Midsomer Murders to move with more pace than this.

Reunion video. Sunday. Send me confirmation you're prepped for it, all right?

Thanks, D

Thursday 31st October
RIGHT. *SEEING AS I'VE NEVER KNOWN YOU TO MISS A DEADLINE, YOU'VE EITHER SLIPPED THROUGH A STONE CIRCLE AND RUN OFF WITH A HULKING HIGHLANDER OR YOU'RE ACTUALLY, LITERALLY DECEASED. PLEASE – FOR THE SAKE OF A POTENTIALLY RUINOUS LITIGATION CLAIM AGAINST THE WEBSITE YOU STILL TECHNICALLY WORK FOR – LET US KNOW THAT YOU'RE STILL BREATHING (and send us your big reunion video – due on Sunday, as discussed).*

Thanks, D

I dash off a reply that once again outlines how furious I am about his 'light touch' edits and follow it up with a statement about ethical editorial practices. I read it back and sigh. I'm still one step above a nobody back in the office. If Duncan's my boss, who's he accountable to? Coming from the man who once commissioned a piece called 'The Homeless Doppelgangers of Hollywood Stars', I'm not holding out much hope for a comeuppance through conventional means.

The last email is far less concerned with my mortality. Disturbingly, it's come from Ginger's address: redhotgingermilf@gmail.com. Jesus.

The Sister Surprise

Tuesday 29th October
Ava!

I snipped the top of my finger off trimming back the buddleia so Ginger is typing this for me. Nothing to worry about. They stuck it back on at the surgery, but it does sting, especially when I zested a lemon for some Ottolenghi pancakes that weren't worth the effort.

Is there something wrong with your phone??? I sent you a picture of Sue's new puppy on Saturday but it kept bouncing back. Do you need a new SIM card because you're in a different country? If you roam there are charges, but I didn't think you were leaving Edinburgh?

Pickles's diet is going badly. I thought he was looking a little saggy, so I gave him ham for dinner and the vet got very angry. Something to do with the salt. Anyway, he's now doubly overweight AND dehydrated, like a chubby raisin, so I've had to freeze chicken livers in an ice cube tray as a way to force hydration.

Love, Mum

—Hello, sweets! This is Ginger! I wanted to tell you I have a niece in Edinburgh – Lauren – who works in beauty. If you want your eyebrows microbladed, she can get you fifty per cent off. (Your mum has made it explicit that she does NOT want you to do this under any circumstance, but the offer is there!).

Ginger
XOXO

It's times like this that I'm really glad Mum is incompetent with quite literally any form of technology. She thought I was copywriting for the surveillance industry when I first told her I was working at a website called *Snooper*, which stuck for a whole year because it took that long for her to ask me what I did at work each day. As such, the likelihood that she'll find out I'm rubbing shoulders with the family she scorned whilst freedom fighting is slim.

I open Instagram on my phone and search the Edinburgh geo-tag for an innocuous picture of a flagstoned street gleaming with rain – something I can legitimately claim I snapped on a lunch break from my fictional sabbatical. I screenshot it, crop the edges, and send it over to Mum with the caption 'Wish you were here!' I'd like to think that she'd worry if I left it any longer without replying.

Once I know it's delivered, I flick through the gallery on my phone, not quite ready to drive back to the farm. I linger on a picture of Pickles on my window sill, his legs tucked beneath his pendulous belly. A dull ache twists between my ribs as my thoughts jump to various images of home: Pickles snoring on the back doorstep in the brief winter sunshine; the smell of sweet potato simmering in the slow cooker; and Mum in her faux fur coat, a plastic tub of craft materials balanced on her hip. I bite my lip and swallow. I'm not used to this feeling. In fact, the last time I was this homesick, I was watching a live feed of the road I'm now sitting on, the same seagulls plaguing the sky, and the same ache in my stomach.

Chapter 29

The noise of a landline ringing cuts through the hyper-ventilating honks of the farm's two geese, Penelope and Princess Bianca. Christened by Kian's grandfather, they make the perfect guard dogs because of their keen desire to attack all other creatures. I wave my arms and they lift their wings in retaliation, hissing as I open the back door to retreat inside. I snatch at my laces to undo my mucky boots, then stride across the kitchen in slippery socks to catch the phone on the last ring.

'Braehead Farm. Ava speaking.'

'Hi, is Kian Brody there at all?'

'No, he's out until –' I lean backwards to read the kitchen clock '– about four or five. He should be back for the evening rounds on the farm.'

'Ah, we were hoping to catch him. Do you work on the farm?'

'Yeah, I'm a volunteer. For the time being.'

'A volunteer? He must have forgotten to put that on the form. That's great! It's nice to hear that farms are taking on outreach work already. It's better than starting from scratch.

Sorry, I'm getting ahead myself. I've just come off paternity leave and I'm on my third coffee today. I've got a four-week-old baby at home who sleeps in forty-minute blocks. Where was I? Outreach! Yes. I'm from the school of Geosciences at The University of Edinburgh. We had a grant application come through for a partnership project, but unfortunately Kian's application reached us just after the deadline.'

I stand up and start paying attention, looking around for a pen and something to scribble on. Dammit. I could do with that mess on the kitchen table now.

'That's such a shame. He'll be gutted. He's really keen on eco-agricultural science stuff. Like, *really* keen. He won't buy proper washing-up liquid because it does something dodgy to the waste water. There's a list of approved products on the back of the cupboard door that we buy from instead.'

'Well, I *might* have some good news for you. The McCulloch farm over in Moray pulled out of the programme. We did a survey and found some undeclared produce in a polytunnel behind the main farm. I can't say what it is for legal reasons, but it's not supermarket produce if you catch my drift.'

'I'm with you. As far as I know, Kian toes the line of the law. He's more into drones and truffle hunting.'

'That's great! We'd like to send a couple of representatives up at the weekend to do a survey, talk logistics, that sort of thing. If it suits, will you ask him to let us know in the next couple of hours? I'm going through our back-up list, so if he's changed his mind, I'll move on to the next application.'

I say goodbye, hang up, and break into jazz hands whilst

slipping across the kitchen doing the running man, my socks fluffy with dust by the time I've completed my third circuit. The fact that the university want to progress Kian's funding application kicks thoughts of The Big Chat to the side, if only for a little while.

An hour later, I spot John bouncing up the farm track, his hand-painted taxi sign rattling against the grille of his car, I open the front door in anticipation and grin as Kian plods across the yard.

He looks awful, like he's just attended his own funeral. His shirt is half tucked in, the collar bent beneath his chin, his shoulders sloped like he's carrying a bucket of water in each hand for the pigs.

'Come down The Banshee tonight, Kian,' calls John, who hovers by the gate, his window rolled down. Kian nods and raises a hand. When John drives off, Kian rubs his forehead and frowns at me.

'What's up?' he mutters, looking between me and the floor, where I hop from one foot to the other.

'The floor is really cold.'

'You're letting all the heat out of the house.'

'Come in then. I've got some news.'

'No offence, but if it's another theory about the cockerel being gay, I'm not in the mood for it.'

'It's not. But I stand by that theory. Quick, come on,' I say, chivvying him through to the kitchen. He pulls out the end chair, slumps into it, and rubs his temples.

'Someone called whilst you were out,' I say. Kian says nothing. After a moment, he swallows hard.

'The bank are refusing to extend the loan repayments,' says Kian. He looks at me, his eyes bloodshot with fatigue. 'They want full payment by the end of the year or they'll repossess.'

I rearrange my expression, taken aback.

'Why?'

'They said the business plan I wrote was "too speculative at this stage to confidently support with financial backing". The lad who held the meeting couldn't have been older than eighteen. He had a script next to him, so my responses were fucking pointless, because they didn't fit with what was on his shitty piece of paper. They'd made the decision before I got there. Two hundred years we've had this land and it stops with a wee bawbag in a short-sleeved shirt on work experience. It wasn't a meeting at all, it was a total fucking farce.'

'That sounds really unfair,' I say, wanting to sound sincere but bursting to tell him about the university.

'If Granddad had been honest about our cash situation, I would have moved back earlier to help turn it around.'

'He might not have wanted you to worry. Even before he got kicked in the head, didn't you say he was a bit ... umm ...'

'Senile?'

'Mmm.'

'He tried poaching an egg in the kettle, so I'd say he was the wrong side of eccentric, yeah.'

I tap the kitchen counter impatiently. 'You got a phone call whilst you were out. I picked it up just in case it was important.'

'If it was PPI, tell them that yes – I have had an accident that wasn't my fault – taking on this fucking farm.'

'It was the University of Edinburgh. They wanted to talk about the partnership grant we put together.'

'Great. Another one to add onto the list of rejections.'

'They want to come and do a survey this weekend to assess our application.' I lean forward in my chair to pull out the receipt I scribbled on with a blunt pencil. 'They used these words, but I can't remember what order they were in. You might be able to make sense of it. "Saturation", "hummocks", "accommodation", and "quick turnaround". I only understand the last one, but I looked up "hummocks" on Urban Dictionary and it's quite perverted, so I hope for your sake it doesn't involve pick-up trucks and a gimp mask. They want to get things going because their initial partner dropped out. If all goes well, you could have that grant money in the next couple of months.'

Kian doesn't say anything but lifts his head slowly like he's heard an unfamiliar noise. He pushes back his chair and reaches for a box file on the shelf, flips it open and flicks through a section marked with blue tabs. He runs a finger down the page, his eyes darting across each line.

'How much was the grant for?' he asks.

'£92,000 over six months, with another £15,000 if you can provide accommodation facilities for students who need to stay for research.'

Kian bends over the table and scribbles down a few figures as though he's adding paint to a canvas, stepping back to analyse the result from a distance.

He looks up and points at me with the end of his pencil. 'We might – and it's a huge might – be able to pull this off.'

'Might?'

'It's going to be tight. This barely covers basic running costs.'

'But it might buy you some time.'

Kian nods, biting his lip.

'Better start training those pigs to truffle hunt if you wanna top up the ol' income,' I say, grinning.

'Come here.' Kian walks around the table and pulls me into a hug. A few seconds later, he stands back, his once drained cheeks flushed with their usual pink. 'Thanks.'

I dither on the spot and hold the back of a chair, relieved that a black cloud has drifted out of the room.

'I was acting like a prick this morning,' says Kian.

'I wouldn't say you were being prickish, just a tiny bit ... sullen.'

'I'll take that. It wasn't you; it was all of this,' he says, motioning to the file (excellently arranged, if I do say so myself). 'John told me at the station that one of the McCulloch lads is planning on asking Moira out, which really rattled me and all. Don't know why. I've had the same problems whirring on in the background for so long that it all turned to white noise. I didn't think anyone else had a perspective worth listening to. Granddad was fucking terrible with money, but he knew how favours worked round here and managed to get by. Jacqui, too. I always keep a tally in my head of what I need to do for her in return, to pay her back, but she disnae want anything.'

As much as I don't like her, I can't dispute how much Jacqui takes on to lighten the load for others.

'She's a good egg, isn't she?'

'Aye. You're not so bad yourself. I wouldn't have applied for this grant if it weren't for you. I definitely wouldn't have been this organised,' he says.

'Acknowledgement accepted. Just so you know, I would have charged at least ninety quid for a service like this down in London,' I say, my chin aloft in mock pride.

'Well, it's a good job you've eaten more than ninety quid's worth of Tunnock's Tea Cakes since you've been here. Don't think I haven't noticed.'

I laugh and eye the pantry door, where I left a half-eaten box this morning, the opening pressed against the wall to disguise my activity.

'You better phone the university back. They're going to ask someone else if you're not keen,' I say.

'I know how to hook them in. I've been teaching one of the pigs to sit on command. That'll win them over. I'll have to lock Babs up, mind. She doesn't like strangers.'

'Don't I know it.'

'When do they want to come and do the survey?'

'The day after tomorrow.'

'Post ceilidh? That's a bastard. I'll still come but I'll have to take it easy. Moira wouldn't forgive me if I bailed. She's fanatical when it comes to reeling. It's sweet, she has this skirt that she *only* wears to ceilidhs. You haven't seen tartan 'til you've seen this thing.'

My stomach swoops. I pinch my hand under the table.

So far as I know, the articles with my name in the byline are still on the *Snooper* website.

'Hey, you'll love it. The band are great, and there's this fella James, right? He's ninety-one and is on his feet from beginning to end even though he's had two knee replacements. Moira's coming round in the morning to teach you the dances.'

'Is she?'

'Yeah. Best be prepared for it.'

'Aye.'

'"Aye"? You're turning Scottish.'

Chapter 30

'Honestly, it's not as complicated as you think,' says Moira, twisting the lid on a tub of chicken feed.

Kian leans against the coop and pushes the sleeves of his jumper up, squinting in the sunshine as it breaks through a cloud. A wave of sunlight crests the hill, stretching our shadows across the ground. I smile from my seat on an upturned bucket, hens crooning by my feet. Babs pecks at my laces and looks up at me with mean eyes when she realises they're not edible. Some chickens are so hard to please.

'How come you know all the dances already?' I ask.

'PE,' they say together. Kian grimaces, but Moira is soft with nostalgia. She bumps Kian with her hip.

'Who still holds the high school title for longest sword dance without falling over?' Moira raises a hand and jigs on the spot, jumping back and forth over a rake on the floor.

'Aye, and you won't let us forget it,' says Kian.

As I look at Moira, her body angled towards Kian, I see an opportunity to help out a little. I'm sure that Kian has a soft spot for Moira, but if he claims that he's got no time for a girlfriend 'until the farm's sorted', they'll both be dancing round each other until the fields learn to plough themselves.

'Hey, give us a demonstration, would you? Then I can turn up at the ceilidh without being identified as so cripplingly English that I can barely put one foot in front of the other without apologising to someone.'

'Ah, I don't know,' says Kian.

'Oh, come on. You're not a bad mover, Ki,' Moira tells him.

'There's no music.'

'I've got it, don't worry,' I say, slapping a dull beat onto the side of a bucket.

'A basic hold: left hand by your side, right hand crosses over my front, then I link in at the back,' says Moira. They face the same way, arms interlocked. Moira can't see him, but I notice the silly grin on Kian's face as he looks down at her, unblinking.

'What do we do now, hop forward four times?'

'I don't want to kick the chickens,' says Moira.

'They'll move,' says Kian. They skip forwards and back, scattering the seed we threw down for the hens moments before.

'Then you spin.' Moira pirouettes like a ballerina, her wax jacket flapping as she goes. 'Hook arms, and you're on your way with someone new.'

Kian grins whilst Moira bounces from one foot to the other.

'God, I love a ceilidh. I'm mad buzzing for it. It's been *way* too long.'

'How does the partnering work? Do you have to write people's names down? Book them out?' I say, excitement stretching up through my chest like a cat clawing a scratch pole.

'No, it's really casual. Chaotic-casual,' says Moira, zipping her coat up. 'But Kian always saves me the first waltz.' Moira smiles at Kian, who raises his eyebrows in admission. 'After that you end up swapping all the time, anyway.'

It's got to be tonight. If Moira's buoyed up about the ceilidh, I'll be able to tell her that we're sisters without it being awkwardly intense. I want it to be good news, the kind that deserves a celebration. What's better than a torrent of foot stamping and ale swigging? Doing it with your sister, for sure.

Once Moira knows, I might finally have the courage to talk to Mum about her time in Kilroch like we're actual adults. I won't have to decode Rory's bizarre postcards in secret anymore. My butchered *Snooper* diaries? That one I've yet to figure out. Baby steps, Ava, baby steps.

***

'Why can't you go in your trainers?' says Kian. I step back out of my room and throw a look down the corridor. Kian stops chewing his toast quite so aggressively. 'That wasn't the right thing to say, was it?'

I groan and look down at the crumpled clothes draped over my arm. 'If I wear any of these I'll look like bad origami.'

'As soon as your body gets warm it'll work out the creases,' says Kian, grinning through a mouthful of toast.

'I'm sure that's not a thing.'

'It's like ironing, but from the inside out.'

'As helpful as you are, this is why Moira should be here.'

'Weren't you guys going to do girly stuff before we left? Drink cocktails and gossip?'

'Yeah. Not got much time for it now. It's weird for her to turn up so late, isn't it?' I say, tapping the bannister. 'Have you had any texts from her?'

'Nope. I've not had a dot of signal all day.'

'No, me neither,' I say, holding my phone aloft. 'Do you think she's OK?'

'Oh, aye. Moira's fierce independent. That's no strange.'

'Hmm. Do you think we should check the animals are safe before heading off? Jacqui said we need to turn the sheep out onto the upper paddock before it gets bogged up.'

'I was planning on it, but there's no point doing it tonight. It means taking them onto the road and it's too dark for it,' says Kian, ducking down to look at the sky through a narrow window at the top of the stairs. I scrape a hand through my hair and frown.

'I'm going to check that the coop isn't leaking,' I say.

'It's fine. I put some tarp over it.'

'Babs won't forgive me if I let her nest get wet.'

'You've changed your tune.'

'She knows what she wants and she wants what she knows. That's quite admirable.'

Kian rips off another mouthful of toast and yawns, his

arms juddering. Inside the bedroom I've occupied for nearly a month, I empty my suitcase on the floor. It's stuffed with newly washed socks and half a tub of Nutella that I've been eating by the tablespoon each night before I go to sleep. I've got to have packed something that'll do for a night out in the church hall.

Rolled up beside a handful of loose tampons is a mustard-coloured jumpsuit, which, although inappropriate for the rollicking wind and rain outside, is the only thing I have that I can confidently say is free from straw and faeces. I lay my outfit on the bed and place a belt and earrings beside it in a flatpack version of myself. It'll have to do.

***

'Where do you think she is?' I ask, zipping up my raincoat. Outside, rain lashes the windows in gusts so violent it's like a caricature of terrible weather.

'I dunno. She might have gone straight there with Jacqui. Ha' you seen outside?' he says, pulling on his mud-streaked work boots. 'Would *you* want to walk over in this?'

I shake my head and check my phone again, if only out of habit. 'And you're sure the animals are fine? We don't need a sheep floating in the brook when they come to do the survey tomorrow.'

'Ava, dinna fash yersel'.'

'Hmm?'

'Sorry, English translation: stop worrying.'

Chapter 31

'Oh, aye! Is that Kian with a lass on his arm?' says a voice from the illuminated porch of the church hall.

'All right lads? Just helping Ava navigate the potholes. How you doing, Gary? Allan, good to see you.'

'I'm fine from here,' I lie, my heel sinking into a puddle rippling with droplets of rain.

'So, this is the reason you're not down The Banshee anymore?' says Gary or Allan. I've taken an instant dislike to them both, seeing as they're referring to me through objective pronouns despite the fact that I'm standing right in front of them.

'No, boys. Got a lot on at the farm. Ava's been volunteering.'

'Oh, aye? Not even paying you? You've got to save money somewhere, right, Kian? He buys all the runts destined for the sausage factory when we're down at the cattle market, so it figures,' says Gary, finally addressing me. Well, someone's already won the Biggest Bell-end of the Week Award.

Kian drags a hand through his hair and forces a smile.

'Any chance we can go inside? It's freezing out here,' I say.

'Oh, aye. After you.'

I nod to the two men and step over the threshold, where the metallic fizz of rain is replaced with the thwack of a drum and the chattering of voices greeting each other. The strip lighting that illuminated my corned-beef legs during aerobics has been replaced by fairy lights wound round the ceiling beams. Below, plastic tealights on each table flicker with an almost believable flame. A man at the back of the hall plucks violin strings and plays with amplifier dials, as other musicians pause every now and again to sip ale, stepping forward in turn to test their sound levels. Ross chats to an accordion player, his arms folded over the instrument like it's a protruding belly. I shuffle out of my coat and hang it on a peg as Ross snatches a glance at me. He rolls his sleeves up to the elbow, something I've noticed he does when nervous.

'Hey, thanks for that,' says Kian, nodding towards the porch.

'Oh, no worries. Thought you might need a good excuse to flee.'

'It's all banter, but it does get boring after a while. They've been dining out on the fact that I'm vegetarian since I came back to Kilroch.' He pauses, raising a hand to John, who has a small child balanced on each hip. 'Ah, best say hello. John never gets a night off. Shout if you see Moira, all right?'

Kian heads over to one of the tables set up around the edge of the hall, paper tablecloths scattered with cardboard coasters, bowls of crisps, and salty peanuts. Everything looks better with fairy lights and bunting. It's the cheapest way to disguise the peeling magnolia paint of community halls. Mum knows this fact well, which is why we have an entire cupboard full of them at home.

I step to the side as Allan and Gary push past, each with a keg balanced on their shoulder. There's a whoop of support from the men in the room, but it's only now that I notice how outnumbered they are by women. It's the most people I've seen in one place since I left London. Three red-headed boys run from one side of the hall to the other, dropping down to their knees to see who can slide the furthest across the parquet floor. Concerted as their efforts are, they're beaten by a small girl with a mass of curls that flops in front of her eyes as she skids across the floor in thick woollen tights. She comes to a halt near my feet with a sudden loss of momentum that forces her back onto her heels. I offer a hand to help her up, which she takes, glancing over her shoulder to grin smugly at the boys who have lined up at the back of the hall to try again, their elbows up by their armpits.

'I'm the best at this,' she says, pushing her hair off her face with a flat palm.

'You are. I bet you can get even further next time.'

The little girl nods vigorously and runs off, leaving me squatting on the floor.

'You all right down there?' says Ross.

I stand up and reach for his arm, which I use to pull him into a hug. He raises a hand behind my back to acknowledge some newcomers. Oh. We haven't done this in public. I shift my stance and pat him on the back.

'If I linger here for too long, will Eileen have words with me?' I whisper, on tiptoes. By the kitchen hatch, Eileen folds her arms and makes a comment to Jacqui, who tightens her apron strings and catches my eye. Hmm. If Jacqui is here, Moira must be.

'If Eileen asks you to try the sausage rolls, say no,' says Ross.

'Why? Did someone leave them next to a radiator?'

'She may have tucked a razor blade between the pastry layers. Take out the competition, you know?' he says, his eyes drifting down my body. Dear Lord, give me the power to get through an evening without gaining the reputation of a village harlot.

'Oh, have you seen Moira?'

'No, actually. I thought she was really keen for a ceilidh.'

'I'm telling her tonight,' I say, dropping my voice. 'As soon as she arrives.'

Ross breathes in slowly and squeezes my arm. 'Good luck. You'll be fine, just be honest. And patient. She'll have a ton of questions, I'm sure.'

The drummer taps out a staccato beat and there's a whoop from the edges of the room as the band kicks into a folk song. Amongst the noise of shuffling feet, there's a groan from a handful of middle-aged men who anchor themselves to their pints, draining their glass like there's someone drowning in it before being physically dragged away from the table.

'Need a partner?' says Ross.

I nod and follow him to the middle of the room, where

we join four others in a circle, all of whom look far more prepared than me.

'I haven't got a clue what I'm doing,' I say to the woman next to me.

'Ah, you'll be fine, lovie. Just don't stand on my feet, I'm fresh out of a bunion surgery.'

I nod, a little put off.

By a trestle table bowed under the weight of three kegs. Allan takes a shot glass out of his coat pocket and hands it to Kian. Still no Moira, or I'm sure she'd be at his shoulder, insisting that she could match him drink for drink.

Ross jumps up on the plywood stage to thank everyone for coming, leaving me to run over the steps in my head from this morning, but it's a blur of footprints against a backdrop of inky clouds.

The caller announces the opening dance and after a brief run-through of the steps, the band kick off and we're hopping in a circle, hands clasped, boobs bouncing (in my case, anyway). I didn't think to wear a sports bra, which was a gross oversight. Each time I jump up, they seem to be going down, resulting in a slingshot manoeuvre designed to cause maximum discomfort. Between looking at gaps in the crowd for Moira and changing direction every few seconds, I've chest-bumped with so many people I could pass as a frat boy.

As the fiddle playing becomes less frantic, I disentangle myself from the mass of interlocked limbs and clap the band, grinning despite my inability to follow the steps. I clutch Ross's shoulder, catching my breath as two women I recognise from aerobics head in our direction.

'Need a drink?' he says, eyeing them nervously.

'Definitely.'

We head to the kitchen hatch, where a plastic ice-cream tub acts as an honesty box for the makeshift bar. Two dozen glasses are upturned on a tea towel, a row of Iron Bru and boxed wine beside it. Everything is laid out with uniform precision. It's the most organised refreshments stand I've come across, and I've seen my fair share. The PTA mums would be wild with envy.

'A white wine spritzer and a Tennent's, please, Eileen.'

Eileen shifts from one foot to the other, her nostrils flared. She looks from me to Ross and glowers, her burgundy lipstick disappearing in the thin line of her pursed lips. I scratch my arm and turn to smile at Ross, but he's been sidetracked by John, who flicks peanuts in his mouth after each sentence. Inside the kitchen, Jacqui turns from the sink and peels off her Marigolds. She wears a deep green wrap dress and her signature scowl, which she aims in my direction.

'Hi, Jacqui. Is Moira about?'

'No.' She opens the fridge and pulls out trays of beige food, garnished with clumps of parsley like a vintage Delia Smith cookbook.

'Oh ... is she OK? She was supposed to come over earlier.'

'She hasn't been out of her room all afternoon. In short, I don't know if she's coming. She barely said three words to me before I left,' says Jacqui, using a fish slice to transfer the canapés onto a tray wrapped in tin foil.

Eileen drops a single ice cube in my glass. I pick it up

with trepidation, but after a sip it's clear that the ratio of wine to soda water is so disproportionate that a mosquito would struggle to get drunk if it fell inside. Ross leans over my shoulder, his wallet in hand.

'I'll get this,' he says.

'Honestly, let me.' I stuff a fiver into the tub. 'Cheers.'

We tap our glasses together and sip. It's lukewarm and has a vinegar aftertaste, but it'll do.

'All right?' Kian leans against the window sill, an empty glass in his hands. He has a loose stance, like his joints have been over-oiled.

'Yeah, not bad. Hey, have you heard from Moira? Jacqui said she's not coming,' I say.

'Eh? That's odd. She's never missed a ceilidh. She didn't speak to me for bloody ages because I couldn't come to the one she threw for her eighteenth birthday.'

My heart thumps and a prickly warmth creeps up the back of my neck.

'Do you think she's all right?'

Kian nods and tips beer foam into his mouth from his near-empty glass. He swallows a burp, his hand on his chest. 'If she's not here in fifteen, I'll call her landline from the phone box outside.'

'I'll be back in a second, guys,' says Ross, squeezing my hand before walking shoulder first through the crowd.

'You look really tired,' I say to Kian.

'Nah, I'm fine.'

'She's great, isn't she?'

'Who?'

'Moira.'

'She's one of the best. Always has been. Always happy,' he says, his lips twitching with a smile.

'You two work so well together. You're like Kilroch's power couple.' If she's not here, the least I can do is talk her up. 'Have you ever thought about giving it a proper go? With Moira?'

'Ah, that ship is long gone,' says Kian. 'We're family friends, you know? It would be weird. If I fucked it up, that would be that. You can't go back to what you were before, right?' Kian says something else, but I can't hear him over the band.

'What?'

'Do you want to join in?' he says, gesturing to the dance. It's a couples dance I don't recognise from our chicken coop rehearsals, but Kian assures me it's an easy one, so we slot onto the end of the row. As the music builds, the dance gets faster and faster until Kian and I are cheered down the length of the hall, spinning in tight circles until we reach the fire exit. I laugh and clap along, gasping for breath, but Kian hasn't fared so well. He bites his bottom lip, hands on knees, positively green.

'Do you need some air?' I ask.

Kian nods, his cheeks puffed up. I guide him out of the side door onto a pea-shingle path that lines the graveyard. Vomiting in public would be a real mood killer. I should know.

Kian paces like Big Bertha when she's trying to find a good spot by the slops trough. He puts his hands on his hips and exhales a measured breath.

'I've overdone it. It's the lads, they always rib me if I can't keep up shot for shot.' He puts a hand over his mouth, pausing on the spot. An owl hoots from above, but I can't remember if this is a good omen or a bad one. Instead of belching, he swallows and rubs his eyes with the palms of his hand. Thank you, my little owl friend.

'I'm good,' he slurs.

'You sure?' I ask, glancing back to the doors to see if it's necessary to enlist support. Kian nods, closes his eyes, and tips forward to prop himself up against the wall, his hand beside my head. He's well within my personal space, but just as I'm about to slip under his arm, I notice a trickle of blood on his forehead.

'You're bleeding,' I say.

'Nah,' he says dismissively.

'You are! What happened?' I say, reaching up. I push his head to one side, exposing a two-inch cut along his hairline.

'Scythe fell off the wall in the barn this afternoon. My fault.'

'Have you tried to stick yourself back together?' I say.

'Yeah. No time to go to the doctors,' he says, smiling stupidly. 'Superglue.'

'That's not meant for your head!'

He opens his eyes, but his gaze is unfocused and hazy. As I step away, Kian loses balance, falling in the same direction, which results in him headbutting my cheek.

'For fuck's sake! Ouch!'

'My tooth!' cries Kian, clutching his mouth.

'It landed on my cheek! Fucking hell!' I clutch my nose

and rub my face to divert the pain, my palm covered in balmy pink. Oh, blusher. You were good whilst you lasted.

'Have I walked into something?' says a voice from the direction of the graveyard. Kian squats by my feet and heaves by the drainpipe.

'Moira! You're here! Where's your tartan ceilidh skirt?'

Moira steps in front of an ornate tomb criss-crossed with ivy, dramatically lit from the disco lights thrown from the church hall windows. Her face is pale, eyes puffy and pink. I take my hand away from my cheek and take a step towards her, but she tenses.

'What happened?' I ask.

'What *happened*?' she says in a tone I've not heard her use before. 'Shouldn't you tell me? Or am I really the last person in the world who knows that you're my sister?'

Chapter 32

'It was meant to be tonight. I was going to tell you tonight.'

Moira doesn't look angry. Instead, she glances from Kian to me, her eyes wide with confusion. I wince from the after-effects of Kian's drunken headbutt, but other than saying 'sorry' in between heaves, he's too preoccupied to lend his attention elsewhere.

'Were you?' says Moira, biting her lip. She twists the wrist strap of her jacket in her hands, not wanting to meet my eye. I feel entirely sober, more so than I ever have done in my life. It's like my insides have shrivelled up, gone black, and been plucked out with a cocktail stick.

'It looks like you and Kian have had a proper laugh tonight. Can't say it's been so fun for me.'

'No, that's not what this is. Moira, honestly, I planned to talk to you about it tonight. It was supposed to be nice. Special, even. I know how much you love ceilidhs, so I was going to tell you here, honestly.'

'Can someone tell *me* what this big secret is?' says Kian, looking over his shoulder at us like Gollum squatting beside The One Ring.

'No ... yes. Later, I need to—' I stutter.

'Ava's my half-sister,' says Moira. She walks towards me. John spots her from inside the hall and gestures for her to go in, but she shakes her head and looks up at the branch of a pine tree, blinking.

'What?' says Kian, dropping back onto his heels.

'Moira, I asked Jacqui where you were and she wouldn't say. I would have come over to the house if I'd known that you found out like this.'

'Ah, you spoke to Mum? Is she the one you refer to as the ... hang on a minute, I took a screenshot.' *Oh, shit. No, no, no.* '"The Hilltop Sasquatch of Kilroch"? Because I can't think of anyone else who was on the cliff the day you almost drove the quad bike onto the rocks.'

Moira's face is lit by the backlight of her phone, her hair in rat-tail tendrils from the rain. She scrolls with her thumb, eyes scanning the screen. I simultaneously want to hug her and kick the phone out of her hands.

'I sent the diaries in, but that part is *not* me. I didn't use those words; someone else did. I'm going to fix it. I'm so sorry.'

'Did you or didn't you come up here to write about us?'

'I did. But I didn't have an agenda,' I explain. 'I know that sounds bad, but – *shit*. This isn't coming out properly. Moira, I came up here to meet *you*. As soon as I got to know the village, it felt ... grubby to write about everyone in that way, especially you. What I wrote *isn't* what ended up on that website. Duncan – my boss – he edited it without telling me. But I'm going to fix it. When I get back to London, I'm going to sort everything out. I'm sorry. This was meant to be a celebration. I didn't mean for you to see it.'

'What do you mean, "you didn't mean for me to see it"? Do you think we're all so thick here in Kilroch that we can't figure out how to open a web page?' says Moira.

'No, that's not what I meant. I know I should have said something straightaway. I know that, OK? But I wanted to do it properly. Those articles are awful, I'll be the first to admit that. My colleagues at *Snooper* ... they don't understand everyone here. I know they come under my name, but they aren't my thoughts.'

She bites her lip and shifts from one foot to the other. Her body language isn't bitter, but protective; wide-eyed, forlorn, shoulders round like she's trying to form a cocoon.

Kian kicks at the gravel with his heel and tries to sit up straight. He scrubs his head with his knuckles like a gorilla, forearms propped on his knees. 'So, Andrew's your dad,' he says, pointing to Moira. '*And* your dad.' He points to me. I nod. 'And you knew this before you got here?'

'Yes, but only for a week or so. We did ancestry tests at work for a video I was presenting. I didn't think anything would come up. Moira did one too. That's how we were linked up, but the only thing I knew was her name and the village, that's all.'

'Aye, I did one a while back. A friend at college gave it to me for my birthday.'

I nod and swallow the prickly lump in my throat.

'I know you grew up with Andrew, for a while anyway,

321

but you have to understand that I came into this blind. I didn't know anything; not his name or how he met my mum. I thought if I got some clarity first, then I'd have a handle on it and be able to introduce myself in the right way, but the more I've learned, the messier it's got. I held back because I didn't want to cause any more hurt, not after finding out how hard it's been for your family and how much Jacqui has put up with because of him.'

'I saw your video,' says Moira.

'The one with the, err ... vomit?' I ask. Moira nods, her expression unreadable. 'Mm. Not my finest moment.'

'A lot of this is not your finest moment,' snaps Moira. As though shocked at her own brazenness, she turns on her heel to break eye contact.

'Moira, wait!'

Moira turns back and takes one step closer, poised to speak. When she doesn't, I fill in the gap.

'I held back from saying anything because I really, truly care about you. I didn't want to send you a message out of the blue and risk it being taken the wrong way. Then when I met you during the pig vaccination, it didn't seem like the right time to bring it up.'

Moira swings her arms back and forth, her cheeks a little brighter.

'Does my mum know?'

'Honestly? I'm not sure. I've had suspicions because she's been quite ... standoffish around me ever since I got here. Eileen doesn't seem to like me either, but that one's more of a mystery.'

'It's because Ross fancies you and not her,' chirps Kian, grinning.

'Feeling better, are we?' I ask. He gives me a thumbs-up, wiping his mouth with the back of his hand.

'I feel like I'm intruding, but I don't think I can stand up yet,' he says.

Moira takes a deep breath in and shakes her head. 'This is mad.'

'I know.'

'And really weird.'

'I know.'

'And I'm still angry.'

'Understandable.'

'But ...' Moira pauses. Foot stomping and big-bellied whoops drift outside, popping the delicate bubble around us. 'It's completely amazing,' she says, scuffing the floor.

I break into a smile.

'Can I give you a hug?' I ask.

'I'm still mad.'

'OK, yep, too much.'

She steps forward, her jacket saturated and stiff like the damp canvas of a tent.

'Are you going to go inside?' I ask.

'Not sure. Not really in the mood.'

'Neither am I,' I admit.

'I've got a lot to sort out in my head, but I think this one needs to go home,' she says, gesturing to Kian.

He shakes his head in defiance before thinking better of it, circling round to a nod of agreement. We lift him up by his armpits and walk round the side of the hall like unco-ordinated competitors in a three-legged race. Our reflection is mirrored in the window, lit alternately in pinks and purples from the mobile disco that accompanies the band.

When we reach the porch, Moira stops abruptly. Her hand grips the back of my jumpsuit so tight that it's stretched across my chest. I follow her gaze to three men grouped around the open passenger door of a pick-up truck.

'Are you OK?' I ask. Moira blinks. Kian's head slumps against my shoulder.

'That looks like ... No. It can't be,' she says.

One of the men licks the paper of a roll-up cigarette, sealing the tobacco inside. He slides it behind his ear and taps the arm of a tall man beside him, jerking his head in our direction. Realising they have an audience, the tall man turns to face us, his turtle-neck jumper strained over broad shoulders. His salt-and-pepper hair peeks from under a beanie hat. Although covered in week-old facial hair, the chin is distinctive as ever.

Moira drops Kian's arm. I stumble, my hip jerked to one side as I try to distribute his weight in a way that's easier to manhandle.

'Dad?' says Moira.

Chapter 33

'Oh my God!' I say, my hands jumping to my mouth. Unsupported, Kian slumps to the floor beside me. 'Moira! That's Andrew?' I hiss.

'Ava, chill out, he can hear you,' says Moira, muttering through gritted teeth.

'Why aren't you freaking out?' I ask, as it dawns on me that she's not reacting like her father has just come back from the dead.

'Why *are* you freaking out? Just say hello like normal and we'll figure out how to do the introductions later.'

'I can't. Oh God. What the fuck? Moira, I thought—' I grab her hand as she steps towards him. The door of the truck is slammed closed, as the motion sensor flicks off the outside lighting, the amber glow from a cigarette jumping at mouth height in the dark. 'I thought he was in *there*,' I say, gesturing behind me.

'What, the ceilidh?'

'No, the *graveyard*.'

'What?!' says Moira, turning towards me.

'I thought he'd ... passed away. Blown up. In the oil rig explosion? My mum said ... Oh God, I feel light-headed.'

Moira pinches my arm. 'Shhh, he's coming, just—'

'Guys, I think I'm going to be sick again,' says Kian.

Andrew joins us underneath the porch light, his posture stooped and softer than I remember from the photograph. He wears jeans tucked into steel-capped work boots; arguably a hazardous choice of footwear for a ceilidh, more so than my bog-stained trainers.

Moira hugs him, but Andrew doesn't make it easy for her. He lifts his elbows to allow her space as though he's getting frisked, his eyes unfocused, staring into the middle distance as though willing himself elsewhere.

'I didn't think you were back until next month,' says Moira, releasing him.

'Job ended early. They switched the crew at Aberdeen, so I drove up with Albie. Who's this then?' says Andrew, glancing me up and down. 'I recognise you ... Did you use to work behind the bar at The Black Sheep near Melkirk?'

'No ...'

Andrew's eyes narrow. 'Nah, you're too young now I think on it.'

'This is Ava. Are you sure you don't recognise her?' says Moira, her words tumbling out, froth-like.

'Oh, sweet Jesus, give me some *warning*,' I say, clutching my forehead.

'Eh?'

I turn to face the wall. There's no point avoiding it now, especially considering my terrible track record when it

326

comes to issues of timing. I take a deep breath and ball my hands, my little fingers interlocked at waist height. My heart beats so hard I can hear it pounding in my ears.

We stand in an awkward triangle, the sound of frantic accordion playing and periodic whooping forming an ill-fitting soundtrack. I can't believe this is him. I've spent my whole life not knowing he was alive. It never formed a big, traumatic milestone, because his absence featured far more heavily than his inclusion ever did. He can't know I exist. If he did, he'd have reached out at some point. That's what a father would do, isn't it?

'I know this is weird, but you know my mum, Lorrie. Lorrie Atmore?'

Andrew chews his lip, his jowls pronounced as he ponders my statement. 'No ... I think you might have got me muddled with another bloke. Name doesn't ring any bells. Not loud ones, anyway.' He scratches his chin, the sound like a match on striking paper.

'You don't remember?' I ask.

Andrew shakes his head and shrugs. 'When would it have been?'

'1991.'

'Christ, that's a while ago. Met all sorts of people back then. Sorry, I can't help you out.'

I know that Mum and Andrew's relationship was of the brief kind, but even so, at the very least, I would have thought he still remembers her.

'Is your mum inside?' Andrew asks Moira.

'Yeah, she's in the kitchen,' she says.

Andrew nods slowly, rocking back and forth on his heels. He looks between the two of us and turns to walk away, his mullet flicked up like a duck's bum at the nape of his neck.

'No, hang on. I'm *not* wrong,' I say.

Andrew stops. He folds his arms and scratches the corner of his eye, as though I'm making a fuss over small change.

'You do remember her, don't you? She worked in a bar when she was here with The Earth Mamas and I think you know that.'

'Look, can we not do this here?' says Andrew, looking over his shoulder to where his friend stands smoking by the pick-up truck.

'It's coming back now, is it?' I say, shivering so much I can barely keep upright.

'Ava,' says Andrew. He runs his thumbnail down his palm, cleaning muck out of the creases. A long breath hisses through his teeth like a punctured tyre. 'If I'm honest, this has caught me off guard. I didn't think for a second you'd be turning up here.'

'You knew?' asks Moira.

'Eh, it's not quite as simple as you think. Her mother told me, back when she first knew about the, err ... situation,' he says, looking to me.

'So why does she think you died in the oil rig explosion?' I ask, my throat tight.

Andrew shrugs. 'I can't answer that. She knew I worked on them. It's how we came across each other. Don't look at me like that, Moira, it's complicated,' he says. Moira drops her gaze, but I can feel her bristling.

'It's a long way to come. London is it? I don't know what your mum has said –' says Andrew, waving his hand between us '– but after she wrote and told me about you, I thought it would be best to leave it.'

'It?' I say, stung.

I'd imagined this situation so many times growing up, but not once was it like this.

'Albie, I'll be back in half an hour. I've got to run the lad back. He's had too much to drink. Typical Brody,' says Andrew, gesturing for us to follow him.

Kian appears at my shoulder, frowning.

'What did he say? I thought I heard my name,' he asks, swallowing a belch.

'Nothing. Dad's giving us a lift, that's all,' says Moira, her eyes tight.

I can't do anything but frown, because if I relax a single muscle I'll start crying and I won't know how to stop. I reach for Moira, who wraps an arm around me as we help Kian over to the truck. We're both hurting, I can feel it. The worst thing is knowing I caused it all.

Moira pulls open the back door, but Andrew flaps her away.

'I've got bits in there that I've got to drive over to the McCullochs' in the morning. If you want a lift, you can get in the back.'

'Seriously?' says Moira. We both look at the flat bed of the truck, where a folded tarp sits next to a gas container and half a dozen lobster pots.

'I've got one seat in the front and you can't all pile in there. Get in or don't get in, but you'll not find a taxi at this time.'

'All right. Thanks,' says Moira, far more appeased than she ought to be, considering the ridiculous demand Andrew's just made. She gives Kian a leg up into the back. He grips the sides and immediately rocks onto his face like a baby attempting to crawl for the first time. I grab hold of the railing to climb up too.

'Get in the front, Ava. I'll keep Kian upright,' says Moira. 'I'm used to this anyway.'

'Oh. Are you sure?' I ask, largely hoping that she'll say no. The thought of sitting up front with Andrew for a whole ten minutes is daunting to say the least.

'Yeah. Go on,' says Moira. She sits back against the cab, pulls the tarp over her legs, and guides Kian's head onto her shoulder.

As soon as I slide into the passenger seat, Andrew flicks the ignition on, reversing the truck with more haste than I'd recommend, considering that there are two adults perched in the back.

We lurch forward and I hear Moira shout an obscenity through the glass as her head hits against the back windscreen. Andrew and I both open our mouths at the same time, followed by 'You go first,' then silence.

'Why did you never call us?' I blurt out. My brain dial has ticked from pain to anger so quickly I've surprised myself. 'Do you realise how fucked up it is to let someone think you died in an explosion?' I turn to look at him side

330

on. Andrew's fingers clench and unclench on the steering wheel, knuckles white.

'It's a bit bloody hard to tell someone you're alive when you never realised you were dead in the first place.'

'But ... nothing? You didn't think I was worth getting to know? That was acceptable for you, was it?'

'That's down to Lorrie, Ava. Not me,' he replies, equally sharp. 'We weren't in a relationship. She didn't seem the settling type, to be straight with you. I didn't know who else she was familiar with and I wasn't keen to fork out for a baby that might not have been mine.'

'Sorry to disappoint, but I took a DNA test so it's pretty conclusive.'

'All right, if you say so. But back then there was no way of knowing for sure.'

We bump along the road in silence and sway in time with the motion of the truck. If vitriol frothed at my mouth before, a trapdoor has now slammed it shut. Poor Moira. No wonder she walks on eggshells around Andrew, worrying if the wrong word could set him off. Sod him. There's no way I'm going to grovel.

'Ava,' he begins, but I turn my face to the side and look out of the window. I don't want to hear anymore, not when it's a straw man defence that manages to slut shame Mum in the process. The headlights map our journey back in silence.

We pull up at Braehead a few minutes later. I open the door before we've come to a full standstill.

Andrew hops down and unlatches the back for Moira and

Kian as I hover by the gate. They both look shellshocked, with pink cheeks and wide eyes. It's clear that the journey has slapped Kian sober. He slides out, stumbling a little as his feet hit the tarmac.

'What's the story, then? You staying or going?' says Andrew, as Moira swings her legs over the side. She looks between us, her usual sunny disposition muddled beneath a cloud of doubt.

'Just putting it out there,' says Kian, far more coherently than before. 'I know for a fact that we have all the ingredients for a shit-ton of cheese toasties inside.'

Moira nods, her lips pressed tight.

'I'm going to stay here tonight,' she tells Andrew.

'Suit yourself. I'll let your mum know,' he replies, pulling himself back into the driving seat.

'Ava, I – I guess we'll talk?'

I don't have the energy to reply. An intention that woolly doesn't deserves one. Andrew clearly agrees, because it's not long before his taillights retreat down the lane, tracing a thread between the dry-stone walls that lead back to the village.

Moira breaks into a weak smile and rubs her thumb on the back of my hand. 'Duvets on the sofa?'

I nod. 'Let's go.'

Chapter 34

The next morning, Moira and I wake up in a duvet cocoon. After Kian's insistence that he'd see to the animals himself, I uncurl myself from the covers to make tea and another round of cheese toasties. Moira lifts the duvet to let me back in, my laptop balanced on a pillow between her knees. My original, pre-edited articles are on display, one tab behind the other.

'It still feels proper weird reading about everyone I know,' says Moira, scrolling down the page. 'You're sure there's no way you can get the edited ones taken down?'

'I've tried, but Duncan's not budging. I've phoned every day since I found out, but he's screening my calls. Oh, *and* he replied to my complaints email with a copy-and-pasted section from my contract, highlighting the part: "editorial changes are the sole discretion of the employer". Seeing as *he's* my employer, there's not much I can do about it. If all else fails, I've got a Plan B.'

Moira frowns, distracted. She scans the screenshots on her phone. 'What does "yokel" mean?'

I groan and try to think of a diplomatic way to say it.

'Umm, someone who doesn't know much about the "real world" because they're a bumpkin.'

'That doesn't sound so bad. I *am* a country mouse, really.'

'It also implies they're *really* thick.'

'Ah, OK,' says Moira, her lips pursed. 'Objectively, I disagree, but sometimes the country lets itself down. I knew this one guy, right. He did a naked belly-flop into a hay baler a few years back. That was pretty stupid.'

'What happened?'

'He chopped off all the fingers on his left hand because he didn't realise there was a rotating blade in the machine. Idiot. It's swings and roundabouts really, because he won £250 for getting the clip featured on *You've Been Framed*. Nowadays, it's the first result that comes up when you Google him, so it hasn't made job applications easy, I'll bet.'

I lean over to the coffee table and rip off a corner of my cheese toastie, snatching glances at Moira, who reads the rest of the articles in silence, unlocking her phone every so often to compare extracts. After a few minutes, she shuts the laptop, puts it on the floor, and leans back with her fingers interlocked in her lap.

'Do you see what I mean?' I ask, trying not to sound desperate. 'I may have exaggerated little things here and there, but not to the extent that Duncan did. He ran a bulldozer through everything I wrote.'

Moira looks at me like a cocker spaniel puppy, her head tilted to one side as she weighs up her words.

'OK, three things. One: you're right, your boss has made a *lot* of changes. Two: no one actually says "Och, aye" in

Scotland. It's a common misconception. Three: I like how impressive I sound in your version of the diaries,' says Moira, 'Particularly the section that said I had "the core strength of a Californian yoga instructor and the finesse of a matador for the new age of pig vaccination",' she says, using a 1950s broadcasting voice. 'Lastly, can I put that on my CV?'

'If you use my version, sure. Duncan's angle is more *Hot Fuzz* than *Line of Duty*.'

Moira nods, tucking the duvet more tightly round her leg. 'He sounds awful to work with.'

'That's what's so weird, he's actually not. I barely saw him until this whole DNA fiasco started. There's a lot of people I thought would stoop this low before he did. The man wears tank tops to work every day. How can you lack a perceivable code of ethics and wear hand-knitted bloody tank tops?'

'People surprise you.'

'Isn't that the truth,' I say, pushing my plate onto the coffee table. I don't want to give Moira the impression that I'm forcing normalcy on to a completely abnormal situation, so I hang back and let her dictate the pace. She bites her thumbnail, her eyes flicking left and right as though tennis is playing on the ancient box television opposite.

Moira drops her hand and faces me.

'Why didn't you send me a message on The Ancestry Project? Right back at the start? That would have been easier than coming all the way up here.'

'I thought about it. I don't know, it didn't feel right. I

wasn't sure I'd even find you, but I clearly underestimated *quite* how small Kilroch is. Besides, Mum has always given me an ambiguous answer as to what she was doing here, so I wanted to find out myself. I only knew that she'd been involved in the occupation of the oil rig when I saw her in a newspaper clipping at the church, then when Ross explained the damage it caused the village, I started to understand why she might have been keen to distance herself from it.'

Moira nods slowly. 'And you've got that to deal with when you go back?'

'Yeah,' I say, my mouth tight. 'Speaking of which, when are you going to talk to Jacqui?' I ask, running a finger along the plate rim to scoop up the last oily smears of cheese.

'Today, I guess. The thought makes me feel all weird and squirmy, like there's a giant slug writhing around in my stomach. If she knew about you and didn't tell me, I want to know why. Eurgh, it's horrible. I can't tell if it's the coffee or the thought of that conversation that's making me need a nervous poo.'

'Welcome to my world,' I say. 'I don't think food has stayed inside me for more than a few hours since I found out about you.'

'Sorry about that,' says Moira, wrinkling her nose. 'This is a lot to face up to. You've had a head start.'

I nod. 'I couldn't anticipate how that live stream would go. Straight afterwards, I had so many messages from people at work asking me what I was going to do but I couldn't tell my arse from my elbow. When I came up on the sleeper train, I still hadn't processed it all. I'd compartmentalised this trip as a work assignment and only the "proper journalists" got to go on those, so I stupidly thought that it was a sign I was progressing in my career. It sounds so *lame* now. The thing is, when I found you, it felt like everything I valued was at risk, including whether you'd accept me as a sister. I was such a control freak about it – who I was going to tell, when I was going to tell them. I thought I'd be able to manage the consequences, but I was only finding new ways to cut off my feelings.'

Moira pushes her overgrown fringe back, thinking. 'You see, that's *so* alien to me because I can't help but overshare. I'll tell anyone anything. I told Old Bert down the docks about my first period and I still don't think he's recovered.'

I laugh, tension easing from my knotted shoulders.

'I wish I could be more like that.'

'You can be. Look, answer this question and imagine that you're me. What was it like meeting Dad last night?'

I groan. 'I don't want to upset you. He's your dad, you have a relationship with him.'

'That's by-the-by at this point,' she says, her face sympathetic.

'OK. I felt *completely* overwhelmed, mainly because I thought he'd come back to life.'

Moira snorts, but holds her hands up when she catches sight of my face. 'Sorry, sorry,' she says. 'It is a *tiny* bit funny, though.'

'You kept talking about him in the past tense!'

'Yeah, because he's worked offshore for the last ten years.

337

It's complicated between us. Anyway, we're not talking about me.'

I compose myself, closing my eyes. 'I also feel ... willingly misled by him. I'm not just angry for me, but Mum too. It's pretty fucked up he let her assume he was dead. At the very least, if he didn't want to take on any parental responsibility, he should have owned up to it. It makes me feel like I wasn't worth the effort.' Moira bites her lip and nods along, encouraging me. 'And ... disappointed. Then I felt *guilty* about feeling disappointed by him, because he doesn't owe me anything and I've had a nice life.'

'You were hardly going to feel indifferent, were you?' Moira smiles, but I can tell this is difficult for her as well. 'Phew, someone open a window, there are too many emotions in here!' she says, laughing. 'I know we're adults, but my parents are arguably more adult than we are and so they owe both of us a few explanations. I've got an idea, but I have a feeling you're not going to like it. I don't either, but it's got to be done. Come with me to talk to Mum and Dad. There's too much that's been left unsaid. We'll get it all out in the open and if it's a car crash, me and you can get fish and chips and drink vodka mixers until we have vinegar tears. How's that for an offer?'

My stomach lurches, but seeing as I've got less than forty-eight hours until my train leaves from Inverness, I nod, my mouth stuck between a grimace and a smile. 'You're right. I don't want it to be really bloody awkward in the future. What we need is to be more American.'

'What do you mean?'

'Talk it out.'

'Then hug it out?' says Moira, her eyes bright.

'Baby steps, sis,' I say, grinning.

Moira smiles and slaps her thighs. 'Right! We'll have to do it today. Dad's over in Fort William on a job from tonight and I never know how long he'll be away for, so it's the only chance we've got.'

I stretch, breaking into a yawn so wide it makes my jaw hurt. I look at the ancient VHS player on the TV cabinet, the clock blinking back at me. Ross will be partway through the All Saints' service by now and he still doesn't know what happened at the ceilidh. Should I have gone to church, to show support? Sing hymns extra loudly from the front pew? Is that what the not-quite-girlfriends of ministers do? Probably not. It's another minefield to deal with, but not right now.

'Have you got the day off?' asks Moira.

I look outside, where the wind had blown the sodden trees dry. It's still so early that lilac streaks across the sky, the sunrise cutting through the room in marmalade hues.

'Technically, yes, but I want to help Kian get the farm spruced up for the inspection later.'

Moira stretches and tucks the duvet tighter round us both.

'Before that, how about another coffee and a quick episode of *Gilmore Girls*? I know for a fact that Kian owns all seven seasons on video and I'm in no rush to go home.'

'Sounds perfect.'

Chapter 35

'I knew it was a bad idea to give you a clipboard,' says Kian. His eyes are ringed with dark circles but there's a glint behind them like broken glass buffed smooth in the North Sea. He leans against the fence and pulls his hood up, smiling contentedly as the sun breaks through the cloud, making us squint. Moira arches her back in a stretch and yawns so widely that she stumbles.

'Ouch. I definitely pulled a muscle in my groin at aerobics this week,' she says, rubbing the top of her thigh.

'That's because you tried to keep up with Eileen when Whitney Houston came on,' I say.

'I've never seen a person perform a grapevine so aggressively,' says Moira, looking up to Kian. 'She's like an angry crab.'

Ever since Max's phone call, I've woken up each day with one foot planted in Kilroch and the other tap dancing with anxious thoughts of returning to London. Thankfully, I've been up before sunrise for the past couple of days to help Kian prepare the farm for today's university survey, which has eaten into the 'dead time' I'd usually reserve for sliding down a helter-skelter of neurosis.

Kian picks up a bucket of dirty water and sloshes it into the wallow, which we've tried to make inaccessible by fencing it off for the day. If the vaccinations had been hard, washing the pigs with an extendable hose and a bottle of dog shampoo was worse. I'm wet through and the padding of my bra has soaked up so much water that it's like I'm carrying two medicine balls on the front of my chest. The pigs, on the other hand, loved it. What started out as an organised system quickly descended into a scene reminiscent of the one foam party I'd attended whilst at university. The pigs writhed and squealed, bubbles frothing, and bodies jostled against one another whilst I blasted them with a hose and Moira scrubbed the worst offenders with a Brillo pad.

'All right,' says Kian, slapping his cheeks. 'What's left?'

I run my finger down the list. 'We've done everything apart from ... Is this right?' I look between Kian and Moira. 'Rub coconut oil on the pigs' ears?'

Kian vaults over the fence and disappears inside the shipping container, returning with a tub tucked under his arm.

'Yep. I read about it on a forum. Well, technically it was a Crufts forum and the thread was about showing miniature dachshunds, but it's got to be the same concept, right?' he says, unscrewing the lid.

'They'll end up eating each other,' says Moira.

'Nah, this is way too refined for them,' says Kian, smearing some on the back of his hand. Moira grabs his wrist and pulls it towards her, inhaling.

'Mmm. Yeah, I'd eat *you* if you were covered in that.' Moira relinquishes her grasp, her neck growing pink. 'I mean, it smells good. It smells like it would taste nice, but I'd have to cook you first. Ha! People taste a bit like pork, don't they? Apparently.'

Moira fixes her gaze at a spot on the floor, her lips puckered like she's bitten into a lemon. Kian rubs his hands clean on his trousers and flings an arm over her shoulders.

'I'll bear it in mind, little one,' says Kian. 'I better let you guys get off for the big family reunion.'

'Ah, don't call it that,' I say, screwing up my face.

'It's going to be *absolutely* fine,' says Moira, rolling her eyes at Kian. 'Now everything is *sort of* in the open, we're just going to talk it out, aren't we, Ava?'

I nod like the Churchill dog, but my stomach twinges with nerves.

'What time are you meeting?' says Kian.

'Four o'clock at the tearoom,' says Moira, glancing up at the sun. 'We've got a little while yet.'

'I'll finish these lot,' says Kian, the tub of coconut oil pinched between his knees. 'I'll see how long the university lot stick around for, but I'll come find you guys afterwards.'

'Wear your posh overalls!' calls Moira over her shoulder.

'They're the same as my regular overalls,' replies Kian, as half a dozen pigs trot towards him.

'They're less mucky!'

We head back up the track as sharp squeals erupt from the pig enclosure. Moira hooks her arm through mine and sighs.

'That was ... an interesting technique,' I say.

'Why can't I flirt like a normal person?'

I laugh and squeeze her arm. 'Well ... offering to *eat* him isn't what I'd call subtle, but I think he needs a more direct approach. Just specify *which part* you want to eat next time.'

Moira gasps and smacks my arm, making me laugh. As we near the farmhouse, a pick-up truck loaded with a small forklift bumps into the yard and pulls into a circle. John climbs out of the driving seat.

'All right? Ava, Moira,' he says, nodding to each of us. 'I didn't know your old man was back. I passed him in the harbour just now.'

'Yeah, he is, but he's heading off again tonight,' says Moira.

'Must be why Jacqui's had her hair done. It's always a giveaway. I'll have to catch him before he goes,' says John. He folds his arms, a wry smile hidden beneath a wiry beard. 'He still owes me for a blackjack game last spring, but he says he can't get his head around PayPal. That's likely, eh?' says John, giving us a nod as he heads down the lane on foot. 'Tell Andrew to look me up before he heads off, will you?'

Moira pins a smile to her face until he disappears.

'Are you going to do that?' I ask.

'No. It causes more hassle than it's worth. I like John, but he has these weird "alpha male" moments. It's all the guys I grew up with. They cringed at their dads for doing the same thing. Not Kian, though.'

We scrape the mud from our boots on a metal plate by the kitchen door. As I bend down to pull off my boots, my back pocket buzzes, as does Moira's hoodie pouch. We both scramble for our phones, dependent on the ever-changing wind direction for updates from The Beyond.

'Eurgh. My course mate is freaking out about our group project,' says Moira, scrolling through her phone. 'Even though I've already submitted it. What have you got?' she asks.

'OH MY GOD,' I screech, causing a trio of softly scratching chickens to jump in the air, stubby wings flapping rogue feathers loose.

'What? What is it?' says Moira.

'My mum,' I say, verging on a whisper. 'She's in Scotland.'

'Why's she up here?'

I read her message again.

Good morning, darling! Guess who got the sleeper train up! Me! My cabin mate (Ricardo) helped me recover your number because I pressed something and it disappeared. Anyway, Grace got in touch. Earth Mamas Grace—Grace who made pitta breads on a camp fire? That Grace. She's living near Leith so I thought that I'd come up seeing as the two of you are in the same place. I'm just getting off the train! Tell me where you are and I'll buy us some lunch. XOXO MUM XOXO

Another text comes through, sent last night but only now reaching my phone:

RED ALERT! LORRIE'S ON THE WAY TO SCOTLAND. Mum just got back from yours – completely twatted – and told me. I know this might be Bad News but I CANNOT COPE WITH THE DRAMA OF IT ALL. LOVE IT. As your oldest friend I hope that everything is fine and dandy but this is also the most exciting thing to happen in my sad single life since I found a bluebottle in my panko crumbs at the Whitechapel Wagamamas. UPDATE ME ASAP. Love you!

'What am I going to do?! Mum thinks I'm in Edinburgh working in an office.'

'Weird-looking office,' says Moira, looking around. 'Maybe you should go there? Head her off?'

'I can't! This is the only chance I've got to talk to Andrew before I have to leave again for I-don't-know-how-long. I need to be here.'

'Well, the only other option is to get her up to Kilroch.'

I bite my lip so hard I almost give myself an edgy piercing.

'I'll go check the sheep; you call her back whilst you've got reception. Stay calm.'

'I'm feeling the opposite of calm.'

'This could be a good thing. Phone her!'

I shiver on the doorstep and hold my phone to my ear, hardly moving for fear of losing reception when I step inside. Mum picks up on the third ring.

'I thought that would get your attention!' she says. 'Surprise!'

'Mum. There's 501 things I need to explain to you, but before I do, you need to get on another train. One to Inverness.'

Chapter 36

'I'd have packed a balaclava if I'd known I was heading this far north,' says Mum, stepping out of the car. Ross walks round to the boot and flips it open, taking out a small suitcase with a big purple ribbon tied around the handle. I step off the kerb and scoop her into a hug. She's wearing one of her favourite jumpers rolled up to the elbow, paired with a woolly hat that has slipped over her eyebrows. She tightens her arms around my shoulders, even though I'm a few inches taller than her and it should really be the other way round.

'I've missed you,' I say into her hair. It smells of the cottage, beeswax conditioner, and the stale air that lingers in community halls, but it's delicate enough to cut through the farm smells I've been enveloped in for weeks now, the ammonia and straw, damp turf, pine trees, and petrol.

As I step away to look at her, Ross lightly touches my shoulder. 'Hey, I'm going to head back to the church. Call me if you need to, OK?' He kisses me on the forehead and I notice for the first time that he doesn't give a furtive glance up the road to see if anyone is watching.

'Thanks. Honestly. I really appreciate it.' I reach for his hand and he folds my fingers into his palm, his thumb grazing my knuckles. He steps back, keys in hand.

'Hey, no worries. Glad I could help. Lorrie, it was a pleasure. Speak soon?'

'Hope so!' she says, perky all of a sudden.

He drives up the hill, leaving us clutching each other on the pavement. Mum takes a deep breath and looks up and down the road, fiddling with the zipper on my coat.

'Of all the things I couldn't predict, you and that priest is at the top of my list. I didn't raise you to be religious.'

'He's not a priest, but he *is* a minister. The rules are different. Our relationship isn't ... spiritual, as much as it is—'

'Say no more. They didn't make them like that when your grandma marched me to church twice every Sunday. I probably would have been more enthusiastic.' For two people who have candid conversations about the menstrual cycle over tea and cake, we've never been so good at The Big Topics. Tiptoeing around them in a conversational Morris dance is more our style. Here, there's no time to waste.

Mum slips on a pair of mittens, the wind buffeting her wild hair, like she's in the epicentre of a hurricane. 'I think you're getting more use out of my old raincoat than me.'

'Mum, I'm so sorry I didn't tell you I was coming here. I don't know how much you—'

'Ross explained some of it. It started with that video, didn't it? The day you came back with a migraine?'

I nod and fold her hat back so she can see properly. I lighten my voice in an attempt to diffuse awkwardness.

'The fun news is that we're a tiny bit Russian and Great-Grandma might well have been secretly working for the KGB. The *not* so fun news is that I found out I had a sister during a live broadcast and then I vomited everywhere, which is now preserved on the internet, for time immemorial.'

Mum's lips are pursed, but her eyes are doleful and soft. She cups my jaw and looks at me like she's trying to recognise the parts that belong to her.

'Why didn't you say anything?' she says.

'Because I knew you'd be upset. And you are, aren't you?'

'Of course I bloody am,' she says. She shoves her fists in her pockets and scowls. 'I'm fuming.'

'This is why I didn't mention it at the time,' I say, forcing a smile as Jenny the Wink walks past, a bag of M&Ms poking out of her raincoat pocket. 'I was going to, the night before the live stream, but then Ginger came in and it wasn't the right time. I knew basically nothing about my father and whenever I brought him up you got all weird and sad.'

'We didn't need him,' says Mum with an edge of stubbornness.

'The fact that *you're* the one who gets to say that is exactly the problem. But this isn't about him anymore. It's about Moira. Oh, you're not going to like it, but there's someone else here—'

'Who? Oh ...'

'Ava!'

I turn around, looking up the street to where Moira

stands with one foot out of the tearoom. She waves with a swooping arm, giving us a double-handed thumbs-up before disappearing back inside.

'Let's get on with it then,' says Mum, picking up her suitcase.

'Don't be like that.'

'I'm not being like anything.'

'Let me carry it,' I say.

'No, I'm fine.'

'*Please* let me carry it.'

'I said I'm *fine*.'

'Stop being difficult!'

We jostle on the spot, each with a hand on the suitcase, our fingers curled tightly around the handle.

'This is like one of those god-awful episodes of *Chucklevision*,' she says, putting on an accent. 'To me, to you—'

'How dare you take the Chuckle Brothers' names in vain. I won't stand for it. Not on my watch.'

We stop jostling, the suitcase poised between us. She stares at me and I stare back, unblinking, until we crack and burst into laughter. We laugh for so long that my cheeks hurt, the wind pulling tears from my eyes. Overhead, seagulls squawk at a pair of fishing boats. The sound is just as shrill as the two of us, gasping for breath on the cobbles below.

'Stop. I'm not wearing my TENA ladies,' says Mum, clutching me for support, one leg crossed in front of the other.

'This is why I wanted to bring you up here,' I say, when we've both composed ourselves. 'Moira wants to meet you. Jacqui's had less warning, but I've got a feeling she knows who I am, so ...'

'Oh, Christ. Is she here?'

I clench my teeth and nod. 'Like it or not, we're a family now, of sorts. A blended family. Actually, a curdled family might be more accurate. It depends on what happens when we get in there,' I say, nodding towards the tearoom.

'And this Moira ... she's Andrew's daughter? His other daughter?'

'Yep. She talks about ten different things at the same time, is totally bananas, and *completely* brilliant.'

'If she's related to you, she's going to be at least a little bit off the wall. You're a two-person portion of banana split yourself.'

'Thanks, Mum.'

I zip my jacket up and try to rub warmth into my hands. The wind blows up the cobbled hill from the bay, where the oil rigs sit on skeletal haunches, crouched behind a veil of sea mist. 'I didn't mean to drag you into this,' I say. 'But I couldn't think of how else to move forward. I can't *unknow* the results of that DNA test.'

Mum tucks her hand into my pocket as we walk up the hill.

'If anything, I dragged *you* into this. Twenty-eight years ago.'

'No need to go into the biology of it ...' I say, twitching

with a smile. 'Wait a second, there's something else I need to brief you on.'

'Can we do it inside? My toes feel like ice cubes. Come on,' says Mum. She steers me by the shoulders before I get a chance to object, a bell tinkling above our heads as we step inside the tearoom.

Chapter 37

I push a chain-link curtain to one side and head through to a small back room. The shelves are lined with industrial-sized bags of flour and sugar, unusual cake tins, and flattened takeaway boxes. In the corner, there's a wooden table that Moira has laid with crockery and napkins, a tiered stand of fresh scones, and two huge ramekins of cream and jam. A quiet hubbub of overlapping chatter, clinking teaspoons, and babbling toddlers filters through from the main room. It's comforting to know that there are witnesses a few feet away if I have to grab a handful of flour and launch it as a smokescreen to sneak Mum and myself out in one piece.

Moira turns to greet us, a half-folded tea towel in her hands. I can tell she was in a rush when she washed and dried her hair because it's fluffy like a baby blackbird. Mine has stuck to my scalp, the unfortunate result of wearing a fleece-lined hat for nearly ten hours today.

'Mum, this is Moira. Moira, Lorrie.'

Moira barrels forward and squeezes Mum to her chest.

'Lorrie, it's so nice to meet you! Ah, this is amazing. And

odd. I barely know what do with myself. I made scones. Ava said you like them, so I gave them a go and I think they turned out all right, but if you pile up the cream you won't be able to tell either way.'

Moira laughs and pulls back. Beaming, she slips her apron off and hooks it by the back door. Mum stays in the doorway, reluctant to come further inside.

'I *am* sorry for intruding on you. I don't think any of us expected the day to turn out like this,' says Mum, clearly nervous.

'It's not an intrusion,' says Moira, batting flour off her jumper. 'It's nice to have you here. Ava's told me so much about you.'

I stand beside Moira, my heart thudding beneath my fleece.

Mum's eyes jump from my face to Moira's. 'Look at you two. Sisters. I mean ... I can't quite believe it. All this time and you were at opposite ends of a train line. I never considered it, which is bizarre, really, knowing your father.' Mum catches herself. 'Sorry, sweetheart. I shouldn't have said that.'

Moira's about to reply, but instead she looks past Mum's shoulder to the kitchen archway. Jacqui stands behind us, her raincoat unzipped and a shrink-wrapped crate of milk tucked under her arm.

'I went to get some milk from the McCulloch farm,' she says, sliding the crate onto the counter. Jacqui's expression irons out as she looks Mum up and down, a hand resting squarely on her hip. Mum pulls off her hat, stuffs it into the pocket of her coat, and fluffs her hair up with her fingertips.

'I've got half an hour,' says Jacqui. 'Dot said she'd hold the fort until half past, but she can barely work the toastie machine without setting the fire alarms off, so I can't be away any longer than that.'

Mum walks forward and extends a hand. After an excruciating couple of seconds that sees Jacqui analysing it, she shakes it slowly like she's pumping water from a well.

'It's a shame you've got to head back so soon,' says Mum. 'I gather there's a fair amount the girls want to talk about.'

'Yes, well. I can't afford to take the whole afternoon off to sit about chatting over tea.'

Jacqui pulls the nearest chair out and sits down, her body language hunched and stiff like she's been called into a tribunal. We follow suit, our elbows almost touching around the circular table.

'These scones look lovely,' says Mum, 'did you use baking powder? I'm always in two minds ...'

'Mum,' says Moira, her voice soft and insistent.

'I'm sorry,' says Jacqui, throwing her hands up. Her tone suggests this is a preface to something she's not sorry about at all. 'But I thought we'd all left this in the past. I've done my best. I know we're not perfect, your dad and me. I made a choice when we got married and I've had to make a lot of them over the years but I have the family I have and that's the family I'd do anything for. I know he's had some slip-ups, but we've taken it on the chin.'

'You don't need to defend him, that's not what this is about.'

'Isn't it? That's why you came here, Ava? To find him?' says Jacqui, looking at me.

'No, not at all,' I say, my stomach flipping over itself with adrenaline. 'I didn't even know that Andrew was alive.'

'He's what?!' splutters Mum, her cup dancing in the saucer as she places it back down.

'I'll get onto that,' I garble, putting a hand on Mum's forearm. 'I came here for Moira.'

Moira splays her hands on the table. 'This is why I asked Dad to be here, so he could speak for himself. There's been too much left unsaid.'

'You could be right, but there we are. He's not here,' says Jacqui.

'Hang on,' says Mum, swallowing her mouthful. 'Can we go back a few steps? Andrew is – in fact – alive and well?'

'Yeah ... I'm just realising that I should have told you this before we came inside,' I say.

'You've got to be kidding me,' says Mum, lifting an eyebrow.

'That explosion you thought he was in? He wasn't on the rig,' I say.

Mum looks to the window and shakes her head, her fingers tapping out a beat on her cardigan.

'Ah. I mean, that wouldn't explain why the child support payments never came through, but I'm sure he'll be able to explain that when he gets here.'

'Christ, I don't know where to start with all this,' says Jacqui, hanging her head.

'I do,' says Moira. 'Mum,' she says, looking at Jacqui. 'You keep saying that you've left things in the past, but you haven't, otherwise you wouldn't have treated Ava like she's an invasive grey squirrel set on wiping out the native species.'

Jacqui sits back and folds her arms across her chest.

'You have to admit that Dad hasn't –' she pauses, chasing a crumb around her plate with her little finger '– that he hasn't exactly stepped up to the things he should have.'

'He's had his problems. He's been working on it,' says Jacqui.

'I know,' says Moira, choosing her words carefully. 'But that's just one part of it. Things have to be different now. You've got to stop blaming other people for the choices Dad made.'

Jacqui bites the inside of her cheek and glances up at Mum.

'I'm one of those mistakes, aren't I? That goes without saying,' says Mum, her eyes glassy. 'Truly, I did *not* know that you were together at the time him and I ... you know. Think what you like, but I'm not that kind of person.'

I let out a breath that I didn't realise I'd been holding in, relief unplucking the tight thread of worry stitched between my ribs. Mum looks at Jacqui, her chin held high.

'I thought he had a right to know, so I sent a couple of letters. It's not like I knew where he lived, so I looked up the firm he worked for and sent them there. I called his office to check he'd picked them up, which he had. I stopped trying after that. I'm no homewrecker.'

Moira clutches my hand under the table and glances at me. I squeeze her thumb in the hope that it communicates that the bulk of this is new information for me, too.

I assumed that Mum left Kilroch in a hurry because she'd stepped on someone else's turf and wanted to flee before the pitchforks were out. If Andrew was the one who adopted an 'Ask me no questions and I'll tell no lies' approach, he needs to shoulder the consequences. When it comes down to it, he didn't want to know me. At that point, what other choice did Mum have? I think back to the times we'd awkwardly sat through adverts for Father's Day on TV, the over-compensating when it came to birthdays, the obstinate self-reliance. She was trying to protect me from the disappointment she'd already borne the brunt of. In a different way, that's exactly what Jacqui had protected Moira from too.

'How much did Andrew tell you?' Mum asks Jacqui.

'He told me that you and he had ... been familiar. And that was that. You were gone, he was back, and I didn't want to think about it anymore. I didn't know about Ava until I saw her on the cliffside, then I guessed your age roughly and put two and two together.'

Jacqui tilts her head to the side and looks at me. 'You said you came here for a change of scenery, but the only folk that come up here to work on farms are the fruit pickers and the farm tourists who think it's all bottle-feeding lambs and drinking home brew. They don't last as long as you have. I underestimated your sticking power. That's a compliment,' she says, although she's still scowling.

'Oh right. Thanks,' I reply.

'Then there's the small matter of you looking like him,' says Jacqui, her voice less clipped and curt.

360

Mum nods in agreement.

'I needed to know. Whatever the circumstances were,' I say.

'I still can't believe you came all the way up here and didn't tell me. You won't even go out at the weekend without giving me an itinerary of where you'll be and when to expect you back,' says Mum.

'I didn't want you to worry about me,' I say.

'It's the other way round, sweetheart. *You* worry about *me* worrying and it causes this angsty cycle of hand-wringing that's not good for someone your age.'

'Aye, that sounds familiar,' says Jacqui, propping her elbow on the table. 'This one does the same thing,' she says, pointing to Moira with a butter knife. 'I tell her all the time. Take when she was on placement down in Inverness, she came home every weekend,' says Jacqui.

'Yeah, but there was a good reason for that. You took on way too much between the tearoom and keeping Braehead afloat before Kian came back,' says Moira.

'I know, you bonnie thing. But Moira – you mother me too much. You need to get away for a while, see some different things. I don't know what's holding you back.'

I look at Moira, knowing exactly how she feels. If there was ever a perfect time to bring up the equine dentistry course, it's now, but her candour is failing her. I can see it in the way she pulls her sleeves over her hands, her hair tucked tight behind her ears. I find her foot under the table and kick backwards with my heel, clipping her shin.

'Ouch!' she yelps.

'Sorry! The rubber on these boots are so thick I can barely feel the floor,' I mutter. 'Tell her.'

'About what? Oh. No, not right now ...' she trails off.

'I think you should.'

Moira screws her face up as though she's trying to teleport somewhere else.

'Christ, there isn't another sister, is there?' says Jacqui.

'No! I don't think so. It's something else. A course I've been offered a place on, but it's down in Surrey and—'

'Stop right there, lassie. Don't go into any "buts" until you've told me all the good parts.'

Moira's words tumble out of her mouth in a tangled mess, like nylon tights in the washing machine. She pauses, closing her eyes as though she's lost a bet and is waiting for the consequential slap in the face.

'It sounds great, you silly goose. When do you start?' says Jacqui, her cheeks pink. 'A dentist! Oh, me!'

'Not a proper dentist, a horse dentist,' says Moira.

'I don't care. Horsey people throw money at their animals, especially in Surrey. Sounds good to me.'

'Yeah, but I still can't afford it. Even with a bursary the rent down south is bananas, and—'

'Let's talk about it later. We'll figure something out,' says Jacqui. 'You're holding yourself back and I won't be the reason for it, all right?'

Moira bites at a hangnail and nods.

'So,' says Jacqui with purpose. 'Are we going to eat these now, or shall I wait for them to go stale for the magpies?'

Chapter 38

The four of us step out onto the flagstones, seagulls gliding in gusts of wind like shrill kites. Moira and I walk a few steps ahead as Jacqui speaks to Mum in the porch. I can't make out what they're saying, but when Jacqui puts her arm on Mum's shoulder and it's not to steady herself in preparation for a headbutt, I relax.

'Our mums are laughing,' I say, my arm hooked through Moira's. She follows my gaze.

'No ... Oh, they are!' says Moira.

Jacqui folds her arms and nods. They look down the hill towards us, a look of quiet affection etched on their faces.

'They're definitely talking about us.'

'So obvious.'

Mum says goodbye and trots down the hill, pausing as she joins us.

'Has it changed much?' Moira asks Mum. 'Compared to last time you were here?'

'Not at all. Feels a bit like déjà vu. We weren't that popular with the locals. I can understand why, but it did mean we couldn't nip in the shop for a can of Coke and a packet of Monster Munch.'

On the corner, the sign above The Wailing Banshee creaks in the wind, the roughly carved wood of a screaming woman with hollow eyes staring uphill. The kind of laughter that accompanies back slaps and bad jokes leaks out into the street as the door swings open. Out steps Andrew, raising a hand to someone inside as he turns on the pavement towards us. Mum stiffens, but she's composed, as though she's about to dive off a high board.

Moira shouts to get his attention from across the street, breaking into a jog to meet him halfway.

'Does he know I'm here?' says Mum, her eyes fixed on Andrew like he's a fox in the front garden about to ransack the bins.

'No ...' I say.

'He hasn't aged well,' says Mum, out of Moira's earshot. 'He looks old.'

'Well, it has been a fairly long time ...'

'Like a pickled anchovy.'

I make hushing noises as Andrew slopes towards us, his hands deep in the pockets of a lumberjack sweater.

'I was just coming up to the tearoom,' he says, somehow managing to look everywhere apart from directly at us.

'We were supposed to meet at four,' says Moira.

'Ah, right. I must have ... Yeah. Well I just popped in for a quick pint. Jim's stopped by on his way to Aberdeen and I owed him one.'

Andrew looks at Mum and stands up taller, his once curly hair cropped short. 'Didn't think I'd see you up here again, Lorrie. Last thing I remember, your peace and earth loving lot were being pulled off the rig by the coastguard.'

'Mmm, that's right. I couldn't stomach another dry oatcake by that point.'

Andrew chuckles and looks up at Mum beneath wiry eyebrows. 'So, have you, err, sorted everything out?' he says, gesturing between us.

Before Moira or I say anything, Mum pipes up. 'Yes, I'd say so. There is the *small* matter of why you didn't think to get in contact about your first daughter, but—'

'Well, hold on. You never asked me to.'

'I sent you a letter. I sent you two, actually, and I know you got them.'

'I thought you were just *telling* me, you know? You didn't give me any sign that you wanted me to do anything, as such, so ... There's not much I could have done from up here anyway. If I'd have known—'

Mum puts up her hands in defeat. 'Andrew, it's all right. Really, there's no point going into it. I'm not in the habit of poring over the past with a nit comb. You don't owe me anything. Truly.'

Andrew runs his tongue along his lower lip and rubs the back of his neck. Moira nudges me with her elbow and gives me a look as though she wants to leave.

'You've done a good job, by all accounts,' he says.

'Thanks.' Mum holds her chin high and looks to me. 'But I knew that already. Shall we get going?' says Mum.

Andrew waves a finger in my direction. 'Oh, Ava. Can I have five minutes?' he says.

Mum bites her cheek and takes her suitcase off me. 'Chuck us the keys and I'll put this in your car.'

'I'll come with you,' says Moira, bunching her hands inside her pockets as they walk away.

When they've disappeared around the corner, Andrew walks half a pace ahead of me, each step slow and deliberate. I follow him and try not to make it obvious that I'm staring at his features and trying to figure out which parts made their way over to me.

'Has your right eyebrow always grown upwards like that?' I ask.

He answers hesitantly. 'Yeah ... I think so. Can't say I've studied it up close.'

'Interesting,' I add lamely, silently blaming him for all I've endured after years spent trying to ensure mine lay flat. I can't think of what else to say, so we walk in strained silence until the road pulls level with a concrete slipway that tips down towards the waves. Around us, boats lay on their sides like slumbering seals, a sun-bleached trunk of driftwood cast ashore between them, its branches twisted and worn smooth like fuzzy felt. Andrew sits down and leans his forearms on his knees.

'I just wanted to say that I'm sorry. I grew up without a dad, so I know what it's like.'

Well, this makes it worse. He addresses a tangle of fishing nets hung from a barbed-wire fence.

'I want to do something. I can't make up for ... all that

366

business in the past, but I'll try and meet you halfway. I'm leaving for a job tonight, but if you want to come out on the boat for a few hours, that'd suit me just fine. We can put the spinning rods off the back, see if we can catch some mackerel.' Andrew looks up and quirks the corner of his mouth in a smile. Out in the bay, a small trawler is followed by a flock of seagulls who screech and squawk, swooping as the fishermen dump fish scraps overboard.

I take a moment to analyse how I'm feeling, poking and jabbing at the recesses of my brain. There isn't much left to consider. I reached a conclusion when Moira took me up to her room and showed me the photograph she kept tucked away in her wardrobe.

'I'm not the person you should be asking,' I say, facing the wind so it blows the hair off my face. 'It's Moira. I mean this in the kindest way possible; it would mean so much more to her than it would do to me.'

Andrew bites his cheek. When he looks at me again, it's the first time that that things don't feel painfully awkward between us. He nods. When I smile, it feels heavy and I realise how bone-tired I am. For the first time since I ran out of the studio in London, the muddy waters I've been wading through have started to clear, like silt settling into solid ground.

Chapter 39

It's definitely far too early for bubbles, especially drunk from a mug with chickens painted on the side.

Kian has his back to us. For once, he's stayed in pyjamas past six o'clock. He flips a thick slice of eggy bread in a cast-iron pan and slides it onto a plate, sprinkling brown sugar on the top that caramelises, soft and gooey from the heat.

'I thought you said that working on the farm has been *really hard*,' says Mum, drawing out her sentence to make it sound like it's come from a six-year-old's mouth.

'Uh, it has been, thank you very much,' I say, sipping coffee so creamy and sweet that it's more like cheesecake than a hot drink. 'Kian, how many times have you made breakfast since I've been here?'

'Every day,' he says, gesticulating towards me with the egg flipper. 'Don't you go telling porkies.'

'I knew you two would gang up against me,' I say, spearing a forkful of eggy bread as Mum laughs into her giant cup of tea. 'What are we celebrating, by the way?'

Kian tops his orange juice up with the last of the

prosecco, his grin set squarely like it has been for the past hour. 'Well, we've had the lovely Lorrie come to stay, which is reason enough.'

'Hmm. I have a feeling there's something else behind all this ...' I say, eyeing him over the rim of my mug.

Kian could smile for the next week and it wouldn't be enough. Yesterday, we pulled up to the farmhouse as he waved off representatives from the University of Edinburgh, their neat hatchback splattered with mud. By the time they'd dipped out of sight, Kian was partway through a lap of the courtyard, fist-pumping the air like Tyler Durden in *Fight Club*. He greeted Mum with a smacked kiss on the cheek, looping us under his arms in a jostling circle, cheekbones clashing in uncoordinated jumps.

Kian takes a fork, spears a green, meatless sausage from the tray on the table, and bites the end.

'I've just got a good feeling, y'know?' he says, waving his fork around. 'I can't call it, but the fact that we can accommodate three sets of students a year must help. Well, hypothetically we can. I'll need to sort the rooms out and get someone in to help, probably. They were completely sold by the pigs.' Kian slides a notebook over. 'That's the third bullet point,' says Kian, jabbing the page, '"the best example of saddleback swine seen this side of Sterling." This side of Sterling! And they're going to help with the woodland maintenance, which means—'

'Truffle hunting!' I say. 'Yeah, check you out! You're diversifying! Just think – Braehead – the future of farming.'

'Steady on,' says Kian, but I can tell he's excited by the

thought. I push my chair back to get milk out of the fridge. As I shut the door, Moira appears in the doorway wearing an oversized hoodie that reaches her knees.

'Morning,' she says.

'I thought you called John to take you home last night?' I say.

'I, err, yeah. I didn't go back, in the end,' she says, her cheeks pink.

Mum coughs, catching my attention. She raises her eyebrows and flicks a glance at Kian.

'Oh! No way. Yes! Did you? No, don't answer that. But you guys? Eh?' I blurt, as Moira bursts into laughter.

Kian tucks her into his chest, one arm wrapped around her shoulders, the other holding a mug of tea away from her head.

'Don't answer that. We can't discuss it, not now you're my official baby sister.'

Moira laughs and sits cross-legged on a dining chair, her hair a homage to Kate Bush in her *Hounds of Love* days. She tucks her legs up inside the hoodie, propping her chin on her knees.

'What are you guys doing before you get the train back to London?' says Moira.

'Shouldn't I be asking what *you're* doing?' I ask, wiggling my eyebrows.

'I'm going fishing with Dad.'

'Oh. Sorry, I made that unnecessarily weird,' I say.

Moira rolls her eyes, her smile as broad as Kian's. I take a mental photograph as he puts a plate down in front of her, wanting to capture this golden moment before we're at opposite ends of the country again. 'I would suggest a wee tour of Kilroch, but I doubt much has changed since you were last here, Lorrie.'

'Not from what I can gather,' she says. 'But there is something I'd like to see before I go.'

***

On our way to Kilroch Point, Mum regales me with stories from her time with The Earth Mamas. I knew that she was a tambourine-wielding, henna-haired activist before she settled in Dulwich, but this is something else. The tale of three women and how they washed themselves with a flannel and one bottle of water between them goes some way to illustrate the unglamorous side of occupying an oil rig in the North Sea.

In turn, I tell Mum about Braehead: the way the house rattles when it warms, the territorial guard geese, and how I've learned to predict the next day's weather based on where the sheep huddle before sundown.

We squelch alongside the hedgerow as dull winter sun pokes through gaps in the bramble. Without warning, Mum stops, taking both my hands to pull me round to face her.

'Ava, I'm not sure I ever said this to you. Not out loud, anyway.'

'Oh, God. What now? I'm not sure I can handle any more life-changing news, unless it's that Pickles is in fact half-cat, half-slug, which would explain his lack of mobility and tendency to leave slobber trails near food.'

Mum rolls her eyes and sighs. 'No, nothing like that. Honestly, I'm trying to build a *moment* here.'

'Oh, right. As you were.'

'I wanted to say that I'm proud of you.' We stand there, crows cawing in the cropped field behind us, linked by our fingertips and a thousand other things.

'I'm proud of the decision you made to come up here. I'm proud of that silly grin you have when you complain about the animals. I'm proud of the way you've established yourself without me. I'm proud that you've figured out what *your* version of happiness looks like.'

'I can also carry an egg in between each finger. Are you proud of that?'

'Yeah, we'll add it to the list,' she says with a smile.

She squeezes my fingers. When she lets go, I open my palm. A tiny glass-blown dolphin sits there, barely a centimetre long. She curls my hand back around it.

'I've kept this in my purse since I left Kilroch. I wish I'd been more open with you about your dad from the start. I do. But I don't have any regrets about coming here. How could I when this place gave me you?'

Mum blinks, her bottom lip quivering as I enclose her in my arms, interlacing my fingers at her back.

'I'm struggling to breathe here,' says Mum, her voice muffled by the excess of knitwear bundled at her chin.

'Sorry,' I say, releasing her. I take a deep breath.

'Mum, I ... I think I've realised something.'

'What's that?'

'I have this feeling that I'm ... that I'm not meant to

leave—not yet, anyway. I want a chance to be myself here, to spend more time with Moira before she starts her course. I'm not sure how it'll work, but I thought I'd try the "see what happens" approach. For once, the thought doesn't terrify me as much as it once did.'

Mum scans my face. 'Are you sure?' I nod. 'You know how cold it gets here in winter?'

'I've heard tales,' I say, my voice thick.

I look up as Mum's eyes fix on a point in the distance. Through a break in the thicket, I see him too. Ross. He walks between graves in the churchyard, head down, leaving a trail of emerald footprints behind him where his boots have kicked a path through the dewy grass. Mum tugs my forearm and gasps.

'Oh, he's got a nice Heathcliff feel, don't you think?' she says in a whisper. 'The right amount of brooding without the disturbing violence. I can see why you don't want to leave *that* behind.'

'Mum, don't say anything, don't—'

'Coo-ee! Ross! Morning!' Mum trills off a laugh and I groan, my cheeks flushing. Ross stops to raise a hand.

'Morning! Cold one for a walk,' he says, tucking his hands in his pockets. 'I was just on my way to Braehead, actually.'

'For Kian?'

'No, for you.'

Mum pulls me back behind the bramble and pulls her mittens on with purpose, her voice hushed. 'I'll go on without you. It looks like he's keen to talk.' Just as I'm about to protest, she puts a woolly finger to my mouth. 'Go on! Fingers crossed you don't burn up if you decide to have a snog in God's house.'

'Honestly. You give me a reputation and I don't even have a reputation,' I say.

'I don't know ... Cavorting with priests? Sounds like a good scandal to me,' says, poking me in the ribs until I squirm. 'See you later, sweetheart.'

'If this gets back to the Dulwich WI, I know who to blame.'

***

I try and stomp the circulation back into my toes as Ross weaves around parcel-taped boxes inside the parsonage kitchen.

'Are you going somewhere?'

'Yeah,' says Ross, 'back to Edinburgh. Doug Dingwall has made a miraculous recovery from his hip operation and, apparently, he's more than ready to take up his duties again. Going by the tone of the care worker I spoke to on the phone, they want shot of him as quickly as possible.'

'Why?'

'Let's put it this way, they had to remove the antibacterial gel dispenser from his bedroom. Suddenly it's not so strange that I've found six mini bottles of gin stowed in hiding places around the church. There was even one slipped down the spine of a King James Bible. Worrying, as it's the one we use for the children's service.'

'Wow. I expect Eileen will be back on dinner duty. Have you told her yet?'

'Yeah, she knows. In fact, she offered to move down with me as a "housekeeper", so it's nice to know I've got options.'

'The woman has *no* shame,' I say, sitting on the corner of the table.

Ross grins, but his smile falters as he steps closer. He's let a beard grow, which suits him exponentially, despite it hiding half his face.

'So, this is it,' he says.

'Is it?'

I put my hands on his hips and he covers them with his own, rubbing the back of my hand with his thumb.

'You know I'll be in Edinburgh, right?'

'Yeah. I'll let Mum know. She's stopping over for a couple of nights whilst she visits her friend.'

'What about you?'

'I thought I'd stick around,' I say, my gaze drifting up to the spider webs hooked around the ceiling beams.

'Aye? How long for?'

'I haven't decided.'

After weeks spent inhabiting different versions of myself depending on who was in front of me, I've settled into quiet contentment. Now that Mum and I no longer need to tiptoe around The Dad Issue, I sense a new kind of trust between us – one that sees our messy, blended family and embraces it anyway. With the truth of our sisterhood out in the open, it's like Moira and I have met for the first time all over again. I don't want to leave when we're only just getting started.

'Hold on. Is this Ava without a plan?' he says, jokingly

patting me down as though I've got a concealed weapon. 'You haven't got a highlighter tucked in here, have you?'

He grins and puts his hands on either side of my face. It's a shame because I was quite enjoying the frisking.

'If you want to see me, I'll be here. If you don't, I'll understand. There's no pressure.'

Ross scratches his newly adopted beard and frowns. 'I'll have to think about it.'

'We don't need to decide anything. Let's worry about it later, okay?' I say, worried that I've pushed him too far.

Ross slides his hands in his pockets and moans under his breath in a way that makes my thighs feel three-glasses-of-wine-fuzzy. 'I'm done worrying about it,' he says, bending down towards me. I thread my fingers through his belt loops and arch my back, reaching up to meet him.

If it's possible for a kiss to be polite, this feels like the opposite. Each kiss overlaps into the next until I'm clutching onto the lapels of his coat like it's the only thing keeping me upright. I break away, our foreheads touching, and flick his collar. The remnants of a bar code are printed on one side.

'Have you still not upgraded the milk carton?'

'Shh,' he murmurs, kissing me again. This time I push him back with my lips, sliding off the table, one step towards the door.

'I should catch up with Mum,' I say.

'Let me drive you,' he replies.

'All right then. But take me on the scenic route.'

Chapter 40

'How are you doing that?' says Kian, taking a break from his continuous pacing of the driveway to stare at Mum with a look of mild horror and awe.

'She just needs a gentle touch, don't you sweetheart?'

Mum sits on the front doorstep with a doleful Babs on her lap, who tucks her wings in and wiggles her corpulent backside into a more comfortable position. Mum runs a hand over her speckled back and smiles.

'It's like she's had a lobotomy,' I say, just as disturbed as Kian. 'I haven't managed to get within two metres without her launching a talon at my throat.'

'Do you think I could squeeze a coop in the back garden?' says Mum, smiling down at Babs.

'Probably, but there wouldn't be space for much else.'

'It's the foxes I'd worry about.'

'Really? I doubt they'd know what to do with a live chicken. They're too busy working through the bins behind KFC to bother with something they'd have to actually kill.'

I lean sideways to allow Moira past, as she carefully steps out of the front door balancing a tray of tea. She places it on an upturned terracotta trough, each mug billowing with steam in the chilly afternoon air.

'Are you going to stop pacing for five minutes to drink this? Kian? Kian!' says Moira, motioning to the mug in her hand. He drags his eyes up and joins us by the front door, his nervous energy spilling tea over the lip of his mug.

The noise of wheels splashing through puddles reaches us from across the yard. 'If we don't get the grant, it's fine. I'm not bothered. I'll start on your business plan anyway, Ava. If we look at next month's invoices, maybe we can get by without—'

'Would you stop with your contingency plan?' I say, as Jacqui's car trundles across the concrete drive. Before she's got her door fully open, Jess the border collie leaps over her lap and greets us by crouching down to release an over-excited wee. Nice.

'All right, are we?' says Jacqui, her raincoat crinkling as she gets out of the driving seat. 'Thought I'd come by for the big news. Going by the state of your knees knocking together, you haven't heard yet, Kian?'

'No, not yet,' he says, rocking back and forth on his heels.

Jacqui pulls two weighty loaf tins out of a plastic bag and presents them to him. 'If it's not the news you're wanting, I made a lemon drizzle to console you. If it's a celebration, you've got pineapple and whisky.'

'Ah, Jacqui, you're a peach,' he says, planting a kiss on her cheek. She waves him away, her dimples on show.

'Ah, go on wi' you,' she says, bending down to pat Jess, who sits with her ears pricked up, eyes darting between the sheep in the distance. When Kian's phone pings with an alert, we all jump.

'Oh God, I can't cope. My insides feel like a cement mixer,' says Moira. Kian tries his best to look cavalier, but his expression is oddly vacant, like he's just this moment wondering who put the alphabet in alphabetical order.

'Open it, lad!' says Jacqui, kicking the toe of his boot. Roused from a stupor, he takes his phone out and walks away with it at arm's length as though it's a grenade with the pin removed.

'What do you think?' I whisper to Moira. 'Oh ...' My gaze follows hers to where Kian stands, his foot propped on a broken lawnmower. He buries his face in his hands, shoulders up by his ears. My heart drops to my stomach where it dissolves into deep, slick disappointment. I knew the grant application was a long shot, especially considering how quickly we'd pulled together a two-year plan from a decade of poorly kept files, but we couldn't have done any better. I couldn't have done any better.

'Shit,' I say, scolding myself.

'It's not your fault,' whispers Moira, stepping towards Kian.

Just as Moira reaches a hand out to rub his shoulder, he turns and pumps the air, his eyes bright and triumphant. He scoops Moira into his arms and spins her with such velocity that one of her wellie boots flies off like a shotput, narrowly missing Jacqui. Mum stands up to perform a jaunty box step with Babs clutched to her chest, her feathered head bobbing like she's grooving to a song no one else can hear.

'Did you get it?' I shout, somewhat redundantly.

'We got it! Ninety grand! Get in!' he shouts.

Jacqui and Mum explode into a cacophony of whoops and cheers, joined by Jess, who shows her support through a fit of frantic barking.

'See this!' says Kian, grabbing my forearm and pulling me over. We lean down to get a good look at the screen, foreheads touching. '"The strength of your application was supported by apt facilities and scope for growth, which together with *exceptionally thorough* records make Braehead Farm an ideal partner for the next two academic years,"' says Kian.

'Well, you can relax now, eh, Kian?' says Jacqui.

'Hardly,' he says, one hand on his hip, the other swung round Moira. 'There's the guest bedrooms to sort out, turning the north field, new piglets, finding an ethical shearer to come and do the sheep ... That's it. Ava – I'm not letting you go back to London. You've got to stay here and help me, or I'll sharpen Babs's talons and pack her in your suitcase.'

'You don't need to convince me. I'd already decided to stay.' My heart thrums in my chest.

'Hang on, you're *what*?!' squeals Moira.

Kian laughs, but it putters out when he scans my face and sees that I'm serious. Moira stands squarely in front of me, her eyes wild with half-restrained glee.

'I want to stay,' I continue. 'For a bit longer, anyway. I haven't thought about the details yet. I've only scratched the surface here, what with you guys and the farm. I've spent so many years not knowing I had a sister. The thought of stepping back into my old life feels weird, like squeezing into shoes that don't fit anymore. Besides, there's so much we haven't covered yet.' Moira bites her lip as though she's trying to restrain her smile from being quite so broad.

'Like watching the director's cut of *Titanic*?' she says, sidling alongside to bump her hip against mine.

'Exactly. I want to eat Ben & Jerry's until we're sick.'

'And borrow each other's tops.'

'Then leave passive-aggressive comments on each other's Instagram posts when we spot the other one wearing it,' I add in a dreamy voice.

'We haven't even made up a secret handshake,' Moira says. I laugh and hook her around the waist. 'Got to make up for lost time, haven't we?'

'There's no part of me *whatsoever* that wants to go back into the *Snooper* office. I want to work at Braehead. I can liaise with the university, do the filing, management stuff, you know? At least until you find someone more permanent. I'll even write you a press release when you're featured on *Farming Today* as Scotland's Face of Ethical Farming,' I say, catching Kian's eye.

'That's my girl,' says Mum, squeezing Babs a little too hard, going by the slight bulge in her eyes. A warmth floods my chest and settles beneath my ribcage like a trampoline, bouncing each heartbeat up my throat until I want to laugh.

'Oh, and your place doing horse dentistry down in Surrey? You need to take it up,' I say to Moira.

'She's right,' says Jacqui, although she doesn't meet my

eye when she says it. She pulls Jess's silken ear through her hand, a flash of conflict on her face.

Moira glances between us, her smile wavering. 'I can't afford it ...'

'So take my room,' I interject. 'I've been thinking about it for ages. If I'm here, you can be there, learning how to be the best horse dentist Kilroch has ever seen.'

Moira bites her lip and draws a staggered breath, her face contorted in angst as she looks between us. She zips her fleece up and over her chin, as though disappearing inside it might make her decision easier.

'Don't worry about us, we'll be here when you get back,' I say, squeezing her fingers. 'There's a few months before the course starts anyway. Plenty of time to get sick of me.'

'Am I going to do this?' she says, peeking at me with one eye.

'Yes, you're going to do this!' says Kian, clutching her to his chest from behind. She hooks onto his forearms like she's clipped into a rollercoaster.

'I'm going to do this,' Moira repeats.

'You'll have to come down before your course starts. Get acquainted with the place and all that jazz,' says Mum, smiling at Moira.

'I'll come and give you a crash course in How to Be a Londoner. If you spend your first day standing on the wrong side of the escalator, you'll be ejected beyond the M25.'

'Really?' says Moira, doubt flashing across her face.

'Nah, just kidding. Although you might get a few

passive-aggressive tuts. We'll do all the naff touristy stuff as well. I'll even take you to M&M World, but bear in mind you can only visit once before consigning it to the ninth circle of hell, where it belongs.'

'Sounds horrible,' says Moira, her dimples set like two full stops either side of her lips. 'I can't wait.'

'And you're set on staying?' says Mum, jiggling Babs up and down like she's soothing a newborn.

I nod and look out towards the field, conscious of the sheer amount of space around me that I'm not ready to swap for zebra crossings, beeping train doors, and swathes of people walking in a thousand different directions.

'I'm staying,' I say.

'My Ava. On a farm. Couldn't have predicted that one,' says Mum, a smile pinching her mouth.

Everyone slips into chatter: Moira with her head tilted towards Kian like she's in *Gone with the Wind*, Jacqui talking with her eyes on the horizon, Mum nodding. I look at them and smile: my new, muddled family.

My pocket buzzes. I pull my phone out and see a message from Max on the lock screen:

You ready?

I type a message back, my thumbs slow and clunky from the cold:

I'm ready.

Chapter 41

I climb up onto the bottom rung of the gate and swing my leg over, the metal rattling on a rusty hinge. There's a chance this won't work, but the wind is quite literally blowing in the right direction, so if I don't do it now, I might not get another chance.

As I march up the sheep trail that follows a line of thick gorse bushes, my phone buzzes.

> *Duncan's in a meeting. Not sure for how long. You've got a window.*

I take a staggered breath, partly from nerves, partly from the incline, which hasn't gotten any easier to hike no matter how many times I do it. As I crest the hill, the sun breaks a sharp line through inky clouds that have tickled the hill all morning, sending sunshine across the patchwork fields in a Mexican wave of light.

I turn around. A gaggle of sheep scatter, their eyes bulging behind a fringe of tightly curled wool. I find a good spot and pull out my phone, open *Snooper*'s home

387

page, then paste the log-in details that Max sent me. As curiosity takes over, the sheep form an audience around my knees, bleating and jostling like a football crowd.

I flip my camera on and hold the phone aloft. My pink cheeks are mirrored back at me, the wind whipping my hair back and forth. My multiple scarves are wound so tightly it's like I've donned a neck brace, which will be useful if I stack it on the way back down to the farmhouse. I close my eyes, breathe, and press 'go live'. It's only now I realise that I haven't got a script, but at this stage, I don't need one. Numbers count down like an old-fashioned Hollywood reel: five, four, three, two, one ...

I'm in. A red button blinks above the image of my face. Viewer numbers steadily click through but I try my best to ignore them as my stomach flip-flops. Boy, do I regret pouring unpasteurised milk in my coffee this morning. I grin at the camera but the wind is so sharp it makes my gums hurt. There's no turning back now.

'Greetings, from a hilltop in the Highlands! It's Ava here. You might remember me from a previous live stream – the one who did a DNA test and found out she has a secret sister? And then spewed everywhere? Yeah, you got it, that's me! It was *such* a laugh, wasn't it? I know a bunch of you have been reading my diaries and waiting for the big reunion, so I'm sorry it's taken this long, but hey, whoever said families were simple?

'The thing is – confession time – those diary entries *weren't exactly* authentic.' A sheep head-butts my thigh and I stumble. I stroke a mad tuft of wool from its face and look back at the camera, my heart thrumming like a diesel engine. 'OK, I'll be honest, they were a *complete* fabrication and that's down to *Snooper*'s *delightful* editor-in-chief – drumroll, please! Duncan Wyatt! You probably don't know who he is, but if you can imagine Mr Tumnus crossed with a particularly droopy basset hound, you're in the right ballpark. That's the thing, isn't it, Duncan? It's not nice to be held up for a cheap laugh, is it?

'As you once said to me, "Journalistic integrity is the bread and butter of our industry," which is why I've made a complaint to the Press Standards Organisation. I won't list all the clauses that were broken when you decided to butcher my diaries before publishing them online, so let's just say that you'd get a decent *Countdown* score if I penned them on a whiteboard.

'I'm sure there was something else ... Oh, yeah. I quit.'

One of the sheep emits a low, guttural *baa*, setting the others off in a chorus of bellows that reverberates around the farm like off-kilter church bells. I raise my voice.

'That's Ava Atmore, *not* reporting for *Snooper* ever again. Over and out!'

I press the red button to close the stream and bury my face in my hands. Adrenaline floods my chest like I've been pumped full of helium. My phone buzzes. I squint at the home screen and bite my lip as messages flood in, the first from Max:

I'll miss our dumpling dates. You made a good choice.

I stand on the hill for a few minutes as the sheep nudge me to get at the grass beneath my feet. For once, I know exactly where I'm supposed to be.

Acknowledgements

Wow – we're here again! I can't bloomin' believe it!

I heard tales of The Difficult Second Book and didn't believe it until I found myself staring into the void of my laptop screen having completely forgotten how to write a novel. Every book is its own beast, as they say. The trick is to learn how to conquer it. Thankfully, I have some exceptionally brilliant book tamers who pushed me back into the ring and bolstered my confidence when I needed it.

The majority of this book was written during lockdown, so although we couldn't dine out on white chocolate mash (seriously – try it) the brilliant Team Fajita took to Zoom instead. To put it mildly, a global pandemic hasn't been the easiest context in which to write a comedy novel, but my agent Hayley Steed and editor Tilda McDonald made the process fifty thousand times better. Hayley is a relentless cheerleader for my work and has helped me understand who I am as a writer, which has made such an impact on how I approach fiction. The goodest of eggs is she!

I feel incredibly lucky to work with Tilda, whose insight and clarity when it comes to story wrangling really is second to none. I *genuinely* feel excited when I get notes back from her. Somehow, she just gets it, you know? Thanks for letting me know when I'm genuinely being funny and when I've taken it too far. It's not always clear when you spend hours each day in a basement trying to make yourself laugh.

Huge thanks go to my copy editor, Sharmilla Beezmohun. When you've spent weeks trying to figure out dates and timelines, copy editors really do feel like fairy godmothers. Your insight and clarity had me blinking in awe.

Is it possible that the One More Chapter team contains the nicest people in publishing? I think so! Thanks to Claire Fenby, Melanie Price, Bethan Morgan, Charlotte Ledger, and everyone else who has championed the book. Also, huge thanks to Sabah Khan, who is a total boss when it comes to publicity. I can't wait to sip fizzy wine with you all again!

There are only a few people who witness the rough points of writing as well as the highs, and Joe has seen it all. Thank you for dragging me away from my desk and pushing me outside when I was being a worry worm. It's not easy to make me laugh when it's 10 p.m. and I've still got 1,000 words to write, but you manage it somehow.

To Mum and Dad – wahey! I did it again! My love of farms and rural life has largely come from the summers spent at The Buzzards growing up. I have a confession: it was me who let the piglets escape. But, hey! It inspired a scene in this book, so …

To Linford, Rachael, and Cassidy. Thank you for all

your advice over the past year and for always having onion rings ready when I come round. I love you all immensely.

To The McKibbens, who have allowed me to be a writing gremlin in their basement for the past year. Thanks for letting me off dinner duty when I was close to a deadline and celebrating with me when I hit a milestone. Extended thanks go to my pet housemates, Wally the cat and Maddie the border collie. You might be able to spot them in this book ...

I've got some stupidly brilliant friends whom I often spam with questions and extracts from dodgy first drafts. So, huge thanks to my Norfolk Girls, who are relentlessly funny, supportive, and kind. I bloody love you guys. Also, thanks to Emily. I will always have a Choco Leibniz in my heart for you.

I want to say thank you to all the authors in the Debut 2020 group. Being published is full of unknowns, but we've banded together in what has arguably been the most difficult year (ever??) to bring out your debut. Our community is so special and I hope we're still supporting each other for mannnnnyyyy years to come.

Finally, thanks to my readers. This wouldn't be here without you. I'm eating a box of Tunnock's Tea Cakes in homage to you.

If you enjoyed *The Sister Surprise*,
don't miss Abigail Mann's
laugh-out-loud debut

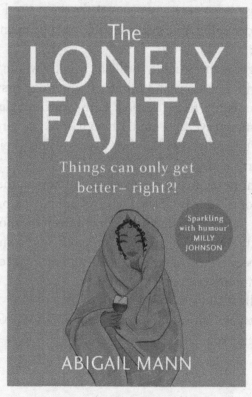

Out now!